THE EYES OF INNOCENTS

-- A WATCHTOWER THRILLER--

MIKAEL CARLSON

WARRINGTON
PUBLISHING

DANBURY, CONNECTICUT

The Eyes of Innocents
Copyright © 2022 by Mikael Carlson

Warrington Publishing
Danbury, CT
www.mikaelcarlson.com

WARRINGTON
PUBLISHING

Printed in the United States of America
Second Edition
ISBN: 978-1-944972-99-8 (paperback)
         978-1-944972-89-9 (hardcover)
         978-1-944972-88-2 (ebook)

Cover designed by JD&J

OTHER POLITICAL THRILLERS AND DRAMAS BY
MIKAEL CARLSON:

- THE MICHAEL BENNIT SERIES -

THE ICANDIDATE
THE ICONGRESSMAN
THE ISPEAKER
THE IAMERICAN

- TIERRA CAMPOS THRILLERS -

JUSTIFIABLE DECEIT
DEVIOUS MEASURES
VITAL TARGETS

- WATCHTOWER THRILLERS -

THE EYES OF OTHERS

For all the survivors of human trafficking and the brave members of law enforcement who bring the perpetrators of this evil to justice.

CHAPTER ONE
DETECTIVE BRESHION HURLEY

SUSPECTED SEX TRAFFICKING STASH HOUSE
PHOENIX, ARIZONA

The SWAT team prepares for the raid as Breshion watches the house's windows for any sign of movement. The blinds are closed, and they stay that way. He checks the surroundings for any telltale signs of trouble. This small, single-family home is like any other in the area. None of the neighbors could know from appearances what nightmarish secrets it must hold.

"We're ready," Jamecca says, all business.

Breshion waits for a few beats. It's after three in the morning, and there has been no movement spotted in the house since before midnight. If there is a guard posted, he isn't doing anything that would attract attention from outside. It's now or never.

"Let's move in."

Jamecca instructs the team to move into position, and Breshion joins the breaching team as they cross the street. This is about the time that the detective longs for the days of no-knock warrants. He understands people's concerns over the practice, but the politicians who wrote that bill never had to storm a house full of armed human smugglers in the dead of night. The moment they yell "Police," their life expectancy shrinks.

The team stops at the front step as the breachers move up the stoop to the front door.

"Report," Jamecca commands.

"Back in position and ready."

"Overwatch ready. No activity."

"Front ready," the SWAT commander says, looking at Detective Hurley.

He nods. "Breach."

"Police! Open up!"

The burly officer waits three seconds before slamming the steel ram against the wooden door, sending it flying open. The SWAT team charges up the stairs and barrels through the door, their rifles up. Breshion, decked out in body armor with "Police" emblazoned across it, follows them in.

A man who was probably fast asleep on the couch seconds ago fumbles for his pistol resting on the coffee table. Three rounds from one of the rifles find their mark and put him down. The second team enters through the back door into the kitchen. A single shot rings out from the adjacent hall before their rifles open up and end the threat.

"Living room clear," the SWAT team commander says.

"Kitchen clear."

The successful entry does nothing to stop Breshion's heart from pounding in his chest. They are only half-finished, and they need these men to surrender, not be lugged out of here in body bags.

The backdoor team forms up and moves down the short hallway, a man with a shield leading the way. A figure emerges with a shotgun and fires off a slug that pings off it. It's followed by a second and third as the man screams at the top of his lungs. Three seconds later, he has joined his buddies in the afterlife. Three down, one to go.

"Bedroom one clear."

"Bedroom two clear."

The team creeps to the master bedroom and awaits the signal before pouring into the room with weapons raised. A lone man stands in the corner near the bed. He looks at the officers warily as panic sets in.

"Don't move. Show us your hands." The man doesn't move, and Breshion repeats the order in Spanish. *"Quieto. Manos arriba."*

The man stares at Breshion with a mix of fear and hatred in his eyes. The detective tightens his grip on the SIG Sauer. Cornered animals fight the hardest.

"Sabe como esto termina, amigo."

Fight or flight means only one thing when cornered. The man reaches for the long gun leaning against the bed. Two members of the SWAT team open up, dropping him.

"Damn it!" Breshion exclaims, hitting the wall next to the doorframe. He moves into the hall as the team goes about their business securing the floor.

"Any sign of the children?" Jamecca asks over the radio.

"Negative," Ritter responds, joining Hurley in the hallway. "First floor is clear."

"Check the attic," Breshion commands his junior vice squad detective. "Front entry team, follow me to the basement."

Builders in colder climates dig the foundation below the frost line, making cellars and crawlspaces ubiquitous. In Arizona, the required depth is about eighteen inches. As a result, many homes in the area don't have basements. The ones that do are either in pre-World War II neighborhoods like this one or newer, high-end developments.

The team descends the rickety wooden stairs to find nothing but old furniture and junk. There are paths through it, and they fan out. It only takes a few seconds for them to cover the home's footprint.

"It's empty," the commander says, his eyes sweeping the room.

"No, they're here somewhere. Trust me."

Breshion checks the corners of the basement. This space feels smaller than the house above. After finding where the foundation tucks behind a wooden wall, he knows why. He traces it and finds an area with disturbed dust and scuff marks marring the concrete floor. He moves some debris and finds a hatch low to the ground.

"Over here," he says, getting the attention of the team.

Breshion nods at the commander, who covers him as he unlatches the sliding bolt. He slides the door open and shines his flashlight into the narrow space. Three pairs of terrified eyes stare at him.

"Children located," Breshion radios in. "Basement level. We could use some help down here."

"On the way," Jamecca responds.

Breshion backs away from the hatch. The odor emanating from it is overwhelming. There are no bathroom facilities down here. The stench of feces and urine makes his eyes water.

"It's okay. You're safe now. Come on."

The children don't move. They only stare back at him with glassy, frightened eyes as they cling to each other.

"Todo esta bien. Ahora estas seguro. Vamonos."

One by one, a dozen children climb out from the coffin of a room. None of them looks older than eight or nine. They are dirty, disheveled, malnourished, and terrified of the men with guns surrounding them. His heart quickens again, but the emotion behind this reaction is much different.

"What's the word?" Breshion asks Ritter as he arrives in the basement with Jamecca following right behind him.

Phillip Ritter is one of the new guys on the vice squad. Plucked out of Cactus Park precinct, he's spirited and lively, almost to the point of annoyance. A squirrel amped up on Red Bull in the middle of an interstate isn't as neurotic and energetic as Phil is on an average day.

"All four subjects in the house are dead."

Breshion shakes his head. "We needed at least one of them alive."

"They weren't going down without a fight. It's a fate better than whatever consequences they faced from getting caught by the police."

"Yeah, I know. It makes you wonder what kind of scumbag they were working for."

"Someone more terrifying than we are," Jamecca concludes as she wraps the abductees in mylar blankets.

The motherly instinct is a powerful one, and hers is kicking in. Detective Robinson slowly encourages the twelve children to follow her upstairs. Some of them will have families looking for them. Others were sent to the U.S. unaccompanied. He's willing to bet one or two are orphans. Those are the easiest to prey on for human traffickers.

"I hope the guys up there had the good sense to cover the bodies."

"I'm betting these kids have seen worse on their journey here. Besides, it looks like they have them drugged."

It's a sad but true statement. The children's lethargy and lack of responsiveness could be paralysis from fear, but they have likely all been drugged to make them compliant. And to keep them quiet.

"Are the ambulances here yet?"

"They're on the way."

"Tell Jamecca to get them loaded up and off to Salt River Valley before the media arrives and camps outside. Tell the ER that the children experienced significant trauma and were found in horrifying conditions. They know the drill."

"Roger that."

"Detective," one of the SWAT team members says, getting his attention. "Here are the IDs we pulled off our traffickers."

Breshion looks at them for a half-second each. "Fakes. Get their prints and run them through the ICE database and see if we get any hits. We need to know all we can about these assholes."

The detective goes upstairs and walks into the master bedroom. He doubts the dead man in the corner was a big fish, but it would have been better had he been alive to talk. Now a three-month vice squad investigation is in jeopardy of being a dead end.

The media will gush over this raid as a win over human traffickers. Politicians will take a victory lap as if something important was accomplished here. It wasn't. This is the tip of the iceberg for human trafficking, and they're no closer to answers about who is running the operation in Southern Arizona.

CHAPTER TWO

"BOSTON" HOLLINGER

WATCHTOWER TRAINING CENTER SHOOTING RANGE
SOMEWHERE IN VIRGINIA

Out of all my daily training activities, this relieves the most stress. The physical conditioning only manages to wear me out, and Nadiya uses me as a punching bag during our Krav Maga sessions. The rest is dull tradecraft and investigative techniques taught by the best agents the CIA, NSA, and FBI can offer. Weapons training gives me a semblance of control and an outlet for my frustration.

I relish the feel of the Glock in my hand as I pump out nine rounds. I always preferred SIG Sauers, which is why I owned one. Having fired everything from Smith & Wessons to Berettas since I've been here, I've settled on this piece of forged steel as my favorite.

The slide locks to the rear, and I clear the weapon before setting it on the tray. Not too shabby, or so I thought. Emma isn't impressed.

"You're mashing the hell out of the trigger again. You need to let it reset before pressing it for another shot."

"I am."

"No, you're not," she argues. "It's not a NERF gun, Boston. Every time you physically abuse that trigger, the Glock moves in ways you don't want it to."

I look back at the silhouette hanging seven yards away. "I'm still hitting the target."

"Oh, big man. You can shoot a stationary piece of paper. Here's your gold star. Don't find out what I'm talking about when you are forced to engage a target ducking behind cover and shooting back at you. Again."

I shake my head and put my ear protection back on. "Are you always this difficult?"

"Again!" Emma demands, donning her own muffs.

I replace the magazine and press the bolt catch. I hold the weapon close to my chest and thrust it out, lining up my sights and emptying another magazine into the target. I think I did better this time. The optimistic thought is quickly dispelled when I see Emma rubbing her forehead.

"Now what?"

"You're anticipating the shot breaking."

"How do you know?"

"You're right-handed. All your shots are landing low left because you're compensating for the recoil before the bullet leaves the barrel. Go again."

"What's the government's budget for ammunition?" I ask, replacing the magazine with a loaded one.

"Something we'll need to double if you can't pick this up."

I send another nine rounds downrange.

"Reload and engage!" Emma yells next to my head.

I do as instructed, performing a quick magazine change. Just as I push my weapon out, I feel a punch to my kidney that causes my leg to buckle.

"What the—?"

"Engage the target! Now!"

I fire my rounds and remove the magazine before setting the weapon down.

"What the hell was that?" I shout, yanking off my ear protection. If this was her idea of a joke, it wasn't funny. Fortunately, she isn't laughing either.

"Training."

"On what range is that safe?"

"This one," Emma says, flipping the toggle to retrieve the target. "You don't get into firefights in perfect conditions. You need to know how to react to the unexpected."

Emma replaces the target with a fresh one and sends it back down the range. She studies my shot group or lack thereof.

"These are all over the place."

"What did you expect? You kidney punched me." She taps the center of the target, making the expectation clear.

"What would happen if I did that to you?" I ask.

Emma smirks and taps it again. "First, Nadiya tells me that you don't pack much of a punch."

"Haha."

"Second, I know more about handling a weapon than you will learn in three lifetimes."

It's an arrogant statement, but I know she can back it up. Watchtower is made up of people from countless three-letter agencies. Emma is one of the premier firearms instructors in the FBI and was reassigned here specifically to train me. That doesn't mean I don't give her a hard time.

"I was in the Army," I say, offering a weak defense. I knew plenty of soldiers who couldn't shoot worth a damn.

"I know. Military Intelligence. Make that four lifetimes."

"You should think about a career as a stand-up comedian."

"I'm trying to get you to loosen up. You're frustrated. Don't be. Shooting is a skill that requires constant practice and refinement. It takes years to get comfortable with it and even longer to gain proficiency. What did you see when you engaged after the punch?"

"Uh, the silhouette," I say, surprised I even answered her dumb question.

"I thought so. Where were your sights?" I pause. Okay, maybe it wasn't a dumb question after all. "Don't answer that. You'll embarrass yourself. You don't know where they were because you weren't using them."

"What will it take for you to develop a bedside manner?"

"That depends. What will it take for you to hit a target center mass with any regularity?"

"Putting Forte at the end of the range," I mutter, opening a fresh box of cartridges to start reloading my magazines.

"My job is to train you to shoot, not solve your self-esteem issues. That's Asami's job," she says, getting close coming up alongside me and leaning against the ledge of the firing point. "You're still blaming him?"

I press my lips together and cock my head. "Zach locked me in this cage, changed my face, and let my friends think I'm dead. Yeah, you could say that I still have an ax or two to grind."

"All true. Of course, without Agent Forte, you'd be dead. Ever think of that?"

"Every day. Put yourself in my situation, Emma. Would you make the trade? Answer honestly, not as an FBI agent."

My lovely instructor picks up an empty magazine and some bullets and starts loading magazines with me. She is a petite dynamo who wields firearms with the precision of a neurosurgeon. When she isn't scolding me for doing everything wrong, she has a soft side that's mysterious and alluring.

"When I was a kid, my father would always say 'get busy livin' or get busy dyin'.'"

"*Shawshank Redemption.*"

"What?"

"Tim Robbins said it to Morgan Freeman in *Shawshank Redemption*," I add as an explanation.

"Whatever. My point is, for all intents and purposes, your life ended on your living room floor. Your fiancée, a woman you wanted to spend the rest of your life with, murdered you in cold blood. I wouldn't want to go back to that life for anything. Since death isn't appealing, I would do everything to make that second chance worth it. But that's just me."

Emma completely missed the point of the line, at least in that movie. It's something I take to heart now. She's right. I am existing, and every day it becomes more untenable.

"You sound like the doc."

"Like I said, Asami is only looking out for you," Emma says, covering my hand with hers. "So am I."

It lingers for a few beats too long before she pulls it away. It was a tender moment from a woman with ice water running through her veins. She is complex, and at the same time, simple. Any man would be lucky to have her, assuming he realizes that she could put a bullet through his heart from thirty yards away.

Emma blushes and picks up her hearing protection. "That starts with giving you the tools you'll need not to get yourself killed. I'd hate to see you squander your second chance because you can't hit the broad side of a barn. Let's go again."

CHAPTER THREE
SSA ZACH FORTE

WATCHTOWER TRAINING CENTER SHOOTING RANGE
SOMEWHERE IN VIRGINIA

Zach and Matt stand at the window overlooking the range from the floor above. This training facility was purpose-built for instructors and evaluators to watch every aspect of training. Whatever that purpose was no longer exists. Now it's the primary proving grounds for Watchtower members, and the two men make full use of their ability to monitor Boston's progress.

"Is it me, or is she crushing on him?" Zach asks as Emma covers Boston's hand with hers and stares into his eyes.

"Does it matter?" the head of Watchtower asks.

"Not really, until a point comes when it does. Why did you invite Brass here?"

"I didn't invite him. He wanted to see Boston for himself."

Matt Remsen is far more political than Zach will ever be. It's why he holds his cards so close to his vest and rarely shares information voluntarily without a subpoena in hand. There is more to this visit that his long-time friend isn't sharing.

Zach has only met David Brass a handful of times. He works for the Department of Agriculture's foreign service on paper, responsible for bringing American farm goods to international markets. It's a cover. Most likely, Brass is CIA. Despite being the program's director, he takes a hands-off approach to Watchtower. That suits Zach just fine, and his absenteeism caters to Matt's resentment of micromanagers.

"In person?"

"Observing from a distance. Boston can't know who he is or that he's unimpressed with his progress thus far."

"Our boy has made incredible strides. His skills are improving every week."

"It's not enough. Brass already thinks we're exceeding our charter and wants to shut this down. We have one opportunity to convince him that he's wrong. Come on."

Forte frowns. Matt shared some information, after all. The two men leave the range and head for one of the training areas converted into a conference room. The facility isn't massive, but it isn't tiny either. It hosts indoor and outdoor training areas, a cafeteria, sleeping quarters, and a well-outfitted operations area to train for tactical and reconnaissance missions.

"You know, when I joined Watchtower, I didn't think we worked for anyone."

"Everybody works for somebody, Zach. Brass is okay. He's just covering his ass in case someone asks questions," Matt says as they walk.

"Who's gonna ask? Nobody knows that Boston is alive."

"That's true, but some senator could easily ask why Agriculture is spending millions of dollars on ice exports to Sweden."

"Please tell me that isn't an actual line item in the budget."

Matt smirks. "What's the doc going to say in here?"

"I don't know. Asami stays tight-lipped about her sessions with Boston. I'm just as in the dark as you are."

Matt rubs the back of his neck. That wasn't the answer he wanted to hear, but it's the truth. Asami is the best psychologist the government has and insisted on her independence when she agreed to this assignment. Despite their pleading for information, she is steadfast in remaining tight-lipped.

"Zach, this project is important. We've dedicated a ton of resources to it."

"*You* dedicated them," Zach says, correcting him.

"It was a calculated risk."

"It was a gamble, and you know it, Matt."

The director frowns but doesn't argue the point as the two men round the corner and bump into Nadiya outside the conference room. One of the instructors here, her remarkable beauty is only surpassed by her hand-to-hand combat skills. The last guy who got handsy with her found himself hospitalized for a week. That incident didn't go over well with her CIA bosses, but her fiery attitude makes her fit right in on this Island of Misfit Toys.

"How did it go today?" Matt asks.

"Fine. Boston's getting there."

"He looked a little unsure of himself while you were kicking his ass," Zach laments, having watched much of the session from afar with their director.

"Most newbies are," Nadiya says. "Any idiot can learn the techniques. It takes time to develop the confidence needed to put them together."

"You would think a military guy wouldn't struggle with that."

"He's not Rambo, Zach."

"He seems distracted," Remsen interjects. "Does he talk to you about anything?"

Nadiya lets out a sarcastic chuckle. "No. He spends any words he has cursing me. Good luck with this, boss."

The two men watch her head back down the corridor. Even without makeup and clad in workout attire, she's a vision. Zach can only imagine what she would look like dolled up for a date.

"Did you surround Hollinger with the most beautiful instructors you could find?"

"Can you think of a better way to get him over Tara Winters?"

Zach won't argue with that, even though he wants to. Tara and Boston have a history together. The Persian trauma doctor he was on the run with was the last person to see him alive before his traitorous fiancée shot him in the head a year ago. They were never intimate, but there was an undeniable connection between them. Unfortunately for Boston, he'll never see or talk to her again.

"No, but that doesn't mean this will work. What happens if Boston develops a relationship with one of them?"

"Then our Tara Winters problem is solved," Matt says enthusiastically.

"And ten more are created," Zach mumbles before they enter the room for the meeting.

David Brass is seated at the table, looking over some files. He doesn't acknowledge the two Watchtower agents as they take their seats. Dr. Asami Kurota is already there, waiting patiently with her hands folded on the table.

"All right, thank you for hosting me today, gentlemen. Director Remsen, I have reviewed Agent Hollinger's training progress. It's slow, but that's not my first concern. Dr. Kurota, can you present your findings?"

"Yes, sir," Asami says, sitting a little straighter. "Boston's gift is no longer a theory. The car accident aggravated a previous head trauma he suffered during a mortar attack in Syria. We can confirm the result with one hundred percent certainty. It defies medical explanation, but Agent Hollinger can see and interpret memories of other people when in an unconscious or near-unconscious state. In fact, he recognizes the memory eighty-three percent of the time."

Brass rubs his chin. "But he has to be sleeping to do it, correct?"

"Not necessarily. Over the past year, Boston has developed meditation techniques that allow him to identify and access strong signals in the room if he relaxes."

"Signals?"

"For lack of a better word, yes. Dr. Winters had the best theory I've seen in her early research. Human beings emit undetectable brainwaves, much like a wi-fi signal. Boston unlocked a neural pathway to tap into them. He can see their darkest secrets and most profound memories. It's apparently possible even if the subject is recently deceased, although we haven't tested that. We don't know the mechanics of how he does it. Only that he can."

"Fair enough. Can Hollinger see memories in high-stress situations?"

"We're not there yet."

"It's been a year. Agents can't just take a nap when the shit hits the fan. He needs to be able to do this in real-time to be a viable asset."

"Sir, with all due respect, he has progressed incredibly far in a short time," Asami argues. "This is uncharted medical territory. It may take time to develop, but the sky's the limit in terms of what he may be capable of in another year, two years, or five."

"Anything else, Doctor?" Brass demands.

"Yes, I'm concerned about his mental state. Agent Hollinger has a lot of...baggage. I'm not sure if he is adjusting to his new reality or just going through the motions. He's struggling to overcome a deep resentment."

Asami goes on to explain her psychological findings. None of it is beneficial to their cause, but it is honest. Zach thinks that she is getting too personally involved. She is more protective of him than a mama grizzly is with her cubs. It is above what would be expected in a doctor-patient relationship.

Brass glances over at Matt, who doesn't react when Asami finishes. He scans the file before turning back to the doctor.

"Will he be a viable field agent?"

"In my professional medical opinion, it's too early to tell."

Brass nods a few times slowly. He closes the file and leans back in his chair.

"I expected to see better results today. This was worth exploring, but it might be time to move on from this experiment."

Now it's time for Matt to work his magic. "Sir, every worthwhile endeavor has had setbacks. The Manhattan Project took years to create the atomic bomb. The Apollo program had countless failures, including a fire that killed three astronauts on the launchpad before anyone ever walked on the moon. Are we really saying we want to give up now and leave ourselves wondering what could have been?"

Brass stares at his subordinate. "This is neither of those. The United States has invested millions in programs like this before and achieved zero results. Watchtower is too important to jeopardize with a man who hasn't developed any of the traditional skillsets and can't use the one advantage he has with any effect. I'm sorry. We have to pull the plug on this and get back to work defending this country."

Matt gave it his best try. Zach partly agrees with the director but has invested too much into Boston to go down without a fight. There is one more card to play, and it's up to him to throw it on the table.

"I understand your conclusion and how you reached it. I agree with you that this sounds crazy, and it seems wasteful because you're looking at this from a traditional angle. Agents who don't develop the tools they need wash out of training programs, whether at Langley or Quantico. Boston is different. We haven't yet begun to understand his capabilities because we haven't seen them in action yet."

"Agent Forte, are you suggesting that we make him operational?"

"Yes. I'm not talking about infiltrating North Korea or the Iranian nuclear weapons program. We can start with a small domestic mission. We need to see real-world results before determining if the investment is worth it."

Brass leans back in his chair, unable to argue with that logic. There is a tense silence in the room. Everything hinges on what he says next.

"You can't put the genie back in the bottle. Once Hollinger is operational, it's sink or swim. Is there a way to block this memory recall if things go wrong?"

"Sedatives can inhibit them," Dr. Kurota says. "We have only begun testing to see which ones are most effective."

"Why do you ask, David?" Matt asks.

"You're training an agent to tap into people's memories. I'm certain you appreciate how dangerous that is. He's under our control for now, but what happens if we ever lose it? A safeguard must be in place, or an alternative prepared for that possibility."

"Alternative?" Zach asks, feeling a surge of nervous energy roll up and down his spine.

"A weapon this dangerous needs to have a safety. Find one and make Boston operational. Present your results when you have them. And Matt, don't bullshit me on this. I want an honest assessment of his performance. If you sugarcoat it, you will find yourself busting meth dealers in the Mississippi boondocks."

"Yes, sir."

Brass leaves the room. Asami doesn't stick around either, undoubtedly knowing that Matt isn't happy with her prognosis. The two men stay seated at the table, weighing the stakes.

"Don't say anything to Boston about this yet," Matt commands. "Increase his training schedule and focus on critical skill development. I'll look for something that we can sink our teeth into."

"You heard what Brass said about—"

"We need to make sure it doesn't come to that. Let's get back to work."

CHAPTER FOUR

MAYOR ANGELICA HORTA

CITY HALL OFFICE OF THE MAYOR
PHOENIX, ARIZONA

Angelica Horta is no different than most other big-city mayors. She earned the support of Phoenix's citizenry by running on a bold platform that articulated a grand vision. After assuming office, Angelica immediately went to work on turning her campaign promises into action. That was when she discovered the cold hard truth about executive leadership: it's a tough job with lots of moving pieces.

The art of managing a big city like Phoenix is a gargantuan effort, but voter expectations pose the biggest challenge. A mayor acts as the check-in agent, security screener, refueler, pilot, and air traffic controller simultaneously. She may sit atop the pyramid, but egotistical city council members and ambitious department heads must constantly be dealt with. That doesn't matter. When there is a problem, the responsibility for addressing it falls on her shoulders. Fortunately, she has two trustworthy aides she can lean on.

"The press about the vice squad's raid of the stash house has been very favorable," Katy Bowlin says. As communications director for her office, she is the mayor's primary conduit to the news media.

"Twelve children," Angelica murmurs. "Lord knows what kind of horrors they saw."

"It was a small victory against sex trafficking, but an important one."

"I agree," Adrian adds. "The people need to see us taking action on this problem."

As her community relations director, Adrian Finley's job is to keep his fingers on the pulse of the community. As many people in leadership positions often learn, it's easy to lose touch with the people. Examples are aplenty on the national, state, and local levels, especially where large cities are involved.

Angelica presses her lips together. "The good press also provides us an opportunity to make some needed changes. We need to work with the police chief to reshuffle personnel around the department."

"You are suggesting the vice squad get rewarded by gutting them? "That won't be received well in the media," Katy warns.

"Or the community," Adrian adds.

"I know, but there are consequences if we don't. Our crime rate is almost one-and-a-half times the national average and worse than over ninety percent of all U.S. cities."

"Homicides dropped," Adrian offers, cocking his head slightly as he makes his point.

"Yes, and so did property crime, but violent crime increased. People feel less safe, and they will blame me. We live in the fastest-growing city in America. Our police response times average over seven minutes, with some calls taking fifteen to twenty. We need more officers patrolling the streets."

"Ma'am, your opponents will remind everyone that you balanced the budget on the backs of rank and file cops while you were on the city council. You promoted the six-year hiring freeze," Katy argues.

"We were facing a severe fiscal crisis. People need to be educated about why that decision was made," the mayor argues, glancing over to see Katy cross her arms.

"I understand that," Adrian says, no more enthusiastically, "but sex trafficking is one of the most heinous crimes there is, and it's thriving. We should be dedicating more resources to combating it, not fewer."

Angelica leans back in her chair and rubs the bridge of her nose. He's right, but there's a bigger picture. If an opponent in the next election makes crime an issue, she'll undoubtedly be vulnerable. That's the political angle. Morally, she has a sworn duty to protect the life, liberty, and pursuit of happiness of all people in Phoenix.

"If we had more resources, I would wholeheartedly agree with you. I'm not saying that we should abandon our efforts. I'm simply stating that it's hard for people to sympathize with the victims of one crime when they become victims themselves of others. We need officers on the streets."

"The community won't look at it that way," Adrian concludes.

"Katy?"

"You'll take a hit. We will need constant messaging to convince people that this is the right move. It's a tall order."

"Adrian, set up a meeting with the chief of police. Katy, start putting together a press release and draft some talking points. The media will have questions, and I want to be ready."

"Yes, ma'am."

Angelica moves back over to her desk and stares out the window. Nobody said this job would be easy. The chief will fight her on this, and the city council will try to score political points at her expense. That's the game. She played the same one when she was a lowly councilwoman. Like most things in life, the view is much different once you're on top of the mountain than when you're climbing it.

CHAPTER FIVE

ALEJANDRO SALCIDO

CORONADO NATIONAL FOREST
SANTA CRUZ COUNTY, ARIZONA

There is nothing quite like a quiet, undisturbed desert. The Coronado National Forest, with its twelve uniquely distinct mountain ranges and eight designated wilderness areas, abuts the Mexican border for sixty miles. Alejandro takes a lungful of the desert air and scans the rough terrain around him. While there are trees and other vegetation, it wouldn't meet most people's definition of a forest in any traditional sense.

Coronado's isolation makes for the perfect place for him to conduct his business. The Border Patrol's Tucson Sector has the highest incidence of cross-border violators in the United States. Nearly half a million illegal immigrants were apprehended crossing the border here last year. The government's efforts to control the border focus on either side of the Coronado National Forest, providing smugglers a less dangerous route into the U.S. for those who can handle the treacherous journey.

"Ya estan aqui, Jefe."

The man has good ears. Alejandro quiets his breathing to hear vegetation rustling in the distance as the human caravan climbs up to the dirt road that he and his men parked alongside. It will be another five minutes before they reach the rendezvous.

Alejandro tilts his head skyward. It's what he can't hear that's the most threatening. The American government uses drones to patrol the border with Alejandro's homeland of Mexico. There is no hiding from their infrared sensors and night vision should one of them venture this far north.

The coyote is the first to emerge as one of Alejandro's men shines a flashlight to mark their position. A rag-tag group of people who paid an exorbitant amount for the shot at a better life emerges behind him. Some may realize that dream. Most won't. A select few will come to understand that Alejandro has other plans for them.

"Helio. Es Bueno verte otra vez. Como estuvo el viaje?" another of his men asks the guide, handing him a bottle of water.

"Sin ninguna inconveniencia. Todos llegaron bien."

The usual group of Guatemalans and Hondurans are lined up, tired but all smiles. They have reached the end of their hike. The rest of their journey will be in the back of a truck. Once at the final destination, they are freed and on their own to make way to family members or start new lives.

"I'm glad your trip was uneventful," Alejandro says in English, nodding at the border.

"Thanks. I didn't expect to see you here, *Patrón.*"

"Did you hear about what happened in Phoenix? We lost four men and a houseful of product. The rest of the teams are lying low in their stash houses until we know it is safe for them to resume operations."

"That's unfortunate," the coyote says.

"Es la verdad."

The raid on the stash house was costly but could have been worse. Alejandro needs to protect his assets and manpower. That means personally handling tonight's selection.

"Bienvenidos a Los Estados Unidos," one of his men says to the group as he distributes bottles of water that they eagerly gulp down.

"See anything you like?"

"Are any of them on a payment plan?"

"The two at the end," Helio says, pointing to a mother and her small child.

The woman is no good, but the girl has potential. "Only two?"

"Sí. Humanitarian groups in Nogales are funding transport to the U.S. now. Does it matter?"

"No, it doesn't matter," Alejandro grumbles, smirking at the irony as he studies the faces of the migrants.

He could easily take them all. Nobody would ever know, but that's not how his business operates. Excess inventory costs money, and he needs profitable selections, not additional liabilities. After decades of working in this world, he knows what sells and what doesn't.

Alejandro points to his first choice. Two of his men grab the thirty-year-old woman, who screams until she is gagged. The rest of the migrants become restless, but running away is futile. Even if one should successfully evade a search, this is not a hospitable place to find yourself lost in.

He makes three more selections. Two of them are teens, and one is a young woman he's willing to take a chance on. He purses his lips before making his final choice.

"Llevense al pequeño. Dejen ir a la madre."

His men nod and grab a young boy, trying to wrest him from the death grip his mother has on him. With each side pulling at him in a tug-of-war, another of his men pistol whips her. She loses her grip as she tumbles to the ground before climbing back to her feet undaunted.

"Mama! Mama!"

The woman begins screaming in rapid-fire Spanish between her sobs. Alejandro has a hard time keeping up with the cursing in his native tongue. A man next to her jumps into the fray. He pushes one man and another in the back of his head before going for his gun.

The traffickers bring their firearms to bear on the maverick, but Alejandro is faster. He unholsters his weapon and shoots the man in the shoulder. Some of the migrants whimper and cower, while others scream. All of them freeze in place.

"¡Cállate!" Alejandro demands before turning to his right-hand man. *"Subanlos. Terminamos aqui."*

His men take the chosen to their truck. The remaining migrants are brought to another that will transport them to the designated drop-off point.

"What about this one?" Helio asks. "Do you want to just leave him here and let fate decide if he lives or dies?"

Helio has succeeded in getting the man to the United States. He was already paid in full with no balance due upon a successful border crossing. What happens north of the border isn't his concern, including the man dying here for being stupid.

"It's tempting, but he could find help. I don't want to risk him running to the police."

"¡No! Porfavor no lo haga—"

Alejandro levels his weapon at the man and puts a round into his forehead. He drops face-first into the ground.

"Find a place between here and the border to dump him," Alejandro commands one of his men in Spanish. The coyotes and vultures will eat well when they find him."

"Okay, Jefe."

Alejandro bids farewell to Helio and climbs into his vehicle as the group prepares to split up. He checks his watch. The sun will rise in a couple of hours. He'll drive north to a stash house on the outskirts of Tucson and spend the day there. Once his newfound merchandise gets subdued with drugs and cleaned up, he can find buyers. Within days, these migrants will be trafficked through his distribution channels. Their lives will change forever. For him, it's all in a day's work.

CHAPTER SIX

"BOSTON" HOLLINGER

WATCHTOWER TRAINING CENTER QUARTERS
SOMEWHERE IN VIRGINIA

Sleep is a demon. It stalks me during the day and haunts me at night. No matter how hard I fight, it still comes for me in the darkness. It's a battle I fight every day, and tonight is no different.

I pop another couple of ibuprofen to derail the freight train running through my head. I don't know if this raging headache is from my condition, stress, or Nadiya pounding on my face during today's training. Whatever the reason, over-the-counter painkillers aren't putting a dent in it.

At least there are no sensors connected to my head tonight. For once, Asami isn't asking for more data, whatever that means. If a year spent collecting it hasn't yielded answers about how I can see memories, I doubt that we'll ever find them.

It's more uncertainty in a world full of it. Something is going on with Watchtower, not that either Zach or Matt is cluing me in. I'm nothing more than a slave to the machine now. The government can't violate someone's civil liberties if they're legally dead. Only I'm not dead. I'm alive, if not living.

The glowing LEDs on the alarm clock read just after one a.m. In six hours, I'll be doing this all over again: physical conditioning, training, shooting, classroom work…it's like *Groundhog Day*, without the love interest. I would like nothing more than to kidnap Forte and drive off a cliff with him like Bill Murray did with Punxsutawney Phil. It'd be fitting.

My eyelids finally start to get heavy as I settle into the mattress. With my last conscious thought being a wonder about what cruel journey my dreams will take me on tonight, I clear my mind and drift off.

A man in a suit leans back in his chair. It's a conference room, maybe even the one at this facility. The fogginess that was the hallmark of these dreams a year ago is gone. My vision is not high-definition, but it's not the 1969 moon landing either.

I can feel the tension in the room as nobody speaks. It radiates through my body as I watch and wait for the man to say something.

"You can't put the genie back in the bottle. Once Hollinger is operational, it's sink or swim. Is there a way to block this memory recall if things go wrong?"

"Sedatives can inhibit them," a familiar voice says. It must be Dr. Kurota. Her sweet tone, laced with incredible intelligence, is unmistakable. "We have only begun testing to see which ones are most effective."

"Why do you ask, David?" another man asks. That sounded like Matt. I am looking through Forte's eyes.

"You're training an agent to tap into people's memories. I'm certain you appreciate how dangerous that is. He is under control for now, but what happens if we ever lose it? A safeguard must be in place, or an alternative prepared."

"Alternative?" I hear myself ask with incredible trepidation. The man only stares at me.

"Make him operational. Present your results when you have them. And Matt, don't bullshit me on this. I want an honest assessment of his performance. If you sugarcoat this, you will find yourself busting meth dealers in the Mississippi boondocks."

"Yes, sir."

My eyes click open. I sit up and close them, allowing the scene to replay in my head. After a year, it's much easier than when I searched for the mole and was led to a confrontation with Gina that forever changed my life. I know what I saw. Best of all, I understand what it means.

Content that I have extracted all the information, I open my eyes and let them settle on the wall. So that's what today was all about. My fate is in the hands of a man who doesn't know me or appreciate my capabilities. That won't do. It's time to take some control back in my life. One way or another, *Groundhog Day* is about to come to an end.

CHAPTER SEVEN
DETECTIVE BRESHION HURLEY

PHOENIX POLICE HEADQUARTERS
PHOENIX, ARIZONA

Breshion rubs his neck as he leafs through the report. The tedious work began once the house was secured, the children were removed, and the bodies were hauled off to the morgue. Evidence was collected, photographed, and cataloged. A thorough search was conducted, including inside the walls. Not a single inch of that place was left uncovered for as much good as it did.

"We got the identification back on the four heroes we killed during the raid," Ritter says, tapping a folder against his hand. "They were all illegals."

"Shocker," Breshion says. "There was nothing useful at all?"

The junior detective drops into the chair across from Breshion. "Nope. One of them was deported five times if you want to count that. These guys were just low-level thugs. What have you found?"

"Nothing of use. There is something odd, though. None of these guys had a cell phone."

"What? How is that possible? Traffickers move their merchandise around all the time. How did they coordinate pick-ups and drop-offs?"

Breshion grimaces. "They didn't. Someone else did."

"Someone who wasn't there during the raid."

"This was all for nothing."

"We got twelve kids back. That's something," Ritter argues.

"Yeah. How many more could we have saved? There were over three hundred reports to the sex trafficking hotline in Arizona last year alone. That's a twenty-five percent increase from the previous year and a fraction of the actual trafficking going on. A raid that saves twelve kids is like shooting at a tank with a BB gun."

"Not to those children."

Hurley can't argue with that. They made a difference in these kids' lives. It's a small victory, but it isn't enough. Not by a long shot.

"What other leads do we have?"

"Not many."

"These guys aren't ghosts, Phil. They're flesh and blood human beings, and they're out there."

He nods. "Yeah, somewhere in the desert. Pima County alone is the size of Vermont."

"We can't worry about what happens down there. Our charter is to stop traffickers from using Phoenix for their distribution. We're a boulder in the stream, not the dam on the whole river. We exist so that the mayor can say that they are doing something about the problem."

"Yeah, and in the meantime, people are sold in the sex trade under our noses."

"Detective Hurley?" Jamecca Robinson asks in an exasperated voice after she rushes over to the two men.

"What's up?"

"The boss lady wants to see you. It sounded important."

"How do you know that?" Breshion asks.

"Something in the way she said, 'Find Hurley and get his ass in here right now.'"

"Subtle as a chainsaw."

"Good luck," Ritter says as Breshion rises from his chair and grabs his coat.

The Phoenix Police Department has five assistant chiefs in charge of specific divisions. As the senior detective of the vice squad, he reports to the fiery Jada Fulcher. A twenty-eight-year veteran of the force, she has done and seen it all.

Her strategies tend to focus outside of enforcement by leveraging non-profits and community groups to help victims and nurture an atmosphere that prevents teenagers from joining criminal ranks in the first place. The programs have gotten wide acclaim from the community and the media. Time will tell whether her more ambitious projects will actually work.

"Take a seat, Detective Hurley," Jada says, getting down to business. "First, nice job on that stash house raid. I know the result isn't what you hoped for, but it's something."

"You're not the first to say that to me today."

"I'm sure. You need to hear it, though. You have a tendency to take these things personally."

"Sex trafficking is the modern form of human slavery. We both have some family experience with that," Breshion says, knowing that their great-great-grandparents worked on Southern plantations before the Civil War.

"Yes, we do. Hopefully, the favorable news coverage will help keep a spotlight shined on the problem."

"If you read the statement that the mayor released, you'd think we won the war."

Breshion might not bother himself with national politics, but knows all too well what happens at the municipal level. Politics here is a shell game. They keep their constituents' eyes on a decoy when the ball is really hiding under the shell you least expect.

"Yeah, about that," Assistant Chief Fulcher mumbles before frowning and fidgeting.

"What?"

She sighs deeply. "I'm going to start by saying that you aren't going to like this. For the record, I don't either, and I told that to the chief."

Breshion steels himself against the news that is about to be delivered. Jada has never shown any concern for his feelings before. His hard-nosed chief traded in her empathy with the last promotion for an old-school, tough-love approach. Whatever gem she's about to deliver is going to be terrible. Breshion shifts in his chair, feeling like another bomb is about to be dropped on him.

CHAPTER EIGHT
SSA ZACH FORTE

WATCHTOWER TRAINING FACILITY
SOMEWHERE IN VIRGINIA

Zach pulls off the main road onto the long gravel driveway that leads to the gate and the facility beyond it. He doesn't know why he bothers maintaining an apartment, having practically lived in this place for the past year. His tasking from Watchtower to supervise Boston's training has become life-consuming.

There are worse ways for someone to spend their time, and it beats the hell out of dealing with the bureaucrats in the FBI field offices. Nobody bothers him here except Matt. It's about the only advantage of this job.

After getting admitted through the gate, Zach parks his car outside the main facility. His identification is rechecked, even though the guards all know who he is. The first order of business is to check in with the nerve center of this place and find out what's in store for the day. The training schedule changes based on availability, and they are the keeper of it.

"Zach, where's Boston?" Nadiya calls out to him from down the hall. She's dressed in workout attire that makes her look like a Peloton spin instructor.

"I thought he was with you," he says, checking his watch.

"He was supposed to be. Boston never reported for training this morning. The cooks said he didn't show up for breakfast at the mess hall, either."

"It's not like him to skip a meal. Did you check his room?"

Nadiya cocks her head sarcastically. "Oh, gee, I never thought of that. There was no answer at his door. Nobody has seen him."

Forte pulls the walkie-talkie off his belt. "Ops, Forte. Give me the location of Boston."

"He's in his quarters, sir."

Everyone in this facility has a GPS tracker that is monitored from a centralized location. The buildings on this campus aren't large, but the training areas are hundreds of acres in size, and it helps knowing where people are.

"Roger, thanks," Zach says, turning to Nadiya. "Let's go wake up Sleeping Beauty. You can go extra hard on him today."

The pair walk to an adjacent barracks building reserved for trainees. Zach doesn't bother knocking when he reaches Boston's quarters. He swipes his facility identification badge on the door entry pad and hears the click as the lock disengages.

He expects to see Boston passed out in bed. Instead, it's empty. A sharp jolt of anxiety rattles him. Nadiya moves over to the desk, finds the watch that contains his GPS tracker, and she holds it up. He never leaves his room without it.

"Hi, Boston," the doctor says, answering the phone after Zach picks it up and dials her extension.

"Asami, it's Forte. I'm in Boston's room with Nadiya. Is he with you by any chance?"

"No, our session is later today. Why?"

"Did you monitor his sleep last night?" Zach asks, ignoring her question.

"No. What's wrong?"

"Nothing. Thanks," Zach says, hanging up as she starts to protest and dialing another extension.

"Ops."

"Boston isn't in his quarters. Only his GPS is. Contact all sentry posts and find him. This place isn't that big."

"Wilco," the man says, using the military lingo for "will comply."

"Let's head to the command center," he says to Nadiya, who beats him to the door despite his head start.

They travel to the beating heart of the facility in silence. The training center has a replica operations room where they train analysts via countless simulations. They can also run joint exercises in the training areas while feeding real-time data back to the room to see how they react. It is only staffed by two people during this off-cycle. One of them is talking to a guard who looks nervous as shit.

"He went for a run."

"What time?"

"Two forty."

"And you didn't think that was odd?" Zach asks, inserting himself into their conversation.

"No, sir, I didn't. Boston isn't a good sleeper. He's done it before on countless occasions."

"Pull up the surveillance video and track his route. Start with the cameras in the barracks."

"On it," the other technician in the room says. "Here."

"What's the time stamp?"

"Just after two thirty this morning."

Zach frowns. It lines up with what the guard admitted. At least he isn't lying to cover for Boston. The analyst deftly tracks him to one of the training areas. He hasn't picked up his pace at all.

"Does that look like a run to any of you?" Zach asks.

"Maybe he's sleepwalking," Nadiya offers.

"Where is this?"

"Urban Training A."

There are three urban sites located on the facility's grounds that are used on a rotational basis. One is used for scenarios, the second for familiarization and tactics training, and the third is always under construction. Crews, mostly Army engineers, are brought in to change the replicas so that agents don't get too accustomed to them. Area A is under construction right now.

Work is just starting on the dozens of buildings and asphalt streets found in any small city. These locations are perfect for situational training using "simunitions," paint-tipped bullets fired from real guns that result in splatters and painful bruises, not death. Better to learn that way than the alternative.

"Boston, what are you doing?" Zach whispers as he watches the shadowy figure move through the area under the infrared-enhanced night vision camera.

Boston pulls a tarp and a set of cutters from one of the buildings. The feed changes to a different camera, and the team watches as Boston begins cutting the links on the fence.

"Shit. Yeah, some sleepwalker. Where do those woods lead?"

An analyst brings up an overhead satellite image of the facility. He zooms out and shows the training area and woods beyond it that stretch for nearly a half-mile. Then he spots the road.

"Contact Watchtower Operations. Tell them that we have a real-world mission. We need to find Boston and fast. Get me the director on the line."

"Remsen," he answers on the first ring after the analyst dials.

"Matt, it's Zach. I'm in the command center."

"I'm five minutes out. What's up?"

Zach closes his eyes, not wanting to be the bearer of this news. Remsen is going to go ballistic.

"Boston made a break for it. He's no longer at the facility."

CHAPTER NINE
ALEJANDRO SALCIDO

DEZRT FYRE NIGHTCLUB
PHOENIX, ARIZONA

He should be more tired than he is, especially after staring at inventory reports for the past hour. Alejandro leans back and stretches. Today is a busy day made worse by constant interruptions. His bodyguard knocks on the door to signal another one.

"Birch Barron is here to see you."

"Send him in," Alejandro says, glancing at the clock on the wall. Seven a.m. is an unexpected hour for him to want a meeting.

"Do you ever sleep?" Birch asks, entering the office.

"Are you my doctor?"

"I'm the last person anyone would want medical advice from."

That part is true. Birch is well-known around Hollywood and Las Vegas. He's a concierge for some of the most influential people in business, entertainment, and sports. He makes in a day what Alejandro does in a month and isn't shy about flaunting it.

Impeccably dressed in an Italian silk suit with no tie and custom "BB" monogrammed cufflinks, Birch is one of Alejandro's best-paying and highest-profile clients. It's the only reason that he agreed to hold this meeting here.

"This is a beautiful place," Birch says, staring out the large window behind the desk down at the dance floor and bar beyond it. "You have what, six clubs and bars?"

"Seven."

"I imagine you make a lot of money from them."

"I do okay," Alejandro says, already not liking the direction of this meeting. He gestures Birch to a seat before taking his own.

"You do better than okay. How else would you justify making generous donations to groups around the city? You fund every political campaign and rub shoulders with the city council and the mayor."

"Is there a point you're trying to make?" Alejandro asks.

"No, not a point. I'm just curious why you do what you do. With thriving legitimate businesses, why cater to morally ambiguous endeavors?"

"You ask too many questions, Mr. Barron."

"I like to know who I do business with."

Usually, this is when Alejandro would be suspicious that the man is wearing a wire. Fortunately, he has a capable bodyguard who has already checked for that. The office is swept for listening devices daily, and there is no way a directional mic could pick up a conversation in the windowless office.

"I see. My father was a good man. An honest man. He ran several restaurants in Irapuato, where I grew up. He worked hard and had me back in the kitchen as soon as I could walk.

"Irapuato is not a safe city. Rival cartels were always fighting for control. My father wanted to be left alone, but that just wasn't possible. He heard and saw too much, so he went to work with them."

"Which one?" Barron asks, riveted by the story.

"All of them. It started off as brokering information. Then, my father diversified. You see, the drug lords had many needs, and he found ways to fill them. In return, he was left alone and became a wealthy man in the process."

"What happened to him?"

"He made one mistake," Alejandro admits. "He failed to pay off the politicians. One day, the government came for him. He didn't cooperate, but the cartels couldn't be sure of that. He was killed in the kitchen of his first restaurant, and I watched from my hiding spot under the counter."

Barron shifts uncomfortably. He was born with a silver spoon in his mouth and could never know that level of violence and pain.

"I'm surprised you didn't seek revenge."

Alejandro collects the inventory sheets and arranges them in a neat pile on the desk. "Who says I didn't? You are aware of my nickname. Where do you think I got it?"

"Is that a message to me?" the concierge says, suddenly defensive.

"No, Mr. Barron. I am simply explaining who you're doing business with. What do you want?"

"Your merchandise hasn't been of good quality lately. I'm a valuable client of yours – probably your most valuable. My customers demand the best."

"Which is why you get the first choice of everything in stock," Alejandro says, keeping the conversation metaphorical.

"That isn't good enough. My customers have discerning tastes, and they can afford whatever their hearts desire. I can make it worth your while for you to give me what I need to satisfy them."

Alejandro studies the man. He knows where this is going.

"My business is specialized."

"Diversify."

"Please, tell me how you expect me to do that."

"It's simple. You own seven hot spots, all brimming with young women every night. That's what my best-paying customers are looking for. Not the trash you keep peddling me."

"I understand. What do you think will happen when young women start disappearing out of my clubs? Do you have any idea how much attention that would attract?"

"Let's not pretend that matters. You took the lesson of what happened to your father to heart, and you wield considerable influence with city leaders. I assume you own the police as well. It's nothing you can't handle."

Alejandro leans forward in his chair and plants his elbows on the desk. "That's not how this works."

"As your most important client, I'm afraid I must insist. If you cannot satisfy my requests, I'll be forced to shop elsewhere. That makes you useless to me. *Comprende?*"

The Mexican stifles a scowl. This gringo has a pair of balls. It's insulting and disrespectful for him to use his eighth-grade Spanish vocabulary in this conversation.

"Perfectly. I value our relationship, so you offer me no alternative. Let me see what I can do."

Birch is all smiles. He got what he wanted and is content to wait for results.

"Thank you, Alejandro. I look forward to continuing our business together," he says as the men shake hands. "I will show myself out."

There was one part of the story about his father that Alejandro left out. The government came after him because he got greedy. No matter how much he made, it was never enough. That was ultimately what killed him, not the hitman's bullet.

"Do you want me to take care of him?" the bodyguard asks as Alejandro stares down at the empty club below.

"No. Barron is too powerful and connected for that. I have something else in mind."

CHAPTER TEN
MAYOR ANGELICA HORTA

CITY HALL PRESS BRIEFING ROOM
PHOENIX, ARIZONA

The mayor enters the room through the side door to the clicking sound of camera shutters and pops of light from flashes. Phoenix doesn't host packed press conferences like the White House does, nor do they have the media saturation of Chicago or New York. It doesn't mean they don't get any coverage.

"Thank you all for coming," Mayor Horta announces from the podium featuring the city's seal. "I am joined by our distinguished chief of police to announce our latest initiative to make our streets and neighborhoods safer. I have worked with the Phoenix Police Department on a plan to reallocate one hundred and eighty officers from specialized positions to patrol duty, effective next month."

Cameras erupt as the reporters in the room covering the event scan the faces of the uniformed police officials standing on each side of the mayor. All remain stoic and unflinching.

"Phoenix is a dynamic and rapidly growing city. Keeping our public sector staffing at the needed levels is challenging without raising taxes and placing undue burdens on our residents. As a result, overtime costs are skyrocketing, officer burnout has increased, and the morale of the entire force is suffering.

"I have discussed this measure at length with our chief of police. He agrees that this reallocation is necessary to ensure the safety of both our community and our officers. Our manpower peaked in 2008 with almost 3,400 sworn officers. That number has dwindled considerably since then, and the department has scrambled to find solutions to the problem. I think they have done a fantastic job, and I applaud them for their efforts."

Angelica turns and claps, prompting applause from the staff along the walls and a smattering of reporters. It's an orchestrated show of solidarity. Community groups, opposing political parties, and activists will use anything she says to advance their agendas. Often, those agendas are detrimental to the city and the people living in it.

"I'm happy to take your questions.," Mayor Horta announces.

"Why not increase the budget for law enforcement instead of shuffling personnel around the department?" a reporter asks from the front row.

"Our budget has already passed for this fiscal year. The city council is discussing the appropriate level of funding for the coming year. Unfortunately, the police department has already spent almost eleven million out of its allotted annual overtime budget."

"What is the amount of that budget?" another reporter asks.

"Twelve and a half million?" the mayor turns and asks the chief. He nods.

That exchange was orchestrated. Angelica knows precisely how much it is. She wanted to appear to engage their well-respected police chief as much as possible to show that he is actively involved in the decision-making. It's a show that every political leader puts on for the benefit of the reality television-loving public.

"Where will these additional officers be drawn from?"

"Thank you for the question. The short answer is the entire department. We are trying to minimize the impact to our specialized units to the extent possible, but no group will be left untouched."

"Madam Mayor, isn't this just a desperate ploy to cover up the fact that your administration has continued the hiring freeze instituted under your city council leadership prior to your election?"

Angelica bristles at the tone of the question from Vincent DiPasquale. There has never been a more despicable yellow journalist in this town. A shill for her political enemies, he can always be counted on to take even the best of news and provide an apocalyptic spin.

"We inherited a serious fiscal situation in this city, and—"

"Ma'am, your critics will point out that you've done nothing to rein in unnecessary spending during your term. Millions are being wasted, and our first responders are continually being asked to do more with less."

"I would not characterize it that way."

"Crime rates continue to rise in the city, yet the budget continues to shrink. How can it not be characterized that way?" LaCugna asks, pressing the subject.

Angelica clenches her teeth. Nobody in the media will help her on this one. They like division and tension, which is why even the friendlier reporters in the room are letting this grilling play out without interruption. Headlines about a heated exchange result in clicks. Clicks equal dollars.

"The budget is not shrinking, as you state," the mayor argues. "We are taking the necessary steps to protect our residents and maintain our healthy police department with the resources we have."

"Will you be asking the city council to increase the PPD budget in the next fiscal year?" another reporter asks, stealing the limelight.

"It is being looked into," Angelica says, sensing that this is starting to go sideways.

"You were critical of the police when you ran for mayor," another reporter says from the back of the room. "Is this simply a way for you to address the rising crime rate in the city without going against your pledge not to raise the budget? In fact, you ran on cutting it. Have you changed your mind?"

"As I stated, we will look at funding and work with the council to make appropriate adjustments."

"You didn't answer the ques—"

"I am going to invite the chief up to the podium to discuss how this personnel realignment will be achieved and provide greater detail about what teams will be impacted. Chief?"

Angelica steps aside as the police chief assumes the podium. She makes eye contact with Katy and blinks twice. It's the signal to her communications manager to end this press conference promptly after the chief and the councilmember speak. If they want to take questions, fine, but she won't be taking any.

It is amazing to her that every issue has to be politicized. She is addressing a need, and reporters are going after her for it. The flipside of the coin is equally applicable. If she does nothing and allows the crime rate to continue to rise, they would criticize her for inaction. She can't win, nor can she please everybody. The best she can hope for is to rally allies and supporters in the community to applaud her actions, and that's all she needs for another term.

CHAPTER ELEVEN
"BOSTON" HOLLINGER

LINCOLN MEMORIAL
WASHINGTON, D.C.

It was easier than I thought it would be to get to Washington. There are still people willing to offer strangers a ride, even in this day and age. I would have thought hitchhiking died in the nineties and that people would be more fearful of carjacking or worse. That wasn't the case. Now comes the tricky part.

The National Mall is one of the most touristy areas in the entire country. It's also among the top five heavily monitored places on Earth. I need to avoid cameras, but they're everywhere, and Watchtower can monitor the closed-circuit television feeds. That isn't my only problem.

Unbeknownst to most Americans, the government can also monitor social media uploads in real time. It's how they determine whether events need to be elevated on their threat matrix. Warnings were going out about the January 6th Capitol incursion days before it happened and were ignored. Much of that intelligence was generated from accessing social media.

If Watchtower has figured out I'm here, and I assume they have, they can use facial recognition to pinpoint my location. If they catch my face in a picture, the stopwatch starts. Tourists are among the most prolific of posters.

That's a problem for later. First, I need money to get anywhere from here and have none. There was no use for it at the training center. I can't exactly go knock over a souvenir shop without attracting unwanted attention. This is the Lincoln Memorial. I could throw a baseball and hit two dozen cops, and those are the ones I see. Watchtower is secretive and will keep the search for me in-house. That doesn't mean I won't find myself in a holding cell if hold up a hot dog stand for twenty bucks.

Tourists are less aware of their surroundings and the easiest targets to rob. I scan faces and look for targets of opportunity. They're everywhere. I now see how it's so easy to pickpocket in the big European cities. Purses and bags are open or unzipped, and men have wallets stuffed in their back pockets. People put their phones down next to them as they eat or talk, paying them no mind. I could spend an hour here and make a week's pay with what I've been taught so far. It wasn't a skill that I expected to use, but I'm glad I paid attention.

A busload of Asian tourists walks past me, all staring in awe up at the white edifice of the monument. Most of them have cameras around their necks or iPads open and pointed as they walk. A guide leads them, and I spot one particularly inattentive one. There's my huckleberry.

I walk ahead of the gaggle until I'm about twenty feet in front of them and stop, checking my pockets theatrically. With a groan and grimace to a young girl standing near me, I swivel quickly on my heels and take a step when the count in my head reaches zero.

I bump the small man harder than I intended, almost knocking him down. There was no way he could tell that I lifted his wallet from his jacket pocket. It's incredible what the CIA trains its agents to do.

"I'm so sorry," I say, holding my hands up to show no offense after I tuck his wallet into my windbreaker.

"Okay, okay," the man says with a series of short bows.

All is forgiven. At least, it will be until he notices his money is missing. I open the wallet and remove about half of the bills. That ought to be enough. I don't touch the credit cards, not wanting to make the rest of the man's vacation miserable. I take a chance and walk over to an officer, testing the theory that Watchtower hasn't contacted local law enforcement.

"Excuse me, sir. I found this lying on the ground over there. I think someone from that group dropped it."

The cop accepts the wallet and pulls out an identification before turning his attention to the tourists walking up the stairs.

"Okay, I'll handle it. You're an honest man. Thank you."

"No problem. Have a good day." I grin. Mostly honest.

The two hundred dollars will get me where I'm going. Now it's a matter of how to get there. Rideshares are problematic without a phone, app, and credit card. Watchtower will be watching mass transit closely, so that's out. That leaves taxicabs, which should be fine so long as I take a few precautions.

A designated cab stand sits next to the MLK Memorial, so I hustle in that direction without appearing to rush out of the area. It's not busy at this hour in the morning, so I don't have to wait for one to turn up. Time is getting short if I want to make it to my destination on time.

"Dupont Circle," I say, climbing in.

The driver doesn't bother responding. Taxi fares are computed by zones, but that's not why I'm stopping there. If a camera did pick me up in the Capitol Area, Watchtower would query every taxi company and check for pickups and drop-offs. Dupont Circle has a Metro station and other travel options they'll be forced to monitor. With taxis frequenting the countless hotels in that area, I can quickly get into a different cab for the second leg.

Content that the plan should work, I settle in for the ride as the driver takes Independence Avenue to Southwest Ohio Drive. Getting to my destination is no longer a problem; deciding what to do when I arrive is another story entirely.

CHAPTER TWELVE
SSA ZACH FORTE

INTERSTATE 66
WEST OF MANASSAS, VIRGINIA

Nadiya presses harder down on the accelerator, pushing the black Suburban down the interstate even faster. They're taking a shot in the dark. If Boston disappeared into the Virginia woods, they'd never find him. Their only hope is if he went to Washington, and even that will be searching for the proverbial needle in a haystack.

"We won't find him in D.C.," Emma says from the back seat.

"Boston has no money and no identification," Zach says, trying to stay optimistic. "He can't travel. All he can do is go to ground."

"We've been training him for a year. He knows how to get money. He can hotwire a car. There are multiple ways to get a fake ID. The CIA has brought in countless experts to teach him all of that, and he's a good student. If he wants to disappear, he can."

"Thank you, Miss Rosie Sunshine," Zach grumbles, not wanting to admit that Emma is probably right.

"I'm just saying that Boston knows we're looking for him. He knows how surveillance in this country works and how to avoid it."

"He's not a ghost," Zach argues, not fully believing it himself.

"He might as well be," Nadiya says from the driver's seat.

Zach's phone rings, and he answers it, placing it on speaker. "Forte."

"It's Matt. I have you conferenced in with Watchtower Ops."

"Tell me you have a lead."

"We have nothing. We think Boston might be heading toward Washington based on traffic in the area, but it's only an educated guess. We're casting a wide electronic net. We'll get him."

Nadiya looks at Forte and shakes her head. He doesn't need to check the back seat to know that Asami and Emma are doing the same thing.

"Okay, keep me posted."

"Take me off speaker."

Zach complies, turning his head to stare out the window. "Done."

"Forte, we need to find him."

"Yeah, no shit. Are you bringing in additional resources?"

"Not yet," Matt says after a long pause. "We have to keep a lid on this as long as possible. You know what will happen if Brass gets a sniff of this."

"Roger that. I'll be in touch," Forte says with a sigh before hanging up. "I'm open to suggestions."

"I'm with Emma," Nadiya says. "We're not going to find him using traditional methods. We need to anticipate him."

As good as Watchtower is, they aren't capable of monitoring an entire metropolitan area. With every passing moment, the radius that Boston could have traveled from the training center grows. The ladies are correct: If Boston is going to be found, it's because they effectively reduce the search area.

"Okay. I want to go someplace I can't be found. Where would I go?"

"You're assuming his motivation," Asami says. "What if that's not it at all?"

"What else would it be?"

"He saw the meeting with Brass," Asami concludes. "He sees memories of stressful situations. If he wasn't looking through my eyes, I'm betting he experienced the memory through yours."

"You don't know that, Doctor."

"It's a reasonable assumption considering the timing, and you know it."

"What was said that would make him run?" Emma asks.

Forte turns and looks at Asami, who returns his stare before continuing to look out her window. The meeting was sensitive. Despite their security clearances, neither of the two trainers in the vehicle is entitled to know what was discussed. This isn't a time to pull that card. He needs their help.

"Let's just say that parts of that conversation taken out of context would make any of us run."

"Why do I work for the government again?" Nadiya moans.

"I ask myself that every day. Okay, let's assume our dream warrior went to Washington. Why would he go to one of the most surveilled cities in the country?"

"Better travel options?" Emma suggests. "You can get anywhere from Washington via multiple modes of transportation."

"There are plenty of empty apartments to hide in," Emma adds. "And it's a city that provides a degree of anonymity. He won't stick out there."

"Unfinished business," Asami concludes, causing Zach's eyes to light up.

"Son of a bitch."

"What is it?" Nadiya asks.

"Only fools fall in love."

"What, are we quoting the Drifters now?"

"When it's applicable," Zach says, calling Watchtower Ops. They pick up on the first ring.

"We haven't found anything yet, Agent Forte," the man who answers the phone says without preamble or even waiting for a question.

"And you probably won't. I need the current location of Dr. Tara Winters. Call me when you have it."

Zach ends the call and sets the phone down in one of the cup holders. He rubs his chin and takes a deep breath. One encounter with her could ruin everything. With that thought, Forte opens his secure tablet, logs in using the biometric scanner, and calls up a file.

"You don't think…"

"Yeah, Emma, I do. Nadiya, get us to Chevy Chase."

"All right. How will Watchtower find her?"

"They've been keeping tabs on her since Boston arrived, haven't they?" Asami asks.

It wasn't Zach's idea, but he didn't disagree with it, either.

"We keep tabs on all of Boston's former friends. If any of them started digging, we need to know. The success of this project relies on Boston's anonymity."

Eric Williams works for the Defense Intelligence Agency and has contacts throughout the intelligence community. His friend Louisiana is a drifter who seems to stay a step ahead of trouble and has an extensive network of his own. Tara Winters is a doctor with the most reason to hope that Boston is still alive.

"Wait a second. Tara doesn't live in Maryland. She has a townhouse in D.C. What's in Chevy Chase?"

Zach stares out the window as the SUV chews up the road.

"Old memories."

CHAPTER THIRTEEN
DETECTIVE BRESHION HURLEY

CITY HALL OFFICE OF THE MAYOR
PHOENIX, ARIZONA

There are "career-ending" moves in every occupation. They are the actions employees take that will get them fired without hesitation. Sometimes, irrationality drives the behavior. However, there are moments when someone stands up for a principle. This is one of those. Let the consequences be damned. Breshion has seen enough.

"Is she in there?" the detective asks, barging into the outer office and passing the administrative assistant's desk.

"You can't go in," the woman screeches, startled as she awkwardly tries to get out of her chair to stop him.

"Watch me."

Breshion throws open the mayor's office door and stomps in, stopping just short of her desk. Her eyes grow wide at the intrusion as she cradles a phone between her shoulder and neck.

"Marjorie, let me call you back," Mayor Horta says, placing the receiver back in its cradle. "What the hell do you think you're doing?"

Hurley's mouth goes dry. This seemed like a good idea all the way up to this point. Now that he's in the position to vent his anger on the leader of their city, the words he so carefully crafted in his head escape him.

"I told him you were busy, Madam Mayor."

"You put out a press release gushing about how invaluable vice is in the war against human trafficking," Breshion says, recovering from his anxiety-triggered laryngitis. "You claimed that our raid the other day gave twelve children their lives back. Then you gutted my squad. I demand to know why."

"I'll call the police," the admin says.

"Don't bother. We're already here," Breshion says, keeping his eyes locked on the mayor.

"No, it's okay, Cynthia. Tell the councilman when he arrives that I'm running late and will be with him shortly." The major watches her assistant leave and close the door before glaring at the detective. "I'm not accustomed to having the police barge into my office and issue threats."

"I didn't threaten you, Mayor."

She flashes a brief smile. "That's a matter of perspective. If I tell your bosses and the media that you did, who do you think they'd believe?"

"Another lie," Breshion says, shaking his head. "Just like you lied about giving a damn about those kids. About all the victims of human trafficking. They are just more props in your political theater, aren't they?"

"Are you trying to get yourself fired, Detective?"

"If that's what it takes."

"I admire your passion," the mayor says, grinning and nodding. "For the record, I do care about human trafficking. You only think I don't because you measure my convictions against your own. I understand. You lead the vice squad and see the worst of society every day. The struggle to make this city a better place lights a fire inside you."

"Someone has to."

"Unfortunately, as mayor of this country's fifth-largest city, I have to balance every issue that comes across my desk. I don't have the luxury of focusing on just one, regardless of how despicable it is."

"Have you seen those children, Mayor Horta? Have you gone to the hospital and looked into their eyes? Seen their shattered innocence?"

"No, nor have I met with all the families of murder victims in this city over the past year. There is nearly twenty percent more of them than last year. Nor have I met property crime or rape victims. Both of those crimes are on the rise. I haven't talked to families we've raised taxes on or all the business owners who have lost revenue so we could cover our growing expenses. I can't speak to every person in this city who feels it's less safe here. Do you know why? I don't need to meet or speak to them to know the truth."

"What truth would that be?" Breshion asks.

"That we have a surge of crime in Phoenix and limited resources to fight it. I didn't gut your team as you insist, Detective. I trimmed it down. I know that you don't like it. For the record, I don't like it either. Trust me when I say that there are no good alternatives. I need more cops on the streets. The academy is barely producing enough officers to replace the ones we lose through attrition, and there is no money to surge more through."

"That's bullshit," Breshion utters.

Mayor Horta stares at her city's insubordinate vice officer before narrowing her eyes at him.

"Don't test my patience further by calling me a liar. I don't really give a damn whether you believe me or not. Understand this: So long as I sit in this office, I will make the best decisions I can for the people of this community. Right now, that means reducing your headcount to help keep those people safe, and asking you to do more with less. You don't like it? That's too damn bad. I may not understand the horrors you face, but you sure as hell don't understand the challenges I do."

Breshion has heard enough. He nods sarcastically and tightens his jaw. He looks around her well-appointed office, complete with framed pictures of her posing with dignitaries, celebrities, and other career politicians. This is the center of power in Phoenix, and it reeks of careerism.

"I understand that politicians in this city, state, and the country don't want to talk about this issue. Nobody wants the people to know that the United States is one of the leading nations for sex trafficking. Or how Arizona only trails Nevada in the number of cases. It's an invisible problem, and you need to keep it that way to help your reelection chances. A hundred more officers patrolling the city is a Band-Aid that won't do jack to stop rising crime. You care more about the perception of action than addressing the actual problem."

"Fair enough. You've stormed in here and made your contempt for me very clear without consequence. Now let me respond with some of my own. Get the hell out of my office before I have another police officer to replace."

There's nothing to be gained by continuing this confrontation. Breshion fully expected to lose his job after this. The fact that he still has his is a blessing...and a curse. He scoffs and swings the door to her office open, startling the councilman and her administrative assistant waiting in the outer office. He storms out, having accomplished nothing more than getting his frustration off his chest and making an enemy in the process.

CHAPTER FOURTEEN

MAYOR ANGELICA HORTA

CITY HALL OFFICE OF THE MAYOR
PHOENIX, ARIZONA

Angelica closes her eyes and lets out a long, slow exhale. It's on these days that her meditation and yoga classes pay dividends. A knock on her door jamb interrupts her brief moment of solace as her assistant announces the next contestant on "Pin the Tail on the Mayor." She nods and stands behind her desk as her smug archnemesis enters the office.

"Good morning, Mayor Horta."

"Mr. Councilman."

Andres LaCugna is as pompous and arrogant as they come. How he manages to convince anyone to vote for him escapes Angelica's rational comprehension. He's slick, lies daily, and will exploit any opportunity to gain influence and power. There are no limits to the man's ambitions, and nothing is off-limits for him to reach them.

"That detective looked mildly upset," Andres says, pointing over his shoulder.

The mayor was hoping that he didn't see or hear that. "Not everybody likes change."

"Not everybody likes what you just did," he says, taking a seat in front of her desk and making himself comfortable.

"Am I to assume you are one of them? I expected you to host a press conference of your own. It's not like you're allergic to the media."

"Oh, shots fired," he says, plastering on a sarcastic smile that she wants to slap off his face.

There is no love lost between him and the mayor. He's one of her most outspoken critics, and not just because they disagree on most issues or because he wants her job. They served on the city council together and personally can't stand each other.

"Am I wrong?"

"That I have a good relationship with reporters? No. That this reshuffling will have any effect on street crime and won't hamper the police – you couldn't be more wrong. That's okay. The people have come to expect that from you."

"I didn't accept your meeting request to trade smears with you."

"No, you did it hoping to somehow earn my support, which is honestly futile since you won't. Your inability to focus on the real problems in the city is becoming legendary."

"I just did," the mayor snaps.

"You did nothing of consequence. Sure, you can point to this and say you tried, but it's meaningless. We both know it. Apparently, so does that detective."

Angelica shakes her head. It was a long shot to think that LaCugna would support anything she did. If she discovered a vaccine that cured cancer, he would find a reason to say something against it. That's just the way modern politics works.

"Something I'm certain you won't hesitate to point out. Why did you want this meeting?"

Andres leans forward and balances his elbows on his knees as he steeples his hands over his lips. He's trying to look thoughtful and diplomatic. The chicanery makes Angelica suppress a grin. She knows he's neither.

"To formally ask you to reconsider this new personnel realignment."

"You know that I won't. That means you are only here so that you can run to the media to politicize the issue and slander me for being unreasonable."

"It's good to know that we hold each other in such high regard," Andres says after a sarcastic laugh. "If explaining to people why this move is rash, irresponsible, and dangerous is politicizing it... then yes, I am."

"Whether you believe it or not, shifting our police resources is in the best interests of our city. If you want to politicize this attempt to combat a rising crime rate, fine, we'll see who comes out on top."

"Human trafficking and illegal immigration are the two fastest-growing crimes in Phoenix. You respond to that with deep cuts to the two departments most responsible for combating them."

Angelica knew he would bring that up. It's untrue, not that the councilman cares much for facts that don't support his narrative. The cuts came from across the entire department, not just vice. He would have a more difficult time selling that in a sound bite. It's flashier to package it the way he did, truth be damned.

"I have the full support of the police chief," Angelica argues, changing the context of the discussion. There is no point in giving him a warning about any possible rebuttal to his nonsense.

"Yes, you have your allies. My sources tell me that the chief thinks the move is boneheaded but refuses to go against you publicly."

"I asked for an honest assessment. That's what I got."

"Yes, yes, I'm sure that's it. I'm certain that you weren't placated by a man who just wants to keep his job for a few more years until retirement."

Angelica smiles pleasantly. "You're in Fantasyland again, Andres."

"And if you think you did anything to make the streets safer, so are you."

This discussion is going nowhere. Andres has made his position clear, not that she needed him to. It's time for them both to get on with their day. Whatever happens next will play out in front of cameras and microphones, and the people will decide.

"Is there anything else?"

"Yes. I'm reintroducing a resolution to increase funding for the police department and other critical services that the city council cut years ago."

"Ah, yes, where you'll make deep cuts to education, raise taxes, and gut public-sector benefits to help pay for it. That's a death sentence for many of our residents, most of whom are staunch supporters of mine."

"There you go playing politics again," Andres laments. "And here I thought you got elected because you didn't play them."

Angelica bristles at the line, more because of its truth than anything. Her reputation as a no-nonsense city leader who didn't engage in political chicanery carried her to this office.

"We both know that you don't care one iota about police funding, Andres. You're trying to hurt me. I take bold steps toward solving a problem, and you forge wedge issues for the next election. That's all your resolution is."

"It's a shame that you've developed such a jaded view of the world. You never used to be that way when you were on the council," Andres says, rising from his seat and buttoning his jacket. "I hope you'll give it your full consideration, Angelica. It's likely to pass, and this isn't an issue you want to be seen on the wrong side of. Good day, ma'am."

Andres shows himself out, and Angelica moves to the window to look out over her beloved city. Everything is a battle in government, and both sides fight for ground. The casualties are the innocent people caught in the crossfire. One side wins, and another loses in the zero-sum game that is the never-ending political war. In Phoenix, the newest front is about to open up.

CHAPTER FIFTEEN

ALEJANDRO SALCIDO

DEZRT FYRE NIGHTCLUB
PHOENIX, ARIZONA

The counting is taking forever. Boxes must be checked and relocated as the totals are annotated on a clipboard. Alejandro doesn't have time for this. He folds his arms impatiently as the last ones are completed. Sometimes the only way to ensure a job gets done is to oversee it yourself.

"*Veinte.*"

The club manager annotates the total and does the math, checking it twice. He swallows hard.

"How many are missing?" Alejandro asks.

"Five."

"Bottles?"

"Cases," the manager croaks.

"*Vamanos,*" Alejandro orders the workers, shooing them out the door with his hands. They leave the two men alone in the cellar. They don't want any part of whatever is about to happen next.

"I hire you to run my club. I trust that you are capable of keeping things in order. This is the result of your work? Five missing cases of alcohol?"

"I manage this place closely. We've never had anything like this happen before."

"Which is always true until the first time something happens. It's why I demand constant vigilance and attention to detail. Take your eyes off *los hijos por una momenta*, and the children cause mischief," Alejandro says. He often switches between English and Spanish when he's upset. "I started from nothing and managed to build these businesses. When my responsibilities exceeded the time I had available, I found reliable people to help. Now I own seven bars and nightclubs in the greater Phoenix area. Do you know how many of them have missing inventory?"

"*No, Jefe.*"

"Just yours."

"I will find out who did this," the man sputters.

"And then what? Fire them? Hand them a pink slip? No, no, no, that's not how this works. I can't have the word on the street that it's okay for people in my employ to steal from me. There must be repercussions. Serious ones. You understand that, right?"

"Yes, *Jefe.*"

Alejandro puts his arm around the manager and moves his face inches away from his. "You will find out who is ripping me off. You will bring me irrefutable proof of his acts, and then you will bring him to me. I will take care of the rest. If you fail to do that, or you decide to find an innocent man to scapegoat in the hope it will save your ass...well, make sure your will is in order."

"Y-yes, *Jefe*. I won't let you down."

"*Bueno.*"

His bodyguard, who has a neck as thick as a sequoia, escorts his lieutenant and another man down the stairs. The pair heads toward them with dour looks on their faces. This cannot be good.

"We are done here. Go back to work and do not disappoint me."

His club manager wastes no time leaving the dingy stockroom and scurrying across the basement to the stairwell. He got the message. Now it's just a matter of whether he can deliver before Alejandro decides that he needs to find a replacement. Javier's arrival is more disconcerting.

"I assume this is important. What's the problem?"

Javier nods at the man. "Go ahead, tell him."

"We had a problem this morning," the man says with fear in his eyes. "One of the girls we were transporting escaped from my men. She went to the police, forcing us to abandon the entire shipment."

Alejandro stares at the ground as he absorbs the news. "What are the losses?"

"Seven women, ages fifteen to twenty-seven," Javier says. "All migrants."

"A girl escaped? Tell me, how exactly does that happen? Was she armed? A black belt in Karate? Batwoman?"

The man looks at the ground. "*No, Jefe.* One of the men...he—"

"He tried to sample the product and got caught with his pants down. *Sí?*"

The man's body language says everything Alejandro needs to know. It's not the first time he's had to deal with this as his business has grown.

"She was getting mouthy with him," the man says, almost pleading. "He wanted to teach her a lesson."

"I see. This is not the first time this has happened? Correct?"

"*Jefe*, I—"

"Answer my question!" Alejandro demands.

"No."

"No? Are my rules unclear? Why did this man think that he had the authority to teach anyone a lesson? Hmm?"

"I...*no lo sé*...I don't know," the man says, breaking into tears.

"You run that crew, yes? Where were you when this unfortunate escape happened? Were you teaching a lesson as well?"

"No, I was..."

Alejandro cocks his head as the man's voice trails off. Alejandro can spot a liar from across the room. He recognizes swindlers and thieves just by looking into their eyes. He is *El Hombre Magico* because of those tricks and many more.

"What is happening today?" he asks his bodyguard, who may be short on brains but looks like he could bench press his car. "Everyone thinks that they can run my business better than I can."

"It won't happen again. I swear it!" the man says, pleading for forgiveness.

"No, it won't."

Alejandro pulls the gun out of his bodyguard's holster and fires a single round into the man's forehead. He is angry enough to fire the entire magazine into his corpse, but doesn't want to make any more of a bloody mess on the floor than he already has. He hands the weapon back to the bodyguard, who holsters it without uttering a word.

"Would you have done that, Javier?"

"No. I would have put two in his chest first."

Alejandro smiles, knowing he picked a good lieutenant. "Did this man have a family?"

"Yes. A wife and a child," Javier says.

Alejandro nods. "Get someone to clean this up and take the body to his home. Murder-suicides are tragedies that happen too often in this country. Then make the other men disappear. Let me know if they make it to the police first."

"I will see to it. And the girls?"

Alejandro presses his lips together. "They know nothing of value. They're the ones who got away. Good for them."

Alejandro heads back upstairs to his office. What a mess. The men responsible will realize the cold, hard consequences so that others can learn a harsh lesson. There is a price for failure in this business, and it doubles for incompetence.

CHAPTER SIXTEEN
"BOSTON" HOLLINGER

THE CHASE IS ON COFFEE HOUSE
CHEVY CHASE, MARYLAND

I sip a coffee and check the clock on the wall before staring out the large picture window. It's almost noon and a little late for coffee, but it's the only spot with a clear line of sight to the entrance. Workers in business suits pour out as their lunch break begins on this sunny, warm day.

It's been over a year since I've been anywhere outside of the Virginia woods, much less Chevy Chase, Maryland. This place looked much different at night. I never forgot the world outside of the constrictive confines of the sterile training center, but I started to miss it less.

This place brings back a lot of memories. The office building across the street was where I learned that my fiancée was a traitor. It's the last place I raced home and was shot and left for dead. It's also where I shared my only kiss with Tara, so one of the memories is pleasant. That was something I had wanted to do since meeting her, and that was the only moment I could pursue that ambition without guilt.

I shift in my chair at the table alongside the window. This is a long shot worth taking. My backup plan requires me to go up to the Solvasön Sleep Center, and I'd rather not do that. I can't be sure Tara even works there anymore. At least I can remain here in relative anonymity and plan my next move – possibly a trip to her home in Adams Morgan.

That proves unnecessary when I catch a glimpse of Tara breezing out the doors in her white lab coat. My heart practically jumps out of my chest. She's still the vision I imagined she would be.

I scramble from my table to the door and walk down the opposite sidewalk. My heart thunders like a bass drum in my chest despite imagining this moment a thousand times. I've rehearsed in my head what I want to say, using different words each time just to hear how they sound. I never settled on the right approach, even in the cab ride up here. Now it's time to pick one.

Tara crosses the street and angles toward the deli ahead of me. I pick up my gait. The door swings open hard, and a woman with an open soda cup careens into her. The drink ends up all over the doctor as both women recoil at the shock of the impact, and the doctor stares down at her soaked lab coat.

"Oh my God! I'm so sorry!" the blonde exclaims.

"It's okay. It was an accident."

"Let me help with that," she says, grabbing napkins off the bar and running them over Tara's coat. "I can't believe I did that."

Tara has her back to me as I walk closer. A brunette materializes next to her friend and grins. I stop cold. Emma.

"You are such a klutz," Emma says as Nadiya eyes me over Tara's shoulder.

My anger rises as I stare at my two instructors. How did they track me here? It doesn't matter. They can't stop this.

"Let me pay for your dry cleaning," Nadiya says, keeping Tara's full attention.

"No, really, it's okay. I have a change of clothes at the office. It's no big deal."

"Are you sure?"

"Yes, thank you for the offer, though."

I need to regain my composure. This is my moment. Emma and Nadiya block my path to the door as Tara turns to enter the deli. She pauses, turns her head, and stares right at me. Our eyes lock on each other, and she offers a warm smile. I'm fixated on her and become paralyzed in the process. I will my legs to move, but it feels like I am standing in wet concrete. My voice works, though, and I'm about to call out when a man steps in front of me.

"Hey, buddy. Whatcha think you're doing?"

CHAPTER SEVENTEEN
SSA ZACH FORTE

THE CHASE IS ON COFFEE HOUSE
CHEVY CHASE, MARYLAND

Boston tries to peer over the senior agent's shoulder as Tara disappears into the deli. There's desperation in his eyes. He is capable of anything.

"Get out of my way, Zach."

"Yeah, that's not going to happen."

Boston starts to push his handler aside so he can follow the doctor. Forte expects that and slides over to the left to block his path. Boston clenches his teeth and tightens his jaw.

"Don't even think about it," Zach orders. "Even if you manage to get past me, you'll still have to deal with Emma and Nadiya. My money is on you not getting past them. You know that better than anyone."

Boston's shoulders dip as he relaxes. Zach is thrilled that he relented without making a scene. He also can't believe how fortunate they are. It's a miracle that they arrived in time and that this tactic worked. Asami came through for them.

"How did you find me?"

"Intuition," Zach says.

"I thought maybe you had a GPS locator sewn into my face."

"No, but you might have one after this stunt."

Boston nods. "So, what happens now? Are you going to spirit me back to my prison in chains?"

"No. Let's go back to that coffee house you came out of and have a chat," Zach says, gesturing Boston back up the street.

After a quick check at his two teammates, he complies. His window of opportunity is shut. The two men walk back to the shop, order coffees, and take a seat away from the window. Boston glances at the door to see Nadiya standing there. Emma selects a table only a dozen feet away.

"You timed that perfectly," Boston says.

"Thank Asami for that. She went up to the sleep center and learned when and where Tara was going to lunch. We just didn't know where you were hiding until you walked out of the shop. You should try looking more inconspicuous."

"I'll remember that next time. Tara looked right at me and didn't have a hint of recognition," Boston mutters after Zach sits and stares at him in silence.

"Nobody will recognize you. Even if they somehow spot the resemblance to the friend they once knew, everyone thinks you're dead."

"I thought… Tara smiled at me."

"You look like Matthew McConaughey. Almost every woman on the planet would flash a smile at that man."

"If you're so convinced that nobody will recognize me, then what's the harm in having a conversation with her?"

Forte sighs. "She can't know what happened, Boston. Your face has changed, but your words and mannerisms haven't. There's a chance she could figure it out. Even a slim chance is more risk than we can afford."

Boston leans back and folds his arms. "Why? Nobody has bothered to explain to me what you people want. You've violated every civil liberty I have to turn me into a science experiment. Not once has anyone asked if I want to do this. Even David Webb was given a choice to become Jason Bourne."

Zach shakes his head. "I thought we covered this months ago."

"We did. You talked about this gift, or curse, and all the people it could help. I listened. I never agreed. Look, all I want to do is talk with her. That's a reasonable request considering my position."

"No, it's a lie. You want to rekindle a past romance. You came here hoping that Tara's still pining for you more than a year later. That's what you've imagined all these months, right?"

Boston doesn't say anything. That's precisely what he wants. Zach has an excellent bullshit detector, and any denials will be pointless.

"She isn't pining for you."

Boston's head snaps. "How do you know?"

Zach pulls out his tablet, opens it with a biometric scanner, and slides it across the table. Boston stares down at the open file with Tara's picture on the side. He begins to scan its contents.

"Because she's about to get engaged."

"If you tell me it's that dweeb Steven from the sleep center, I will throw myself in front of one of Emma's targets."

"That won't work – she'll bend the bullets around you. To answer your question, no, it isn't Steven. Their relationship has stayed platonic, so far as we can tell," Forte says as Boston scrolls down and then opens attachments containing pictures of Tara and her boyfriend.

"He must love that."

"This guy is a medical services strategist, whatever that is. She met him at a conference about three months after you died. They've had a slow romance that has gotten hotter with each passing month. He bought a two-carat diamond engagement ring three weeks ago. Tara is booked on a flight to Aruba with him next month. I'm betting he proposes during that trip."

Boston turns off the tablet and pushes it back across the table. "Why are you telling me this?"

"You need to know."

"No, Zach. I needed to know months ago. Why now? Did it have to take my breaking out to get Watchtower to give me any information?"

"We are on the same side, Boston," Zach argues, wishing he had chosen his words more carefully.

"Then start proving it."

"You're right. I should have told you. I underestimated your feelings for Tara, and I apologize for that. It doesn't change anything, though."

"Maybe not for you. Tara moved on. I don't have that luxury."

Zach wants to ask why he ran, but at the same time, doesn't want to know. If Boston saw the meeting with Brass in a dream, it confirms everything he feared. Once confirmed, the information gets reported to Matt and then up the chain. Not asking buys time, or so Zach hopes.

"That's about to change. You asked if I was going to take you back to your prison. We're not. You're not going back to the training facility, at least right now."

"What do you mean?"

"We have our first assignment."

"Yeah, I don't really care," he says, staring back out the window.

"I know you don't, but you're going anyway."

"Fine. Whatever. When are we leaving?"

Zach looks at his watch. "Right now. We packed you a bag. It will be waiting for you at the airport."

"Where are we going?"

Forte grins. "Someplace warm."

CHAPTER EIGHTEEN
MAYOR ANGELICA HORTA

CITY HALL OFFICE OF THE MAYOR
PHOENIX, ARIZONA

Angelica stares down at the city out her office window. It's not the world's prettiest view, but that's hardly the point. It's a reminder of her obligations. Only one person in the city has it, and that person is responsible for the welfare of the people living in this fast-growing desert metropolis.

Adrian and Katy stand patiently on the other side of her desk. Neither of them wanted to deliver this news. Now they can only wait for instructions as to what to do about it.

"Ma'am?" Adrian asks, piercing the long silence. Angelica doesn't move, her mind still racing.

"The timing isn't good," Katy admits.

"Who requested assistance from the feds? The chief? Vice squad?"

"I don't think so," Adrian says. As her community affairs liaison, he would know best. "Those requests would have been funneled through the Phoenix FBI field office. My contacts there said that they were as surprised as we were. They still haven't been officially notified by the Hoover Building."

"Did the city council go behind my back?"

"Why would they?" Katy asks, turning her head to stare at Adrian.

"It's something LaCugna would do," the mayor offers.

"No, ma'am. He doesn't have anywhere near that much clout."

Angelica leaves the window and returns to her desk. She stares at the paperwork on it, but her mind is stuck on this newest development.

"Options?"

"We could try to bury it," Katy says. "Treat it as business as usual."

"Someone will leak it. You know that," Angelica's community relations director argues.

"Adrian, we can't bury our heads in the sand and say nothing. The mayor announced the reassignment of vice squad resources. How will it look when a special FBI team shows up to combat human trafficking? It makes us look incompetent."

"Or strong," he insists. "Like we brought in federal resources that our citizens don't have to pay for."

Angelica's head snaps up. "You think we should take credit for the request?"

"Why not?"

"We'll get challenged on it," Katy argues. As the staff member in charge of the mayor's messaging efforts, she knows the circus that could turn into.

"By who? The FBI won't confirm or deny the information. Everything else is a rumor."

"Not a good one. The city council or even the police department could refute it. The media will start digging. Worse, the mayor would be outright lying."

Angelica paces behind her desk. Her two staffers remain silent as their eyes track her movements. They know better than to climb on the tracks while her train of thought gets up to full speed.

"I've been in politics for a while now. The one thing I've noticed over those years is that everyone lies. It's the type of lie you tell and who it hurts that makes the difference. The arrival of this special FBI team is a benefit for the city. A white lie hurts nothing, assuming anyone bothers sniffing it out. What it does do is cut my political enemies off at the knees. Their lies are only designed to enhance their own power. They don't give a damn about anything else."

Both of her aides nod. Whether they agree is irrelevant. They are here to serve their mayor, and she has made her decision.

"How do you want to do it?" Katy asks. "Another press conference?"

"No, I don't need the media asking questions that I'm not ready to answer. Let's release a statement and then find out why this team from Washington is here. Most of all, I want to know who sent them and why. See if they'll meet with me so I can formally welcome them to Phoenix. Once we know what we're dealing with, we can answer whatever questions the media has at our next event."

"I'll draft the release and have it on your desk within the hour," Katy says, spinning and exiting the office. Adrian follows her out after a respectful nod.

Angelica sits at her desk and stares at her calendar and to-do list. There aren't enough hours in the day to plow through all this work. With all the political distractions surrounding her and this office, it's incredible anything gets done. This FBI team is just one more thing for her to deal with.

CHAPTER NINETEEN
DETECTIVE BRESHION HURLEY

PHOENIX POLICE HEADQUARTERS
PHOENIX, ARIZONA

Despite having different missions, there are a lot of similarities between the military and police. They both have specialties, wear uniforms, and carry firearms. They also have rank structures and a chain of command. When you run afoul of it, you land in an office to get chewed out. That's where Breshion finds himself now.

He wasn't in the squad bay for more than fifteen seconds before being summoned by his furious superior. The call Jada received was likely made before he hit City Hall's front door. His incursion into the city's seat of executive power may have been fulfilling, but it comes at a price. This is it.

"Please, help me understand because I really don't get it. How can a man as smart as you be so damn stupid?" Jada asks, following a five-minute tongue lashing that had Breshion wondering how she was even breathing between shouts.

"Something needed to be done," the detective murmurs.

"Really? And that was your solution? Barging into the mayor's office and confronting her? How did that go, by the way? Did you get what you wanted?"

The questions were all rhetorical. Breshion made the mistake of answering them the first time he landed in this position years ago. He wouldn't make the same mistake this time, even if he had good answers, which he doesn't.

"No, I didn't think so," Jada concludes.

"At least I'm not sitting on my hands and taking this lying down," Breshion says, no longer able to hold back.

"Seriously? Is that what you think is happening? Understand something, *Detective*. Nobody is just accepting this. We fight our battles strategically in the PPD."

"How's that working? Are you getting what you want?"

Jada's face contorts as her emotions change from disbelief to anger to rage. She's a competent leader who stomachs rants from subordinates asked to do a difficult job during trying political times. There is a limit to that, though, and she doesn't tolerate insubordination. Breshion is walking that line and teetering in the wrong direction.

"If your purpose is to get suspended or worse, Detective Hurley, just say the word. I'm already three seconds away from taking your badge and tossing it in my desk drawer."

"Then why don't you?"

"Because I need every warm body I can get, including insubordinate little shits like you. We have guests coming."

"Guests?"

"The FBI has taken it upon themselves to dispatch a special team from Washington that can help with the human trafficking epidemic in Arizona."

"I'm glad the feds finally noticed the problem. It only took a couple of decades. Why get involved now?"

"It's the Federal Bureau of Investigation, and trafficking is a federal crime. What do you think?"

It's another loaded question that Hurley doesn't bother answering. FBI agents are big-game hunters. If they're coming to Phoenix, it's because they think a big fish is running the show and want the credit for taking him down.

The relationship between the FBI and local law enforcement in many places across the country is frosty, to put it generously. Individual agents can have excellent working relationships with state and municipal police, but it rarely extends beyond that. In his experience, federal involvement only makes matters worse.

"What do you want me to do?"

"Your job. In the process, you will give the agents whatever they need."

"Great," Breshion says with a sneer.

"You were just complaining about resources. This is a gift, even if you don't like the wrapping paper."

"If you consider a bag of coal a gift."

"Quit your bitching," Jada demands. "You wanted help. Now you have it."

"The feds don't help. They dictate. When things go wrong, they pass the blame. Then take all the credit when things go right."

"Do you care?" Jada asks in an eerily calm voice. She has the upper hand in this argument, and the detective knows it.

"That's not the point."

"It is now. I'm all for whoever can help break up a major human trafficking ring in this region. If you aren't, you might want to take a step back and ask yourself whether you care as much about these victims as you say you do."

"When do they arrive?" Breshion asks, knowing that he's lost this round. Only a fool would voice objections further, given the circumstances.

"They're already on their way. How fast does a Gulfstream fly?"

Breshion shakes his head. "Must be nice."

"You know, you're a brilliant detective and one of the most passionate men I have ever met, but you're a hothead. I put up with your crap because you're an asset. Don't let that dynamic change. Don't pull a stunt like you did in City Hall ever again. And play nice with the FBI, or I will relieve you of your duties in front of them. Understood?"

"Completely."

"Good. Now, get the hell out of my office," Jada commands, glaring at her subordinate.

Breshion complies without another word. Getting thrown out of offices is his thing today. At least what happened in Mayor Horta's office was unique. What just happened in Jada's office is a rerun of an old classic.

The detective returns to his desk and collapses in his chair. The squad bay is quiet, and the few other officers here avoid eye contact with him. The dressing down has earned him the mark of Cain, at least for the time being. Only Ritter has the balls to pay him a visit.

"That sounded tense."

"Yeah, well, I probably deserved it."

"Ya think? At least you still have your badge. So, now what?"

Breshion rubs his face and exhales. "Pull out the fine china and the good wine. We have distinguished guests coming. We'll take turns entertaining them long enough to get real work done."

"Guests? Like the Kardashians?" Ritter asks, his mouth curling up at a joke only he would think is funny.

"No – different divas this time."

CHAPTER TWENTY

ALEJANDRO SALCIDO

PHOENIX CHILDREN'S ACTIVITY CENTER
PHOENIX, ARIZONA

The tent provides some relief from the unrelenting sun beating down on the city, but not from the oppressive heat that comes with it. Alejandro isn't used to it. His job requires him to be a night owl and awake long after the sun sets and the temperatures fall. Once in a while, he has to mainline caffeine to stay awake for events like this.

Lantern House is the city's premier child advocacy and welfare group. The non-profit is involved in everything, including afterschool activities, supplementary tutoring, family assistance, and juvenile rehabilitation. It's a noble effort, reliant on successful fundraising to perform their services. Between raising cash and providing services, Lantern House's president stays busy.

"Thank you all for coming out today," Judy Costello says from the small lectern adorned with microphones from local and state media outlets. "It warms my heart to see you all here to support the Lantern House's latest endeavor for the city's children. With me today are some of our most prominent community and political leaders. We have Andres LaCugna and Kevin Demeter from the city council, Adrian Finley from the mayor's office, and countless financial contributors for whom I am eternally grateful.

"This facility is a long time coming. Thanks to the City of Phoenix, who was gracious enough to gift us the property, we took a decaying structure and turned it into a vibrant place where our children can engage in sports and enrichment activities. They are our future, and we owe it to our kids to provide them every opportunity to enhance their development. The Children's Activity Center will go a long way toward achieving that goal."

There is enthusiastic applause from the audience of supporters, parents, and media. Judy Costello is a purist. She doesn't run Lantern House out of a need for love, ego, or a feeling of importance. It comes from a place of love and compassion, and she is grateful that so many others feel the same.

"There is one special man I would like to invite to speak today, although he doesn't know it yet," Judy says, eliciting a smattering of chuckles from the audience. "As many of you know, we fell short in our fundraising for this facility. I honestly thought that all hope was lost, until a guardian angel swooped in. Through his generous donation, we not only reached our goal but surpassed it.

"He is an avid supporter of this community, and of Lantern House in particular. He does all of this without asking for praise or recognition. Too bad, because you're getting some today. Please welcome Mr. Alejandro Salcido."

The well-dressed man steps forward and shakes her hand before trying to settle the crowd. He's smiling, although screaming inside. Alejandro hates public speaking more than almost anything else. It's why he never had any interest in politics.

"I am blessed with dual citizenship in what I consider to be the two greatest nations on Earth: Mexico and the United States. I'm fortunate enough to keep residences in both. While I will always have Mexico in my heart, I consider Phoenix my home and all of you my extended family."

He stretches his arms out and receives warm applause in return.

"I did not have a happy childhood. I had excellent parents, but they had to work hard, and I was often neglected as a result. My hometown was dangerous, and I was not afforded the opportunities that education, athletics, and a stable environment provide. I clawed my way out of those circumstances to become successful, thanks to the many blessings the United States has to offer.

"Because of my experiences, I understand the importance of peer groups and role models. I know how an activity center like this can be more than a place to gather and learn – it can change lives. I agree with Ms. Costello that nothing is more important than our children. They must be nurtured and protected but also challenged to grow and develop. I hope that this center serves to provide those opportunities to the city's youth.

"This is my commitment, and not because of tax breaks. This city has given so much to me, and I want to give something back. It is my distinct honor to be here today, and nothing will give me more joy than to help cut that big ribbon and open this center up for Phoenix."

There is more applause as he steps back and turns to face a beaming Judy Costello. She assumes her place at the podium.

"Well, there's nothing that I can add to that, other than to thank Alejandro for his unbelievable generosity and to do as he wishes. Let's get this center open for business!"

She is handed an oversized pair of scissors larger than a pair of bolt cutters. She holds them with Alejandro, the two councilmen, and the mayor's representative as they mug for the cameras. She nods, and they all take part in slicing through the giant ribbon ceremoniously strung across the sidewalk.

"Please, everybody is welcome. I'm happy to give a tour of the facility and explain all its features for those interested."

Judy helps usher the crowd forward before peeling off to see Alejandro. "Your speech was phenomenal. Thank you so much!"

"It is always my honor to help you and Lantern House. Maybe we can open more of these centers."

"Do you mean that?"

"Of course. It may take some time, but if this center is as valuable to the community as I think it will be, I will happily contribute to opening more."

"I'm going to hold you to that," Judy gushes.

"Great speech, Mr. Salcido," Councilman LaCugna says as the audience filters past them and into the activity center. "Your eloquence was astounding, considering you didn't know you would be speaking."

Alejandro eyes the councilman warily. The accusation is as subtle as a chainsaw. None of this was choreographed or orchestrated, not that he feels compelled to explain that to this charlatan.

"It's easy when you're passionate with your words and what they symbolize."

"The activity center is filling up fast, Judy," Councilman Demeter says, interrupting the conversation. "You might want to get in there to answer more questions."

"If you gentlemen will excuse me, duty calls," Judy says, heading into the building with the politician in tow to commence her guided tour.

"Can his nose get any farther up her ass?" Andres asks.

"There are worse people to suck up to, I suppose. I'm sure you know a few of them."

LaCugna forces a smile. "Rumors were circulating in the council chamber that he was having an affair with a married mother of four. Unfounded ones, of course."

"Of course."

"It was a good turnout for such a hot day."

"Yes, it was," Alejandro says, nodding in a mixture of agreement and pride. "I'm not surprised. People love children."

"Yes, they do. That's why the FBI is sending a special team from Washington to help with the trafficking problem in Arizona. They think there's a ring here led by some big fish that can be broken up."

A shiver runs down Alejandro's spine. He presses his lips together, trying not to react to the information. He didn't know the feds were sending a team here. That's a problem.

"The more people trying to end that scourge, the merrier. How did you learn that?"

"We all have our sources," Andres admits. Alejandro didn't expect the snake to tell him anything useful.

"Did the mayor request them?"

"Nah," the councilman says, brushing the question away with a hand. "She'll say it was her idea, though. I'm surprised she didn't tell you. I know you are a big supporter."

"I have contributed to your campaign in the past as well. You know that."

"Not all contributions are equal, Mr. Salcido. I intend to unseat her in the next election. The cops she reassigned won't make a dent in the rising crime rate. Her mismanagement of this city makes her an easy target. You may want to reconsider what side you're on."

"You would be a great mayor, no doubt," Alejandro says, humoring him. "Who I choose to support is my business. Enjoy your day, Councilman."

Alejandro slaps LaCugna on the shoulder and starts back for his car.

"You're not coming in?"

"No, I have many things to take care of," Alejandro says with a smile that disappears from his face after he turns and makes his way back to his vehicle.

CHAPTER TWENTY-ONE
SSA ZACH FORTE

SOMEWHERE OVER NEW MEXICO

Zach mindlessly stares out the small window of the Gulfstream. Even from thirty thousand feet, he can make out the craggy rocks on the desert floor below. Private jets are the way to travel, but he hasn't enjoyed the trip. Too many things are swirling around his head. With the stakes as high as they are, the slightest misstep on this mission could lead to disaster. The problem is, there are a thousand things that he can't control that could lead to that outcome.

Asami walks back from the galley up the aircraft's short center aisle. He hasn't had the chance to discuss her medical analysis during the meeting with Brass, and she doesn't appear to want to talk now. That's too bad. They need to clear the air.

"Hey, Doc. Have a seat," he says, gently grasping her arm before she can walk past him.

"We're landing soon."

"We have time," Zach says, dismissing her attempt to delay this any further. Reluctantly, she sits in the seat across from him.

"What's up?"

"Did you meet Dr. Winters while you were up in the sleep center?"

It was a guess where Boston was heading, but an educated one. After her adventures with Boston a year ago, Tara quit working with Veterans Affairs and started full-time at Solvasön. Their rogue agent couldn't have known that but was likely to check there first based on history.

Since finding Boston anywhere else with their small team was unlikely, they decided to locate Tara and wait for him to come to them. The doctor volunteered to visit the sleep center under the pretense of requesting information for a patient while Emma, Zach, and Nadiya covered the building's exit.

"I bumped into her to get a lunch recommendation, and we chatted for a few minutes. Why?"

"What do you think of her?"

"She's a beautiful, intelligent woman. I can see why Boston is attracted to her."

The comment was accompanied by a tinge of resentment in Asami's voice and earned a sharp glare from Emma, who's listening in across the aisle. Zach knows that Matt is playing with fire by having these women train Boston, especially if their feelings toward him continue to develop.

"Boston's relationship with Tara was a short but potent one. I don't understand why he is still drawn to her, but he is. Now that he's seen her in person, is he going to be okay?"

"Psychologically or in his dream state?" Asami asks.

"Both."

"I can't say with certainty. Psychologically speaking, Boston will react like any person would. The meeting ripped open emotional scars for him, but that can be dealt with. I don't know about his dreams. There are too many variables. How long were they in proximity to each other?"

"A minute or two. Does it matter?" Zach asks.

"I don't know. If Boston and Tara have a powerful enough bond, he could be in the same city as her and pick up signals for all we know. There's still a lot we don't know about how this works."

Zach looks over at the dream machine, who is passed out in the seat across from Emma. He dozed off not long after takeoff and hasn't so much as flinched since.

"He could be having one about her right now."

"Unlikely. I sedated him when we were on the tarmac, and the drug serves as a natural inhibitor. It's likely he isn't dreaming at all, memories or otherwise."

"Will that stop him from having any about Tara in the future?"

"No," Asami says, grimacing as she shakes her head. "It's a short-term solution. I'm researching different cocktails that could serve as inhibitors if the time ever comes, but using them on him would be experimental."

"And counterproductive to everything we are trying to do here. Let's hope that we never need it."

"Brass's request was completely inappropriate."

Zach meets her accusatory eyes. "So was your summary."

"I'm a doctor. Brass got my professional medical opinion."

"Not colored in any way? Because from my seat at that table, it sure seemed like it was."

"No, it wasn't."

"Bullshit."

Asami recoils before her face flushes red. "What are you implying?"

Zach knows that her emotional attachment to Boston is clouding her judgment. Her briefing to Brass felt more personal than professional. With Emma listening in, Forte doesn't want to get into the specifics about that right now. The other women don't need to know that their love triangle looks more like a pentagon.

"Only that you work for Watchtower, Asami. Every journey has a beginning and end. The only question is how far down ours we are."

"Boston is my patient. His interests are my foremost concern. That's the end of the discussion. If you expect anything less, then find another doctor."

Zach watches her get out of her seat and move toward the front of the plane. She would climb into the baggage hold to get away from him right now. Asami might be upset at getting called out, but her reaction was better than Zach expected. Her attitude is a bigger problem.

Remsen may replace her if things don't go well on this mission or she doesn't toe the party line when it comes to Hollinger. This program means more than any of them. On this plane, Sleeping Beauty is the one person who is not expendable.

"Was that conversation your idea or Remsen's?" Emma asks, leaning into the aisle.

"Does it matter?"

"Yeah, it kinda does. I don't know what happened at that meeting or what Boston saw that made him cut the fence and bolt. I don't really care, either. I just need you to understand something: If I think you are putting Boston in any unnecessary danger, we're going to have a problem."

Emma's eyes tell the story. She is dead serious.

"Fair enough," Zach says. "Since we're sharing, I have no interest in seeing anything bad happen to Boston. He's been through enough. That said, I'm not going to coddle him, either. If you get in my way of me doing my job, calling what happens between us 'a problem' will be an understatement."

"Good. I'm glad we understand each other," Emma says with a nod before returning her eyes to the window as the plane begins its descent into Phoenix.

Zach closes his eyes. This team is being held together by duct tape. It won't take a whole lot of pressure to rip it apart. He can only hope that this mission is not only successful but an easy one.

CHAPTER TWENTY-TWO
"BOSTON" HOLLINGER

SALT RIVER VALLEY MEDICAL CENTER
PHOENIX, ARIZONA

With Nadiya behind the wheel, the team piles into their nine-seat Chevy Suburban and heads out of Phoenix Sky Harbor Airport. The city center lies only three miles to the northwest, so the drive will be short.

"Are you feeling well-rested, Boston?" Zach says from the front seat.

"I'm still a little groggy, but yeah."

"Any dreams?" Asami asks, piquing the interest of Emma seated behind them.

I don't answer, and instead continue staring out the window. "Are we heading for the police department?"

"No. We'll meet them in the morning."

"Where are we going?" I ask.

"The hotel," Nadiya says.

"No, we need to make a stop first," Zach turns to her and says, pointing at a large building off to the left.

Nadiya parks at the massive medical center, and we enter the large foyer. The attendants immediately issue us each a visitor's pass and direct us to the appropriate floor. The pediatric wing is not where I expected to end up, and my curiosity finally gets me to break my silence.

"What are we doing here?" I ask Zach as we wait near the nurse's station.

"You'll see."

Medical staff scurries around, and small families walk past us. Some of them are happy. Others look stressed or sad. It's the daily sight in any modern hospital. There is no worse roller coaster ride than the emotional journey of watching a loved one deal with medical issues. It's worse when a child is involved.

"Agent Forte?" a woman in a white lab coat asks after stopping next to us. "I'm Dr. Catalina Benito. I was told to expect you."

"Yes, thank you for seeing us on such short notice, Doctor. These are Special Agents Emma Farris and Nadiya Jesperssen. The guy behind me is Special Agent Will Smith."

The doctor nods at the group. "Will you please follow me?"

"Will Smith? Seriously? Do I look like one of the Men in Black?" I ask Forte in a whisper as we turn the corner and walk down a long corridor.

"If you play nice on this mission, I may give you a bigger gun than the Noisy Cricket."

"I'm glad you're amused."

"Look, you can't go by your given name outside the training center or Watchtower. Every mission will mean a new alias. This one is Will Smith. Deal with it."

"Fine. I get to pick the name next time."

We enter an outer room with a large picture window peering into a playroom behind it. There are almost a dozen kids in it lounging around. None of them are engaged in the energetic play the room hopes to encourage.

"What is this about?" I ask, still not understanding the point of us being here.

"This is your mission."

"They're only kids."

"Yeah. I see those millions of dollars we've invested into your training are paying off," Forte says, his tone dripping with sarcasm.

"How are they doing, Doctor?" Asami asks.

"As good as can be expected. The children are traumatized but finally starting to feel safer here. They haven't opened up to us yet, but they're interacting with each other more frequently."

"What about their parents?" Emma asks, her voice low and soft as she stares at the children through the window.

"Authorities are hoping to identify them, but it's an agonizingly slow process. Most likely, they were handed over to a coyote and ferried across the border on their own. We may never find their parents, and if we do, they may not want them back."

"That's horrible," Nadiya says.

"It's our reality," Catalina explains. "No matter what happened to them on the journey, their parents probably believe they have a better shot at a good life in America. That's the story with most unaccompanied minors who come across the border."

I slide over and open the door, expecting the doctor to protest. She doesn't. The children glance up at me but don't react to my presence outside of that. I stand along the wall, unable to resist closing my eyes. I clear my thoughts, and poignant images come pouring in.

My body has seized up in fear. I'm paralyzed…unable to move or even breathe. I feel terror in its purest sense.

"¡Dije cállense!"

I feel the smack across my face…the pain…the tears that start pouring out of my eyes. I'm somewhere else. It's dark. I'm being held down. I struggle, but it's no use. Whoever is holding me is too strong.

"Griten y los mato. Aprendera a que les guste esto. Recibira mucha practica."

There is tugging at my clothing. I try to wriggle free, and the man laughs. I begin to sob as a hand caresses between my thighs and reaches between my legs—

I'm in a tight space. My knees are tucked into my chest. I feel woozy but have enough strength to scratch and hit the walls with my hands as I try to stifle sobs. The wood is sturdy, and I feel…helpless. Blood drips down my fingers from my knuckles. I hit the side of the crate again and grimace at the sharp pain. It's almost a relief from the sense of being trapped and unable to escape.

Now I'm in a truck. It bounces up and down…I can smell the diesel and stench of urine and sweat. I feel myself hyperventilating as I begin to sob.

I'm somewhere else. I'm clinging to somebody – holding on as hard as I can. People pull at me and break my grasp.

"Mama!"

"¡Por favor! Es mi hijo. Es todo lo que tengo. ¡No se lo lleven! Por favor…"

I watch as the woman is hit. She falls to the ground, and two men beat her with bats as she struggles to cover her head. A man kicks her in the side. Her eyes lock onto mine. They have an incredible sadness to them…and regret.

I feel a surge of anger and then panic as I'm carried away. I see a figure standing…lights are behind him, and he throws back his head, laughing.

Now I'm in a room. A man is hitting me. More and more – in the head and the stomach and the side. Intense pain comes with each blow. He stops, and I can smell alcohol on his breath as he moves inches from my face. Something sharp is placed against my neck.

"Haz eso otra vez y to corto el cuello, después, te empiezo a cortar en pedazitos, así."

He removes the knife, and I feel the blade slice through the skin on my arm. A hand covers my mouth as I try to howl in pain. My eyes grow wide in horror as a small plastic container is held in front of me. I can't read it, but I see the chili pepper on the package clearly. The man takes some in his hand and rubs it into the cut. I try to scream—

I open my eyes to find the team standing around me with looks of concern. Tears pour from my eyes, and I desperately try to wipe them from my cheeks. My heart aches in a way I've never felt before.

"You okay, Will?" Emma asks, touching my arm softly. Nadiya places her hand on my shoulder.

I stare at the children and notice one of them with bandages on his knuckles. Another young girl has one on her arm. Doctor Benito goes over to one of the children and touches her gently on the shoulder. She jerks away from the doctor like she just gripped the handle of a pan on a hot stove. Another boy stares out the window, refusing to acknowledge anything or anyone around him.

These children have been through hell. They have been abused in every way a human can be. How could anyone endure that? How can anyone inflict that kind of pain on any living thing, let alone a child?

"I need some air."

This is the last place I want to be right now, and I head for the door, shooting Zach a hostile glance. He brought me here on purpose. He knew I would see this.

"Give him some space," Forte says, stopping Asami from coming after me.

I make my way down to the foyer on the first floor and out into a desert garden courtyard. Despite its beauty, I have the entire space to myself and my choices of benches to sit on. Some things cannot be unseen. I close my eyes, and the images of the memories linger in my consciousness. Covering them with my arms doesn't help any.

My respite is interrupted twenty minutes later when I hear someone sit down next to me. I uncover my head to see Zach sitting there in silence, admiring the desert flora adorning the courtyard. At least he had the balls to come and see me himself instead of sending one of the women.

"Checking up on me?"

"You look like you need it," Forte says, still staring straight ahead. "What did you see up there?"

"Exactly what you thought I would: unimaginable horror. Those kids weren't just smuggled across the border. They were being trafficked as sex slaves."

"The Phoenix Vice Squad conducted a raid on a stash house a few days ago. The four men holding the children were killed, and there was no useful information on the kingpin."

I shake my head. "How can anyone do that to another person, much less children?"

"Evil exists, Boston. That's the simple answer."

"Is that why you brought me here? So I could experience their trauma?"

Forte pauses for a long moment before answering. "No."

"Don't lie, Zach. You knew I would share their memories in there."

"I don't understand why you see anything, Boston, let alone know what you will and won't see."

"So, why?"

"Because I want to show you what your gift could mean to this shitty world we live in if you choose to use it."

"Those kids aren't perpetrators."

"No, they're victims, and there are a lot more like them. That's why we're here. I want you to help us find out who is behind this."

"I thought trafficking was a police problem," I argue, leaning back on the bench.

"It's a federal crime, so we're making it ours. You neutralized one of the deadliest moles in the history of American intelligence. Nobody else would have found out about Gina. You did. I want you to do the same here to bring these monsters to justice."

"I don't know how."

"Yes, you do," Zach argues. "I'm sure whatever you saw was horrible, but it wasn't the only thing."

"No, it wasn't. I felt terror, Zach. It was a horror movie that I was in instead of watching on television. It was...I...I can't begin to describe it."

My memories of the dreams come rushing in, and I close my eyes. In the early days, I would forget the dreams moments after I woke up. I would give almost anything for that still to be the case. The techniques I have learned to remember what I see are not serving me well right now.

"Was anything said?"

"Yeah…in Spanish," I say, grimacing.

"Anything you could understand?"

"My training didn't include languages," I snap. I close my eyes and exhale, forcing myself to relax. "It was hard to focus beyond the pain."

"Did you see any of the men who did this in those children's memories?"

"It was dark and blurry."

"Blurry?"

"I was looking through my tears. In some of the memories, I felt drugged. There was one backlit figure that I noticed."

"Was he in a structure, like a house?"

"The man was in front of headlights, I think. They were outside…in the desert. It could have been anywhere."

"And we're going to work to find out where," Zach decrees. "Watchtower uncovered some intelligence that this particular trafficking ring is well-funded and seems to have eyes and ears everywhere."

"And we're still working with the police? If Watchtower is right, you have to believe that they're compromised."

"Yeah, Matt believes that some cops might be involved. We're going to find out for sure and draw them out."

"Great," I mutter, tired of having to work with people who are actually working against me. "So, we can't trust anyone here?"

"Trust is earned, not issued. You know that better than anyone. We'll start unraveling the mystery by assuming everyone is lying to us. I need you to use these memories to get to the truth."

"I don't care what you need," I say, getting up off the bench. "I'm not interested in dirty cops. Whoever did this to those children needs to be taken down."

"I agree," Zach says, also rising. "But we need to rip this out root and stem."

"Okay. Understand that I'm going to do this for them. Not you, and definitely not for Watchtower."

Zach nods. "Noted."

I turn and head out of the courtyard with Forte right behind me. The last thing in the world I want to do is go back up there and face another ambush of memories. Something tells me that it won't be the last time I face those demons.

CHAPTER TWENTY-THREE

ALEJANDRO SALCIDO

DEZRT FYRE NIGHTCLUB
PHOENIX, ARIZONA

This has already been a long day. A few hours of sleep after the activity center's dedication helps, but Alejandro needs some rest. It's time to go home to Mexico for some much-needed relaxation. That is for tomorrow or the day after. He has business to conduct tonight above and beyond just managing his clubs and bars.

The bars start to pick up around this time. The business types who frequent happy hours have all headed home, and the night crowd will begin filtering in. Eight o'clock is when his clubs open, including the Dezrt Fyre, but there is no line to get in. People start coming through the doors, but it will be another two hours before this place begins to resemble the hot spot that it is.

Alejandro makes his way up to his office. His bodyguard remains outside to keep an eye on the entrance. More often than not, anyone coming up the stairs uninvited is just drunk and got lost looking for a restroom. It's the guy who knows what he's doing that Alejandro is concerned about. Sex trafficking is a dangerous industry, and competitors play dirty.

He pulls out a burner phone with the blue stripe at the bottom from the safe built into his wood desk and hits redial. Alejandro has about a dozen of these, each with uniquely colored pinstriping at the bottom. That helps him determine the phone's function without powering the devices first.

"Yeah."

"You're failing me," Alejandro says in English.

"How?"

"Why am I hearing from a city councilman that the FBI is sending a task force before I hear from you?"

"I just found out earlier today."

"How much earlier?"

Alejandro hears a door slam and footsteps echoing off the walls as his contact moves into a stairwell.

"Does it matter? I couldn't get away to call you," he says, the unmistakable sound of someone speaking in a confined space.

"You are my eyes and ears. That is our arrangement, or have you forgotten?"

"I haven't forgotten. I can only report what I see and hear, and only when it doesn't look suspicious. I haven't had the chance."

"Did you take a leak between then and now?" Alejandro argues.

"It's not that simple."

"Why didn't you know this ahead of time?"

"It was kept in the dark until the team from Washington was already in the air. I don't know why the Phoenix FBI wasn't informed."

Alejandro frowns. That's odd. The FBI may not be known for cooperating with state and local law enforcement, but that doesn't apply within the Bureau itself. That's typically where any request for federal assistance would have been funneled through.

"Do you know who requested them?"

"No," his source replies curtly.

"Find out."

"Asking questions like that will draw suspicion. It's above my pay grade."

"I don't care. Be inventive, and let me know what you uncover. This development has come at an inopportune time. There are only so many losses I can endure right now."

"That sounds like your problem, not mine."

"My problems are your problems. Never forget that."

Alejandro hangs up and powers down his phone before replacing it in the drawer and locking the safe. This is yet another wrinkle to deal with. There is so much incompetence around him and so many who dare to threaten his business. He needs to start lightening the load.

CHAPTER TWENTY-FOUR

SSA ZACH FORTE

CITY HALL CONFERENCE ROOM
PHOENIX, ARIZONA

Forte and the team have been waiting in the City Hall conference room for over ten minutes. Politicians always run behind schedule, but it's first thing in the morning. What could be keeping the mayor at this hour?

"How are you doing?" Asami asks Boston, sidling up next to him.

"Fine."

"Are you sure? We need to talk about what you saw in the hospital yesterday."

"No, we don't," Boston argues. "There's nothing to be gained by it."

Asami searches his eyes with hers. She gives a concerned glance at Zach before returning them to her patient.

"I don't think—"

"We're wasting time waiting for a damn politician," Boston interrupts, showing no interest in continuing that conversation.

"He's right, Zach," Nadiya says, walking over to him. "Why are we here?"

"Politics."

"I didn't think Watchtower played those games."

"Emma, don't mention that name in here or any other public area in this city," Zach warns. "You know the protocol. To answer your question, we don't. There's a method to my madness in this instance."

The mayor finally enters the conference room, trailed by a small entourage of staff. Introductions are made, first by Zach and then by her. Angelica Horta seems warm and inviting – traits that must make her popular with her constituents. Absent is the devilish shrewdness inherent in most political types. He's betting Boston notices it as well.

"Now that we've gotten the introductions out of the way, let me formally welcome you to Phoenix. We appreciate the FBI's help with the state's human trafficking issues."

"We're happy to be of service, Ms. Mayor."

"Please, call me Angelica. I understand that the state authorities have made numerous requests to federal law enforcement for help. I'm thrilled that it was finally accepted."

Zach notices Boston close his eyes. The dream machine – the nickname his friend Louisiana gave him over a year ago and that has stuck with the people at Watchtower – has gone to work. It's exactly what Zach was hoping to see. If the kingpin is being protected by corrupt politicians, the mayor is the logical place to start.

"We're not here at your state's request, ma'am."

"Oh, I'm sorry," Angelica says in the fake tone that politicians like to use. Maybe she isn't so genuine after all. "I've been misinformed. It was a local request then?"

Forte searches her eyes. She's fishing for information. That's the point of this meeting. He just doesn't know why, and that has him intrigued.

"No, I don't believe it was."

"Then, not to sound at all ungrateful, but may I ask why you are here, Special Agent Forte?"

"Angelica, are you concerned that there is some sort of jurisdictional issue? Because, I assure you, we have no interest in interfering with ongoing local law enforcement operations."

"I'm pleased to hear that, although I would never make such an insinuation."

"Excellent. Now, I'm sure you're aware that human trafficking is a federal crime. The FBI and DOJ take a keen interest in bringing perpetrators of these crimes against humanity to justice."

"Of course," the mayor says. "Uh, Special Agent Forte, is your agent okay?"

Zach turns his head and sees Boston with his eyes still shut. His eyelids are twitching. It's the one telltale sign of remote viewing.

"I apologize, ma'am. Agent Smith has been working long hours and didn't sleep on the flight here. I wanted to work some rest into his schedule, but he insisted on being here to meet you."

"I admire the work ethic. You know, such federal efforts usually come with an announcement from Justice, the Hoover Building, or even the White House. They like the media attention those efforts get, yet there was none. Can you explain that?"

"I'm a lowly field agent, ma'am. I can't begin to understand why people do or don't do things in Washington. I get handed assignments, and I follow them. You are free to check with my supervisor to see why no public proclamations were made."

"I see," the mayor says, her tone clear that she doesn't believe a word that came out of Zach's mouth.

"If I may be blunt...why does it matter?"

Boston opens his eyes. "The mayor wants to know where the request came from before she orders her staff to take credit for making it."

The stunned reaction on the mayor's face is immediate. "I'm sorry?"

"Did I say anything that isn't true?"

"Yes...Agent Smith, is it? I am drafting a statement that the FBI will be assisting our efforts against human trafficking, but I have no intention of taking credit for a federal request I didn't make."

Boston looks at her and smiles. "'I've been in politics for a while now. The one thing I've noticed over those years is that everyone lies. It's the type of lie you tell and who it hurts that makes the difference.'"

Everyone in the room stares at Boston before turning to see the mayor's face go pale. Emma and Nadiya smile, while Doctor Kurota looks annoyed at the careless use of his gift. Forte is caught somewhere in between those emotions. The mayor's staff have looks that combine shock and indigestion. Whatever he saw and quoted, it was a private conversation.

"Wouldn't you agree, ma'am?" Boston asks, pressing the metaphorical dagger in further.

"Yes, I would. Well, I won't hold you up any longer. I've asked the Phoenix PD to give you their full support. Please be sure to tell me if that doesn't happen."

"We will, ma'am," Emma says.

"Adrian will show you out."

The team files through the door after the aide, who guides them to the elevator. They take it down to the ground floor and walk out of the foyer to the waiting Suburban.

"You saw her memories?" Asami asks, stopping as they reach the vehicle.

"There's a lot of stress in her life, Doc. It wasn't hard."

"You know, your gift needs to stay a secret."

"I know," Boston grumbles.

"Do you? Because you sure didn't act like it in there."

"He was fine," Emma argues.

The doctor scans the faces of the other team members. It seems she is the only one concerned about what happened in that conference room. That annoys her more than what Boston did. It is a complete violation of Watchtower protocols.

"No, he wasn't. He quoted the mayor in a conversation he couldn't have known anything about. You saw her face."

"Yeah, it was priceless," Nadiya says, earning the doctor's ire.

"Is she dirty?" Forte asks, staring up and down the street through his sunglasses.

"I don't know yet. The memory was a specific conversation. I know the mayor has a few secrets and concerns about her political rivals. Don't be surprised if she uses us as pawns."

"You can't be condoning this behavior, Zach!" the doctor screeches. "There is no way the mayor isn't up there questioning how he could know what she said."

Zach ignores her. "You need to keep tabs on Mayor Horta."

"You mean we."

"No. I mean you. Unless I miraculously develop a TBI that lets me tap into people's memories, you're our guy."

"I don't care about her politics. That's your arena. I have monsters to catch and destroy. Mission first, remember?"

Boston pats Zach on the shoulder, opens the door, and climbs into the Suburban.

"Just remember that monsters lurk in the most surprising of places. You worked for Congress once, remember?"

Emma takes the spot next to Boston, forcing an annoyed Asami into the third row of seats. Zach slams his door and slides into the passenger seat. This is going to be a long few weeks.

CHAPTER TWENTY-FIVE
DETECTIVE BRESHION HURLEY

PHOENIX POLICE HEADQUARTERS
PHOENIX, ARIZONA

The frosty reception that the feds are getting from Breshion and the vice squad is causing nerves to fray. The FBI may be regarded as America's premier law enforcement agency, but they're prima donnas who expect everyone to cater to their needs. That's not going to happen here, as these five agents are learning the hard way.

"We just need a place where we can set up that's not this squad bay," their lead agent says.

"Space is at a premium here, Special Agent Forte," Ritter explains.

"You're saying that you don't have one conference room available?" the blonde agent asks. "That's bullshit."

"I'm sorry you think so. What's bullshit is you guys marching in here and setting up shop like you own the place. You have a field office in Phoenix," Breshion interjects.

"Yeah. It's thirty minutes away. Our mission is to liaise with the Phoenix PD. Kinda hard to do that from twenty-five miles away, don't ya think?" Forte asks.

"Fine, if you insist on being here."

"We do."

"Then you'll make do with what we can give you. Phil, why don't you show our distinguished guests into one of the interrogation rooms?" Hurley says, the corner of his mouth curling up.

"You got it."

Detective Ritter puts his hand on Nadiya's lower back and edges it farther south than is appropriate. She doesn't immediately react, but her face tells a different story. It was a power move and one that she isn't about to tolerate.

"I suggest you remove that hand before I break it."

"I'd like to see you try," the vice detective replies.

The challenge is immediately accepted. Nadiya spins and catches his arm. She slides under the detective's shoulder and locks his elbow before clamping down a wristlock that causes him to yelp. She kicks his leg out from under him and pushes forward in one motion, planting his face hard into a desk.

Detective Hurley is about to intervene when Emma holds a hand up in front of him before wagging a finger. He thinks about testing her, but one look at the agony on Ritter's face makes him have second thoughts.

"All right! Enough!" Breshion barks before turning to Zach. "Is this how the FBI acts around their hosts?"

"Is this how the PPD treats their guests? It makes the mayor's words of having support seem pretty hollow."

Breshion slides past Emma and gets into Forte's face. To the agent's credit, he doesn't withdraw a single millimeter.

"Then take it up with her. I really don't give a damn."

"What the hell is going on in here?" Jada Fulcher asks, storming into the squad bay. "Detective Hurley! Stand down. You! Agent whoever you are. Let that detective up."

Nadiya looks at Zach, who nods. The woman was equally willing to rip his arm off and beat him with it. Instead, she releases him and he stands upright and rubs his sore wrist.

"I asked a question. I expect one of my people to answer it."

"Assistant Chief Fulcher, I presume?" Zach asks, seizing the initiative. "I'm Special Agent Forte. Your detectives and my team were just all getting to know each other better."

"Uh, huh. My office, Hurley. Right now."

The assistant chief and her subordinate retreat behind closed doors, which only reduces the shouting volume. The conversation is one-sided. Jada rips him a new asshole for the next five minutes before ejecting him from her office with orders to apologize. Instead of obeying the directive, he heads out of the squad bay. He can't do this anymore.

* * *

Agent Smith walks into the locker room and leans against a locker as Breshion packs a duffle bag. The FBI are some of the smuggest bastards Breshion has ever worked with. This agent doesn't look to be any different.

"Quitting? That's a shame. I would have expected someone working in vice to have more grit."

"You're wasting your time, asshole. Unless you're here to apologize for your team's behavior."

"Nah. It wasn't someone from my team who got handsy with one of yours."

"That's not how I saw it," Breshion argues.

"Of course you didn't, but what would your reaction have been had I done that to Detective Robinson?"

"Jamecca can handle herself."

"I have no doubt. That's not what I meant, and you know it. It's *your* reaction that I'm interested in."

Hurley stops packing and glowers at the FBI agent. He's been here all of a half-hour and can't know anything.

"You don't know what you're talking about."

"We both know that isn't true. Don't lie, Detective Hurley. It's beneath you, and you suck at it."

"Get the hell out of here."

"You've always had feelings for her but tried to keep things professional. You didn't know that they were reciprocated until she kissed you one night. It's the happiest you've ever been."

The detective's mouth hangs open, and his face betrays him. He fights to close it and mask the surprise, but it's far too late for that. The agent smirks.

"That never happened!" Breshion shouts.

"Yeah, you tried to convince yourself of that at first. It's why Jamecca was so hurt when you told her that it needed to be kept a secret. She still isn't completely over that conversation, by the way. Despite her brave face, part of her thinks you'll betray her just like you did in her apartment. You might want to tell her how you really feel."

"That isn't—"

"Possible? I'm very intuitive and know it's the truth. What is the department's policy about relationships for officers in the same unit? Oh, that's right. No tolerance, as you explained to her."

Hurley grabs the agent by the windbreaker and shoves him into the lockers. The loud crash of his body into the thin metal echoes around the cinderblock locker room before finally dissipating. Agent Smith doesn't react at all, further agitating the vice detective. He only looks him dead in his eyes.

"Beating the shit out of me will get you nowhere."

"How do you know about Jamecca and me?" Hurley demands.

"It doesn't matter how, only that I do."

"What do you plan on doing about it?"

"That depends on you."

Breshion eases his grasp on the man. "What is this, blackmail?"

"Of a sort, yes. I don't really care about your relationship with Jamecca. It's not my business or anyone else's. Catching the monsters that are selling these kids into slavery is."

"So, what do you want from me?"

"Let's start with professional courtesy. We can build from there."

"We don't need the feds butting in. That's the end of this discussion. Do what you want with the information you know."

"Your mother was a whore."

Breshion's head jerks around, and he's about to throw a punch before the agent continues.

"Your father was a cop, and that's the first thing he said to you after your mother died of a rare form of cancer when you were sixteen. She went to L.A. to become a model and ended up as a prostitute when the money ran out. She tried to break free, but her pimp wouldn't let her go. Your father rescued her from the street life, and they fell in love." Smith pauses and glances at the ground. "That was the last conversation you had with your dad before he committed suicide."

Breshion stares dumbfoundedly at the agent. The shock wears off quickly, turning into something closer to anger as the scenarios churn through his mind about how this fed could have learned that. None of the conclusions are palatable.

"Nobody knows that. How could you—?"

"That's why you care about this job as much as you do."

"I asked you a question," Breshion says through clenched teeth.

"I heard you, Detective. It doesn't matter how I know. It also doesn't matter how I know that you're in a relationship with a subordinate. Whether you want to believe it or not, we're here to help, not piss in your Cheerios. If it's about credit, you can have all of it when we're done. I want justice for those kids I just met at the medical center. That's all that matters."

Breshion searches the man's eyes. After a career dealing with liars and thugs on the street, he has a finely tuned bullshit detector. In this instance, he finds none. Agent Smith has a conviction that he sees in the mirror every day. For the first time since he heard the feds were coming, he realizes that this might not be the dog and pony show he thought it was.

"Okay. But there's one condition to my cooperation: If you screw me over or do anything that I feel jeopardizes my mission to protect the people of this city, it ends. Understood?"

The agent nods. "I guess you're all out of excuses, Detective."

"There's one more thing, Agent Smith. Before you leave here, I want to know how you knew about my relationship and what happened with my parents."

"I'll tell you right now," he says, stopping at the end of the lockers. "It's one of life's mysteries. I mean that."

The FBI agent leaves the locker room, and Breshion exhales. Even if the FBI could have sniffed out his relationship with Jamecca, they couldn't know about the conversation he had with his father. No amount of surveillance could have uncovered that information. Something is a little off about Agent Smith, and now Breshion is determined to figure out what that is.

CHAPTER TWENTY-SIX
MAYOR ANGELICA HORTA

PHOENIX CHILDREN'S ACTIVITY CENTER
PHOENIX, ARIZONA

Angelica looks around as she enters the activity center. It's already bustling with kids playing games and hanging out. She walks past some smaller rooms where tutors are hard at work helping younger children with their homework. She would have thought there would be primarily Spanish-speaking children here, but the ones she has seen are of all colors and ages.

"I have to hand it to you – nobody else could have gotten this place off the ground this quickly," the mayor says from the threshold of the small office.

"I told everybody that there was a huge demand for this. It's why I want to build more youth centers," Judy Costello says, rising from her desk and giving her friend a hug.

As impressive as this building is, her office is anything but. Not much larger than a standard walk-in closet, it contains nothing more than a desk, computer, small bookcase, and chair. Judy wanted to devote most of the facility's space to the children. With big offices come big egos, and she knows she won't be running this place forever.

"And you should. This place is amazing."

"Thank you, Mayor. Is this a social call or something else?"

"A little of both, actually. First, I wanted to apologize for not attending the opening. The scheduling conflict made it impossible, but I really wanted to be here. What you're doing for this community is really remarkable."

"Thank you. It keeps me plenty busy."

"That brings me to the second reason I'm here. I'm about to ask you to be busier," Angelica says, causing Judy to cock her head. "I've had something in the works for a while, but it has only recently come together. I'm initiating a task force that will take the lead on tackling human trafficking in the city. It's going to have one goal: eradicate sex trafficking once and for all."

"Bold words."

"Yes, I want leaders to repeat them. I think you're the person for the job."

"Why me?" Judy asks.

"Because Lantern House is the preeminent community organization in this city. You help thousands of people every day. Your involvement shows the city that we're serious. More importantly, you know how to get things done."

Judy exhales and scratches her head. Angelica didn't expect an immediate yes to this request. The founder of Lantern House would take on the world if she had the time, but there are only twenty-four hours in a day. Opening this center has added an incredible burden on the gargantuan task of running her organization. Angelica doesn't blame her for balking at taking on more.

"Does this have something to do with the FBI arriving?"

"Not directly, but their assistance provides us with an opportunity to make a real difference. I want to create a synergy among local, state, and federal law enforcement and the private sector. You are the one person I can think of who has the respect of all sides and can bring them together."

"Angelica, this is an honor. It really is, but I can't do it alone. I could never dedicate the time that would be needed."

"I know. Kevin Demeter will co-chair the task force with you."

Judy's eyes light up. "Kevin is involved?"

"As of an hour ago, he is. I have also enlisted Assistant Chief Jada Fulcher from the vice squad, Dr. Catalina Benito from Salt River Medical Center, and countless others. Adrian Finley will act as the task force liaison to my office."

"Why not you personally?"

Angelica grimaces. "If I get involved, things get political. I want real results, not intrigue. I'm committed to its success, so can I count on you to join me?"

Judy sighs and looks around her office. Angelica can only assume she's looking for a reason to say no. Or yes. She isn't sure which.

"I already have my hands full here."

"I know you do. The timing is lousy, and I apologize for that. The FBI committing resources to the fight is a game-changer. I can't let this opportunity pass us by."

"I understand, but I'm already stretched too thin."

"Most people can't do a fraction of what you do in a day. I know that your ultimate goal is to grow Lantern House and raise enough funds to create more activity centers. The free press this earns you will go a long way in helping to meet those fundraising goals. This is a win-win for all of us, Judy. Especially the hundreds of human trafficking victims, too many of whom are children."

Children are Judy's Achilles' Heel. She loves them – all of them. It's hard for her to say no to anyone when the health and welfare of kids are involved. There is no more of an affront to their well-being than a life in the sex trade. She finds it abhorrent, and that's what Angelica is looking to leverage.

"When do you plan on announcing?"

"Tomorrow afternoon. There's no time to waste."

"And if I say no?"

Angelica smirks. "Then I will delay the announcement until you change your mind."

Judy lowers her eyes. Already with too much on her plate, other Lantern House administrators would be forced to pick up the slack. That's what delegation is designed for. The youth activity center is off to a rousing start, and she can pass her duties off to one of a half-dozen administrators or volunteers. She needs to be involved in this task force. Angelica can only hope that she realizes that.

CHAPTER TWENTY-SEVEN
ALEJANDRO SALCIDO

RENTED CACTUS CORRIDOR HOUSE
SCOTTSDALE, ARIZONA

Alejandro arrives at the house in the Cactus Corridor neighborhood of Scottsdale. The community had expressed interest in custom homes situated on medium-sized building lots to maintain a suburban character. They succeeded. This is a lovely area.

He pulls his Mercedes into the concrete driveway and parks in one of the bays in the three-car garage, closing the door behind him. He removes the opener from his visor and clips it on his belt. This house is a rental. It will be the last time he ever uses it.

Barron is on the couch drinking with three beautiful girls fawning over him when Alejandro enters the kitchen. The first floor has an open plan with sightlines into the elegant white-beamed family room from all the other communal areas. Javier nods from the wet bar at the far end of the room. The plan is in motion.

"I see that you're enjoying yourself, Barron."

"I'd say so. This is more like it," he says, caressing one of the women.

Alejandro grins. He can get as handsy as he wants. None of the women are his, and they were paid for the rest of the day. It will be the easiest money they ever made.

"They're only a sample. I have fresh goods in the master suite on the other side of that wall."

Barron looks behind him and takes another long sip of his drink. "Why wasn't I shown them when I got here?"

"You're a valued client who deserves my utmost attention. I wanted to show them to you personally."

The man beams. "They're better than these fine specimens?"

"You can see for yourself and be the judge."

"All-righty," he says, smacking his knee and downing the tequila in his glass. "Please excuse me, ladies."

"If you must," one of the women says as Barron struggles to stand.

"Hurry back, stud," another adds.

Barron stumbles as he moves around the sofa. One of Alejandro's men dressed in a black suit steadies him before he can tumble to the ground. The man is beyond woozy and probably can't see straight at this point.

"Whoa. You okay?"

"Fine. I'm fine. The alcohol is just hitting me harder than usual. That's all," Barron says, slurring.

"It's the good stuff. Follow me."

Javier and one of his men support Barron as the quartet walk down the short hallway leading to the bedrooms. They stop at the double doors at the end, and Javier uses a key to unlock them.

The doors swing open into near darkness. The blackout shades don't make the room pitch-black, but more of a dark brown. Alejandro switches the light on, and confusion registers on his guest's face. There are no women in the bedroom – only a half-dozen men holding blunt instruments.

"What is this?"

"What does it look like?"

"The girls…where are they?"

"There are no girls here, Barron. I don't appreciate people telling me how to run my operation. I'm certainly not willing to compromise my other businesses to appease some washed-up Hollywood hack. Therefore, I'm ending our business relationship. Unfortunately, for you, that means I'm ending your life."

Barron stares at Alejandro for a long moment. He then smiles and starts to laugh as he wags a finger at him.

"You got me. Oh, this is good. Are there cameras in here? I bet the look on my face was priceless."

Alejandro doesn't smile, and Barron's disappears. "We can do this one of two ways. You can die peacefully, or you can die violently. It's your choice."

"You're…you're serious. You can't kill me! You'll never get away with it!"

"I'm the Magic Man," Alejandro says, stretching his arms out. "I make people disappear. You're no different."

"People will miss me."

The men in the room chuckle. Even Alejandro is amused by the comment. "They will notice your absence for about five minutes. Then you'll be replaced. None of them will *miss* you."

Barron looks around the room and pivots, swinging his fist wildly at Alejandro and hitting nothing but air. He gets his legs tangled, causing him to stumble and collapse to a knee. The men in the room pounce and hold him in that position as Javier grabs his arm. Another man puts a rubber restrictor band on Barron's bicep and finds a vein. He inserts the needle and depresses the plunger, and within seconds, Barron is off to La-La Land.

"Heroin is a wonderful drug, wouldn't you agree? It binds to specific receptors in the reward center of the brain to stimulate the release of dopamine. You'll feel a distinct heaviness throughout your body and will fight to keep your eyes open until you slip into blissful oblivion. It will be the last feeling you ever have, so enjoy it."

Barron's head bobs around on his shoulders as the men pick him up and dump him on the bed.

"You sure you don't want to use him to teach a lesson to others?" Javier asks.

"Not this time. Is everything ready at the airport?"

"Yes. The plane and pilots are reserved, and the flight plan back to L.A. has been filed. Per your instructions, there won't be a flight attendant aboard."

"Good. Make sure that he's alive when you get there. The pilots need to see him conscious when you load him on the plane. If he isn't, move to plan B."

"*Si, Jefe.* What if they question me?"

"Say he partied too hard and needs to sleep it off. He already has that reputation, so it's not a hard sell. Give him the lethal dose before you disembark the aircraft."

"Will the pilots check on him before takeoff?"

"I doubt it. The crew close and lock the cockpit door until the plane reaches cruising altitude, if not for the whole flight."

"What about you?"

"I am heading south. I will see you in a few days. If there are any problems, handle them. You're in charge until I return."

The man's face lights up. "I won't let you down."

Alejandro nods and moves over to the bed. He removes one of the "BB" cufflinks from the French cuff shirt, inspects it, and tucks it into a pocket. Even though Barron knows the next hour will be his last, he's powerless to do anything about it. That's the beauty of heroin. It makes even the most ardent person not care about anything in the world.

"Goodbye, Barron. It was a pleasure doing business with you."

CHAPTER TWENTY-EIGHT
"BOSTON" HOLLINGER

COPPER STAR HOTEL & SUITES
PHOENIX, ARIZONA

This run has lasted longer than I thought it would. I needed the exercise, but more importantly, I needed to clear my mind. The problem with seeing people's memories is that it doesn't come with an off switch. I didn't want or need to see what those kids went through again – the first time was bad enough.

It's one thing to hear stories about unimaginable suffering. It's another to live it. I am caught in between – it didn't happen to me, though I feel the pain and anguish as if it did. Physical, verbal, and sexual abuse is repeated over and over. The feeling of being drugged made me powerless to stop it. I've gotten to the point where I don't want to sleep now. Zach picked one hell of a first mission.

I pick up the pace the last mile back to the hotel, sprinting the last quarter mile. Upon reaching the parking lot, I pull up and walk to the main entrance to bring my heart rate back under control. Zach is leaning against a pillar of the covered area that shields the front door from the blistering sun. He tosses me a bottle of water that I eagerly uncap and chug down.

"Did I forget my hall pass or something?" I ask, not appreciating his waiting for me like I'm a teenager coming home an hour after curfew.

"I was beginning to think that maybe you made a run for it again."

"We're in the middle of the desert, so not this time. Is that the real reason you're greeting me at the door at six in the morning, or is it something else?"

Zach looks around. "What did you say to the detective?"

"Who? Hurley? Does it matter?"

"Yeah, it does," Forte snaps. It's going to be one of those conversations.

"He's playing ball. That's the end of the story," I say, feeling disinclined to share the particulars. Zach might try to use the information as leverage himself.

"I need to know what you saw. It had to be something good for Hurley to change his attitude so quickly. Is he dirty?"

"No, I'm sure that he showers."

"Cut the shit, Boston. Is he a bad cop?"

"Not that I know of."

"Then what?" Forte demands. I shake my head, earning a scoff. "Tell me."

"My name is Will, isn't it? Is there ever going to be a point that you'll trust me when I say that you don't need to know?"

"Will there ever be a point that you don't hate me?"

"I don't hate you, Zach. I resent you. There's a difference."

"Do I need to give you an order?"

"You can try."

Zach pushes himself off the column and gets closer to me. I can see the conflict in his eyes. He's trying to be conciliatory and understanding. Another part of him wants to flatten me with a hard right.

"Look, we need to be able to work together. A lot depends on it."

"So I've learned. If you want this to work, you need to stop micromanaging me. If I say I can't tell you something, there's a reason for it. If you can't respect that, we might as well end this experiment now."

I give him a pat on the shoulder and start to walk away. I only get a few steps.

"Okay, under one condition, and it's non-negotiable," he says, causing me to stop and turn.

"We'll see about that."

"You have to ease up on overtly using memories to manipulate people. You can't advertise your gift. Nobody can know what you can do."

"I haven't *overtly* said anything."

"You weren't subtle with the mayor, and I'm sure you weren't with Detective Hurley. Am I wrong?"

"You didn't bring me along for my good looks and charm. I thought you wanted results."

"I do, but the price can't be secrecy," Zach admits.

"You won't get results any other way."

"Of course we will. The FBI isn't known for playing nice in the sandbox with local law enforcement. We still get results. There are ways for us to get what we want."

"So, use my gift but don't use my gift...not that we should be calling it a *gift*. Got it. Anything else?"

Zach reacts like I completely missed the point, but I didn't. I'm just in no mood to listen. They were the ones who turned me into a law enforcement weapon. I don't really care that they disapprove of how I do it.

I head into the hotel's lobby and take the elevator up to my room to shower before breakfast. Watchtower needs to get their house in order. They don't know what they want. I don't have that problem. I know my ultimate goal and just need to find the right time to reach it.

CHAPTER TWENTY-NINE
DETECTIVE BRESHION HURLEY

PHOENIX POLICE HEADQUARTERS
PHOENIX, ARIZONA

The conference room is almost full. Four of the five FBI agents are seated at the table with two of Breshion's detectives. Ritter elects to stand along the wall as Breshion takes a spot at the front of the room.

He launches into his briefing and explains their situation to the FBI team. He's not sold that they will make any difference, but a deal is a deal. As he looks at Jamecca seated at the table, he knows it's worth it.

"That was almost depressing, Detective Hurley," Forte says.

"I wish I could paint a rosier picture for you. This is what we're up against."

"Then it's time to change the math in this equation."

"I appreciate your enthusiasm, Special Agent Forte, but I don't know what you hope to accomplish. There are only five of you. You could mobilize the whole Bureau and still not make a difference. I've been working vice for years, and we haven't put a dent in our human trafficking problem."

"We're going to make one."

The detective looks around the room to find all the FBI agents staring at him. None of them are bored or disengaged. Even the perpetually sleepy Agent Smith seems to be attentive. Maybe they are more serious about helping than he's giving them credit for. Time will tell, but until then, he'll play the game.

Breshion shakes his head. "I don't see how. Human trafficking is an umbrella term. It's like cancer: It manifests in various ways, has unique treatments, and is difficult to eradicate. Most victims are trafficked by someone they know, such as friends, family members, or romantic partners. What we are currently fighting is something different."

"Illegals."

"Yes, although I'm not sure that's the politically correct term anymore, Agent Jesperssen."

"Call a spade a spade," she says, leaning back in her chair. "We don't have time for bullshit."

"Fair enough," Breshion says with a smile. "Traffickers are intercepting immigrants smuggled illegally across the border and selling them to the highest bidder."

"It makes sense as a tactic," Agent Forte says. "Who will report them? It won't be the people who witnessed it since they aren't even supposed to be here, and there could be repercussions."

"All true. The people who are abducted for the slave trade just disappear," Breshion says, opening his hand into the air like a magician would.

"Are we talking mostly young girls and women, or…?" Agent Farris asks.

"Boys and men are just as likely to be victims as girls and women, at least internationally.   Girls face forced marriage and sexual exploitation. Boys become laborers or are recruited into armed groups. Thankfully, you don't see that here. In Arizona, we find the majority of victims are children of both sexes and women."

"So, by the time they reach the city, they're already captives. What if we can stop the trafficking at the border?"

Breshion smiles, appreciating the enthusiasm. "Unfortunately, it's not that simple. Illegals make easy targets for these predators. There is just too much border to watch, and we don't get much help from the federal government these days. No offense."

"None taken," Forte says, waving a hand dismissively.

"Even if we watched the border," Detective Ritter interjects, "we'd only be getting the low-level players. The men running the operation rarely go into the field. Most of the time, the low-level scumbags are hired thugs who don't know their employer."

"What about the victims? Have they provided any information?" Agent Jesperssen asks.

"Typically, they aren't helpful," Detective Robinson says. "These guys aren't afraid to use force and wield that as a threat. Victims are controlled through drug addiction and manipulation. They have no financial independence, are isolated from family, and are fearful of getting deported. They don't talk."

Agent Forte scratches his chin. "What about taking the opposite approach and trying to get to them through the buyers?"

"Who would even think about buying a sex slave?" Emma asks in disgust.

"More people than you'd think." Ritter pushes himself off the wall and joins Breshion at the front of the conference room. "The United States is one of the most active sex trafficking countries in the world."

"That's disgusting," Agent Jesperssen grunts.

"Agreed. It happens in cities, suburban, and rural areas. Most survivors engage in sexual activities in return for essentials such as food and shelter. Others are prostituted or exploited for child pornography. Tracing buyers is a good thought, but the odds of following one back to the guys we are looking for are slim."

Breshion watches the agents at the table intently. They're getting the picture now. He's not trying to be difficult on purpose; if catching the ringleaders were that easy, they would have done it by now.

"You said that you think one big fish is running most of the trafficking in Phoenix."

"Seventy percent of it, give or take," Ritter says.

"At least as far as we can tell," Hurley adds. "The raid we conducted before you guys got here was supposed to net us at least one mid-level lieutenant. Unfortunately, he wasn't there, and the four thugs guarding the house were dispatched to the afterlife."

"Working our way up the ladder from the lowest rung will never yield results. We need someone who can take us to the head of the snake so we can cut it off," Agent Smith says, looking around the room suspiciously.

This guy is so odd. He's engaged but not all there at the same time. How did he ever become a federal agent? Breshion has a three-year-old niece with a longer attention span, even if she lacks his intuition.

"Good plan, Agent Smith, but how do you suggest we do that?"

"Leave it to me," he says, rising from his chair. "Emma, Nadiya? Care to go for a drive with me?"

The two agents look at their boss, who nods. The three exit the room without another word, leaving the PPD detectives clueless about where they are heading and why.

"You wanna tell me what that's all about?" Breshion asks.

Forte shakes his head. "Agent Smith has a gift for getting information out of people. My guess is he knows where he can get some to jumpstart this investigation."

CHAPTER THIRTY

SSA ZACH FORTE

PHOENIX POLICE HEADQUARTERS
PHOENIX, ARIZONA

With Boston, Emma, and Nadiya out of the building and Doctor Kurota doing God knows what, Zach has spent the last couple of hours with the vice detectives poring over files and victim interviews with members of the vice squad. Breshion was right – all their arrests are small fish. No wonder Hurley is demoralized. Zach is depressed just reading through this.

Forte excuses himself and rises from the conference room table to stretch his legs. He makes his way to a break room and pours himself a cup of the horrid coffee they have here. Cops are among the most avid consumers of caffeinated beverages on the planet. You would think that they could at least procure and brew a decent cup of joe.

"Hi, Zach."

"Hey, Doc," Forte says, turning his head to see Asami standing at the threshold of the break room. "What's up?"

"Where's Bos— Agent Smith?"

"He left with Nadiya and Emma a couple of hours ago."

"Left to where?" she presses.

Forte stares at her blankly and doesn't answer.

"He went to the hospital, didn't he?"

"I don't know for sure, but I suppose it's a reasonable assumption."

"And you let him go?" Asami asks, the exasperation dripping from her voice. "Worse, you didn't call me?"

Forte tightens his jaw and squints at the doctor. "I didn't realize I needed *your* permission. He's an FBI agent tracking down a lead. Yeah, I let him go. As for not contacting you, had you been here this morning, you could have gone with him to babysit."

Asami crosses her arms. Forte wonders if they teach that body language in medical school. Every doctor he knows does the same thing when they hear something they don't like.

"Do you think this is a game, *Supervisory* Special Agent Forte? Because I sure don't."

"I don't know what this is, *Doctor* Kurota," Forte says, matching her tone. "That's what we're here to find out."

Asami scoffs. "You still don't get it, do you?"

"Apparently not, so why don't you explain it to me?" Zach says, folding his arms to match her.

"He doesn't just *see* memories," she says, keeping her voice low after checking behind her. "He *experiences* them."

"I know that."

"Do you? Because he's at that hospital living the most terrible and despicable moments imaginable. He will feel those kids' fear like it's his own. He'll know what it's like to be beaten, raped, and chained to a wall. It may not be his life, but while he is experiencing that memory, it might as well be."

Zach grimaces. Boston has a gift that they have tirelessly worked to unlock to its fullest potential. They all hope what he sees in the memories will be valuable. What he experiences emotionally is collateral damage. That's why the doctor is here in the first place.

"He's a big boy. He can handle it," Zach argues.

"Can he? You saw what happened the first time he was there."

"I didn't send him there, Doctor. He made the decision to go himself. I'm sure that Agent Smith wouldn't have walked out of here if it was more than he could handle."

"And I disagree."

"Good for you."

Zach wasn't one of Asami's fans even before the briefing to Brass. The truth is, she's an overprotective mother hen with feelings for him like his other two trainers. Unfortunately, the doctor's attachment clouds her judgment and interferes with her job.

"One of the two of us has been studying his psychological makeup for almost a year now. Do you really think you know him better than I do?" Asami asks.

Zach can't answer that question. Boston's animosity over what happened the night Gina shot him in the head and the year to follow has caused him to shut everyone out, Zach included. The senior agent won't admit it, but he doesn't really know Boston at all.

"What do you think is going to happen, Asami?"

"I don't know, and neither do you. That's what worries me. Do you understand the psychology of heroism?"

Zach rolls his eyes. "You think he's a hero? That'll do wonders for his ego."

"We all have a need to live in the service of something to thrive. Otherwise, a person becomes a rudderless ship aimlessly sailing through life at the mercy of the winds and tides. Agent Smith's service was in the military and then working with Congress. Then it was the search for the traitor which led him to Gina. Since then, he's had nothing."

"That's why we're here. This mission will give Boston a new purpose."

"And might get him killed. Do you know what the prototypical features of heroes are?"

"I'm sure you're about to tell me."

"They're brave, moral, courageous, protective, honest, altruistic, selfless, determined, and inspirational. How many of those traits do you think Agent Smith has? Here's a hint: you don't need to eliminate any."

"You speak as if that's a bad thing. I get that Smith's a good man. Get to the point."

"Many people claim that humans are born good or bad. It's nonsense. We are shaped by circumstances. Look at his," Asami says, checking behind her again. "Boston has equal capacity for heroism and to do terrible things. I don't know where he'll draw that line, assuming he draws one at all."

Zach lets that sink in. Asami has given a hundred assessments of Boston's psychological state since she was assigned to Watchtower. Not once has any of this ever been presented. It makes him question why she chose now to bring it up.

"Are you saying that he's unstable?"

"I'm saying that I don't understand him yet, and you don't have the first damn clue either. I get that you want this mission to be a success. I do, too, but at what price? I have no idea how he'll react to what he sees, physically or emotionally. Now isn't the time to let him do things his way. There's no telling what the consequences will be."

Zach is about to argue when the doctor turns and walks away. Zach swirls the coffee in his paper cup and chugs the lukewarm brew before refilling it. The doctor's concern isn't unexpected, but it is unnerving. As if he didn't have enough to think about on this mission.

CHAPTER THIRTY-ONE
MAYOR ANGELICA HORTA

CITY HALL PRESS BRIEFING ROOM
PHOENIX, ARIZONA

Angelica brushes her hair back as she paces back and forth. She left her office early for some quiet time away from ringing phones. The backroom of the press briefing room may not be the most private place to collect her thoughts, but it works for now.

There is a lot that can go wrong with this. They're putting this together on the fly, and her critics might consider that political opportunism. She will need to find an answer for that. The question is bound to come up.

"Here's the final version, hot off the presses," Adrian says, entering the room with several packets of paper separated by small binder clips.

The mayor flips through the document she's handed before looking up at her trusted staffer. "This is good…very good. You just threw this together?"

"The previous administration left us a draft that they did nothing with. I used it as a foundation and updated it with the information you and Judy provided. Lantern House helped me finish it this morning."

"You look exhausted. There are bags under your eyes that I could use at the supermarket."

Adrian shrugs. "All in a day's work…or night's."

"I can't believe Judy put some of these resources together on such short notice."

"The woman is a machine, that's for sure. She knows everyone in this city, and most of them owe her favors."

Adrian's conclusion is spot-on. Judy has boundless energy and the biggest heart of anyone she knows. She uses her powers of persuasion for the forces of good, and Phoenix is a better place because of it. Few people with those abilities would also qualify for sainthood.

The founding members of the new task force filter into the backroom and chat amiably as they wait for the briefing to start. There are dedicated people in this room, and it's about time they were in a position to work together. This is a good day for Phoenix.

"We're all set to go," Katy announces after poking her head in.

"Excellent. Then let's introduce this to the world," Angelica says with a smile to the group that's instantly returned.

The mayor walks onto the dais and stands at the podium. A decent number of media are present for this announcement. Their attendance is often hit or miss. They must be curious as to what this is all about.

"Ladies and gentlemen, thank you for coming," Angelica announces after the group takes up position behind her. "I am pleased to announce today that the City of Phoenix has created an interagency task force comprised of both the public and private sectors to address and combat the scourge of human trafficking in our community.

"The Compass Rose Initiative will be co-led by Councilman Kevin Demeter and Judy Costello of the Lantern House. To meet our goal to eradicate human trafficking in Phoenix, we have outlined an ambitious five-year roadmap that the Compass Rose team will implement and administer. Kevin and Judy will oversee programs spanning four functional areas, like the four cardinal directions: outreach, training, law enforcement, and victim services.

"The task force will comprise community leaders, residents, business interests, law enforcement, and city government. It's a bold endeavor that will explore and implement innovative solutions to address this critical issue. Through their efforts, the City of Phoenix will lead the nation in combating human trafficking and providing services to its survivors."

The mayor gestures to the pair to her right. "Before I ask Judy and Kevin to say a few words, I'm happy to take a few questions."

"What government groups are involved in the Compass Rose Initiative?" a reporter up front asks.

"The City of Phoenix Police Department Vice Unit, led by Assistant Chief Jada Fulcher, will target human trafficking offenders while linking victims with service providers. We are also partnering with federal law enforcement, prosecutors, and the U.S. Department of Labor, along with tribal and state agencies."

"Who is paying for this?" another journalist asks.

"All non-government employees are volunteering their time. Any incidental costs will come out of the City Hall budget for now. If we need to finance an expansion of this program, we won't apologize for the success, and we'll ask the city council to incorporate it into the budget for the next fiscal year."

"You stated that there are numerous community groups involved. Can you name some of them?" another reporter asks.

"A comprehensive list is available in your press packet, but I'm happy to call out a couple. We'll work with our state university domestic sex trafficking research on areas of prevention and awareness, intervention, and treatment. We can use their data to help reform how we work with victims, identify perpetrators, and train law enforcement, prosecutors, educators, medical, and social services personnel."

"Mayor Horta, isn't this nothing more than a shallow attempt at deflecting attention from the rising crime rate in the city?"

Angelica glares at the man in the front row. Vincent DiPasquale is the biggest scumbag in a profession full of them. For him, the news is secondary to his agenda. His most recent endeavor is to support LaCugna's future bid to become mayor. Who knows what he is getting in return for that cheerleading?

"The safety of all Phoenicians is our top priority," the mayor responds. "We are looking to address the recent increase in property crime by shifting law enforcement resources into the community."

"A follow-up, Mayor," he says, shouting over one of his colleagues. "One of the areas losing people in your ill-advised reassignments is the vice squad. Are you afraid that loss will mean more human trafficking, and that's the real reason behind this task force?"

"We are using every resource we can bring to bear on both problems."

"By leveraging the generosity of outside resources to handle problems that you and City Hall cannot?"

"Madam Mayor, if I may," Judy says, placing her hand on the mayor's arm. It's a good thing. Angelica can feel herself losing her temper before yielding the podium to the unimpeachable head of Lantern House.

"The Mayor and City Council have shown bold leadership in identifying human trafficking as a city-wide priority and embarking on an aggressive plan to address it," Judy says, taking turns looking each reporter in the eyes. "I know many of you would like to make this political, but it isn't. The Compass Rose Initiative is building on successful programs and practices from around the country. That's why I decided to help lead this initiative. Trafficking is a community problem, and it needs all of us to come together to solve it."

"That's all well and good, Ms. Costello, but—"

"But what, sir?" she innocently asks Vincent, silencing a man who rarely stops moving his lips. "Would you rather the mayor do nothing?"

"I don't see how another government task force solves the human trafficking issue."

"It's not just an 'issue.' It's modern slavery, and I would think that you and everyone at the *Phoenix Record* would like to see the kind of bold action the mayor is taking today. Unless you and your paper support slavery, that is. Tell me, Mr. DiPasquale, is that the case?"

"Of course not."

"Then all I ask is that you set aside your apprehension about the creation of Compass Rose and help us. We are not going to have instant results. The short-, medium-, and long-term actions laid out in our charter will improve the overall response to human trafficking over time. However, these actions alone will not solve the problem.

"It will require a cultural shift in attitudes toward human trafficking. It must be clear that it's unacceptable and won't be tolerated under any circumstances. This requires buy-in from every individual and the mobilization of private-sector resources to help augment the city's efforts. The mayor, city council, and law enforcement are committed to this. So is the community. I sincerely hope you all are, too. The media will be instrumental in bringing our message to the people."

All eyes in the room turn to Vincent to measure his reaction. He was shown up, and as much as the reporter would love to lash out, he knows he can't. Judy Costello is as much an institution in this city as the group she runs. Any attack on her will look petty.

Judy looks directly at the reporter. Vincent offers a reluctant nod, and Angelica suppresses a grin. Convincing Judy to help chair the Compass Rose Initiative and bring the resources of Lantern House with her was the most crucial moment in her political career. She couldn't have asked for a better ally in this fight.

CHAPTER THIRTY-TWO
ALEJANDRO SALCIDO

SALCIDO MEXICAN RESIDENCE
SAN CARLOS NUEVO GUAYMAS, SONORA, MEXICO

San Carlos is a beautiful port city across the bay from Guaymas, where the desert meets the sea. The summer months are hot and humid, much like Texas, and the city is renowned for the clarity and warmth of the ocean water that make it popular with divers. Many Americans and Canadians live in San Carlos during the winter, but none are here now, shrinking the population to under seven thousand.

Alejandro moves out onto the veranda and stares at the glistening water on the Sea of Cortez. San Carlos is about a six-hour drive from the United States along Mexican Interstate Highway 15. With an airport only fifteen minutes away, he prefers to take a private jet back and forth from Phoenix to this dream house on the coast.

"*Patrón, su huésped ya llego*," his bodyguard says from the door, announcing that his visitor has arrived.

"*Trae me lo.*"

He didn't intend on taking meetings while he was here. Alejandro rarely does business in his home, either here or in Arizona. Compartmentalization is essential in his line of work. Home, legitimate business, and trafficking are kept separate to the extent possible. There are exceptions to the rule, like with Barron Birch. This is another of those occasions.

Alejandro sizes the American up as he watches him emerge from the kitchen. There are dozens of non-governmental organizations working in Mexico, and some of them are nothing more than fronts for intelligence agencies. He thoroughly vetted the man in the white suit but is still apprehensive about falling into a trap. The key to survival in this country is never trusting anyone.

"This is a beautiful home, Mr. Salcido," Jai Snyder says in English despite being fluent in Spanish.

"Thank you. What brings you to it?" Alejandro asks, shaking his hand and offering him a seat.

"I know you've done your research. You know who I am and what I do."

Alejandro knows everything he needs to. There are few people he discusses his business with. Jai has been involved in trafficking for a decade now, just never with Alejandro. With those bona fides, it was worth hazarding a meeting. It doesn't mean there isn't a backup plan.

"I do. Would you care for a drink?"

"I wouldn't mind a beer if it's no trouble."

"*Cerveza*," Alejandro instructs the bodyguard before turning his attention back to the pompous American. "Why don't you tell me why you are here anyway?"

"I organize caravans, starting with the early ones arranged by *Sin Fronteras*. Every few months since, especially in the spring, I arrange for groups of four to seven thousand people to make the long journey to violate American immigration laws."

In Spanish, migrant caravans are often called the "*Viacrucis Migrante*" or the "Migrant Stations of the Cross." In Catholicism, the Stations of the Cross reenact Christ's last steps and crucifixion. Many migrant caravans begin their trek north around Easter, drawing comparisons of their persecution with Christ's suffering. Jai is unknowingly their Pontius Pilate.

"I'm aware of your activities."

"Then you're also aware of what I can do for yours," Jai says, leaning forward.

"You seem to believe I have an interest in expanding my operation."

"How you run your business *is* your business. I'm here to provide you with options."

The bodyguard arrives with a glass of beer and places it on a tray next to the outdoor sofa. He steps back and retrieves a garrote from his pocket, allowing Alejandro to see it as Jai takes a sip. The trafficker shakes his head, wanting to see where this conversation goes.

"What options are you referring to?"

"The caravans have increased exponentially in size over the years. People think that there is safety in numbers when the opposite is true. It makes people more vulnerable to extortion, rape, and other criminal activity. These people are vulnerable, and there is no accountability in the caravan. People come and go daily. That also means nobody misses them when they disappear."

"Mr. Snyder, can you please get to the point?"

"Who buys a fifteen-year-old child for sex? The answer is ordinary men. Americans would be shocked to learn it could be their co-worker, doctor, pastor, or even their spouse."

"When I asked you to make a point, I did not mean a lecture on the consumers of the sex trade."

"That is not my intent, sir. You do not have a demand problem, *Señor Salcido*. You have a supply chain problem, and I have a solution."

Alejandro offers him a sarcastic grin. "And what solution would that be?"

"I will help you find people earlier in the process. You currently make your selections after the border is crossed. It reduces smuggling risk but also limits your inventory. You are the Magic Man, Alejandro. There are countless stops during the voyage in Mexico where migrants could be siphoned off. The net result is your tripling or even quadrupling the quality and quantity of your merchandise."

Alejandro leans back into his seat on the adjacent sofa and rests his arm along the top of the cushions. This is not the first time he has been approached with an offer like this. It is the first time by someone who could pull it off without attracting attention.

"It solves one problem and causes another. I assume the risk of transporting product across the border."

"That's where I come in. I have relationships with various shipping concerns – ones that won't ask questions. Transport can be arranged. For a small fee, of course."

"Of course."

"I have developed a sizable network while organizing the caravans."

"Yes, I'm sure UPS and FedEx will love transporting live cargo," Alejandro says with a sneer.

"These companies are much smaller than them, but all reputable enough with American Customs and Border Patrol to avoid scrutiny."

"Tell me, Mr. Snyder, why would they?"

"Simple. Morals go out the window for businesses when money is involved. That's the most valuable lesson I have learned over the past ten years. I'm sure you will agree."

"You make an interesting sales pitch, Jai, but that's all it is – a pitch. I have no idea if you can deliver what you say you can."

"Then let me prove it to you. Send two trusted men down to Mexico to make selections for you. We can then make arrangements to have them delivered to the place of your choosing in the U.S. I would assume it will be a new stash house for security reasons. If you are happy with what you see, we can talk about future business."

Alejandro mulls the offer in his head. It's not a horrible arrangement. He gets free merchandise, and he knows that Jai will deliver the best he has to offer. Even better, he can dispatch a second team to watch the activist to ensure he isn't setting up a trap. It's a win-win.

"Deal," Alejandro says, shaking the man's hand after they rise from their seats. "I will make the necessary arrangements and contact you with the details."

"I look forward to this being the start of a lucrative relationship," Jai says, beaming.

Alejandro watches him leave before turning his attention back to the glistening sea. The mayor can start all the blue-ribbon initiatives that she wants in Phoenix. If this works out, nothing can stop the tsunami he is about to unleash.

CHAPTER THIRTY-THREE
"BOSTON" HOLLINGER

SALT RIVER VALLEY MEDICAL CENTER
PHOENIX, ARIZONA

The hardest part is maintaining my focus. Tara's initial hypothesis concluded that the memories I see are traumatic or stressful moments in someone's life. Asami confirmed that during testing in the cozy, controlled confines of the training center over the past year. I'd prefer more joyful moments, but that's not how this curse seems to work.

My current problem is that the raw emotion of these children's traumatic memories crashes into me like a tidal wave. There is no order or chronology to them. I could be seeing events from the journey through Mexico or life in a stash house. I have to listen, watch, and feel their agony until my brain picks up on a new signal to get to what I need.

Focusing on any one child is another challenge. In the two hours I've been doing this, less the thirty-minute break I needed to clear my head, none of the memories have yielded anything useful. It's a tiring exercise, and the energy drink I chugged down is failing to reduce my fatigue. Determined to get something, I close my eyes and clear my mind for another attempt.

* * *

I feel exhausted and thirsty. The low brush smacks against me as I crawl through it. Loose rocks slide under my feet, and I stumble to the ground, letting out a yelp.

A slender man comes up next to me and squats. He pulls out a knife and holds it in front of my face. In the moonlight, I can see the white ivory or pearl handle as he runs the tip lightly down my cheek, stopping near my mouth.

"Cállate o te arranco la lengua," a man threatens in a low voice.

I feel a shockwave of fear course through my body. I look into his eyes. They are confident and determined. My heart races, and I start to shake as he stands and continues up the slope.

"No está mu lejos. Vamos, mijo," a woman says, consoling me as she rubs my back. Her words soothe me, but I can still feel the crippling fear tearing at my soul.

I am still walking when things get blurry. I refocus. This time it's dark. I can hear a truck engine rumbling. I bounce on the rough road. It's tight in here. I feel claustrophobic. My knees are tucked into my chest. Light pours in through three quarter-sized holes and disappears. I feel tears roll down my cheek.

Now I'm back in the desert, standing beside a road. Four lights shine on us, and a figure stands silhouetted against them. A girl is pulled from the group by a man. She's screaming. I clutch someone around the waist. I'm scared. I don't want them to choose me.

A man steps up to me and squats. He's different than the man from before. The side of his mouth curls.

"¿Tienes miedo, niño? Lo deberías estar. Ese es El Hombre Mágico. Te va a desaparecer y a tu madre Tambien."

Hands grab at me. I resist, and the woman screams.

"¡No!"

She is grabbed from behind. I lose my grasp on her. I am being pulled away…

I jump when I feel a tug at my shirt, and I open my eyes. A boy, no older than eight, shyly stands in front of me.

"*Hola.*"

"Uh, *hola,*" I say, wishing I had paid more attention to my Spanish teacher in high school. "What's your name?"

"*¿Cuál es tu nombre?*" Dr. Benito asks, translating for the boy when he looks up at her.

"Adelmo."

"It's nice to meet you, Adelmo. My name is Will."

Dr. Benito translates and looks back at me after Adelmo sheepishly responds. "He wants to know if you're here to help him. His mother was taken by the same men, and he hasn't seen her."

The road. The man in front of the lights. The boy climbing the crest of the rocky ridge. I saw all of that through Adelmo's eyes. It may have even been him in the box, although I can't be sure.

I've been told repeatedly that I can't do anything that would betray my abilities to anyone outside of Watchtower. Now that I'm in the field, that rule works better on paper than in practice. To hell with it. I need information and can't get it without her help.

"By the Magic Man?"

Adelmo's eyes grow wide in surprise after she repeats my question in Spanish. I even get a puzzled look from the doctor.

"*Si. El hombre la hizo desaparecer. ¿La puede encontrar?*"

"Yes. He made her disappear. Can you find her?" the doctor translates, mimicking Adelmo's sad tone in her own voice.

It'd be too easy to lie. It happens all the time in these situations. Words meant to reassure or console often translate differently, not because of the differences in languages but the filter of emotion. The odds aren't good that the boy's mother will ever be found, but I need to give him some hope without crossing a line I can't retreat from.

"I don't know," I say, prompting the doctor to translate as I speak. "I will make you a promise, though, Adelmo. I will do everything I can to find your mother and bring her back to you. Then I am going to stop the Magic Man so he can't take anyone else. Okay?"

The boy nods again when the doctor finishes speaking. He wraps his arms around me, and I fight to stop tears from cascading out of my eyes. I don't know where this boy's father is. I don't know if he ever had one, at least in the parental sense. The only male figures he has been exposed to on the journey here were bullies who did unspeakable things. For him to emotionally connect to me like this…I lose the battle. A stream of tears rolls down my face.

He breaks his embrace, and I rush to wipe my moist cheeks. The doctor offers another puzzled look. I can't tell her about my past or explain away this sudden connection with a young boy I just met from another land. She may have already learned too much about me.

"Cute kid."

"You're the first person he has spoken to since he's been here. That's why I rushed over. You have a way with children. Do you have any of your own?"

"No. Not yet, at least."

"Well, when you do, I already know you will be an amazing father. Who is the Magic Man?"

There it is. When we arrived yesterday, I'm sure that Forte told her we were only starting our investigation. She didn't need to Sherlock Holmes this too hard to uncover that I knew a lot for being here a day.

"I'm not sure. I think it's who abducted him."

"How do you know that?"

"It's a really long story, Doc."

"Okay. I won't press you to tell it. Do you think you can find Adelmo's mother?"

"I don't know, but I'm going to do everything I can. Now I have an idea where to start looking."

CHAPTER THIRTY-FOUR
DETECTIVE BRESHION HURLEY

KINGSNAKE FITNESS
PHOENIX, ARIZONA

There is nothing easy about being a detective. Days are long, hard, and stressful. At the end of most of them, Breshion likes to blow off steam at the gym. He found one on his route home and always keeps a gym bag in his trunk. He doesn't have his mid-twenties physique, nor does he try to regain that sculpted look. For him, this is therapy as much as it is exercise.

Breshion finishes his fourth set of bent-over rows as a man approaches in workout clothes that look like they just had their price tags removed. Under normal circumstances, he would have left his earbuds in and ignored the man. It's too late now, so he pulls them out when the politician reaches him.

"Detective Hurley, how are you?"

"Councilman LaCugna. I'm good. I haven't seen you in here recently."

"I rarely come at this time. I prefer to exercise in the morning."

Breshion flashes a fake smile as his internal BS meter redlines. Not only does he rarely frequent any gym, as anyone with two functioning eyes could figure out, but this meeting also isn't coincidental.

"Then I'll let you get to it," the detective says, hoping his quick exit strategy is successful.

"Since I'm fortunate enough to run into you here, can I ask a question?"

Breshion shifts to a different tactic after his first epically failed. "I'm in the middle of a workout after a long day."

"I understand. I promise not to take too much of your time."

"Okay. What do you want, Councilman?"

"We're at the gym, not the city council chamber. Please call me Andres. Answers. I want answers."

"To what?" Breshion asks, picking up a set of large dumbbells and settling onto an upright bench for some shoulder presses.

"You know about the mayor's Broken Compass program, or whatever it's called?"

"Compass Rose Initiative. Yes, I'm aware of it," he says, hefting the weights rhythmically over his head and back level with his shoulders.

"What do you think?"

"It doesn't matter what I think."

"I want to know."

Breshion drops the weights and stares up at Andres. "Why? So you can run to the media with a quote if I agree with you and ignore my opinion if I don't?"

He thought that would wipe the goofy smile from the councilman's face. It doesn't. If anything, it has the opposite effect.

"I'm glad you know how the political game is played."

"I'm losing my sense of humor about this conversation, Andres."

"Then let me get to the point. Mayor Horta gutted vice and then announced this initiative in the same week. Those two things are diametrically opposed. For all intents and purposes, she pulled resources away that could make a difference. Then she doubled down on the mistake by replacing them with some community outreach mumbo jumbo that will talk tough and do nothing. You must have an opinion about that."

"Sex trafficking is a scourge, Councilman," Breshion says, hefting the weights from the floor to his quads and readying himself for another set. "It should be treated as such. If this initiative accomplishes what it has set out to do, then I'm all for it."

"And if it doesn't? If this fancy blue-ribbon commission turns out like I predict?"

"Then we're in the same place we were in before it was created."

"That's true. Only the politics are different. I've known Angelica Horta for a long time. This is a smokescreen and nothing more."

Breshion rocks out a set of twelve repetitions, hoping LaCugna will get the hint and walk away. Instead, he waits patiently for the detective to finish.

"How long have you been on the city council?"

"Does it matter?"

"You wanted this conversation and asked your questions. Let me ask mine. How long?"

"Seven years...and change."

"What have you done to fight sex trafficking in that time? It's not like this problem popped up last week. It's only an issue for you now, despite our previous attempts to get the council's attention. Then you cut the PPD's budget."

"That wasn't me," Andres says reflexively. "It was Horta's idea."

"Look, I know that you're looking for something to run against her on. I don't really care about city politics. I'm just going to warn you not to make human trafficking that issue. Don't politicize slavery."

Breshion starts to walk away, forgoing the remaining two sets and the rest of his lifting routine. He cannot get out of here fast enough. If dealing with the FBI wasn't bad enough, now he is being accosted by a slimy, baby-kissing jackass.

"Are you working with the FBI, Detective?" Andres calls out, forcing Breshion to stop.

"Yeah. They have a team from Washington here."

"Did they arrive before or after the mayor's announcement?"

"I don't remember," Breshion lies. He knows damn well that it was before.

"Have the agents you're working with mentioned the Compass Rose Initiative?"

"Not to my knowledge."

"Don't you find that suspicious?" Andres asks, walking over to him.

"Not really. So long as the feds are here to help, I don't much care why. Neither should you. Have a good workout, Councilman. It'd be a shame if that gut causes you to have a heart attack. You should work on losing it."

Breshion gives LaCugna's belly a couple of taps with his hand and walks away much faster this time. He hates politicians. LaCugna doesn't care about the traffickers or the people being trafficked. They are tools for him to reach his goal: the mayor's office. If he wants leverage on Horta, he can find it elsewhere. Breshion already has enough to worry about.

CHAPTER THIRTY-FIVE

SSA ZACH FORTE

WHITE ROCK CAMPGROUND
CORONADO NATIONAL FOREST, ARIZONA

This is a beautiful part of the country. The Coronado National Forest has elevations that range from three thousand to almost eleven thousand feet in twelve mountain ranges that rise from the desert floor. The views are spectacular from these heights, and Forte imagines that he could experience all four seasons during a single day's hike. He will have to put Arizona as a possibility on his list of retirement spots.

Bathed in moonlight at this remote campsite, everyone is getting antsy waiting for something to happen. The Phoenix cops haven't been silent about their opinions that the feds are wasting their time. Boston has taken the criticism in stride, not offering up anything more than scant details. That will have to change in a hurry if he expects everyone to keep waiting in the dark, literally and metaphorically.

"Why exactly are we here, Boston?"

"I told you. The RVs. One was pulling out of this campsite in the memory, and the truck almost hit it."

"How do you know?"

"The door opened, and Adelmo saw it."

"Who the hell is Adelmo?" Zach asks.

"One of the kids at the hospital."

"You said you saw all their memories. How do you know it was his?"

Boston shoots Zach a nasty glare. "Because I do."

Zach isn't sure what he's more concerned about: Boston's emotional stability following his hospital visit or his insistence on coming down to the border. He didn't provide details other than a list of needed resources, including a reconnaissance drone and location that they would use for staging. He was even aloof with Emma and Nadiya, and Zach is convinced they could charm the code to the Fort Knox vault out of a security guard.

"You know, Watchtower had to call in a lot of favors for this. Do you have any idea how much that drone costs to operate per hour?"

"I don't manage our budget. You want results. I'm getting them for you."

"You had better be right about this."

"I am."

Detective Hurley walks over, effectively ending the conversation. The vice detective has been a good sport about this excursion thus far. That might be attributed to this being a win-win for him. If they succeed in capturing some traffickers, they make progress tracking down the ringleaders. If nothing materializes, he gets the satisfaction of the FBI having egg on its face.

"I hope you know what you're doing, Agent Smith. This is a 1.7-million-acre forest with sixty miles of border with Sonora, Mexico. Fifteen hundred illegal aliens pass into the United States here each day."

"Yeah, I saw the 'Smuggling and illegal immigration may be encountered in this area' sign on the way in. Very helpful."

"Hey, I didn't write it. This isn't even our jurisdiction. I'm only saying that you are looking for a needle in a stack of needles. There is a difference between smuggling and trafficking. The odds are slim of finding the people we're looking for."

"We're not looking for people."

"We have something," Emma announces. "Go ahead, Looking Glass."

The entire task force gathers around the laptop perched on the Suburban's hood. Watchtower Ops is going by the name "Looking Glass" for this mission to maintain some semblance of secrecy. Zach has already had to explain too much to the vice detective.

"This is Looking Glass. We have three vehicles on thermal with headlights off."

"Two small box trucks and a pickup truck?" Boston asks.

"Stand by…roger."

All eyes turn to Boston after the creepy premonition. "Follow the road and see if you can find anyone waiting for them."

"Wilco."

"There they are," Emma says, pointing at the image on her laptop. "Four clicks away. A small group huddled off the road between these two outcroppings."

"It's a 'lay-up' site," Detective Robinson says. "Smugglers will make travelers wait at them before they get transported to Tucson or Phoenix. Authorities find backpacks and clothes left behind so that more people can be packed into vehicles."

"All right, Boy Wonder. Now what?" Hurley asks.

"Keep monitoring the feed. If they separate the immigrants on the two trucks, we move into position at this bend on Ruby Road. They won't see us until it's too late."

"How do you know all this?" Robinson asks.

"Yeah, it's creepy," Ritter adds, earning a stern look from his superior.

"It's one of life's mysteries," Boston says with a grin.

"Let's load up," Forte says before the vice squad can ask any more questions he can't or won't answer.

* * *

The headlights on the Suburbans are activated at the same time. The three trucks rumbling up the dirt road lock up their brakes and come to a dead stop thirty feet away. Detectives Ritter and Hurley shout commands in Spanish for the drivers to exit their vehicles as guns are trained on the occupants of the lead vehicle.

The two men jump out of the vehicles and immediately fire their weapons wildly at the team. The response is immediate. Emma takes down the driver with one shot. Zach needs three to drop the passenger. More shots ring out from their right as Ritter and Nadiya engage from the uphill flank.

A man exits the pickup truck and sprints across the dirt road, diving into the brush that dots the downhill slope from the road.

"Shit," Zach says.

"Oh, that's not gonna happen," Boston says, darting out from cover behind the SUV and launching himself down the hill after him.

"Smith! Get back here!"

The order falls on deaf ears. Zach races into the brush after them, desperate to close the gap and only succeeding in tripping on the unstable hill beneath him. He falls forward and plants himself on the ground. The last time that happened, Zach was entering Boston's house a year ago. It saved his life back then when Gina opened fire at where his head would have been.

He looks up from the ground in time to spot Boston tackling the suspect. Their momentum carries them down a slope until they tumble out of sight.

Zach pushes himself back to his feet and navigates down the moonlit crag to find the two men squaring off against each other. Zach pulls his weapon as the man threatens Boston with a switchblade. As much as he wants to shoot, he's too far away for his fire to be effective. And they need him alive. It's up to Boston.

The man holds the switchblade out in front of him menacingly. He thrusts it forward, and Boston turns his body to move off the line of the strike while raising his forearm parallel with his torso. He deflects the thrust and secures the wrist of the man's knife hand as he pops him in the face with a right jab. He then joins his hands together and twists the man's arm hard, exposing his midsection long enough to land a kick to his lower abdomen.

With a hard twist, the assailant is torqued off-balance and collapses to the ground. Boston ratchets down on his wrist, causing the stunned coyote to lose his grip on the knife, which Hollinger relieves him of. Zach relaxes as he moves his weapon to the low ready. Boston uses the wristlock to force the man onto his stomach, expertly cuffing him in less than five seconds.

"Damn," Zach cries as Emma and Nadiya arrive alongside him.

"Look at you go," Nadiya cheers her pupil.

"He was much easier to take down than you are."

"How would you know? You've never taken me down."

"Exactly."

"I'm actually impressed," Emma adds. "Have you frisked him yet?"

"I'm just getting to that." Boston starts with the back pocket and pulls out a worn wallet with some cash and an Arizona driver's license. "Helio Cervantes Lozano. Well, Helio, we're going to have a little chat."

"I want a lawyer," he says in English.

"People in hell want ice water," Zach says. "You should listen to what we have to say before making demands. There's one chance for you to not end up in prison, and asking for a lawyer ain't it."

"Whatever, *puta madre.*"

Boston finishes checking the coyote for weapons, and the group escorts him back up the rocky outcropping. The vice squad has already searched the two men they took down, and Detective Robinson is doing her best to keep the illegals who crossed the border calm. Seeing their guide emerge on the road in handcuffs has the intended effect.

"What do we have here?" Detective Hurley asks, searching the young man with his eyes.

"Contestant number one," Boston says.

"Excellent! Arrangements are being made for CBP to pick up our country's newest guests. State police will help clean up this mess. Ritter will hang back here to handle the details. Let's get this *hijueputa* back to Phoenix."

Zach doesn't bother asking what that means before they load up in the vehicles —but he assumes it isn't pleasant. He can only hope that Boston's memories led them to something worthwhile.

CHAPTER THIRTY-SIX
MAYOR ANGELICA HORTA

THELDA WILLIAMS PUP PARK
PHOENIX, ARIZONA

When local pet charities helped transform a small patch of grass outside Phoenix City Council chambers into the city's first downtown dog park, residents in the area were elated. It was cleverly advertised as a "paw-pup," a temporary pop-up park that organizers hoped would become a well-utilized and -maintained permanent neighborhood fixture. Angelica is thrilled with that outcome.

"All animals deserve our love. I mean, really? Who can resist this face?" the mayor asks, holding up the Labrador retriever puppy she's cradling.

Several photographers move closer to get shots. Sometimes her job requires her to do things she doesn't want to. This isn't one of those days. Puppies are better therapy than most other things she can think of.

"This group does amazing work for our community. I urge everyone to come to the pup park today or tomorrow and help these animals find their forever home. When you rescue a pet, you're saving a life—more than one. By adopting, you're helping make space for another animal in need of becoming a beloved pet. Shelter animals have so much love to give. So please, I urge everyone thinking about opening their home to a pet to consider coming here and finding their new best friend. Thank you."

The media is packing up when Adrian and Katy approach. A shelter volunteer thanks the mayor and offers to take the puppy from her, but she isn't eager to give it up. If her schedule weren't as demanding as it is, this guy would be going home with her today.

"Well done," Adrian says, with Katy nodding her approval.

"This cutie pie did the heavy lifting," she says, nuzzling her face into the puppy's neck. "Why don't either of you have a dog?"

"Our hours are crazier than yours are, Mayor," Katy says with a smile as she pets the teething puppy, who tries to nibble on her finger.

"A word, Mayor Horta?" Vincent DiPasquale asks after breaking away from the other jackals in the press corps.

"That depends. Is it about pet adoption? You look like you could use a best friend."

"Uh, no, ma'am, it isn't."

"I didn't think so."

"He looks like he kicks puppies," Adrian mutters, earning a nasty glare from the reporter. There is no love lost between Vincent and her staff.

"I'd like to ask you about the FBI involvement in the Compass Rose Initiative."

"Are the FBI involved?" the mayor asks.

"You said so."

"No, she didn't," Katy interjects. "Why do I always have to set the record straight for you, Vincent? You have a functioning recorder on your phone. The mayor said we were receiving federal assistance."

"That means the FBI, Miss Bowlin."

"It means a lot of federal agencies in a position to help," Adrian interjects.

"How do you know?"

"I helped write the charter."

Vincent grimaces. He didn't know that, although a toddler could have connected the dots to figure it out.

"The FBI has a team from Washington in Phoenix," the mayor discloses. "We would prefer to keep that out of your reporting."

"Why?"

"The less the traffickers know about who is hunting them, the more likely they are to be brought to justice. You do want to see them taken off the streets, don't you?"

"I do. I also want government transparency."

"Nothing can reach the transparency of your motives, Vincent. Ask me what you really came here to ask."

"You slashed vice's manpower and then convene a blue-ribbon initiative—"

"For a reporter, your word choice leaves much to be desired. It's not a blue-ribbon anything. This isn't a group studying the problem. They're charged with doing something about it."

"It's just coincidence that this all happened when the FBI team from Washington arrived?"

The volunteer collects the puppy the mayor is holding. She gives him a kiss on his forehead after reluctantly handing him over. She prefers dogs to people. They are loyal and love unconditionally. She has yet to meet a human who can meet those lofty standards.

"The Compass Rose Initiative has been in the works for some time. The previous administration worked on the idea."

"And it happened to all come together now."

"I don't know what you're fishing for, Mr. DiPasquale. I thought Judy made it all very clear for you during the press conference."

Vincent's face contorts in anger. He was humiliated by Judy in front of his peers, and the mayor has no doubt that they won't let him forget that anytime soon. Journalism is a cutthroat business. She is surprised more of them don't go into politics. If they believed at all in accountability, the halls of government might be full of them.

"You look sad, Vincent. Do you want a puppy?" Katy asks, spreading her hands to gesture around them.

Without another word, the reporter storms off. The mayor still doesn't know what he was after, but there is no doubt that LaCugna is trying to make a scandal out of the FBI's arrival in Arizona.

"What was that about?" Katy asks, coming up alongside the mayor as Vincent disappears down the sidewalk.

"LaCugna knows we have the high ground with the media, and he is trying to find something to knock us off the hill. He sent his loyal attack dog to scare us."

"That guy…"

"It's just politics, Katy. Keep your ear to the ground. We're going to get hit with something soon, and I'd prefer not to get blindsided by it."

"Yes, ma'am."

Katy moves off to join Adrian in talking to the head of the shelter. The mayor looks around the small dog park. This is what governance is about: recognizing a problem or need and mobilizing people to do something about it. That's what the Compass Rose is, even if the timing was forced on them. She only wishes others could see that.

CHAPTER THIRTY-SEVEN
"BOSTON" HOLLINGER

PHOENIX POLICE HEADQUARTERS
PHOENIX, ARIZONA

I open the interrogation room door and find a place along the back wall to lean against. Besides the coyote and Detective Hurley seated at the table, Zach and Nadiya stand along the side. Emma and other vice squad members Ritter and Robinson are watching from the other side of the two-way mirror.

Forte scowls at my appearance but doesn't say anything. I focus on Helio, determined to ignore my boss's withering glare. For whatever reason, Zach didn't want me in this room. As if they would have found Helio without me. I played along while they got nowhere for over an hour in their interrogation. No longer content to sit on the sidelines, I have every intention of intervening.

"We can do this the easy way or the hard way," Hurley says, leaning across the metal table. "There are enough charges against you to put you away for a long time."

"Lawyer. Now."

I think back to the movie *Basic* with John Travolta. He moves a detainee out of the interrogation room because he knows that subjects clam up while seated in one. Helio may not be an American, but he understands his rights in these circumstances. "Lawyer" is the subject of every sentence he has uttered since he's been here.

"We've explained to you why that's a bad idea," Detective Ritter says from beside the wall.

Helio nods. "I want a lawyer anyway."

Breshion looks at Forte, who shakes his head. Helio isn't talking because he doesn't feel he needs to. It's time to change the math. I close my eyes. It only takes a moment for a flood of memories to come in. The force is strong with this one.

I am out of breath…being chased. I can see flashlights behind me. A hand reaches up from the ground and grabs my leg. I look back and see the pursuers growing closer. I strike the man, sending him sprawling back to the ground. I continue to run as people scream.

I open my eyes and still see shadows of the memory in my vision. It's less crisp but still there. A wall. The feel of metal and the smell of desert air. My panic begins to subside. I'm safe.

The memory fades before my eyes as I stare at the young man seated at the table across from Detective Hurley. That's an interesting development. I've never been able to experience a memory with my eyes open. I close them again.

I feel pain: not emotional, but physical. My cheek and ribs hurt. I'm sitting somewhere…a bench or log. Houses are around me. Cars honk their horns. The sun is setting, but the heat is still unbearable. A young girl comes up to me. She might be a teenager.

"Si vas a pelear, tienes que ganar," she says, grabbing my chin and studying my face.

"Ellos eran mucho mas grandes."

"Ells siempre serán mas grandes. Ellos siempre serán mas fuertes. Tu tienes que ser mas inteligente que tus enemigos o perderás."

"Pero no se como."

"Papá dice, 'Lo que hagas como de niño, definera quien eras como hombre. No dejes que el hombre viva con remordimientos."

The memory continues to play. I'm a small boy. Helio as a child? Who is the girl? Is that his sister? And what the hell are they saying? I really need to learn some more Spanish. Papa dice – dad says. I manage to figure out the rest. With that thought, I close my eyes again.

I'm at a camp of some sort. There are people seated in groups and vehicles. Is this some kind of staging area? I need to take a leak. I walk over to the shrubs and see two men holding a woman down with a hand covering her mouth. A third man has her pants off and is having his way with her. I watch with no emotion. She stares at me with pleading eyes to help. Without a word and feeling nothing, I finish my business, zip my pants, turn, and walk away.

I feel the surge of anger and push myself off the wall. The hollow, wounded eyes of the woman staring at me are seared into my memory. He did nothing about it. To him, she was garbage, not another human being violated in front of him. He didn't care.

My emotions take over. I lunge across the table, knocking Helio backward in his chair. We slam to the ground, and I get my balance and straddle him. I land five sharp blows to his face before being jerked backward.

Strong hands hold me as I try to fight through them. I am almost free when Nadiya grabs my wrist and wrenches it forward. I almost drop to my knees at the pain before the pressure is released. Hunched over, I stare up at her before Forte grabs me. He slams me into the wall and presses his forearm against my chest.

"*¿Que diablos, hijo de puta?*" Helio lashes out. "You're crazy! An animal!"

"I'm an animal? I didn't leave people behind at the border. I didn't watch a woman get raped in front of you while taking a piss!"

Helio's eyes grow wide. "I did none of that!"

"You're lying, coyote. *'Papa dice, no dejes que el hombre viva con remordimientos.'* Are you living up to your father's words, or do you need your sister to keep reminding you?"

I butchered the pronunciation, but the words ring true. The man's mouth hangs open. When it moves, it takes several attempts to find some words.

"You can't… You are *el Diablo!*" Helio shouts, stunned and shaking his head.

"Everyone out!" Hurley bellows. "Now!"

Nadiya doesn't need to muscle me out. I jerk my arm to break her grip and walk out the door. Emma and the other vice squad members meet us in the squad bay.

"What the hell was that?" Ritter asks. "Are you trying to force us to let him go?"

"He wasn't talking, so Agent Smith shook him up a little. That's all," Nadiya argues.

"That's all?" Ritter asks. "He just violated that kid's civil rights."

"Yes, I'm sure you've never done anything like that," Emma argues, meeting the young vice detective's glare.

"All right, settle down, everyone. We're all on the same team," Detective Robinson says in a calming voice.

"Are we?" Hurley asks as he and Forte join us from the interrogation room.

"Yes, we are," Nadiya says, quick to challenge the detective. "I think we've already proven that."

I stay quiet, having already done enough damage. We're supposed to be a team, so I'm content to let my fellow agents do the damage control.

"No, you really haven't," Hurley says, shaking his head. "I want to know what that was in there, and I want the truth."

"He lost his temper," Zach interjects.

"No, the thing about his sister. I speak fluent Spanish. 'Do not let the man live with regrets.' That's what you said to him. When did you learn it?" the detective asks me.

"I'm picking some things up."

"Uh, huh. We didn't know that Helio Lozano even had a sister. How did you?"

"It's in a database," Forte argues.

"Bullshit," Ritter argues. "We ran his information in every state, federal, and international database there is. There is no mention of a sister in any of them."

I don't need dreams, memories, or an ounce of intuition to know that the vice detectives are pissed. I know impossible things without any permission to explain how. That's probably why Forte didn't want me in the room in the first place. Too damn bad.

"Anyone? I mean, we are on the same team," Hurley chimes in, staring at me.

"It's one of life's mysteries," I say with a smile.

"Okay, cut the crap. I don't know what the hell is going on or where you guys are really from, but you're not sharing. You had better start talking, or I'm taking this to Jada. She'll be far more inquisitive than I am."

"No, you won't."

"What?"

"You won't," I repeat.

"Are you testing me, Agent Smith?"

"Yes. You're free to go to your superior. We could have Nadiya stop you in your tracks, but it would only be a temporary solution. But if you do that, you won't get the answers you so desperately want."

"Why not?" Detective Hurley asks.

"Because I will go home."

Hurley scoffs and folds his arms as he closes his eyes and shakes his head. I understand his frustration. Whether Zach and the rest of the team know it or not, they would be equally annoyed if the roles were reversed. Since I can't tell him the truth, I need another tactic and I hope it's effective.

"Helio is a run-of-the-mill coyote, but he moonlights for someone called *Hombre Magico.*"

"Magic Man."

"Yes. Once the coyote guides his flock across the border, the Magic Man selects people he wants to traffic. They are separated from the group, and the rest are filtered into the traditional migrant networks in Arizona."

"Magic Man is the kingpin we've been looking for," Robinson explains.

"That kid in there is the key to taking him and his whole network down. I want to find out who this scumbag is as badly as you all do."

"How do you know all this?" Detective Hurley demands.

"You can accept that I know things that you don't, and we'll get this piece of crap together, or we can stand here and keep arguing about it."

"Not good enough."

"Fine, then run off and whine about it to your superiors," Zach argues, finally understanding what I'm doing. "I can have this team on a plane back to Washington tonight."

"And you'll spend the rest of your days lamenting the one that got away," I say, finishing the threat. "The choice is yours, Detective. Decide."

Hurley glares at me, but there's thought behind his eyes. Like any good detective, he's contemplating his options. He would love nothing more than to drop the dime on us, but it's self-defeating, and he knows it.

"Fine. I only want two of us in that room. Me and you."

"No way," Forte says, stepping into the conversation. "That kid is terrified of Agent Smith and won't talk. We should keep him out of the room."

"Are you kidding? I want him in there for everything."

"No."

"I'm going in there. If Agent Smith doesn't join me, you guys should all just pack up and go back to Washington."

Hurley retreats into the interrogation room. His fellow detectives don't stick around either, but instead file into the adjacent observation room. The two women on my team shift their heads back and forth, waiting to see who says something first. There's nothing to be said.

I wink at Forte and brush past him. The bell just rang for round two with Helio. It's time for me to take some swings and put this scumbag on the mat.

CHAPTER THIRTY-EIGHT
DETECTIVE BRESHION HURLEY

Breshion watches the FBI agent enter the room and stand along the side. He wasn't sure if they would meet his demand. Smith seems to be here for the right reasons. He can't say the same for the rest of that team.

"I want a lawyer," Helio demands, shifting in his seat as he eyes the agent.

"So you keep saying," the detective mutters. "We'll get you one. He will get you out of here, maybe even threaten to sue the FBI and PPD in the process. Then you'll be set free on the streets. Only you won't really be free, will you?"

"¿Que?"

"The Magic Man," Smith says. "He makes people disappear, right? How long before he makes you vanish?"

"He has no reason to. I'm loyal."

Smith grins. "Yes, I'm sure you are. You were loyal when the Magic Man executed a migrant in front of you. You said nothing. He trusted you after you first learned who he was. He put his arm around you and warned you never to talk. You swore on your parents' lives that you wouldn't."

Breshion studies the shocked look on Helio's face. How does this agent know all that? He was spot-on, and it has the coyote spooked. If Smith's plan is to scare the kid into talking, Breshion has every intention to keep setting the table to allow him to do just that.

"El diablo," Helio whispers.

"Si. Yo soy el diablo," Smith says, practicing his high school Spanish. "I am the devil, and I will drag you straight to hell with me."

Helio scoffs. "Sure."

"You doubt me? What do you think is going to happen when Detective Hurley here releases details of the Magic Man's operation that he couldn't possibly know; at least know without your help?"

"You know nothing. He knows I would never betray him."

The agent takes a seat at the table next to Breshion and stares directly into the kid's eyes. "Really? Are you sure that he won't seek retribution against your parents in Nogales?"

Smith plants his elbow on the table and snaps his fingers once.

"Maybe he won't find your sister working for one of the cartels and have his men rape her over and over."

He snaps his fingers again.

"Maybe he won't sell her in the sex trade. The same one you've been working for going on three years. Wouldn't that be something?"

Helio lunges at the FBI agent on the third finger snap. Smith doesn't flinch as Hurley intercepts the kid and forces him back into his chair. The detective looks at the fed, who stares at the coyote impassively. It's an impressive show of restraint and confidence.

"Don't make me restrain you," Breshion warns Helio.

"When you dance with the devil, be prepared for the music to change. Talk, or my vision becomes your reality."

"I don't know who he is. I don't work for him," Helio says in a defiant voice, leaning back and crossing his arms.

"No, you're a subcontractor for your sister's cartel in Sonora. That doesn't mean you don't know exactly who he is."

"This isn't legal. You can't threaten my family, *diablo*."

"I'm telling you what's going to happen. I didn't say I would do it myself."

"He won't touch my family. He won't mess with the cartels."

Breshion shares a look with the agent before taking his turn. "So, you do know more. Why won't he mess with them?"

"They have a partnership," Helio says with a sigh.

"Do you think that will save your sister or parents?" Smith asks.

"What do you want from me?"

Agent Smith leans forward again and touches his cheek. "Everything. *Tu tienes que ser mas inteligente que tus enemigos o perderas.*"

Helio looks like he has seen a ghost. Breshion translates the expression in his head. "You must be smarter than your enemies, or you will lose." What does that mean? Nothing to him, but something to the young coyote sitting across the table. He's terrified and suddenly more cooperative.

"I told you. I don't know his name."

"Tell me what you do know."

"He's American."

"Caucasian?"

"No, Hispanic. He splits his time between here and Mexico."

Smith closes his eyes and says nothing for what feels like minutes. When he opens them, he leans back. "What else?"

"That's it."

"No, it isn't. How do we find him?"

"Nobody finds him. I meet his men at a prescribed place. I don't even know where until we cross the border."

Smith closes his eyes again. "What did you do with your cell phone – the gray one with the sticker?"

"It's gone, man."

Smith nods. "What does Magic Man do for a living?"

"This."

"That's not the whole story, is it, Helio? Tell me what else he does."

Breshion doesn't know where the agent is going with this. From the sounds of it, the kingpin is an American citizen. That means he pays taxes. With the money he earns from trafficking, he needs a way to launder it. That means cash businesses. Maybe that's what Smith is trying to get out of their detainee.

"What? I don't know. I've only met him a couple of times."

"Don't lie to me, Helio. What your father did to you when he caught you lying will pale in comparison to what I'm capable of."

Helio leans forward, his eyes a mix of surprise and confusion. Somehow, this agent has gotten inside the kid's head and is living there rent-free. With every revelation, more information comes.

"He owns bars or something. I don't know which ones."

Smith leans back and stares at Helio. The two stare at each other before the coyote breaks eye contact. Breshion thought he'd be scared of the man sitting across from him because of their altercation. He never thought knowing those things would be the actual reason.

"Well, that's something at least," Breshion admits. "There are a lot of bars in the Phoenix metro area. We'll narrow down the list. We can start by—"

"Don't bother," Agent Smith says, rising from his chair and straightening his suit. "Get everyone in the conference room. I know who the Magic Man is."

CHAPTER THIRTY-NINE
SSA ZACH FORTE

PHOENIX POLICE HEADQUARTERS
PHOENIX, ARIZONA

Zach is biting his tongue so hard that it starts to bleed. He would love nothing more than to yank Boston out of the room and choke the life out of him. Unfortunately, that would cause more problems than it solves.

Asami walks in and gets the attention of Ritter, who has joined his colleagues and the FBI agents watching the interrogation from behind the one-way mirror. There's no doubt that Hurley and his detectives have to be wondering who she is and what she's doing there. The answer to the second question is not much.

Zach nods at the door, and she follows him out and past the desks to the break room. It's one of the best places to have a conversation with some degree of certainty that it won't be overheard. It's also the place they had their last argument, so why break tradition?

"This assignment is going off the rails," Zach declares.

"Didn't he just identify Public Enemy Number One? That's what you wanted."

"And barely covered up how he did it. Boston doesn't understand the word *subtle*, and the PPD is starting to figure things out."

"That was always a risk."

"Now's really not the time for you to be so cavalier," Zach says, eliciting a sigh from the doctor.

"What's more important? Secrecy or the mission?"

"Stop! It's not that simple. They're connected. If we round up every sex trafficker in America and Boston's gift gets discovered, the mission is still a failure."

Asami nods. "Okay, what do you want me to do?"

Zach turns and leans against the countertop. He stares for a long moment at the coffee machine. He's already had too much caffeine today. Any more, and he might jump out of his skin. He turns and faces Asami. She isn't going to like this one bit.

"We need to consider drugging him."

Asami's mouth hangs open. "You can't be serious."

"I am."

"Then we fail," she says, slumping her shoulders in defeat.

"No. We just slow things down. You have to have something that will inhibit his memories for a short time."

The doctor gets closer to Zach and speaks in a whisper. "It's all experimental, Zach. Not to mention that there's no medical reason for it."

"I just gave you one. Boston's life could be at stake."

"I don't know what that means," Asami says, turning her palms up and shrugging.

"You have to trust me on that one. I wouldn't ask if it weren't important," Zach confesses.

"I wish I could believe you, but I don't. I'm not even sure whose side you're on anymore."

Zach closes his eyes. He isn't sure, either. Matt has put him in a bad situation, and if he weren't a friend, he'd have knocked him unconscious for it. Unfortunately, Zach is stuck with keeping Boston out of trouble during this mission, for better or worse.

"Can you do it?"

"Can I? Sure. Will I?" she asks, shaking her head. "I'm his doctor and won't break that trust with my patient. Boston knows the rules. If he breaks them, it's on him. As his friend and mentor, you should recognize that, too."

Asami leaves the break room, effectively ending the conversation. He's oh-for-two. The three women who accompanied them down here all have feelings for Boston. They are trying to protect him in their own ways. Zach is doing the same. Unfortunately, only he knows what the stakes of their failure could mean. By protecting Boston, they may be sealing his fate.

CHAPTER FORTY
ALEJANDRO SALCIDO

SALCIDO MEXICAN RESIDENCE
SAN CARLOS NUEVO GUAYMAS, SONORA, MEXICO

The television is on, but Alejandro isn't watching it. He fled to his coastal retreat from Arizona for some relaxation. Despite lounging in his favorite spot on the veranda, he isn't getting much of that. The time spent mulling over Jai Snyder's offer of a business association was filled with a different concern when his lieutenant reported that their primary crew didn't arrive from the border last night.

That's cause for alarm. Alejandro has run hundreds, if not thousands, of smuggling operations. There have been a few police and CBP chases, but no team has ever failed to return. That's a problem. Worse, he has contacts everywhere within law enforcement communities on both sides of the border, and none of them are checking in. If U.S. Customs and Border Control had scooped them up, he should have heard by now.

Alejandro stares at the water as the sun begins its dive toward it. It's his favorite time of day. Unfortunately, it's interrupted by the imposing mass of a man who serves as his bodyguard.

"Javier Barerra has arrived. He requests to see you." The Russian-accented announcement catches Salcido off-guard. "Show him in."

Javier has been Alejandro's right-hand man for several years now. He has been with the organization almost since the beginning and has worked in every role. It makes him the perfect operations officer, and the only man he trusts to fulfill his responsibilities when he isn't able.

"I didn't expect you to come here, Javier," Alejandro says, rising from the cushioned sofa to shake his hand.

"My apologies, *Patrón*. This information is sensitive, and I thought it best to deliver it in person."

"You drove here from Phoenix?"

"I left as soon as I had the information."

"That is a long trip. Please get my friend some water and ask Jose to prepare a second meal for dinner tonight."

The bodyguard nods and retrieves a bottle, tossing it to Javier before heading off. The beefy man probably doesn't like acting as a butler, but serves the role without complaint. Alejandro has done a lot for the man's family, and he's enormously grateful. Enough to place his life on the line to protect him, although both men hope it never comes to that.

"Thank you, *Patrón*," Javier says, bowing his tired head.

"Is your information about our team at the border?"

"Yes. Our men were ambushed. They fought, but most are dead."

Alejandro gestures toward the patio furniture, and the two men sit. "Customs and Border Patrol?"

Javier shakes his head. "FBI."

"FBI? There was nothing from my source in Phoenix warning me of any operation."

"And there still isn't any word from him. My information comes from a friend in the Phoenix Police Department. It was that special team from Washington. They conducted a joint operation."

"And that source gave no advance warning either?"

"During the report, it was conveyed that any warning would have pointed to a leak. I agree. Had we been told in advance, it would have compromised the source."

Alejandro rubs his chin and clenches his teeth, trying to hold back his anger. Javier doesn't deserve to be the target of his rage. Still, he needs to lash out at somebody.

"I pay for timely information. If sources get burned, so be it. We can cultivate new ones. What else was said?"

"The coyote was captured and is in their custody."

Salcido frowns. "Which one?"

"Helio."

Alejandro leans into the back of the sofa and rubs his temples. Most of the coyotes he works with are only tools that can be disposed of and replaced. Helio is an exception.

"He knows much about our operation."

"*Sí, Patrón*. And he knows you."

"We cannot have him speaking to the police or the feds."

"I agree, but he is also our most loyal coyote. I don't think he'll talk."

"Are you willing to bet our freedoms on that? Our lives?"

Javier lowers his eyes and remains silent.

"I don't question Helio's loyalty, but he will talk eventually. The FBI has ways to secure his cooperation. They are worthy adversaries and excellent at what they do, despite their apparent bungling. Do not underestimate them."

"What do you want to do, *Patrón*?"

"He has a family?"

"*Sí*. They live in Nogales."

"I will arrange transportation up there. We will leave after dinner. You rest until then. There is another long drive in your future."

Alejandro pats his lieutenant on the shoulder and heads into the house to check on dinner. The idea of losing Helio bothers him. He doesn't like what that can mean for him, and for his operation, even less.

CHAPTER FORTY-ONE
DETECTIVE BRESHION HURLEY

BRESHION'S APARTMENT
TEMPE, ARIZONA

Their relationship is still somewhat new, but work demands forced Breshion to stop impressing his love with fancy dinners. Jamecca was okay with that. She seems content with pizza, beer, and cuddle time on the couch in front of Netflix. It's one of the many things that have made him fall for her.

"You're quieter than usual. What's on your mind?" Jamecca asks.

"Today."

Jamecca nods as she takes a bite and sets her slice down. "Is Agent Smith right?"

"About Salcido being the kingpin? I don't know. He knows a lot. More than he should."

"Is that what's bothering you?"

"Partly," Breshion admits. "Since they got here, it feels like they're holding back. Something with Agent Smith is off. He knows way more than he should."

"After today, I can't disagree. He knew a lot about that kid. How?"

"I don't know. The only explanation is that the FBI has intelligence that they aren't sharing with us."

"Unless he has ESP or something."

"Yeah," Breshion says, taking a long swig of his beer.

"Wait…you're actually thinking about investigating Salcido," Jamecca says, cocking her head and setting her lager down as he shrugs. "Bresh, he's one of the city's most prominent businessmen. He's also on a first-name basis with the city council and mayor. That's before all his philanthropic work with Lantern House. Do you have any idea of the hell that will rain down on us if we're wrong?"

"You're right. None of those are hallmarks of a sex trafficking kingpin. It's the perfect cover. Think about it."

"I have. Investigating a prominent businessman with political connections is suicidal. Especially without hard evidence and only based on the word of some Looney Tune FBI agent."

"Salcido meets the criteria of a Hispanic who owns bars and nightclubs."

"Yeah, okay, and that's the only criteria. I'm sure he's not the only one. Breshion, Agent Smith could be wrong. If we swing and miss on this, the FBI goes back to Washington. We'll be stuck cleaning people's windshields somewhere for spare change."

"I know. I'm not arguing with you. We need more."

Jamecca's shoulders relax. Breshion eyes her as he takes another bite out of his slice. She's protecting him, and more than that, keeping him grounded. There is no reason to take Smith's word for it, even if a part of him wants to. He's never been on Team Salcido, even if most of Phoenix is.

"Does the FBI have a plan?" she finally asks.

"They're working on one, or so they say. I don't have much faith in them."

Jamecca stares at him. No matter how hard Breshion tries to break eye contact, it's futile. She draws him right back in.

"I know that look."

"Yeah, I know. Yes, I think we need to do this ourselves."

"Are you crazy?"

"Probably, but hear me out. If we can lure Salcido into doing something stupid, we'll have enough to bust him," Breshion concludes.

"Uh-huh. And if he doesn't?"

"Then maybe he isn't our guy. We can wait around for the FBI, but if they don't want to play nice, why should we?"

"This could go bad, fast," Jamecca warns.

"Yeah, that's why I'm going to bring it to Jada. She signed off on this fishing expedition with the feds and agreed to our participation in the Compass Rose Initiative. I've kept her in the dark about the FBI and their fortune-teller, but maybe she can rattle their cages."

Jamecca dabs the corner of her mouth with a napkin before tossing it on her plate. Breshion knows that his love likes and respects Jada but doesn't fully trust her. To make it to that level in any city police department, you have to be somewhat political. Jada will always put her interests above anyone.

"Breshion, I know you're not going to want to hear this, but we've made more progress in a couple of days than we have in a year. Maybe you should consider letting it play out a little longer."

"Are you on their side now?"

"This isn't about sides. You know that better than anyone else. The feds aren't sharing with us. I agree. But they aren't taking credit, either. Their tactics may be unorthodox, but I think they want to see progress as badly as we do."

Breshion isn't sure about that, but maybe going to the assistant chief isn't the right move yet.

"Fine. I won't say anything to Jada for now. We need to shake things up, though, and Helio Lozano is the leverage we need. It's time to beat the grass to see where the rattlesnakes slither off to."

CHAPTER FORTY-TWO
"BOSTON" HOLLINGER

COPPER STAR HOTEL & SUITES
PHOENIX, ARIZONA

I seriously considered asking Asami for something to shut down my subconscious before I left Phoenix Police Headquarters. I've seen enough horrors in the last couple of days to last a lifetime. We have our target, and there's nothing to be gained by revisiting those tragedies tonight.

I decided against it. Watchtower is playing enough games with me. I don't need to assist them in finding a way to shut down my abilities. That's why I'm trying NyQuil. If green had a taste, this is what I imagine it would be. Hopefully, the "sniffling, sneezing, coughing, stuffy head, fever, so you can rest medicine" is enough to keep me in a deep sleep. If it works, I'll write the company to tell them to add "dream suppressor" to their marketing pitch.

I turn down the air conditioning and nestle into the comfortable bed. The alarm clock glows on the night table, telling me that it's already nearing two in the morning. If I don't want to be a complete zombie tomorrow, I need to roll the dice and get some sleep. I clear my mind, letting myself drift off.

It's noisy in here. The constant chatter makes sense when I see the bottles lined up along a mirror behind the counter. I'm in a bar with a woman I don't recognize. She's sitting close to me, which means we're probably friends. Then I spot a black smudge in the corner of my eye. A hand brushes it away, clearing my vision.

"You're more melancholy than I've seen you in a while. What's going on?"

"I had... I had a weird thing happen to me the other day at work. I was getting lunch and saw a man outside the deli."

"Ohh...was he cute?"

"Uh, yeah, but that's not the weird thing. I didn't recognize him, but he felt so familiar to me."

"Felt familiar? That's intriguing. You must have met this mysterious, handsome gentleman before."

My head shakes. "No, I don't think so. He looked like Matthew McConaughey."

"Ohh... that's not cute, it's drop-dead gorgeous. Did you get his number?"

"No," I say, feeling a sudden surge of... What is that? Regret? Remorse? Guilt?

"Why not? You haven't dated since..."

The woman's voice trails off, and she looks at me with sorrowful eyes. I don't know why, but there is a jolt in my abdomen. The comment hurt, even if it was unintended.

"It's okay. You can say it. Since Boston was killed."

Did I just hear this right? Did I hear myself say my name?

"I didn't mean…I just want you to be happy."

I force a smile. "I know. I would have gotten it, but some woman spilled coffee on me before I could talk to him, and then I went inside, and he didn't follow me."

"It's always something. So how was he familiar?"

"I don't know. It was a vibe."

"Tara," she says, leaning in. "Do you think you could be projecting?"

"Are you analyzing me?"

"Someone needs to."

"I'm fine." I can feel that it's a lie. I don't feel fine at all.

"No, you haven't been 'fine' since Boston died. You bottled all that emotion up inside you and have never released the pressure."

"I didn't know him for that long, Sadie. We kissed once. It's not like we were married."

"Yet you had a connection with him that even you can't explain."

I feel an emotion that I haven't in a while: sorrow. A deep, hollow hurt that comes with absence and loss.

"It doesn't matter. He's gone."

"I hear you saying the words, but I don't think you believe that. You haven't been on a single date since that day. Maybe he was your person, and you knew that on a subconscious level. Maybe not. But he's gone — taken from you in something I could only describe as a tragedy. You're still here and need to move on."

I feel a pair of tears roll down my cheeks. I don't bother wiping them away. There is almost comfort in them.

"I don't know if I can. I may never get over Boston. Ever."

I jump out of bed the moment I wake up. I break into a cold sweat as my mind races. I pace the room in darkness and immediately retrace every second of the dream. I commit every word and every feeling to memory until I can play the reconstructed construct over in my head.

I check the time on the alarm clock before switching on the light. That dream came fast. So much for NyQuil. I could drink the bottle, and sleep won't come after that dream. I sit on the edge of the bed with my head in my hands.

"Son of a bitch."

CHAPTER FORTY-THREE
MAYOR ANGELICA HORTA

DEFOREST RESIDENCE
FOUNTAIN HILLS, ARIZONA

Fountain Hills borders the Fort McDowell Yavapai Nation, Salt River Pima-Maricopa Indian Community, and Scottsdale. As the town's name implies, it's known for its impressive fountain that was once the tallest in the world. It's also where Angelica can get some much-needed guidance.

Donna DeForest was a professional political operative for the better part of a half-century. She has run elections at every level, making forecasted blowouts close and dragging frontrunners across the finish line. Her political IQ is off the charts, and her natural savvy for choosing the correct path for a candidate made her millions of dollars. The irascible woman retired from the great game after the last presidential race. Nobody would know how to get the mayor out of this predicament better than she would.

"It must be far worse than I thought if you showed up on my doorstep," Donna rasps before taking a deep drag on her cigarette in the entryway to her house.

"It's good to see you too, Donna."

"Well, come on in. Want some tequila?"

Angelica frowns. It's not her first choice of liquor, but she doubts there's anything else in the house. Donna is a big fan of any spirit made from agave. Rumor has it that she retired here because of her love of tequila, pulque, and mezcal.

"It's not that bad," Angelica argues.

"Yeah, sure. You just got politically ax murdered on the front page of the *Sun Republic*. Almost everyone picked up the story, and LaCugna is gleefully kicking your teeth in every chance he gets. And now you're here. Tell me again how it's not that bad."

"You don't miss much."

"I'm old, Angelica, not stupid."

Donna moves to the counter and retrieves the newspaper. "I read this article three times. They have sources, presumably members of Compass Rose, and no comment from the feds. The media love drama, but they hate LaCugna. If they printed this, he has something on you that's unimpeachable."

"He doesn't," Angelica snaps. "The Compass Rose has been in the planning stages for a while."

"I'm sure it has been. So why implement it now? Why the rush?"

"It wasn't rushed."

Donna shakes her head and sparks another cigarette before sitting back down on the sofa. Angelica hates smoking but would never be audacious enough to say anything as a guest in this house. If she wants lung cancer and to smell like an ashtray, that's her business.

"If you're going to lie to me, we might as well kick back and watch *The Bachelor*. It's just as much a waste of time and probably slightly less annoying."

"Fine. It was the FBI."

"What about them?"

"The feds dispatched a team from Washington to help with the sex trafficking problem in the state."

"And that's a bad thing?"

Angelica exhales. "I just shuffled personnel off the vice squad to help fight the growing crime problem in the city. I thought it would look bad and thought this would provide me some political cover."

"Oh, boy," Donna says, leaning forward. "Who cares?"

"What?"

"You heard me. Who cares if it looks bad?"

"I do!" Angelica says, the tone of her voice getting a little higher. "I didn't want to hand LaCugna a club to beat me with next year."

"So, you handed him a sledgehammer instead? You're an idiot."

"You don't pull punches, do you?"

"Hon, I'm too damn old and tired to worry about having a filter. You should have known that someone would clue him in about the convenient timing of the FBI's arrival and Compass Rose. You also should have known that it would be viewed as hyperpolitical gamesmanship. People aren't used to seeing that from you. That's why it's a story."

"What should I do?"

Donna crushes her cigarette and grabs her tequila before leaning back on the sofa. "You already know what to do. You're just looking for confirmation that it's the right thing."

"Is it?"

"Do you think I'm a tarot card reader?"

"Humor me."

Donna smirks and shakes her head. "If you sit back and do nothing, you look uncommitted while LaCugna controls the narrative. If you go on the attack, you look unsure of yourself and petty for playing politics with sex trafficking. That, and you suck at it."

"Thanks for the pep talk," Angelica moans, taking a sip of her drink and willing the burning fluid down her throat.

"Some politicians are pit bulls. Others are cuddly Shih Tzus. You are somewhere in between…like a chihuahua."

"Are you kidding me with this right now?"

Donna waves her off. "I don't mean any disrespect. Attack politics isn't who you are. Part of me is surprised that you ended up as mayor. You like to work behind the scenes. It's how you get things done, like signing Judy Costello up to co-chair the Compass Rose Initiative. That was a boss move, by the way. You just weren't ready for the blowback from your enemies because you don't think that way."

She's right, not that it's surprising. Donna worked internationally in places like Central America, where losing meant imprisonment or death for the candidate. Her key to winning is to continuously measure every word and action for how they could be used against you. It's no wonder that nothing important gets done in modern society.

"Why does everything have to be looked at like that?"

"Because it's politics," Donna says with a laugh. "Had you been paying any attention at all, you'd know that you made this bed while you were on the city council when you slashed the budget."

"I know you didn't agree with that."

"A lot of people didn't. You defunded the police before it became the chic thing to do. What did you think would happen?"

"It was necessary. We were in a fiscal crisis."

"If you say so. Phoenix is the fifth-largest city in the nation. I'm sure there were dozens of other programs you could have cut. You didn't. What was the vote on the city council?"

"I don't remember. Seven-two or six-three, I think."

"Mmhmm. Did LaCugna vote for it?"

"No," Angelica says, embarrassed that this is the first time she ever thought about that.

The corner of Donna's mouth curls skyward. "And you didn't see his posturing to become the law-and-order candidate coming from a mile away? My God, woman, you've been out in the sun too long."

Angelica looks at her hands. They're shaking, although she doesn't think Donna has noticed. Then again, that woman sees everything.

"At the time, it was about not raising taxes. Spending cuts needed to be made. I was trying to do what was right for Phoenicians, and I still am. I was elected to put their needs above my own."

"Noble words, Madam Mayor. Do you think the people look at you that way? Crime is up in every category, and you covered it up with what will be portrayed as a phony group with a catchy name. That's what you're facing."

"I know. I have a messaging problem."

Donna rubs her temples. "Are you kidding me? The media gives you more free passes than a bouncer on ladies' night. You have a *message* problem."

"What do you mean?"

"I can't believe I need to spell this out for you. Do you believe in the cause?"

"What?"

"Do you believe in the Compass Rose?" Donna articulates each word of the question slowly and deliberately.

"Absolutely."

"Prove it."

"I created the Compass Rose Initiative to best serve—"

"Don't tell *me*, you moron! Get out of my house and go tell the people. Let them see the passion. Let them know that this isn't the farce it's being portrayed as. Go out and win the news cycle back."

Angelica thanks her host before swallowing the rest of her tequila. Donna may be hostile, blunt, and eccentric, but she knows what she's talking about. There is nobody better at the game, even though she is no longer an active player.

The mayor climbs into her car for the drive back into the city with a lot to think about. The first thing is to figure out how to go on the offensive without looking like that's what she's doing. Maybe Katy will have some ideas about that.

CHAPTER FORTY-FOUR

ALEJANDRO SALCIDO

LOZANO RESIDENCE
NOGALES, SONORA, MEXICO

Alejandro pulls up in front of the house and gets out with his men. He stares at the sky and orange glow of the faintly visible horizon. The brighter stars can still be seen above the horizon, allowing sea navigation. This is nautical twilight, where the geometric center of the Sun's disk is between six and twelve degrees below the horizon. At least, that is what he read somewhere.

Gunshots ring out in the distance. It's another beautiful early morning in Nogales. Crime levels in northern Sonora have increased for years as narco cartel-related violence is the source of hundreds of homicides and other violent crimes in the state.

Most crime in the city happens after dark, so visitors are warned to travel throughout the city only during daylight hours. Businesses here close by ten, except for the bars and nightclubs. Those establishments harbor a dangerous mix of guns, drugs, and cartel members. None of that matters as a new day starts.

"Is this it?"

"They're on the second floor," Javier informs him.

Alejandro nods. "Keep an eye out. This won't take long."

"*Sí, Patrón.*"

Alejandro climbs the rickety stairs to the apartment. Even at this hour, he can hear movement behind the wall. He knocks on the peeling paint of the door, and a woman answers.

"Yes? Can I help you?" she asks in Spanish.

"Yes. My name is Alejandro. I'm sorry for the early morning visit. I work with your son, Helio. May I come in?"

"Of course," she says, eagerly gesturing him in.

Alejandro doesn't know if Helio's parents are aware of what their son does for a living. Very few people accept guests this early in the morning without good reason. If his parents know that he works for one of the cartels, it's more than enough of one.

"This is my husband, Raul," she says, introducing her aging spouse.

"It's nice to meet you."

"We were just sitting down for breakfast. Would you like some?"

"No, thank you."

"Then something to drink? Coffee?"

"Coffee would be great, thank you," Alejandro says, joining the man at the table.

"What brings you here?" Raul asks. "Is Helio in some sort of trouble?"

"Have you heard from him?" Alejandro asks, not bothering to answer the concerned father's question.

"No, not since the other day. He is working very hard."

"Yes, I know. You have a daughter, yes?"

"Yes. She's working now."

That's unfortunate timing. Alejandro would have thought he timed this visit so that she was either just ready to leave for work or getting home from it. It's no bother.

"I see. You have a good family. Very hard-working. Very loyal."

"Thank you. We tried to raise our children right."

"Yes, I'm sure you tried. But you failed. Your son is betraying me."

"Excuse me?" Raul says, offended.

Alejandro presses his hands together in front of his face. This man reminds him a little of his own father: proud and family-oriented. That was once the way in old Mexico, and there's little doubt that he won't take this news well.

"He's in the custody of the American FBI. He is telling them everything."

"No, no, no. Helio would not betray anyone."

"Yet I believe he is," Alejandro says, his voice even.

"This is a mistake. I will speak to him, and he will tell me the truth. Is he coming home?"

"I don't know."

"Whatever Helio has done, it must be under duress. He would never turn on his employers."

Alejandro stands, his previous question answered. The parents know what he does and likely know what's coming next.

"I wish that were the case."

"Please, we don't want no trouble," Raul says, his hands up to show no offense.

"I don't want any trouble either."

Alejandro pulls out his gun and shoots the man in the forehead. The sound that echoes through the small apartment almost masks Helio's mother dropping the coffee mug. Salcido wastes no time leveling his weapon and putting a round through the center of her chest.

"No trouble at all," he mumbles, opening the door and leaving the apartment.

His men watch from below as Alejandro shuffles down the stairs. The police in this city are overwhelmed. For every good officer, there are five on the payroll of the cartels. This will be yet another unsolved murder in a violent city. There are many more like them.

The trafficker isn't worried about being caught. The neighbors will not have seen or heard anything. Even if they did, the cartels hold all the power in Sonora, and they are far more feared than the police.

"Job finished, *Patrón*?" Javier asks.

"Almost. Helio's sister isn't here. Find out where she is."

"Consider it done. Do you want to leave a man here to watch the apartment?"

"No," Alejandro says after taking a moment to contemplate their options. "She won't come back here after hearing the news. We will use other means to find her."

The men climb into the vehicles. Alejandro learned as a boy that actions have consequences. The young coyote is about to understand the price of his. Even through his rolled-up window, he hears more shots ring out in the brightening Nogales morning. It's another fine day in the city.

CHAPTER FORTY-FIVE
"BOSTON" HOLLINGER

COPPER STAR HOTEL & SUITES
PHOENIX, ARIZONA

As I predicted, there was no sleeping after experiencing my memory. The rest of the night was spent watching whatever ridiculous shows air on television at that hour, and eagerly waiting for the hotel to start serving breakfast. Now on my third cup of coffee, I enjoy the quiet solace of the small eating area. It's early enough that only a few hotel guests have joined me.

Emma walks up to the table and gestures at the open seat. Despite wanting to find an excuse to say no to her, I nod. She's a good person, a capable agent, a brilliant instructor, and a vision to behold even on a bad day.

"How'd you sleep?" she asks after taking a seat with her own steaming cup of coffee.

"Do me a favor and never ask me that question again," I growl.

"Okay, Rosie Sunshine, I'll take that as not good. I'm sorry, Boston. I know you've seen a lot on this assignment. Probably more than anyone bargained for."

I close my eyes briefly. "You have no idea."

"Do you want to talk about it?"

"No, not really."

"I'm sorry. I truly am."

"I know. It's okay," I say, trying to shrug off my grumpiness. "I'm stuck in a horror movie. All I've seen here is the worst of humanity: rape, torture, kidnapping…every moral crime you can think of. And then there's the deceit and lies."

"You get that with the criminal world."

"I was talking about our side," I admit with an edge to my voice.

"What do you mean?"

I don't know how much I should say. Emma is a mentor and friend, but that could be an act. She could just as easily report everything I tell her to Zach. Eh, screw it.

"How much has Forte told you about Tara Winters?"

Body language is one of the many tools used to read people. Emma clams up. Everything about her reaction screams, "Never say that name to me."

"Not much. Just that you spent time with her before…"

"Yeah, in a previous life. That's it?"

"Forte doesn't talk about her, and honestly, I don't ask questions," Emma says, avoiding my eyes as she speaks.

"Why not?"

"Because I don't want to hear the truth. I don't want to admit that you still feel a connection to Tara, knowing that you can't do anything about it now."

I lean back and study her as I sip my coffee. This is the most vulnerable I've ever seen Emma act.

"What?" she demands, finally reestablishing eye contact.

"Nothing. Your honesty is refreshing. For the first time, someone on this team has opened up a little."

"Yeah...well, you should also know that it's only part of the story."

"What's the rest?"

"Something you'll have to read in a later novel," she says, forcing a smile. "What's this really about?"

I grimace. "When I was working for Congress, the challenging part of my job was figuring out who my allies and enemies were at any given moment. It shifted with the political winds. That's the nature of politics. Even as a staffer, I felt the ripples in the pond when one of them made a splash.

"It was different in the Army. You were part of a team. On the day of the mortar attack, I listened to a guy named Mexico tell everyone a story. He and his driver were hauling ass through the desert trying to evade an Apache helicopter that was messing with him. I remember thinking how close that group was and how I would miss them when the deployment was over. And then the base was hit."

"And Mexico?"

I lower my eyes, not wanting her to see the pain. "He was killed in the barrage. So were Georgia, Colombia, and a few other of my friends. I was lucky to survive. If you can call it that."

"You got a second chance."

"A third, if you count whatever this is."

"Do you?"

"I'm starting to understand what a hammer feels like." I get a puzzled look and opt not to keep her in suspense. "I get used to pound a nail and then I'm dropped back in a toolbox without a second thought."

"Boston, it's not like that."

"What's it like, then?"

"People care about you," Emma says, almost scolding me.

"Who, Zach? This is an assignment for him. Nothing more."

Emma reaches out and takes my hand in hers. She massages the top of it gently with her thumb. I can almost feel the electricity pulsing through her fingers.

"I care about you."

"Am I interrupting something?" Zach asks, walking over to the table and standing over us like an angry father protecting his teenage daughter.

CHAPTER FORTY-SIX
SSA ZACH FORTE

COPPER STAR HOTEL & SUITES
PHOENIX, ARIZONA

Zach watches a startled Emma try to remove her hand from Boston's. He clenches down on it, not releasing her. For whatever reason, she isn't more forceful in removing it. Of course, he knows precisely why.

"Yes, Zach, you are interrupting. We wanted you to be the first to know. We're having triplets. So, we'll be needing some family leave in seven months and some more bunk space at the training center so you can train the children to be pint-sized assassins or something."

Emma closes her eyes and stifles a laugh. It's the only thing that clues Zach in that his petulant agent is only joking. It's a predictable outcome in this little game that Remsen seems intent on playing to help Boston forget all about Tara Winters.

"Funny," Zach snarls.

"No, not really," Boston says, finally releasing Emma's hand. "I'm just tired of you treating me like a child who requires constant supervision."

"Then stop acting like one."

Boston sips his coffee. "Gee, Boston, you did a great job yesterday fingering the mastermind behind a massive human trafficking operation. We could never have done it without you. Here's your gold star and some extra allowance to buy a new toy."

Zach shakes his head. "You need a serious adjustment to your perspective if you think you were helpful yesterday. You have all but blown your cover and compromised this team and its mission."

"I guess we're back to this lecture," Boston says, looking at Emma. "At least I'm doing something for this team and the mission outside of getting in its way."

"I'm going to leave you guys alone to work this out."

"No, Emma, please stay," Boston pleads as she starts to rise from her seat. She stops and eases herself back down, uncomfortable about being caught in this crossfire.

"Emma, go."

"Don't give her commands like she's a terrier."

"I'm her boss."

Boston nods. "Go ahead, Emma. Maybe the big boss needs his obedient secretary to fetch him another cup of coffee before you go."

"What the hell is your problem?"

Boston stands and gets into Zach's face. "Right now, you are."

"Listen, you insolent bastard, everything I have done – everything – has been for your benefit."

Boston nods slowly. "Everything? Are you sure you want to stick to that, Zach?"

"Did I stutter?"

"No, you didn't."

"Good. Then there should be no issue with you hearing what I'm about to say. I know you resent me. I have to live with that. But everything I have done since that day is for you. I hope you realize that someday."

Zach starts to walk away to de-escalate the situation. Boston stands there and watches him go, not saying anything until he is at the entrance to the breakfast area.

"She's not engaged."

Zach freezes in place. He had to have seen it in a dream. It's the only way he could know that. The question is, when?

Boston crosses the room. He stares directly into his boss's eyes when he reaches him. "You lied. Worse, everything you showed me in that dossier was fabricated. Tara isn't dating someone she met at a conference. She isn't going on a trip. There is no impending marriage proposal. In fact, she hasn't been on a date since that day because she's miserable. Tara isn't letting go even though she thinks I'm dead. Imagine that."

Forte glances back at the table to see Emma lower her eyes. She didn't know that Boston figured that out, and it isn't what they were discussing before Zach interrupted.

"Boston, I didn't want to—"

"What? Lie? I see traumatic memories, Zach. If you were torn up about deceiving me, trust me, I'd know."

"You're right. I wasn't. That doesn't mean I wanted to do it."

"Yes, it can be so hard to do the right thing. After all, everything you do – everything – is for my benefit."

Forte can only stand there and face Boston's withering glare knowing that he walked into this ambush. There is no escape. No defense he can offer that will make a difference.

"Not so smug and demanding now, are ya?" Boston leans in and stops only inches from Forte's face. "I'm going to warn you only once: Stay the hell out of my way from here on out."

Alarm klaxons sound in Zach's head. Hollinger was unpredictable before he flew the coop back at the training center. Now that their team is in the field, the risk of losing him has reached a whole new level.

CHAPTER FORTY-SEVEN
DETECTIVE BRESHION HURLEY

HOT AS HELL COFFEE HOUSE
PHOENIX, ARIZONA

Location is the key ingredient to success for any retail endeavor. That's the first lesson every entrepreneur learns. If you want to open a coffee shop, holding a ribbon-cutting on a side road in the woods will not lead to abundant customers and constant foot traffic. If you open one near a police station in the center of a city, you'll get plenty of both.

Breshion pulls open the door to one far enough from the station where most of his colleagues won't frequent it. Distance from police headquarters isn't the only reason: The owners are known for being anti-police. That revelation came to light when employees were caught spitting in coffee meant for uniformed officers, and the owners initially refused to fire them. They eventually bowed to public pressure, but the bad blood has persisted since. It's why he hid his badge before entering the shop.

His contact materializes beside him just before the barista finishes inputting the order for the customer in front of him. It's either lucky timing, or the mayor's lackey planned it that way.

"I recommend the mochaccino. It's to die for," Adrian Finley says.

"I prefer my coffee strong and bitter. It suits my personality."

The aide snickers. "You won't get an argument out of me on that one."

The two men order and wait at the counter. This place is chronically understaffed and very slow. It should give them all the time they need to have this conversation.

"Why did you want to see me?" Adrian asks, keeping his voice low.

"LaCugna is kicking your boss's teeth in."

"Yeah, there's no love lost between those two. It's Katy's problem, not mine."

"Are you sure about that? It will be yours if Horta loses next year's election."

A customer walks over from a table to add some cocoa to whatever froufrou drink she's sipping. The two men wait until she returns to her table, and then resume speaking.

"It's a long time until November. I know you aren't the political type, Breshion," Adrian says, using his given name instead of his title because he knows the reputation of this place as well. "You don't care if Horta wins or loses."

"That's true, I don't."

"Good, now that we've established that, why am I here?"

"Because she needs a win, and so does the Compass Rose Initiative."

"Yeah, that's falling apart faster than it was put together," the staffer complains.

"So, the FBI prompted its creation."

Adrian shakes his head. "Not exactly. They accelerated it, though. Is that what this is about?"

"No, but I was curious. You should know that the FBI team came through," Breshion says, eyeing the barista making his coffee before hazarding a glance at Adrian. "We conducted a joint operation down at the border the other night."

"I haven't heard anything about it. A little out of your jurisdiction, isn't it?"

"It was done in secret, and we had local and state support. We captured a coyote who has fingered the leader of Arizona's largest human trafficking ring."

"Are you kidding?" Adrian asks, cocking his head.

"No, I don't have a sense of humor about these things. I can't release the kid's name or who he has implicated, but will tell you that we are investigating and he's cooperating. We're placing him in protective custody as state's evidence while we corroborate his information."

"Why are you telling me this?"

"I told you. The mayor needs a win, and we need her in our camp. The Compass Rose Initiative is off to a rocky start. We're going to need all the help we can get to bring this trafficking ring down."

Breshion's coffee is ready and served at the same time as Adrian's froufrou chocolate drink. The two men walk over to the condiment bar, more for privacy than a need for cream or sugar.

"The Compass Rose was just formed. It's a little early to expect much support."

"Since when has that ever stopped Judy Costello? That woman doesn't have an off switch. She turned Lantern House into a community powerhouse in four months."

"Okay, yeah, touché. What do you want me to do with this information?"

"Whatever you need to. The coyote is protected, and we need to be seen making progress. It serves all our interests."

The customers behind them retrieve their cups of joe and start to walk over. Breshion did what he came here to do. Now, it's time to get the hell out of here.

"Are you going to put cream and sugar in that?" Adrian asks, grimacing at the thought of drinking any unsweetened coffee.

"Some farmer in Costa Rica worked hard to provide these beans, which someone else roasted to perfection. I wouldn't dare disrespect them by ruining the fruits of their labors. Enjoy your mochaccino."

Breshion smacks him on the arm and grins. There is a lot this kid still needs to learn. At the top of the list is how to enjoy one of the greatest gifts ever bestowed upon humanity.

CHAPTER FORTY-EIGHT
MAYOR ANGELICA HORTA

PHOENIX COLLEGE CAMPUS LOADING DOCK
PHOENIX, ARIZONA

The assembled group shuffles in front of the pallets and mug for the cameras while the program's leader pulls away the cellophane wrapping to access one of the boxes. She labors to open it, making a quip to the media's amusement about how well-packed they are. Once she manages to free the laptop from its box, she holds it up to applause. All eyes turn to the mayor.

"We live in an increasingly networked world. Computers have fundamentally changed society – how we communicate, interact with each other, pay our bills, and how we learn. Children on the wrong side of the digital divide are at a distinct disadvantage. It's crucial to provide the students, families, and educators in our community with the tools they need to thrive. I'm proud to announce that the City of Phoenix has partnered with Virtual Schoolhouse to furnish these internet-enabled laptops to children, to help close the technology gap."

Angelica smiles as the small crowd breaks into applause. She wishes she could enjoy this moment. It has been in the works for a while and only now has come to fruition. Unfortunately, her mind is elsewhere, pondering the answers to questions that she knows are coming.

"I am grateful to the Phoenix City Council for approving almost two million dollars in funding," Angelica continues. "We also accepted countless community donations, including generous ones from Alejandro Salcido, the Chamber of Commerce, and several religious groups. Their contributions helped us procure enough of these laptops to help our students thrive academically. That's assuming we can get the boxes open."

There is laughter and applause among the group of onlookers comprised of teachers and representatives from school PTOs. Reporters join in the laughter – at least, many of them do. The others are too busy plotting the timing of their ambush.

"I'd like to thank Phoenix College for the use of this receiving facility, and the various student groups who have volunteered their time to help our area schools with the setup and distribution of these devices," the mayor says, clapping to invite another round of applause as she wraps this up. "We hope this is the first step of many to continue our reputation as the 'Silicon Desert.' Thank you very much, ladies and gentlemen."

As important a step as this is for education in Phoenix, the crush of reporters covering the event aren't here to talk about kids getting laptops. They have their eyes on advancing a scandal that will guarantee them views, clicks, and circulation. It's what Angelica is counting on, even if she isn't eager to face the questions.

"Did you see the article in the *Sun Republic*, Madam Mayor?" one of the friendlier journalists asks.

"Yes, I've seen it."

"Your office hasn't had any response. Can you comment for us today?"

"Well, yes, but I'm actually waiting for you guys to ask the question," Angelica says sweetly, nailing the line she spent a chunk of the morning rehearsing to get the right tone.

"What question is that?"

"Why a city councilman would come out against an organization designed to combat sex trafficking. Has anyone here even asked why he's playing politics with the victims of sex slavery?"

"So, you reject the assertion that you created this task force to cover the rising crime rate?" Vincent DiPasquale asks.

"Why are you hiding in the back, Vinny? Come closer, so I don't have to yell. I want to ensure you hear me correctly."

He moves through the crowd of reporters who all await the mayor's answer. He was trying to catch her off-guard. It didn't work. Katy informed her the moment the partisan hack climbed out of his vehicle.

"Well?"

"Everybody wants safe neighborhoods and city streets. The rising crime rate is alarming, which is why I worked with our police chief to address that. We decided to shuffle personnel from specialized units to patrol to help put more cops on the street. If that doesn't begin to have the desired effect, we will take additional actions."

"Like what?"

"I'm not going to discuss the options available to us right now."

"Madam—"

"What about his accusation that you only created the group because the Federal Bureau of Investigation sent a team here to help combat the problem?" Vincent asks, cutting off another reporter.

"The Compass Rose Initiative has been in development for some time. It was initially conceived by the previous administration, and my staff continued working on it. The announcement coincided with the FBI's arrival, and we're happy that it did. I will accept every resource given to this city to combat sex trafficking. I would have thought that Councilman LaCugna would feel the same way. Someone should ask why he doesn't."

There is a murmur among the reporters. The idea that they might not have thought to ask him that is bewildering to the mayor.

"What about the accusation that Compass Rose is only a publicity stunt that won't garner any results?" one of her friendly reporters asks.

"It already *is* showing results. An announcement is forthcoming, but law enforcement personnel working together under the Compass Rose umbrella have captured a coyote funneling immigrants directly into a sex trafficking network in Arizona. He is turning state's evidence and is being transferred into protective custody tonight. It's the first win that we hope will lead to many more. Does that sound like window dressing, as the *Sun Republic* article concluded?"

"You think that it's actually Councilman LaCugna who's playing politics over this?" another reporter asks as Vincent stews.

"That's a conclusion that the people should come to for themselves. Thank you, everyone."

The mayor walks away from the press, some of whom are still shouting questions. Katy and Adrian arrive at her side as they exit the loading dock area and head for their SUV.

"Well played, Mayor."

"It helps for now but won't solve our problem. This is all so petty. The people don't care about this crap. They are trying to drum up drama where none exists."

"Maybe it will go away now," Adrian offers.

"Fat chance. LaCugna will search for any angle he can exploit, and the media will eat it up. I need something stronger to hit back with when he does."

"Like what?"

"I don't know. Results, hopefully. Until then, we need to be ready for anything. If LaCugna wants a war, then that's what I plan to give him."

CHAPTER FORTY-NINE
"BOSTON" HOLLINGER

SALT RIVER VALLEY MEDICAL CENTER
PHOENIX, ARIZONA

These children are amazing. After everything they have been through, they still long to be kids. The simple act of playing games with them has broken them out of their shell. Despite our shared language barrier, they still laughed as we played with blocks, toy trucks, and stuffed animals. I've managed to even pick up some Spanish. That was my second most remarkable feat. The first was getting the boys to join the girls for a tea party.

I can't understand how they even function after experiencing what they have. The kids are far more resilient than I am. It's why I abandoned my searching their memories for more information and chose to sit and create some happy ones with them.

Adelmo has helped the rest learn to trust me. He's still shy and hesitant but is the most outgoing one in the group. When he sat down with me to play with the blocks, the others followed. When we started this board game, he learned the rules the fastest. Not that the others haven't caught on. Now I remember why I hate Chutes and Ladders. I land on the long slide every time. It's annoying, but the children find it hilarious when I add the sound effect of sliding back to the bottom of the board.

"Having fun?" Dr. Kurota asks, standing over me.

"For the first time since I've been here," I growl.

"You are late for our…meeting."

"I wasn't planning on going."

"Come, take a walk with me," she insists. "I promise that we won't take long."

I look at Dr. Benito, who nods. I tell the children that I will be right back, waiting for her translation. Although the children show their disappointment, they seem to accept the interruption. Adults should take notes.

The doctor and I don't say much as we reach the first-floor courtyard. It's completely empty, just as it was when Forte found me here. For symmetry's sake, I sit on the same bench I planted myself on that day.

"I'm really starting to hate these meetings."

"Don't be like that, Boston," she says, looking around to confirm that we're alone. "This isn't meant to be torture."

"No, but I'm sure it will be close. What do you want, Asami?"

"To talk. We used to do that every day back in Virginia, remember?"

"Vividly," I moan.

"How are you holding up?"

"I'm fine."

Asami grins. "Yes, the defensive body language and curt response are clear indicators of that."

"You're going to draw your own conclusions anyway, doc, so out with it."

"Okay, we'll cut to the chase. I've been watching you with the children. I think what you are experiencing in their memories is drawing you to them."

I can't stop myself from giving her the blank "Captain Obvious" stare. "And you think that's unhealthy or something?"

"It's a cause for concern," she says, staring at her hands as she clasps them together. "They've seen some horrific things."

"You have no idea."

"No, I don't. That's your job and why I worry about what this exposure could mean for your long-term mental health."

It can't be any worse than having everybody I've ever cared about in this world thinking I'm dead so that I can become a government superweapon, but I don't say that. My mental health is not their primary concern. My doing something reckless that would ruin this experiment of theirs is.

"Tell me, doctor, how long am I expected to access memories after being exposed to a signal?"

"Why do you ask?"

I phrased the question carefully on purpose. I can't mention my dream about Tara to her. Forte probably already informed her, but they don't know the timing of it. She might have me institutionalized if I confirm that it happened days after I ran into her and admit I saw something she experienced after that. It's best to get the answer by other means.

"These memories. I want to know how long I will see what horrors these children have after I leave this place."

"Well, I don't have any hard data on that. Like most things with you, it's uncharted territory. My guess is that it depends on the connection."

"Could it also depend on the depth of the trauma?"

"Possibly."

"So, I could see memories for days, or even weeks, after I leave here?"

"I wish I could give you a definitive answer. It's a possibility."

"The answer is no."

The statement catches Doctor Kurota off-guard. She turns to me with a quizzical look that I notice out of the corner of my eye as I stare at the desert vegetation that adorns the courtyard.

"Okay…what's the question?"

"Not a question – it's the answer to your next demand. You're going to say that my spending time with the children compromises me and that I shouldn't do it anymore. My answer is no."

"Well," she says, recoiling on the bench. "There is nothing wrong with your crystal ball. Boston, I'm only—"

"Looking out for me. I know. Here's the thing, Asami – those kids are what's keeping me going right now. They're my sanity, not the opposite."

I stand, unilaterally deciding that this conversation is at an end. Some people pay for therapy. I would happily pay for it to end. It's one more example of how my world is upside down.

"What about the mission?" the doctor asks, not bothering to move from the bench.

I stare at the door back into the hospital for a long moment before turning back to meet her stare.

"*They* are *my* mission."

CHAPTER FIFTY

ALEJANDRO SALCIDO

DEZRT FYRE NIGHTCLUB
PHOENIX, ARIZONA

Unexpected company is never welcome but must be greeted with an open mind. Alejandro doesn't want to keep breaking his cardinal rule of mixing one business with another. Like his bars and nightclubs, enterprises only stay legitimate if illegal activity is kept out of them. Fortunately, nobody is accusing Jai Snyder of anything nefarious, so the risk of holding this discussion in his office is low. Of course, he said that about Barron Birch as well.

"I'm surprised to see you here," Jai says from the seat opposite Alejandro's desk.

"The Dezrt Fyre is my business. One of seven, to be exact. Why wouldn't I be?"

Jai grins. "That's not what I meant. I heard a rumor that one of your men was captured by the FBI."

"He was a coyote we contracted. It's an unfortunate development."

"You aren't concerned that he could lead the police or feds to you?"

Alejandro laughs and spreads his arms, gesturing at the room. "I have spent decades building this. There's no reason to abandon it based on the capture of one insignificant coyote."

"I've had customers get busted for less."

"I'm sure you have. Fortunately, like my nightclubs, I have invested decades in building up my import business. Safeguards were put in place from the very beginning. The Phoenix PD and the federal agents have a man who may or may not utter a name, and that's it."

"You're much bolder than I would be."

"That says more about you than it does me. What can I do for you, Jai?"

"It's what I can do for you and the supply chain interruption you're dealing with. Three migrant convoys are merging in Lechería. My NGO has convinced them to combine their numbers for safety reasons and take a westerly trip toward Arizona and California. I have access to more product than there is demand for in my current channels. I came to see if we could continue our business negotiation."

Alejandro nods. He knows the area well. Lechería is just north of Mexico City and is one of the most dangerous stops for migrant trains arriving from Mexico's southern border with Central America. Criminal elements run rampant, making it the most hostile and hazardous part of the journey for the tens of thousands of people who pass through each year.

"Are you in a position to deliver?"

"I can have fresh merchandise here in the next couple of days. You judge for yourself."

"And the price?" Alejandro asks, steepling his hands in front of his face. There is always a catch when something sounds too good to be true. The trafficker would bet that is it.

Jai leans back in his chair. "Why don't you inspect them for yourself and determine their value. We can work something out then. Maybe a percentage of the final sale?"

Alejandro grimaces. There it is. "I prefer fixed-price contracts."

"Yes, of course, because that benefits you by reaping the rewards of the high price some products fetch. I understand the logic, but a percentage incentivizes both of us – me to provide high-value stock and you to obtain the best possible price."

"You're pushing hard for this, Mr. Snyder. It sounds...desperate."

"No, you think that this is some sort of trap. Yes, you caught me. I'm really an undercover fed trying to snag you in a sting operation. It doesn't matter that I've worked for years with countless other traffickers. It doesn't matter how many mules I've arranged to carry untold amounts of drugs across the border. You know all this, yet you still question my bona fides?"

Alejandro rubs his chin. "My apologies, Jai. It has been a tough time for us."

"I understand. It's also why I'm here. A partnership would remove a lot of risk for you. You handle the reception and distribution north of the border, and I'll take care of acquisition and transport south of it. That allows both of us to rely on our strengths. But if you feel this is too risky for you right now, let me know, and I'll walk away."

Salcido eyes Javier, who is standing in the back of the room. He hasn't said anything, yet his body language speaks volumes. He doesn't like Jai or his offer one bit.

"You make a compelling argument. Okay. Contact us when your merchandise reaches the border. We can make arrangements from there."

"I will do so," Jai says, smiling. The two men shake hands, and Salcido's Russian bodyguard escorts Snyder out.

Alejandro looks down at the dance floor from the window as Jai crosses it to the exit. Javi steps alongside him.

"I don't trust him."

"Mmm. I don't either, but Snyder checks out."

"I don't care. It's too convenient. Helio gets busted, and this guy shows up a day later? His timing is too perfect."

"That's why I personally spoke with people who have worked with him. He gets high marks. Even the cartels have relationships with him."

"What if the people he works with are setting you up to fall so they can expand their operations?"

"If I go down, so does he. He knows that."

Alejandro likes that his lieutenant is skeptical and not afraid to voice his reservations. It's what he groomed him to do and how they all stay alive and in business.

"So, we take his word for it?" Javier asks.

"Never. We will insulate ourselves from Jai to the extent possible. Put in additional safeguards before, during, and after the transfer."

"I will," his apprentice says, relaxing. "What about Helio?"

Alejandro exhales deeply. "It's business as usual for the time being. If they begin investigating us, I'll know it. Until then, the worst thing we can do is panic. Helio only knows one aspect of our operation. There are no ties to our legitimate businesses, and we will have people protecting us. The FBI will need a concrete case to bring us down."

Javier nods and excuses himself from the office as Alejandro returns to his desk and scans the club's bottom line. He grins. This place might as well have come with a printing press. It's one ray of sunshine on an otherwise dark and ominous day. Helio's capture is nagging at him, despite his display of confidence. Alejandro can only hope that he's right. Complacency is the curse on the Salcido family, and it cost his father his life.

CHAPTER FIFTY-ONE
SSA ZACH FORTE

COPPER STAR HOTEL & SUITES
PHOENIX, ARIZONA

Zach opens the door to the indoor pool area and immediately scans for guests. There are none. The only people here are the two women he asked to speak to, both looking overdressed for a swim.

"Where's Boston?" Nadiya asks, waiting for their fellow agent to emerge behind Zach, only to see the door closing.

"At the hospital with Dr. Kurota. I wanted to talk to both of you without him here."

The women don't react. He expected at least a nod of approval at the precaution. Either they don't care, or more likely, wish it were one of them instead of Asami.

"What's going on?"

Zach pulls up a chair and sits, planting his elbows on the small poolside table. "You both know who Dr. Tara Winters is. She was the reason he left the training center."

"Yeah, the woman he was involved with before his...rebirth."

"Yes. That's who we intercepted in Chevy Chase."

"Is this about the conversation you guys had this morning?" Emma asks.

"Yeah. Unfortunately, there's much more to the story, so that argument you overheard probably didn't make much sense. What you don't know is what happened after Boston and I walked away."

Forte explains the aftermath with Boston, detailing the fake dossier with the made-up boyfriend, impending marriage proposal, and her having forgotten all about him. The glares from the two agents are merciless. He feels about three inches tall.

"You lied?" Nadiya asks, her accent enhancing her contempt.

"And Boston figured it out," Emma adds, equally pissed.

"Yes, and yes. Boston likely had a dream about her, although I don't know when. I'm guessing recently."

"Was anything you told him true?" Emma asks. "Is she still in love with him?"

"Everything was fabricated. I don't know if Tara's still in love or not, but she hasn't let go. That much I know for sure."

"Well, you dug quite a hole for us all, Zach," Nadiya concludes. "Nice job."

"Why are you telling us this?" Emma challenges.

"Because I need your help. Boston is a loose cannon. Even more so after learning the truth. I need you to keep an eye on him and report everything he does."

The two women look at each other before returning to Zach. Both have a noticeable look of disbelief on their faces.

"You want us to report on his activities?"

"I need you to do it. I can't be everywhere, and Boston trusts the two of you."

"No," Emma says, crossing her arms. "I won't do it."

"Me neither," Nadiya adds, matching her body language.

"Ladies, listen, you—"

"No, *you* listen, Zach!" Emma exclaims. "Boston trusts us because we've never given him a reason not to. You and Matt have given him every reason in the world. Honestly, if I were him, I'd try to get as far away from you as possible."

"You guys are so focused on turning him into a weapon that Watchtower can use that you forget he's a living, breathing person," Nadiya adds. "You put more faith in the system than you do in him. I wouldn't trust you either."

"That's not true," Zach says, shaking his head.

"Sure, it is. Take a look at the training facility. It has guards, cameras, doors with biometric locks and is located in the middle of nowhere. Boston was there a year before trying to escape. I would have been outta there the moment I was able to walk."

Forte grinds his teeth and leans forward. "Maybe I wasn't clear: This isn't a request, it's an order. You will report on Boston's activities or find yourself out of Watchtower and off to wherever the CIA or FBI decides to stick you."

Nadiya slides off her stool and tosses her FBI badge on the table. Even though she's CIA, she was issued one during this mission for appearances. Emma follows suit. Hers is the real McCoy.

Neither woman offers any threats or cliché one-liners. There is no banter or snarky quips. The two of them simply walk out of the pool area, leaving Zach to watch them go. This didn't go anything like he planned.

He wants to chalk this defiance up to their affection for Boston, but it's more than that. They think Forte is wrong and are drawing their line in the sand. As he sits by himself, he's beginning to wonder if they have a point.

CHAPTER FIFTY-TWO
DETECTIVE BRESHION HURLEY

PHOENIX POLICE HEADQUARTERS
PHOENIX, ARIZONA

Police-work, especially in vice, is not a nine to five job. Breshion is used to working all kinds of crazy hours and isn't used to being in the office before noon. This week has been a departure from the norm in more ways than one. He also isn't used to working with the FBI. Outside of busting kingpins and heavy hitters, vice crimes typically do not command their attention. Maybe this team from Washington is finally getting bored.

"Where are our friends from the Bureau?"

"They're not here yet," Jamecca says from her desk without looking up.

"That's odd. The feds have been getting here so early that I was beginning to think they're in the military."

Jamecca sets down her pen. "Maybe the Arizona heat is slowing them down."

"Good. It's what we need today."

Breshion scans the room. None of the other detectives or officers here are paying them any attention. He leans in as his love interest stares up at him.

"I arranged the transfer. Lozano is getting moved to county lockup this evening."

"Are you sure you want to do this?"

Breshion lets his eyes linger on the report she's writing, wanting to avoid her pleading eyes.

"No, but I'm going to do it anyway. If Salcido is our guy, we need to do something that draws him or his men into the open."

"And what if he isn't?" Jamecca asks, her tone hard despite the hushed voice. "Or what if he sends henchmen and they don't talk? Or what if nothing happens?"

"It's a risk we have to take. I know it's not a perfect plan, but a good plan today is better than a perfect one tomorrow."

"Save the fortune cookie wisdom, Breshion. You're emotional, and you're reacting to circumstances instead of dictating them. You haven't thought this through."

"You're wrong. It's *all* I've thought about."

"Gee, thanks."

"I didn't mean… You know that's not what I meant. Jamecca, if Alejandro Salcido is the Magic Man, then our chances of convicting him in this city are almost zero. The odds are only marginally better that we could get an indictment, and that's if a judge even approves the warrants we need to make a case in the first place."

"I don't disagree with any of that, but he is not stupid enough to go after Helio himself."

"I know. That's why Lozano is being fitted with a tracking device. If they somehow manage to spring him during the transfer, we'll know exactly where he goes and can take down whoever is there."

Jamecca shakes her head. "Nobody is that reckless."

"The Magic Man will want to know if Helio talked and make him disappear. Dead men can't testify."

"This is a bad idea. Too much could go wrong."

"SWAT will be in the area. They will never be more than a block or two away from the transport vehicle, and it's a short trip."

"That's great. What about the uniforms in the car? Seconds matter, Breshion. A block can be a long distance to cover when bullets are flying. It's a needless risk."

"I think—"

"No, I'm going to tell you what I think," Jamecca interrupts, taking a moment to join him in ensuring that nobody here is eavesdropping. "You're the most passionate man I have ever met, but you're too close to this. You're angry at the feds and even more pissed off that a pillar of the community may be the wolf killing the sheep. You want to get him so badly that any sacrifice is on the table."

"Not true."

"There's no talking to you about this. If you think you have it all figured out, then you should be the one in that car with Lozano. Things look different when it's your ass on the line."

Jamecca starts to walk away when Breshion snags her arm. She's surprised at the move, even though it isn't rough. She glares at him.

"I need to know that you're with me on this."

"Fine."

"Is that a yes?"

"It's not a no," she says, jerking her arm away. "There's one thing I don't understand: Your trap hinges on Salcido finding out that Helio is being moved. How do you plan on managing that?"

"Haven't you been watching the news? The mayor already puffed her chest out and announced the capture and the transfer."

"You leaked it to the mayor? How did you know she would go public?"

Breshion grins. "That's all politicians are good for."

CHAPTER FIFTY-THREE
MAYOR ANGELICA HORTA

CITY HALL OFFICE OF THE MAYOR
PHOENIX, ARIZONA

Ask nearly any American if their job is stressful, and you will get the same response. Work, by its very nature, is demanding. It is no different when you're a public figure, and it's often worse. Angelica doesn't answer to one boss – she answers to a city full of them. When one of them calls to complain about her decisions, it's an annoyance. When that person is a major contributor and staunch supporter, it's nerve-racking.

"You've been one of my biggest supporters, and I value—"

"This is not the time for half-measures, Madam Mayor," the man says, so steamed on the other end of the line that he's breathing heavily into the phone. "I was the one who encouraged you to run when you were an irrelevant councilwoman. I threw my support behind you and helped you win because you pledged to be different. Now I learn that you're more of the same."

"That's not the case. Compass Rose is not a political stunt. That's why I brought in Judy from Lantern House. They're a—"

"I'm fully aware of what Lantern House does and Judy Costello's value. I was at the activity center dedication. I want to know why you created it."

"To keep people safe and help the victims of human trafficking," Angelica blurts out, massaging her temple while she cradles the phone in her shoulder.

"Is that so? I was one of your biggest supporters when you cut the city budget and gutted the police department. That bravery is, in part, what earned you my support. This is how I'm rewarded?"

"I appreciate your support. I did then, and I still do."

"Then prove it."

Angelica snatches the phone from her shoulder and stares at the receiver after hearing the click and then nothing but dead air. He has some nerve.

There is a knock at the door, and Adrian pokes his head in. He looks concerned.

"What is it?" she snaps.

"Madam Mayor, Judy Costello is here to see you. She's pissed," her aide says, lowering his voice to a whisper.

Angelica closes her eyes, desperate to think happy thoughts. They don't come. Whatever her longtime friend wants, it isn't to catch up on city gossip.

"Please show her in," she says, rising from her desk.

The head of Lantern House brushes past Adrian and storms into the office. She slams a copy of the *Sun Republic* down on the desk. Angelica needs only a cursory glance to see what edition she was reading.

"Judy. What a pleasant surprise."

"What is this?"

"The article was a hit piece. Most people knew that in the first three paragraphs."

"Is it true?" Judy demands.

"Are you seriously asking me that?"

"Yes, I am. I want to know if it's true, and don't you dare lie to me, Angelica."

Angelica leans forward, looking directly into Judy's eyes. "Of course it isn't."

"That's funny because during your press conference, you said Compass Rose had been in the works for a while," Judy says, clearly not placated. "If you were looking to have me lead it, why didn't you mention it a long time ago?"

The mayor sighs. "There is nothing nefarious about this if that's what you're thinking. I knew you were busy with the activity center. It's as simple as that."

"Seriously? We've talked about everything from how the Diamondbacks looked in spring training to the best place in the city to get a mani-pedi."

"There is a difference between small talk and asking an already overextended friend to take on yet another project."

"Or you only did this because the FBI showed up right after you shuffled personnel out of PPD special units, including vice. That's the allegation, isn't it?"

"Yes, that's what the reporters doing LaCugna's bidding are alleging. That's politics."

Judy exhales and shakes her head. "Do you know why I never went into politics? I don't like playing games with people's lives. That's what politicians always do. You all have some kind of God complex."

"I ran for mayor to make a *difference* in people's lives."

"So you've said. You can't wax philosophical about the scourge of human trafficking one minute and then sell everyone involved out the next."

Angelica feels her face flush. She's already had a miserable day, and that accusation from a woman she considers a friend isn't sitting well with her.

"Okay, now I'm getting insulted. That article is a complete misrepresentation of what Compass Rose is and why I created it."

"Maybe. Despite your proclamations to the contrary, nothing you are saying convinces me that the rest of this article isn't true. The *Sun Republic* is not some birdcage-lining newspaper. They're reputable, and I doubt they would run with this story unless they have proof. I sincerely hope I'm wrong, and that's not the case. If it is, I will sever my involvement with you and Compass Rose in half a heartbeat."

"Please, Judy, don't do anything rash. I need you to make the initiative successful. Please, do it for the city…and for the victims. That article is filled with baseless lies. You have my word."

Judy offers a slight nod. "If that's true, then you have nothing to worry about."

She pulls the newspaper off the desk, tucks it under her arm, and strides out of the office. Angelica collapses into her chair and spins it to stare out one of the windows at the buildings and sky. She just lied to a friend and one of her closest allies. The only thought that occupies her mind is what this job is turning her into.

CHAPTER FIFTY-FOUR
"BOSTON" HOLLINGER

PHOENIX POLICE HEADQUARTERS
PHOENIX, ARIZONA

Tension has returned once again to the Phoenix Police Headquarters building. I thought we had been making some progress in our relationship with vice, but that was dispelled moments after we arrived. It seems like they have their own way of doing things in this city. Forte is having none of that.

"That is the most boneheaded thing I have ever heard!" Zach bellows despite being only a couple of feet from Hurley's face. "Why weren't we informed?"

"You weren't here," Detective Ritter deadpans.

"Am I talking to you, jackwagon?"

"Don't think you can march in here and treat us like we're the Keystone Cops," Ritter shouts, sidling up next to his boss.

"Then stop acting like them," Asami coolly says from behind Zach.

"Who are you, and what are you even doing here?" Hurley asks, taking a few steps closer.

Against my better judgment, I decide it's time to get involved. This conversation is counterproductive.

"I would love nothing more than to watch you guys throw down, if for no other reason than it would be wildly entertaining. Too bad Nadiya isn't here, but I guess the odds are more even without her."

"Wanna bet?"

I turn to face Hurley. "Yes, but we'll never find out. Detective, why did you move Helio?"

"We can't hold him here."

"What's the real reason?"

"That is the real reason," he says, getting defensive.

I don't need to peer into his memories to know that isn't true, but now isn't the time to press the issue. Whatever his reason, we have a bigger problem that needs to be addressed.

"Which one of you leaked it to the mayor?" I look around when I get no response. Ritter stares at the floor. "Nobody? So, the statement was crafted through extrasensory perception?"

Zach shoots me a glare that I ignore. This being treated like a misbehaving child in the supermarket is getting old. No matter what I say, he will never trust me unless I do things his way. The odds of that happening are less than me drinking a cup of coffee while surfing on the back of a shark as "Stairway to Heaven" plays in the background.

"I don't know how she found out, but it doesn't matter. Helio will be transferred in a couple of hours. What's done is done. I don't take orders from the FBI and I'm not about to let you tell me how we deal with our prisoners."

Ritter smirks and follows Breshion out of the squad bay. Other uniformed officers go back to their business, but the hostility in the room is palpable. Zach and I retreat out of the building to get some air.

"I'm surprised you didn't call him out on the real reason he's transferring the coyote," Zach says after looking around to ensure that we're alone.

"I don't know it. I can only guess."

"You didn't pick anything up?"

"This office is a garbled mess. There are too many lies and too much drama in here to pinpoint any particular memory. I could only manage to access Helio's because they were so strong."

Zach nods, accepting the explanation. "This transfer is going to end in disaster."

"You know a few things about that, don't you?" I ask with a sneer.

"You really want to do this again?"

"I didn't want to do this at all. Any of it. I was forced into it, remember?"

"You had choices."

"Oh," I say, nodding. "Name one. Was being free and getting my life back one of them? Save your breath. It wasn't. And then there were the lies about Tara."

"That was a mistake, Bos... Agent Smith."

"Ya think? The question is, do you only think that way now because you were caught, or were you feeling guilty about lying to me in the first place?"

"I didn't want to."

"Really? Where are Nadiya and Emma?"

Forte bites his lower lip. He has more tells than an amateur poker player. "They are taking care of something for me."

"Okay. I'll find out the truth later. Understand something, Zach – I pick up memories that have *emotion* attached to them. If you were that torn up about lying to me, I would know. Then again, who really knows how this thing works."

I give him a smirk as I reenter the building. I'm keeping him off-guard for a reason. The less he knows about what I do, the better things will be for me. That's my new reality. I'll have to find out what happened to Emma and Nadiya later.

CHAPTER FIFTY-FIVE

ALEJANDRO SALCIDO

DEZRT FYRE NIGHTCLUB
PHOENIX, ARIZONA

Alejandro rubs his hand over his hair and leans back in his executive office chair. He chose to forgo marrying and having a family to dedicate all his time to his businesses. They are his children for all intents and purposes, and his adult life has been dedicated to raising them. That's why he feels so much anguish when he knows one of them is in trouble.

"Sir, here is tonight's VIP list for the Dezrt Fyre and Cactus Club," his manager says after a quick rap on the door jamb.

"Thank you. Just put it on the edge of the desk."

The man nods and does as instructed, retreating as Javier enters the spacious office. Alejandro nods, and his lieutenant closes the door. Once again, he will be mixing his business endeavors in what has become a nasty habit.

"You saw the mayor's press conference, *Patrón*?"

"I helped fund that initiative. I should have been there and I would have had we not had…developments. So, yes, I saw it. What have you learned?"

"A source made contact."

"It took long enough," Salcido grumbles.

"It was worth the wait. We have the details we need. The transfer is happening at eight tonight."

Alejandro looks at his watch. It's just over four hours away. That's not a lot of time to develop a plan, assemble and arm the required manpower, brief them on their responsibilities, and get them into position. Navy SEALs don't move that quickly.

"Can you intercept them?"

Salcido watches Javier kick at the floor as he contemplates the request. "Si, *Patrón*, but it's risky. A lot could go wrong. Are you sure this is worth it?"

Salcido rises and stares out the window at the dance floor. In another six hours, it will be jammed with people. Some will be trying to traverse the crowd with drinks in their hands. Others will be grinding away to the latest electronic dance music. All will be oblivious to the world around them. Americans like to go through life that way.

"Yes, I'm sure."

"Helio can only cast suspicion on you. He can't really hurt you."

"You have learned much about this business, Javier. There's one thing I've neglected to teach you. Reputation is everything in this business. If we don't take care of our business by cleaning up our messes, the cartels see that. They will think we're weak and they will seek to exploit that. And then there's Jai Snyder. He has to know what will happen if he betrays us. That includes any decision to run to law enforcement or federal authorities. That is of supreme importance, as I'm sure you'll agree."

Alejandro looks over his shoulder to see Javi nod. "Then we will get Helio for you."

Without another word, the junior trafficker starts to move off. Alejandro shifts his gaze back out the window, but isn't done with him.

"Javi? Plan carefully. The police will take steps to ensure Lozano gets to his destination. Plan for the worst and use maximum violence."

"What about the community? It will be all over the news."

Alejandro has Mexican blood, but he has spent far more time in America than in his homeland. He's the living embodiment of all immigrants' dreams – coming to a foreign land and living a better life than he would have had he not left. America is the land of opportunity, for things both legal and illegal. He has thrived in both worlds and refuses to abandon either of them.

"It doesn't matter. The nice thing about Americans is their insensitivity to violence and their short attention spans."

"It will be done."

"Bueno," Alejandro says, turning and standing in front of his desk. "Once it is, and you know you aren't being followed, bring the young coyote to me."

"Of course."

Javier exits, pulling the door closed behind him. Alejandro doesn't like the idea of having to do this. It mitigates the risk of inaction by inviting the risk inherent in declaring war against the Phoenix Police Department. Fortunately, he's the unknown enemy and has spent a fortune creating allies in people who can keep it that way.

CHAPTER FIFTY-SIX
SSA ZACH FORTE

DOWNTOWN
PHOENIX, ARIZONA

Forte sits at the light in the Suburban and leans against the arm he wedged up against the window. He doesn't even care about the traffic right now. The time sitting here is being used figuring out how to have this difficult conversation. The hotel isn't far away, so the red lights are an act of mercy.

Zach's phone rings, and he is jarred back into the present. He connects it using the vehicle's hands-free.

"Forte."

"I'd ask you how things are going down there, but I think I already know," Matt says, using the condescending tone he chooses when he's annoyed.

"You've spoken with Asami?"

"No, but I guess I need to now. I checked my inbox and am staring at Nadiya's and Emma's resignation letters. What's going on?"

Zach tightens his hands on the wheel. They didn't wait long to make that move. He can only hope that Matt doesn't bother pressing him on it.

"It's a tactical disagreement."

"Don't BS me."

"I'm not. I told Nadiya and Emma to look after Boston. They didn't like the order."

"According to their letters, you wanted them to spy on him."

Zach presses his lips together, contemplating how far he wants to go with this. "Babysit is a more appropriate description."

"As appropriate as that request?"

That wasn't the right approach, and in hindsight, Zach should have handled it differently. He underestimated their response, which is something that happens when reacting to events. That's what he's doing, having been left no other option.

"You're not here, Matt."

"No, you are. I expect you to handle these things."

"I am. If you don't like it, get your ass on a plane."

"Do you need a refresher 'how important this is' speech? Because, if you do, I'm happy to give it."

"Nope. That's why I wanted Boston watched in the first place. He's insubordinate and combative when I'm standing next to him. Lord knows what he does outside of my line of sight."

"He's not playing ball?" Matt asks, now audibly getting concerned.

Zach chuckles. "He's barely in the stadium. He resents everything. The only reason he's still engaged is the attachment to the children Hurley liberated. I'm sure that Asami already told you that."

"She did. What else is she saying?"

"Not much," Zach admits. "She defends him. So do the other women. They're willing to put their careers on the line for him, which is why you're holding their resignations."

"I admire the loyalty, even if it's misplaced," Matt admits, softening his tone. "What are you going to do?"

"Whatever I need to."

"How about you give me some specifics?" It was an order more than the question it was phrased as.

Zach doesn't have any to give him. He doesn't know what he's going to do.

"Would you like it in a PowerPoint or regular Word document?"

"Lose the attitude, Zach."

"Then stop micromanaging me. I said I would deal with it. You either trust me to do that, or you don't. Either way, there is no way I'm going to let you run this operation from Virginia."

Zach checks to see if the call is still connected after a long moment of dead air. Matt is used to getting his way at Watchtower. Outside of his conversations with Brass, he's the kingfish, and he knows it.

"Fine. Let me know the result," Remsen says before disconnecting.

Forte steers the car into the parking lot. This is worse than working for his old boss, Grimman. There's too much tension. It is only a matter of time before someone snaps, and this experiment ends in a catastrophic collapse.

CHAPTER FIFTY-SEVEN
DETECTIVE BRESHION HURLEY

PHOENIX POLICE HEADQUARTERS PARKING LOT
PHOENIX, ARIZONA

At least the oppressive sun isn't beating through the windshield. It has dipped below the roofline of the surrounding buildings as it continues its journey below the horizon. Night brings a respite from the brutal heat of the day. Breshion watches as Helio Lozano has his shackles checked and is guided into the back of the squad car.

Hurley checks his watch. The transfer vehicle will leave in a minute for the short trip to the 4th Avenue Jail. With over two thousand beds and a full ten percent dedicated to the highest security level inmates in the system, the facility is the main detention facility for the Maricopa County Sheriff's Office. It was designed with public safety in mind, but it's not the jail Breshion is most worried about – it's getting to it.

The radio affixed to his dash crackles to life. "Subject is loaded. Pulling out now."

"SWAT One ready."

"SWAT Two in position."

"Overwatch ready."

Breshion takes a deep breath. It's a lot of manpower for a few blocks of travel, but better safe than sorry. The parking lot behind headquarters empties onto West Adams Street to the north. From there, it's the third right at the theater and a straight shot south down to the county jail. Fourth Street is one-way, so they don't need to worry about oncoming traffic impeding their progress. That means overwatch is paying close attention to the intersections and streets that bisect the route from the traffic court building across from the theater.

SWAT One will move west on Washington and then turn north on third before moving up a block and picking up a trailing position. As they pass, SWAT Two will depart their designated parking area on Madison and move east toward the courthouse, covering the southern part of the trip.

"Rolling," the transfer vehicle announces.

Breshion is not an official part of this observation and doesn't bother checking in. He's an observer and not much more. Jamecca rattled him because, deep down, he knew that she was right – these men are bait in a trap. The detective couldn't live with the guilt if something goes wrong and he isn't here in harm's way with them. He pulls out onto the street thirty seconds later. A few cars are between him and the transport, but he watches them stop at a traffic light and continue once it turns green.

"Right on Fourth."

"Right on Third," SWAT One announces.

"SWAT Two standing by."

"Overwatch clear."

Breshion allows himself to relax. There is nothing suspicious. Maybe Salcido didn't take the bait, and nothing will happen. As much as he wants that scumbag taken down, it wouldn't be the worst thing in the world.

"Shots fired! Shots fired!"

"Last unit, report status," dispatch commands over the radio.

"This is SWAT Two. We are taking fire! Vehicle disabled with rear flat tires. Suspects fleeing east in a brown late-model Buick Century sedan."

"SWAT One, move in!" Breshion bellows into the radio after snatching the mic off the dash. "Move in, now!"

"Wilco," he hears as there is a series of loud bangs behind him.

"This is overwatch. We have a multi-vehicle TA at the intersection of Fourth and Washington."

Breshion sees the accident in his rearview mirror. He missed the carnage by mere seconds after making the right. Cars point in all directions now after a beer truck accelerated through the red light and slammed into them.

"This is SWAT One. I don't think we can get through this mess."

The detective rubs his forehead, coating his hand in the sweat forming on his brow. This is too well-coordinated to be coincidental, and he stomps on the accelerator to get to the transfer vehicle. The engine whines as the car surges ahead.

"Transfer, this is Hurley. I'm moving toward you down Fourth."

"Roger that, crossing – look out!"

The radio goes dead.

"Transfer? Transfer!" dispatch shouts.

"This is overwatch. TA, Jefferson, and Fourth. Transfer hit by a late-model beige sedan. Shots fired! Shots fired!"

"SWAT One moving south on foot."

"SWAT Two, east, same."

Breshion comes up behind the scene and jumps out of his car after slamming it into park. He is immediately met with a hail of gunfire that forces him to duck behind the bumper of the vehicle in front of him. He checks his backdrop and returns fire as he watches two men in helmets and face shields extract Helio through the shattered rear window. Neither of the transfer cops seems to be in the fight.

The detective pops up and draws more fire. All he needs to do is keep them here until a SWAT team arrives. If this turns into a standoff, they can catch the attackers in a crossfire and close the trap. It's a big "if."

Breshion pops up again and squeezes off a round before more return from different directions. He had tunnel vision from being affixed to the targets at the car. He didn't see the man covering them from the corner. The sound of the rifle belching precedes car windows exploding around him.

With a fear of getting pinned down and no longer able to harass the extraction team, Breshion scurries around the far side of the car. When he lifts his head and checks the opposite corner, he knows he made a mistake. Another man wearing a tactical vest and cloth face shield levels his weapon and fires a handgun in his direction. He feels the jolt of adrenaline as the first shots buzz past his head, making a snapping sound as they pass.

The detective should hit the ground. Instead, he brings his own weapon level and moves his finger to the trigger. He's hit with the force of a sledgehammer right to the chest. It's the last thing he feels before collapsing to the ground.

CHAPTER FIFTY-EIGHT
SSA ZACH FORTE

COPPER STAR HOTEL
PHOENIX, ARIZONA

There was no answer at either of the women's doors. Zach checks his watch and tries to ignore the pit forming in his stomach as he punches the elevator button for the lobby. There is no way they left yet. At least, that's his hope.

He returns to the front desk and is greeted by a receptionist who informs him that neither has checked out. Zach relaxes a little. The women are still in the city unless they packed up and left without closing their hotel bills. Since trying to track them down is almost pointless, he wanders over to the hotel bar to think things through. Forte can't believe his luck when he finds Emma and Nadiya sitting on stools opposite a young bartender smiling like he just won the lottery.

"I wouldn't have guessed that I'd find you here."

"We don't work for you anymore," Nadiya says. "What do you want?"

"Scotch, rocks," Forte orders the bartender. "Make it a double."

"I thought you were laying off the sauce," Emma reminds him.

"It's been one of those days."

"I assume Remsen sent you here?"

The bartender delivers his drink and Forte takes a long sip, fully aware that his presence isn't appreciated by the young man. "I spoke with him, but that's not why I'm here."

"We don't want an apology, Zach," Nadiya offers, firing the first salvo.

"Good, because I'm not offering one."

"You still think how you're treating Boston is right?"

"I don't think a single thing we've done with him is right. Do either of you know the story about how I got involved in this mess?" Zach asks, sliding into the seat next to them.

The women shake their heads, and Zach settles into an explanation of his backstory. He informs them about what happened in Operation Beaver Cage and how he was on the cusp of losing his badge. He then explains Grimman's offer, the surveillance of Boston and his friends, and breaking into Tara's house.

Emma and Nadiya listen intently without questions. Zach continues with how he learned about Boston's abilities and teamed up with Matt Remsen to track him down. He concludes with the events at the sleep center, capturing Louisiana and Maryland by accident, and the gunfire at the house. Zach even includes the part about tripping in the front doorway and how that tumble saved his life.

"What exactly happened to Gina? I know that she was neutralized, but I've heard five different versions of how. Even the official records are ambiguous."

Forte smiles at Emma. "Louisiana, Maryland, and presumably Tara blew her off the side of a mountain in West Virginia with an IED."

"Seriously?"

"Yeah."

"Why didn't anyone press charges?" Nadiya asks.

"You remember the circus. Two senators were dead, the White House was in crisis mode, the media was swirling, and the intelligence community was embarrassed. Everyone wanted the truth buried."

"So, they concocted a cover story, and nobody asked questions about Boston," Emma concludes.

"There was no need. He was dead as far as anyone was concerned."

"Zach, why did Boston stick around after he emerged from his coma? He had a new face and a new lease on life. He never wanted to do this, so why stay?"

The senior agent sips his drink, knowing this is a test. Watchtower was built on secrets and generates even more of them on its own. The women are tired of it.

"Boston's fiancée betrayed him. His friends thought he was dead. He was fingered as a traitor. There wasn't much of a life to go back to. As for starting anew, he would have needed a new identity. Matt wasn't about to hand him one."

"Watchtower forced him into this. That's why he fled to see Tara," Nadiya says, seething.

"And you lied to him about her in the hopes that he would accept his circumstances and stay," Emma piles on.

"Yeah. We always thought that Tara would just move on. Only she didn't. And after we concluded that he went to see her, we learned that neither had he. They're from different worlds and only spent a few days together. Nobody could have guessed that their connection was that strong."

The two women look wounded. Both are strong, intelligent, passionate, beautiful, and have deep feelings for him. Zach hates the idea of Boston ever having to decide between the two. It's going to be like choosing between your two favorite flavors of ice cream. Many people would think that it's not a bad problem to have as a man. This bartender would probably be one of them. But the moment Boston dates one of them, he hurts the other.

"You don't know him that well, then," Nadiya says.

"No, you're right. I don't. To be honest, I don't know if Boston likes Tara or the *idea* of her. He has a piece missing from his life."

"A piece missing?" Emma asks. "Like a girlfriend?"

Zach shakes his head. "Purpose. In a way, Gina provided that…until she almost ended his life. Whether he knows it or not, we're trying to give him a new one."

The women fall silent for what feels like an hour. They knew the basics, but Boston never talked to anyone about Gina, and Zach's sure they never wanted to ask. That kind of betrayal is like getting a knife to the heart. Nobody would be eager to force open that wound.

"What do you want from us?"

"Simple, Emma. I need the two of you to protect him."

"From whom?" Nadiya asks.

"Me. Remsen. Brass. Everybody."

"Why can't you do that yourself?"

Zach forces a weak smile. "Because I already serve too many masters. My first allegiance is to Watchtower. Yours isn't."

"We won't spy on him," Emma warns.

"I know. I'm not asking you to. In fact, I'm asking the opposite. I need you to have Boston's six, not report back to me."

Forte swallows the rest of his scotch and drops some money on the bar before sliding off his stool.

"Why the change of heart?" Emma presses.

"I'm supposed to say it's because Boston has been of great service to this nation, and we owe him. That's not the real reason, though. It's that I have never taken the time to look at things from his perspective until now. If our roles were reversed, I would feel like everyone was against me. It's time for him to know that the two of you are on his side."

"Assuming we decide to return," Nadiya says.

"Yes, assuming that. I'm not a salesman. My cards are on the table. The choice is yours, and I will leave it to you to make."

Zach is thrilled to be walking away without any physical damage. He had convinced himself that Nadiya was willing to bash his head in. Emma was likely ready to shoot him on sight. In counterintelligence, he excelled at dwelling on the worst-case scenario. Zach only makes it two steps before his cell phone rings in his jacket pocket.

"Forte. What? Okay, I'll be right there."

"What happened?" Emma asks, recognizing the look for something a person wears after eating gas station sushi or biting into a decade-old Twinkie.

"Phoenix police were transferring Helio Lozano to county lockup. The vehicle was ambushed. Two officers were killed, Helio was taken, and Hurley was shot."

"Is he alive?"

"I don't know."

CHAPTER FIFTY-NINE

"BOSTON" HOLLINGER

SALT RIVER VALLEY EMERGENCY ROOM
PHOENIX, ARIZONA

My heart thunders in my chest. Adrenaline courses through my bloodstream, heightening my alertness. I can smell gunpowder mixed with the desert air. My head moves, but I'm focused on the car a few dozen feet in front of me.

I dart around the rear of a car. I can feel that something isn't right and turn my head. The man standing there is wearing a tactical vest and some sort of covering over his face. My heart jumps into my throat, and a deep sense of fear seizes my legs up. The man points a gun at me and fires.

The snapping sound. I know it too well. The bullets are close, maybe inches away. I should run...find cover. But I don't. I ignore the danger and bring my own weapon to bear at him.

My sights line up. Another moment longer... A crushing force strikes me in the chest, and my legs wobble below me. Darkness closes in, like a tunnel that gets narrower. Then my vision gets hazy before everything goes dark.

I come back to the conversation in the room. We were all relieved to hear that the round fired at the detective was caught by his body armor. The vest saved his life. He'll be sore for a few days, but he's still breathing.

The same can't be said for the transfer officers executed with shots to the head and pronounced dead at the scene. Seven bystanders were hospitalized from the accidents and the shootout. The incident has already made the national news.

My instincts not to trust anyone here were spot-on. Someone provided the sex traffickers with the details of the transfer. Detective Hurley is the only one above scrutiny at this point because no mole would risk death to maintain their cover. At least, I imagine that's the case.

"Is there any news on the assailants?" Detective Hurley asks in a low voice, shifting in his bed.

"A patrol unit responded to a car fire and identified it as the vehicle from the attack," Ritter says. "They torched it and switched vehicles. We're pulling traffic footage from the area, but don't get your hopes up."

"Even if Ritter does find something, positive identification is unlikely," Detective Robinson adds. "We started poring over video at the scene to put together what happened. All the men were either wearing motorcycle helmets or face coverings. They left a ton of shell casings behind, so we may be able to pull DNA or prints."

Breshion grimaces and shakes his head. These guys were careful. They may catch a break – it's not implausible. It's only unlikely. The helmets block facial recognition, and they were wearing heavy leather gloves. Their car will come back as either stolen or junked. There's no chance that they left any evidence on a casing.

"So, nothing."

"Helio is a fugitive," Forte chimes in. "We've engaged the U.S. Marshals. They have the tools and experience to get him back."

Breshion jerks suddenly and grabs his ribs, leaning back on the bed.

"Take it easy," Detective Robinson chastises. "You were just shot in the chest. If not for the Kevlar, we'd all be picking out your casket right now."

"I'm fine."

"You could have been killed," she says, her eyes showing her tender concern. "What were you even doing near that transfer?"

"That's a good question," Jada Fulcher asks, entering the already cramped room. Breshion's team immediately makes room for the assistant chief. "I'm glad to see you alive, but I'd like to hear the answer to that before I kill you."

"I was leaving to go get a bite," Hurley says, hazarding a glance at me.

I know he's lying but I don't say anything. Every cop in this room recognizes the deceit, including their boss. She will press the issue with him, though probably not with us present.

"Mmhmm. We'll talk about this later. I'm happy that you're okay. Now, get out of this place and get some rest. I have damage control to get to and a department to rally. We have two officers killed in the line of duty, and the mayor's office is going nuts."

I can't help but wonder why. Is it because the mayor feels the loss of two public servants, or does she fear how the public will react? Unfortunately, in politics, it usually is the latter over the former. Maybe Mayor Horta is different. Perhaps she's the same. It's something to look into. One memory didn't give me much of a baseline on her.

"Can somebody look into getting me out of here?" Hurley says after a long sigh when his boss departs.

"I'm on it," Ritter offers and disappears from the room.

"Can everyone else give me a minute?"

"We all need to get back to headquarters anyway," Robinson says.

Breshion grabs me. "Hang back for a second."

Forte nods at me, and the room clears. I'm almost afraid to hear what this is about, and am not looking forward to providing a detailed synopsis to Forte when we're done.

"What's up?"

"Agent Smith, I don't know what your deal is, and right now, I honestly don't care. You have some sort of gift, and I need you to use it now."

I fold my arms across my chest. "What do you mean?"

"That ambush was perfect...and I mean *perfect*. The attackers knew where our units were staged, had our routes, and timed the ambush down to the second. The details of the transfer had to have been leaked to them."

"You have a mole," I blurt out.

Detective Hurley leans his head back and sighs. "I knew you were going to say that."

"Because you already came to that conclusion yourself."

"Yeah, I did. Any idea who?"

"No, but you leaked the transfer to the mayor's office. I would start there."

"I didn't leak anything."

"You met with Adrian Finley at a coffee shop. There's no doubt that he told the mayor. She could have gotten the details about the transfer from any one of a dozen people. Not that she did. It's just speculation."

"Smith, when this is all over, you're really going to have to tell me how you could possibly know that, and don't give me the 'it's one of life's mysteries' crap."

I can't suppress the smirk, but there's nothing more to say. The detective can never learn the truth, so he will have to learn to live with disappointment. I turn and start to leave him to argue with a doctor about his discharge.

"Will?"

"Yeah?"

"Thanks."

I nod and head out to join my waiting team. Another thought pops into my mind about something I have some experience with. Nothing changes someone's perspective like getting shot at. Whether he knows it or not yet, Alejandro Salcido made a colossal mistake tonight. A divided house cannot stand. Insofar as the FBI and Phoenix PD are concerned, it's not divided anymore.

CHAPTER SIXTY
MAYOR ANGELICA HORTA

CITY HALL PRESS BRIEFING ROOM
PHOENIX, ARIZONA

This should have been a solemn occasion. No elected official likes delivering bad news to the public or facing the media during a crisis. Two police officers are dead. Both were married with children. They should be honored for their sacrifice, and the city should mourn with their families. That's not what the people in this room are interested in.

Angelica prides herself on her relationship with the police department. It hasn't always been rainbows and sunshine, but it's built on a solid foundation of mutual respect. She also maintains ties to the Arizona State Police and federal authorities. Her decisions aren't popular with the rank and file cops, but the leadership knows they have her unwavering support.

None of that matters to those seeking to turn this into a political issue. News of the two fallen officers hit her hard, but that's not what will be reported. This was a prisoner transfer, not a drug bust or an operation to take down a dangerous serial killer. It was a routine duty that went horribly wrong and has become an opportunity for her critics to cash in politically.

The mayor concludes her statement to the assembled media with members of the police standing behind her. Her words are genuine but sound hollow. The dark mood of the reporters in the room is apparent.

"Our thoughts and prayers go out to the families. I want each of them to know that the City of Phoenix grieves with them. Thank you."

The barrage of questions erupts as the final words leave her lips. As much as Angelica would love to ignore them and step off the dais, she knows she can't.

"Have you spoken to the families of the officers?" a woman in front asks, shouting over her colleagues.

"We have reached out, but they're grieving right now, and we are giving them their privacy."

"You haven't talked to them?"

"As I said, we reached out and did not receive a response."

"Could they be angry at you for the deaths of their loved ones?" a second reporter asks.

The mayor suppresses a scowl. "I won't speculate on a reason that they didn't pick up the phone."

"Madam Mayor, we have sources inside City Hall who allege that you lashed out at the police for this happening. Is that true?"

"I suggest you vet your sources better. No, I did nothing that can be characterized as lashing out. I immediately reached out for details, which the police provided me."

"You're saying that you don't blame the police, then?"

Angelica stares at the reporter. The media no longer exist to inform. They only seek to divide, and when there is no relevant issue to achieve that end, they invent one. There is no division between her and the police, despite how they attempt to depict the relationship.

"I blame the perpetrators of the crime," the mayor responds.

"Are there any details as to who the attackers were?"

It's about time one of the friendlier members of the media threw her an appropriate question. "The police are exploring all leads."

"Do you feel that you are responsible for the deaths of these officers?" Vincent DiPasquale asks.

Angelica wonders if the *Sun Republic* reporter confers with LaCugna before asking his questions at these press conferences. It's a politically charged question and something that she would expect her archrival to ask. The councilman has countless useful idiots like DiPasquale to do his bidding.

"I feel their loss, just like all members of our community do."

"That's not what I asked, ma'am. I want to know if you feel responsible."

"Why would I?" Angelica asks, snapping back at him. The moment the words leave her mouth, she regrets opening the door for him.

"You cut the police budget on the city council, resulting in a significant downsizing. You also made a personnel shift recently, one that many in this community don't agree with, including removing officers from SWAT."

"The personnel shift had nothing to do with what happened. As for the budget, it was a difficult time for the city—"

"You don't believe your actions killed them?"

"I resent that implication."

"Why was a SWAT team on-site, Mayor? Is that standard procedure?"

The mayor expected that question. "I will leave it to the police to comment on the specifics of their procedures in this case. My understanding is that the police wanted to safeguard the transfer of a high-value prisoner."

"So, the police must have some leads on who was responsible for the attack."

"They're exploring every lead, as I mentioned."

"There's a difference between exploring leads and knowing who was responsible. If this was a high-value prisoner who required SWAT protection, and this attack was some kind of rescue mission, the police must have an idea what group or individual is responsible."

"As I said, every lead is being explored."

"Can you at least release the name of the prisoner?"

"We are withholding that information at this time."

"There is a dangerous criminal on the streets of the city, and you won't share that information with the public? Is that your idea of making the city safer?"

"More details will be released at the appropriate time. Thank you, everyone."

Every nerve in Angelica's body is screaming to get the hell out of there. It's a fight or flight mechanism, and now it's time to retreat and fight another day. Questions are shouted as she steps away from the podium and off the dais. One voice sounds out more loudly than the others.

"Why are you lying to us, Madam Mayor? Why won't you be honest and tell us the facts? What are you hiding?"

CHAPTER SIXTY-ONE
ALEJANDRO SALCIDO

DEZRT FYRE NIGHTCLUB STORAGE ROOM
PHOENIX, ARIZONA

The basement level of the nightclub is not unlike what you find under many bars in America. It's musty, dirty, poorly lit, and filled with cases of every imaginable kind of alcohol. It's also relatively soundproof. Any noise that does escape will be instantly drowned out by the thumping bass of the EDM blasting upstairs. It's the perfect hiding place.

Several of the men who conducted the rescue wait with Javier and Helio in the storage room. One of them is getting a bandage applied to his hand. None of the rest shows any signs of injury. It was well-executed.

"Did anyone follow you here?"

"No, *Patrón*. We used several cars and took the scenic route."

"Where's the vehicle you arrived in?" Alejandro asks his lieutenant.

"I had two men take it to the desert to be torched."

"Excellent. Nice work."

Javi nods, appreciating the praise. Alejandro keeps a close watch on neighboring businesses. They know which ones have cameras and where they point. His own closed-circuit system was built with a blind spot for reasons just like this. Since there are no traffic cameras in this area and the vehicles they used don't have internal GPS, it's unlikely anyone could trace them back to this club.

Under any other circumstances, this would have been done at a stash house shielded from Salcido's legitimate businesses. Unfortunately, his team is being hunted, and this was their best chance at evasion despite Alejandro assuming personal risk.

"Thank you for rescuing me."

"We look after our own, Helio. It's what we do for loyal soldiers."

"*Gracias, gracias.*"

"Are you okay? You weren't injured during the rescue, were you?" Alejandro asks.

"I hit my head. It'll be okay. Why am I down here?"

Alejandro spreads his arms out and presents the room. "There is no safer place for you right now. You are a fugitive, and everyone is looking for you. We need to keep you hidden until we can smuggle you back to Nogales. How did they treat you?"

"Okay," Helio says after a short pause. "They interrogated me for hours."

"I'm sure they did. The authorities knew that they had a valuable member of this operation in their custody. What did you give them?"

"Nothing," Helio adamantly decrees.

Alejandro raises an eyebrow. "Nothing at all? No small detail or way for them to track us?"

"No. I stayed quiet. That's why they were transferring me. I wouldn't talk."

"I see," Alejandro says, nodding. "I would have thought that it's because you gave them what they wanted."

"*No, no, Patrón*. I told them nothing."

Alejandro checks over his shoulder and catches Javi shaking his head almost imperceptibly. He has come to the same conclusion that Helio is lying. He either cut a deal or gave them something they wanted.

"Was the FBI there?"

"What? Uh, yes…they were there."

"Did they offer you a deal? Immunity from prosecution?"

"No, they didn't."

"No offers at all?"

Helio shakes his head. "I am loyal. They knew they wouldn't get anything out of me."

Alejandro smirks. "That's great. You are invaluable to my business, Helio. You know that, right?"

"Thank you, *Patrón*. I look forward to serving you again soon."

Alejandro beams. "Soon, *chico*, soon. For now, you must remain hidden. You are too important. I cannot afford to have you get caught again."

Alejandro studies the young coyote's face. There is a sense of relief on it. He doubts that Helio ever intends to work for him again. Despite the praise and assurances of his value, all he wants to do is return to Mexico and disappear. It's in his eyes.

"We will get you set up. You could be here for a couple of days until the dust settles. I will see to it that you are as comfortable as possible."

"Thank you, *Patrón*."

Alejandro smiles. At least the kid is respectful. He turns his back to Helio before stopping. "I almost forgot. There is one thing you can do for me."

"Anything. What is it?"

Alejandro pulls the gun from his waistband and spins. He points it at Helio's forehead as shock registers on the young man's face.

"Die."

Alejandro pulls the trigger. The sound of the shot is deafening in the room. The other men cover their ears as the noise bounces back and forth between the brick and concrete walls. Helio hits the floor, the open mouth and wide eyes forever frozen on his face.

"Say hi to your parents for me," Salcido says, leaning over the body.

Javi walks over, and Alejandro hands him the weapon.

"We could have done that ourselves."

"Some things I prefer to handle personally. Clean this mess up and be thorough. Make sure the body ends up somewhere that even the coyotes will have problems finding it."

"I thought you said this was a safe place for him, *Patrón*," Javi says with a grin as he stares down at the corpse.

Alejandro returns the devilish smile. "This is a safe place from the police and FBI. I found a safer one. They won't be looking for him in hell."

CHAPTER SIXTY-TWO
DETECTIVE BRESHION HURLEY

Jada Fulcher is not political. She didn't get this job because of her connections or ability to schmooze. She earned it by performing better than her peers. Her reputation is one of a competent administrator who doesn't play games or pull punches.

That's what makes this moment so unnerving to Breshion. Most of the time, a summons to her office leads to an immediate verbal beatdown. Not this time. Jada is making him wait in front of her desk while she finishes writing out a note. Breshion almost wants to ask if she's drafting his resignation for him. Almost. Park rangers will tell you there's a reason not to poke the bears.

"Do you have something that you want to tell me?" Jada finally says without looking up.

"Yeah, I think something is up with this Agent Smith character. He knows things that he shouldn't. It's like he has ESP or something. He's always ten steps ahead of us."

Jada peers over her thick black reading glasses. "Look at me, Detective. Does my face strike you as someone who gives a damn about the FBI right now?"

"No, ma'am, it doesn't."

"Because I don't. We have two dead officers, an irate police chief, an angry public, and a mayor getting crucified by the media. So, you're here because I want to know if it was your bright idea to transfer Lozano and then leak the details to the damn mayor's office!"

"I didn't leak the details. I only told them that it was happening."

"I'm glad you feel the need to draw that distinction. I don't. You told Horta's office. Why would you do that?"

"The mayor needed a win."

Jada leans back in her chair and shakes her head. "Out of anyone else's mouth, I might almost believe that. Unfortunately, that crap answer came out of yours, and you suck at politics worse than Horta does. Here's what I think: You were baiting Salcido into making a move. That's why you had SWAT shadowing them and an overwatch keeping an eye on things. It's also why your dumbass was in a trail vehicle. Go ahead – lie to me and tell me I'm wrong."

For some odd reason, Breshion has always liked the movie *Wall Street*. Charlie Sheen's character said something before meeting Gordon Gecko for the first time— something that has always stuck with the detective: "Life all comes down to a series of moments. This is one of them."

If he lies to save his ass and Jada sniffs it out, he's through. If he tells the truth, the result may be the same. In moments like this, a man's character is revealed.

"No, ma'am, you're right. I thought there was a chance that Helio Lozano was important enough that Salcido would either want him back or silence him. So, I took precautions. Unfortunately, the attackers knew every detail of that transfer operation — every detail. I didn't mention any specifics to the mayor's office, yet Salcido's goons knew."

"I see. Do you know for sure that Alejandro Salcido is a sex trafficking kingpin, or are you taking a twenty-year-old kid's word for it? Hmm?"

"We're exploring the possibility. No, we have not yet confirmed that it's Salcido."

Jada nods several times slowly, her eyes staring at a spot on her desk. "I expect the men and women who work for me to have better judgment. You royally screwed up, Breshion. Men have died. The chief wants heads to roll over this, and that likely means yours. I've warned you about getting too close to your cases."

"Yes, you have."

Breshion unclips his badge and withdraws his weapon from its holster. He sets both on the desk and takes a step back under the watchful eye of his boss, who removes her reading glasses and sets them down.

"I'm sorry, but what the hell are you doing?"

"Beating you to the punch. You're going to suspend me, at the very least."

She scoffs. "For such a brilliant detective, you're as dumb as an adobe brick. Pick those up! You will not deprive me of the opportunity to verbally abuse you. That's one of the highlights of this job."

"I'm not sure I want them back now."

"Yes, you do, and for the same reason that I won't take them from you now. We've never been closer to bringing down this sex trafficking network. If it is Salcido, I want nothing more than to see him rotting in solitary confinement for the rest of his natural life. There's nobody I trust more than you to make that happen, despite your uncanny ability to do dumb things."

"And the transfer?" Breshion asks, picking up his badge and gun off her desk.

"You took reasonable precautions under the circumstances. The death of those two officers was a tragedy that will haunt you for the rest of your life. Which would have been short had you not had the common sense to be wearing a vest. There will be an unpleasant inquiry in your future, but you have my support. That's provided you don't do anything to make me reconsider it."

"Thank you."

"Mmhmm."

"There's one more thing. We need a warrant on Salcido."

"You like pushing your luck, don't you? Well, you ain't gonna get one. There isn't a judge in the great State of Arizona that would sign off on one. You have no evidence, and your star witness is a fugitive. Get me something concrete, and we'll talk about your warrant. You have no idea the mesa you'll have to climb to convince one that Salcido isn't the financial guardian angel he pretends to be."

"I can't get the evidence we need without a warrant."

His superior smirks. "Then I suggest you talk to Agent Smith. If you say he's ten steps ahead of you, maybe he can consult his crystal ball or channel Miss Cleo."

"He probably would if she hadn't died back in 2016," Breshion grumbles.

"Which would make the feat that much more impressive. Anything else, Detective?"

"No, ma'am."

Breshion quickly exits Jada's office before she can have second thoughts about letting him off the hook. He still has a job, but his life isn't any less complicated. The guilt over the loss of the officers is overwhelming. Taking down Salcido may ease that pain, but it'll have to be done the hard way. The only thing worse than searching for a needle in a haystack is doing it blindfolded with an arm tied behind your back.

CHAPTER SIXTY-THREE
SSA ZACH FORTE

PHOENIX POLICE HEADQUARTERS
PHOENIX, ARIZONA

It takes a few minutes, but Zach finds Boston staring through the two-way mirror in the narrow observation room at vacant chairs. Maybe in his mind, they aren't empty. He could be reliving the interrogation of Helio Lozano using some visual aids. If that's what's happening, he doesn't want to interrupt.

The dream machine finally glances over at him before pacing to the other end of the room, checking out all the video and audio equipment. If he had any revelations, he isn't sharing them.

"Anything?"

"No."

Forte is about to press further when his phone chirps from his pocket. He retrieves it, checks the caller id, and connects the call before putting the device against his ear.

"Zach, it's Matt. We have a development. Are you alone?"

"Boston is with me. Otherwise, yes."

"Good. Put me on speaker," Remsen orders, and Forte complies. "Watchtower Ops just learned that Alejandro Salcido reserved a private jet departing Deer Valley Airport. A flight plan was filed with the FAA."

Forte curses under his breath. "Where's he going and when?"

"Guaymas International Airport. He departs in three hours."

Zach presses his lips together. Their boy is flying the coop. While there is an extradition treaty with Mexico, their case isn't strong enough to make the request. He could imagine the laughter from Mexican officials when he tells them that their only evidence is the word of a young coyote. Salcido has dual citizenship. If he stays down there, he's out of reach.

"Can you find out why he's going down there?"

"We're digging into that now. Salcido doesn't have any known residences in that area, so we assume he's meeting someone. Maybe checking in with a cartel, and then he'll return."

Zach frowns. "He knows we're on to him. Helio Lozano either told him about his interrogation, or it was forced out of him. Either way, Salcido isn't coming back anytime soon. Has Watchtower had any hits on Lozano?"

"No. He disappeared."

"Magic Man," Boston murmurs from across the table.

Forte rubs his chin, knowing that Boston is right. Salcido has spent a lifetime hiding in plain sight. Lozano is on their radar, so the easiest way to continue avoiding detection is to remove the blip permanently.

"If the trafficker took a page out of the cartel playbook, then he won't leave loose ends untied," Zach admits. "Dead men don't talk."

"Yeah," Matt admits. "Probably."

"Any bright ideas?"

"One. We'll follow the money and see if we can find something to use against Salcido that way. We're getting the financial records from his bars and nightclubs to see if any money was funneled where it shouldn't have been."

"You got a warrant for that?" There is silence on the other end. That's telling…and scary. "Never mind. They're cash businesses. Salcido will claim the credit card receipts to keep him off the IRS radar, but there is no way to track where the rest of his revenue goes, assuming that he's mixing funds at all."

"People make mistakes, Zach. All it takes is one. Are there any leads down there on who attacked the transfer?"

"The motorcycle helmets made facial recognition impossible. None of the casings had fingerprints, and even if they did, the men were likely illegals and wouldn't be in our database. We found the car used in the ambush and possibly a second vehicle they used, both torched. A third burned-out SUV was found outside the city, but we can't confirm it was even involved. All three were old models and lacked navigation systems. A team is going through traffic camera footage hoping to catch a break, but I'm not getting my hopes up."

Forte looks over at Boston, who shakes his head. It appears that even the dream machine doesn't have any useful ideas for leads to explore.

"What about Salcido's network?" Matt asks. "Can he run it from Mexico?"

"From what we've learned here, most traffickers run decentralized operations. Decisions are made echelons below his level, and he only provides strategic guidance."

"So, you're saying that he could run it from the moon with a phone and large enough oxygen supply."

"Bingo. He could leave someone trusted behind to mind the shop and coordinate activities, though."

"Perfect. Get the locals to dig up whatever they can about who he associates with. They don't need a warrant for that. We'll do the same on our end."

"Matt, even with an army working on this, there isn't enough time. Is there any way to hold him up or revoke the travel?"

"Legally? No, not without cause. The best we could do is jam him up for a couple of hours, but what good would it do? What's the progress on your end?"

"Zero."

"All right. Let me know if you find anything. I'll do the same," Matt says a moment before the line goes dead.

Boston wrings his hands as he stretches his neck. "This could take months."

"Most investigations do. This isn't an episode of *Law & Order*. Things don't get wrapped up in an hour."

Boston leans back against the counter that runs the length of the room, and he crosses his arms. "By the time we even get on the right trail, Salcido will have insulated himself by dismantling wherever it leads. If we don't grab him now, it's game over."

Forte wants to argue but can't. That's the likely outcome. Still, someone needs to remain optimistic.

"Watchtower has tools that these guys haven't even dreamed of. We'll get him."

"I need to stretch my legs. I'm going for a walk around the block to get a decent cup of coffee."

"Do I need to send Emma or Nadiya with you?"

Boston stops next to him and grins. The concerned and apprehensive look on Forte's face is almost caricaturish. "I don't know. Do you? I'll be back in a bit."

Forte considers having him tailed but changes his mind. He has to learn to trust, and Boston has too much invested in this now to flee. With that thought, he heads back to the conference room to see if the vice detectives have been able to work any magic.

CHAPTER SIXTY-FOUR
ALEJANDRO SALCIDO

DEZRT FYRE NIGHTCLUB
PHOENIX, ARIZONA

Alejandro glances at the wall clock hanging in his office. It's almost noon, and he will need to head for the airport soon. His eyes wander over to the window and gaze out on the empty dance floor and bar below. He isn't usually this nostalgic. A man in his line of work needs to be willing to drop everything at a moment's notice. His journey to Mexico with no immediate plans to return is making him sentimental. Only now does he realize how much he loves this place.

The firewalls between his legitimate and illegitimate business activities provide him plausible deniability and should hold. Still, Helio likely provided the FBI with a name, and it was his. Nobody wants to be the subject of a federal investigation.

While Alejandro doubts that the feds and Phoenix Police will find anything concrete on him, there's no point in sticking around to find out. He has dual citizenship and can easily pass off his absence in Arizona as a much-needed vacation or a sick relative. Who would know the difference?

A knock at the door shatters his quiet reflection.

"Sorry to bother you, *Patrón*."

"It's no bother. Is the plane ready?"

"*Sí*. We can depart for the airport whenever you're ready."

"Thank you, Javi. Do you have everything you need?"

"*Sí, Patrón*. I won't let you down."

"I know you won't. I have made it brutally clear to the club and bar managers that you're acting on my behalf during my absence. Let me know if any of them fail to heed your orders."

"I think they learned their lesson," Javier says with a grin.

Alejandro nods. The club manager couldn't finger someone for stealing the booze out of the storeroom because it was him. The admission didn't come as a surprise to Salcido – that was his feeling all along, and hence his stern warning not to find a scapegoat. When the truth was finally admitted, justice was swift.

"The same applies to our sales business. I trust you to keep both of our operations running smoothly."

"I don't anticipate any problems."

"It's the one you don't anticipate that gets you in the end."

Alejandro admires the young man's confidence, but arrogance like that could be his downfall. Every world leader who ever experienced a coup probably never saw it coming. How many of them paid with their lives?

"The FBI?" Javier asks. "Our sources are saying they don't know anything."

Salcido frowns. "The Phoenix FBI isn't coordinating with their agents from Washington. I don't know who that team is, but they're different, and that worries me. Until we discover what they've learned, I need you to stay on guard. A raid on our businesses is not out of the question."

Javier doesn't look so cocky now. "A raid? Here?"

"Don't worry. The feds won't find anything. If they arrive with a warrant, invite them in with open arms and let them tear my businesses down to the studs if they want to. Show them every document and every account we have. Hide nothing."

"Very well. Pardon my boldness, but if you aren't concerned, then why are you leaving for Mexico?"

Overconfidence cost Alejandro's father his life. He will not make the same mistake. If that means sacrificing a loyal lieutenant like Javier, so be it. If the choice is between the two of them, the answer is simple.

"The FBI could take years to investigate me. Once they realize that my businesses are legitimate, it will take the heat off of you. Their focus will stay on me because the innocent don't run. That will result in fewer eyes on you while running things here."

"Won't they assume that I'm acting on your behalf?"

"Not if you're smart about things. Don't give them any reason to think that you're involved in my other business at all. Sooner or later, they'll get bored watching you and assume you're clean."

His right-hand man nods. Alejandro knows that the FBI is unlikely to stop watching everyone who works for these clubs, but he doubts his employees recognize that. Every last bartender, bouncer, shot girl, and barback he employs will be scrutinized.

"Javier, you're about to become a rich man. You will be handsomely rewarded for your loyalty. This office is yours until I return," Alejandro says, taking one last look. "Come, escort me to the airport. We can talk more in the car."

CHAPTER SIXTY-FIVE
"BOSTON" HOLLINGER

PHOENIX DEER VALLEY AIRPORT
PHOENIX, ARIZONA

Deer Valley is not a large airport. An access road moves in a square around a central parking area that's smaller than you'd find at a typical Walmart. The main terminal has a flavor of Southwest – arched covered entryways and a cream-color adobe building. I'm not here to scout that.

Watchtower learned that the contracted private jet is departing from the adjacent private charter facility. I pull the "borrowed" Suburban into the spot located along a chain-link fence that leads to the main entrance. I'm not sure what I'm planning to do, but anything feels better than nothing.

An engine winds up on a small jet as it rolls across the apron to the taxiway. I'm betting that Salcido is on the plane. There's only one way to find out if I missed him by a few minutes. I lock the Suburban and head toward the office entrance as three men crossing the street spot the shiny black beast with the U.S. government plates on the back. That gets their attention, and they change direction, their eyes locked on me.

"Hey! You a fed?" the big guy in the middle of the trio asks.

The tiny hairs on the back of my head stand at attention. His words don't alarm me as much as the aggressive tone they were delivered in. All three men exaggerate their "tough guy" walk as they stride toward me. The first indication is that they can handle themselves in a fight and have a swagger that comes with practice.

"Excuse me?" I ask, buying time.

"You deaf? I asked if you were a fed," the trio's leader says, nodding over at my Suburban.

My mind races. This is a public area, and they have no reason to attack me, but they don't need one when it's three on one. I may be able to take them in a street brawl, or at least hold my own, except they're more than likely armed. That complicates things.

"A fed? As in the FBI? Hell no."

The three men surround me. The first one leans in, and I remain as calm and impassive as I can.

"I don't believe you."

"Well, I don't know what to tell you guys, then."

"How about we beat it out of you?"

I hold my hands up in front of my chest as anyone not looking for a fight would do. It's not looking like it's going to have any effect when a thin, well-dressed Latino rounds the corner and heads toward us.

"What's going on here?"

"I think your friends are trying to make me feel welcome in Phoenix."

"What are you guys doing?"

"He's an FBI agent! Look at the plates," the trio's leader says, pointing. The man does take a peek but isn't sold on the conclusion.

"Step back," he orders before turning to me. "I apologize for my guys. They've lost their manners after an unfortunate number of run-ins with law enforcement."

I try to look a little nervous after I recognize the tactic. It's a version of the good cop, bad cop routine. He's trying to get me to admit that I'm FBI by pretending he's saving me. I'm glad I don't wear my badge around my neck or on my belt.

"It sounds that way. Fortunately for them, I'm not a cop or in the FBI," I say, going on the offensive without the expectation that he'll believe my denial.

"No?"

He glances at my belt to see if I have a glimpse of a badge visible. He then rechecks the Suburban.

"These things are a dime a dozen in Washington, but the government keeps fleets of them everywhere. I work for a congressman."

"Which one?"

"Timothy McHale."

"Never heard of him," the man says, shaking his head.

"I wouldn't expect you to. He represents the Ohio 17th district."

"Where the hell is that?" the trio leader asks from a couple of steps away.

"The seventeenth is made up of two counties just outside Columbus. Have you ever been there?" I ask, causing the man to make a face and the slick-looking man in front of me to grin. "Yeah, okay, it isn't exactly a hopping tourist district."

"I didn't catch your name."

There is a good chance this guy, or one of his minions, will whip out a phone and open a browser. Most members of Congress have their own websites that list members of their staff. Fortunately, I worked with many of them in my former life. I mentally pick a guy I know who doesn't have his photo up or at least didn't a year ago.

"Michael Halston. I'm a legislative assistant for Congressman McHale," I say, extending my hand, which the man shakes as one of his friends peels away and pulls out his phone.

"Javier Barerra. What brings you to Phoenix, Michael?"

"I'm on an advance. The congressman is meeting with members of your congressional delegation about a legislative initiative we are co-sponsoring. I was asked to act as a liaison with their staffs for a couple of days."

"Here?" Javier asks, gesturing at the charter aircraft building.

"Most politicians don't fly commercial anymore. Too many confrontations with people in airports that end up on YouTube."

"Pssh. Rich people," one of the thugs moans.

"You don't know the half of it."

"Actually, we do. Our boss is pretty wealthy," Javier says, giving his men the side-eye.

"Oh yeah?"

"Yeah, he's a prominent businessman in the city. His name is Alejandro Salcido."

I knew that name drop was coming and I blank my mind as to not give anything away. There are dozens of tells in poker. The same applies to liars. The cardinal sin is faux curiosity, so I don't even ask any follow-up questions. No congressional staffer would.

Javier checks back with his guy, who gives him a slight nod, satisfied that I am who I say. I'm reasonably confident that I didn't give anything away about his boss, so it's time to end this inquisition.

"From the looks of that suit, he pays more than my boss does. McHale inherited his money and is still as cheap as hell."

Javier grins. "We should let you get to it."

I check my watch, thrilled that it looks expensive, even if it isn't. "Yeah, thanks. I'm due back at the hotel in less than an hour. It's nice meeting you, Javier."

"You too, Mark."

"Michael," I say, instantly correcting his purposeful error.

"Oh, sorry, I'm bad with names."

"No worries. So is my boss."

I smile as I walk past the group. They head across the street, giving the Suburban one last glance. I turn and enter the office and make a show of discussing fictional travel arrangements with the clerk. It was news to them that a congressman was planning an arrival here. He bought the lie, and the story will check out if Javier or his comrades follow up.

I watch their pair of cars depart the parking area out of my peripheral vision and allow myself to breathe. I dodged a bullet. These guys were bold to confront me at a public airport. There was no reservation about grilling me to see if the FBI was sniffing around their boss.

Salcido is an intelligent man, and he hires smart people to work for him. He also has their unwavering loyalty. Some of that is bought through money, but I'm willing to bet that he also treats his people well. No wonder Helio didn't want to give him up. We could investigate Salcido for a decade and come up empty. I need a different tactic if we are going to end this. It's time to take matters into my own hands.

CHAPTER SIXTY-SIX

MAYOR ANGELICA HORTA

CITY HALL OFFICE OF THE MAYOR
PHOENIX, ARIZONA

Her two aides stand there with blank looks on their faces. Angelica has never liked the idea of doling out a dose of verbal abuse, but this is different. The current predicament isn't their fault, and neither Katy nor Adrian has seen the mayor lash out like this, but something needs to be done. These aren't ordinary times. Angelica is under attack, and they haven't lifted a finger to help.

"What do you expect us to do?" Katy asks.

"You are my media rep," the mayor responds, pairing a sardonic tone with a withering glare. "You're supposed to help guide me. You have relationships with every journalist and reporter in this town. Use them."

"I have. This is a story, Mayor, whether we want it to be or not."

"Oh really? What's the story, exactly? What law did I break or oath did I violate?"

"It's not about that," Adrian interjects. "You got elected because people trusted you. They thought you were different. All these accusations are placing that in doubt."

Angelica crosses her arms and lifts her chin. "And you, Adrian? Is your trust in me in doubt?"

"Honestly, I don't know what to think. I...uh..." Adrian hangs his head.

"I see. Is that why you aren't doing your job?"

"Ma'am?"

"You are my eyes and ears in the community and my voice when I can't be there to use my own. I have to wonder if your silence is part of the problem."

"Not at all."

"That's not how it appears. Adrian, if you're unable or unwilling to do your job, don't bother showing up tomorrow. That goes for you too, Katy. Not having a staff is as good as having one that doesn't do their jobs."

"We've done nothing but try to help!" Katy exclaims, her face reddening.

"If that were true, I wouldn't be reading these headlines, would I?"

"I can't control what the media reports!"

"That's not what you told me when I hired you. Either of you. You said you were the best choice because nobody had your connections. You said that people liked you and you would help control stories and shape perceptions. Start proving it or update your resumes."

Angelica studies their faces. They aren't so smug and overconfident now. Both of them made promises during their interviews that ultimately got them hired. The mayor liked their swagger and youthful exuberance. Now it's time for them to back up the words.

"Get out of here. Both of you. I don't want to see you until you're ready to fight with me. If you're not, then I don't want to see you at all."

Angelica watches the pair hurry out of her office. Once they're gone, she plants both hands on her desk to support her weight and hangs her head. That was harder than she thought it would be.

"Well, that sounded like fun. It makes me want to get back into politics."

The mayor's head snaps up as Donna DeForest drops herself into a chair. The political curmudgeon was the last person she expected to see today.

"Next, you're going to tell me that I was too hard on them."

"Hell, woman, that was the most leadership I've seen you display since you were elected. They needed to have their cages rattled."

"They've been loyal until now," Angelica mutters, offering a weak defense.

Donna waves a dismissive hand. "That's because they've had it easy. The media has never attacked you before, and the community holds you in high regard. They're soft, mushy staffers who haven't faced a challenge. Now they're going to find out what it's really like to do their damn jobs."

The political operative digs through her oversized pocketbook and emerges with a pack of cigarettes and a lighter. She sticks the butt of one in her mouth and flips open the Zippo, prompting the mayor to stare at her with a horrified look.

"Put that away! This is a non-smoking building."

Donna frowns. "No wonder everyone is so miserable in today's society. You can't do anything fun."

"What are you doing here?"

"Bingo was canceled," Donna says, earning a disapproving look from the mayor. "You're in a political crisis. I'm here to offer you some pro bono instruction from the school of *been there, done that*."

"I'm not asking for advice this time."

"Yeah, but you should be. I told you that you can either attack or defend. It's a simple choice of two directions. Instead, you stood in the middle of the damned intersection and did neither. Now you're watching the headlights come at you like an idiot."

"What do you expect me to do? You said it yourself. I'm not an attack dog."

"Yes, I'm keenly aware of your chihuahua-ish behavior. Actually, you may be more like a baby deer."

"Okay, I get it."

"No, Angelica, you don't. I checked with some contacts around the city. Andres LaCugna is coming for you. He smells blood in the water and is going to make a move."

"Let him come."

"Ah, brave words said with confidence and conviction. Only you have no teeth to back them up with, Bambi. LaCugna is a snake, but he's also a charmer. While you're sitting on your ass, he's turning the city against you. People who you thought were your friends are hedging their bets in case you don't politically survive this."

"No way. That isn't happening. Not over this!"

Donna shakes her head slowly. "You're a slow learner, aren't you? Your star isn't burning as brightly as his. People like a winner, Angelica. It's the one axiom that transcends party politics in this messed-up world. Right now, you're losing."

Angelica closes her eyes and rubs her temples. She's never had this experience before. She knew that governing a city the size of Phoenix wouldn't be easy but never imagined it would be this hard.

"What should I do?"

"It's not my job to tell you that," Donna says with a chuckle. "I'm only here to prod you to do something. The longer you stand on the sidelines, the further behind you fall. Don't lose the game because you didn't take the field."

"Really? A sports analogy?"

"Yeah, I use them when they fit. Good luck avoiding the hunters, Bambi."

The worst part of having any conversation with Donna DeForest is that the cranky, arrogant old bag is usually right. Angelica has analysis paralysis and needs to pick a course of action. As far as she can see, there is only one avenue that will gain her any ground, and it's not a path she has ever wanted to walk.

CHAPTER SIXTY-SEVEN
DETECTIVE BRESHION HURLEY

MUNICIPAL PARKING GARAGE
PHOENIX, ARIZONA

Breshion has been a cop long enough to remember the endless boredom and lousy food that came with stakeouts. The surveillance age changed those methods, but that's not what this feels like. Lurking near someone's car waiting to pounce is something that a stalker would do. He feels more like a common criminal than a vice detective.

The municipal parking garage serves the public visiting the city center and is where most City Hall staff park. After a quick search of DMV records to find out what his target drives, it becomes a waiting game. Fortunately, he's out of work early today.

Breshion exits his vehicle and quietly closes the door. He moves behind the concrete pillar and patiently waits for his moment. He might as well be standing in plain sight – Adrian isn't paying any attention to his surroundings.

In the history of crime, lack of awareness has gotten more people killed than any other circumstance. The staffer looks stressed out, walking in a gait closer to a perp walk than a busy public servant. If he's distressed before this conversation, just wait.

The detective makes his move. He closes the distance from the pillar to Adrian just as the staffer unlocks his door with the remote. Breshion spins the surprised man around, using his body to keep him pressed against the rear fender of his car.

"You owe me an explanation!" Breshion exclaims, jamming his finger in the man's face.

"What are you talking about?"

"The transfer. The men who ambushed us knew every detail. How?"

"How the hell would I know?" Adrian snaps.

"Because you were the only one outside of the police and prison departments who even knew it was happening."

"Look, I don't know what you want from me, but I'm not in the mood for this."

Adrian starts to slide out of his spot between the detective and the car. Breshion grabs him by the shoulder of his suit jacket and throws him against the vehicle. The aide tries to hand-check him, and his arms are knocked away. The detective jams his forearm into the man's chest and drives him into the car, bending him backward over the trunk. Off-balance, Adrian gives up the fight and uses his hands to steady himself.

"What the hell, man?"

Breshion moves in closer. "I don't give a damn what you are or aren't in the mood for. I want answers, and you're going to give them to me. That, or I'm going to beat them out of you in the middle of this garage. Your choice."

"Is this how the police treat all our citizens?"

"Only a slimy political aide who got two officers killed."

Adrian's face contorts, and he tries to push the detective back. Outweighed and outmuscled, it has no effect.

"I did no such thing!"

"Who did you tell?"

"The mayor and Katy. That's all."

"Don't lie to me," Breshion demands, using his forearm to give the man another shove.

"I'm not! You want answers to what happened, ask the mayor. She was behind closed doors for over an hour after I told her."

"Who was she talking to?"

"Are you deaf? Her door was closed. I don't know. Now, let me go!"

Breshion eases up and lets Adrian stand erect. He grabs the lapels of the suit in case the man has any illusions that this conversation is over.

"Do you think she had something to do with the ambush?"

"No. Well, maybe…I don't know."

"Which is it?"

"Look, she's been acting weird ever since the FBI arrived. Her demeanor changed the day they showed up from Washington."

"Why?"

"I don't know. Horta hasn't said anything to us about it. All I know is that she isn't the same person I went to work for."

"In what way?" Breshion asks, letting the man go now that he's cooperating.

"She's always on edge," Adrian explains. "She just threatened to fire Katy and me because we aren't working hard enough for her. She accused me of being disloyal."

Breshion squints as he studies the staffer. Adrian has no reason to lie, but Angelica Horta has always had a reputation for treating the people around her well. The lack of political baggage or personal scandals is how she coasted to a win. The same couldn't be said of her opponent.

"Are you loyal?"

"That's a stupid question. Of course, but that doesn't mean I don't think the mayor deserves the criticism she's getting. Everything the media has reported about Compass Rose is true. We slapped it together at the last minute."

"How do you know?"

"Because I finished revising the charter the morning of the press conference. Horta only approached Judy Costello and Kevin Demeter to run the thing the day before. The whole thing was finished just in time for the press conference."

"Why so fast?"

"Horta claimed that the FBI showing up was embarrassing after the personnel changes to the PPD. It was an excuse."

"But you don't believe her?"

Adrian shrugs. "Who cares that they showed up? She did what she needed to do to address the rising crime rate. She should have welcomed the feds with open arms. Instead, she panicked."

Breshion rubs his chin. He will never understand why politicians do what they do. Horta may look like a good person, but looks can be deceiving. There must be something more to it. He decides to take a chance.

"What is her relationship with Alejandro Salcido?"

Adrian's brow furrows. "Why?"

"Just asking."

"He's one of the city's biggest campaign contributors."

"To Horta?"

"To everyone. The political class in this city all run in the same circles. He's a major contributor to Lantern House, and the mayor is tight with Costello."

The irony of a possible sex trafficking kingpin contributing to a community non-profit like Lantern House isn't lost on Breshion.

"Could she have called him after you told her about Helio Lozano?"

"She could have been on the phone with the pope for all I know. Why do you care?"

"Someone gave the traffickers every detail about Lozano's transfer. I want to know who."

"You want to know if it was Horta."

"She's near the top of my list, yes."

Adrian shakes his head. "Well, if you're going after her, take a number. The mayor's political enemies are lining up to drag her through the mud, starting with Andres LaCugna. He wants her job and sees a golden opportunity to take her down a couple of pegs."

"Weren't they friends when they were both on the city council?"

"Pssh. Nobody on the council is friends. Politics is a contact sport, even at this level. Horta is a softy who won because she never presented an easy target for an opponent to hit. Now there is one, and she's cracking under pressure."

"All right, thanks." Breshion releases Adrian and starts to walk away.

"That's it?"

"Yeah, unless you have something more to tell me."

"Horta gave the two of us an ultimatum. I'm not even sure I want to work with her anymore, so there won't be more to tell."

Breshion nods. "Be sure you tell me if you do learn something."

This conversation was more interesting than the detective imagined it would be. He walks back to his car, consumed with what could bother the mayor so much that she would threaten her aides. Hanlon's Razor could apply to this situation: Never attribute to malice that which is adequately explained by stupidity. With a politician, even one regarded as benevolent as Angelica Horta, it could go either way.

CHAPTER SIXTY-EIGHT
"BOSTON" HOLLINGER

U.S.-MEXICO BORDER CROSSING
NOGALES, ARIZONA

Border checkpoints are designed to be intimidating. It's a technique to identify people lying to gain entry to cause mischief or engage in illegal activity. As a result, documents are scrutinized and questions asked in a manner that makes people feel uncomfortable. Since I don't care, the immigration official can take his time. After a moment, he stamps my passport and hands it back to me.

"Enjoy your visit to Mexico."

"Thank you," I say, rolling up the Suburban's window. A moment later, I clear the border crossing and enter Nogales.

Historic twin cities, both called "Nogales," straddle the U.S.-Mexican border between Arizona and Sonora. I'm covering the same ground that early Spanish Conquistadors did as the first Europeans who explored western North America. Or so the brochure read, marking the extent of my research before this hasty mission.

Nogales, Mexico is a city of about 200,000 people that caters to the tourist industry. It has restaurants, shopping, and all the sights, colors, and sounds that embody the national character of America's southern neighbor. Visitors can negotiate the prices in English on everything from pottery and glassware to jewelry and handmade crafts in the markets. Not surprisingly, the dollar is the preferred currency.

Of course, the city also has a dark side. It's a major hub in the sex and drug trades, making it violent and dangerous at night when the cartels go to work. I didn't read that in the brochure – that information came from the State Department's travel advisory. The city is safer than the suburbs, for what that's worth.

I planned this excursion just well enough to make it happen. A quick stop at the Copper Star on the way here achieved two things, the first being a change of clothes into something closer to civilian attire. I wasn't about to wear a suit or my FBI windbreaker and stick out more than I do. Fortunately, the bag that Zach packed for me included several clothing options that would help me blend in.

The second part was trickier, as it forced me to break into his room. Getting a key card from the front desk was easy enough. There are still plenty of people willing to help law enforcement in this country, and flashing my badge did the trick. That only left the hotel safe to crack, and I put my training to use in overcoming that obstacle.

The most popular models of room safes have vulnerabilities that I was taught how to exploit. This safe model has an override code of ##000000 which I was hoping the hotel forgot to change during installation. Unfortunately, luck was not on my side, so

I had to do it the hard way. I removed the logo-emblazoned brass cover plate with a screwdriver to reveal the mechanical override. It was a simple cross lock that could be jiggled open with the right tool. An expert picker could have done it in five seconds. It took me close to a minute.

Inside the safe was my passport. The team is carrying theirs, but Forte wasn't about to trust me with mine. That precaution was for good reason because I'm free of Forte and Watchtower. I am in a foreign country that it would be difficult to extricate me from. It's the best I've felt since waking up in that makeshift CIA hospital.

I focus back on driving while trying to orient myself, which is no easy task. This place will not be easy to find, and the clock isn't on my side. It is only a matter of time before the cartels are alerted to my presence. I didn't flash my credentials at the border, but this gas-guzzling beast has federal plates. It wouldn't take any critical thought to figure out whom I work for.

Since I'm alone, the cartels and traffickers may view me as a curiosity and not a threat. Then again, I may be an inviting target for anyone who wants to make a name for himself. It's a coin flip.

This isn't a tourist trip, nor is it official business. I needed Watchtower to know that I was here, and the GPS in the Suburban accomplished that. Now that I am, the hard part is over. The dangerous part has just begun.

CHAPTER SIXTY-NINE

SSA ZACH FORTE

EL BURRO CORRIENDO RESTAURANT
PHOENIX, ARIZONA

The Watchtower team found Hurley's account of his run-in with the mayor's staffer enlightening. It certainly gave the detective and his colleagues in vice a new reason to focus on her. Forte knows that from the beginning, Boston hasn't trusted Horta, and now it may be with good reason. While the PPD starts to throw an investigation together, Forte, Emma, and Nadiya head out for a quick bite while Dr. Kurota heads to the hotel to check on Boston. He isn't answering his phone.

El Burro Corriendo, translated to The Running Donkey, is precisely the kind of restaurant a tourist would expect to see in the desert Southwest. It's Mexican-themed, almost to the point of being a caricature, and serves American interpretations of Mexican dishes. Fortunately, the food is good, the price reasonable, and it's close to Phoenix Police headquarters.

The three agents sit in a booth in a corner as far away as possible from other patrons. The women sip their water, and Zach orders a cola while they eagerly await their orders to tame their grumbling stomachs. Despite the relaxed appearance of the group, Forte can't help but worry about Boston. The women don't seem concerned at all. Sometimes people just need a nap.

"Does vice have what it takes to even investigate the mayor?" Nadiya asks.

"They seem competent enough to me," Forte argues.

"I'm not talking about the cops. Vice specializes in street crime, not political corruption. I'm only questioning whether they should still be leading this."

"She has a point, Zach," Emma concludes. "Politicians may be prostitutes, but they aren't your typical streetwalkers."

"It's not my call. We don't have the evidence to insist on anything. We have a name. We have hearsay and innuendo. That's it."

Neither woman argues. They know he's right, even if they don't like it. Any thoughts of continuing the conversation dissipate as the food arrives and the trio dives in.

Zach only stops when his cell vibrates in his pocket. He pulls it out and grimaces. "Forte."

"You alone?" Matt barks on the other end of the line.

"I'm getting a quick dinner with the team. What's up?"

"The whole team?"

"Yeah, except Boston and the doctor. They're back at the hotel."

"Are you sure about that?"

"Uh…yeah, pretty sure. Why?"

"Because CBP logged him crossing the border at Nogales into Mexico less than a half an hour ago."

Zach drops his fork on the plate. "What? How?"

"How do most people cross an international border? He used his passport."

"Not possible," Zach argues, shaking his head furiously. "His passport is locked in my hotel safe."

Matt sneers. "Not anymore it isn't."

"What is it?" Nadiya asks in a whisper.

Forte presses his lips together out of frustration before speaking. "Boston fled the country."

The two women look at each other. Neither saw that coming.

"Put me on speaker, Zach," Matt orders.

"You're on."

"Boston has made a run for it again. Did either of you two know about this?"

"No," both women answer, indignant at the question.

"How were you alerted?" Forte asks before Nadiya can explode.

"The Suburban's GPS pinged at the border crossing. Watchtower checked with CBP, and Boston's name came up in the system. Instead of leaving our training facility and going to Washington, he left the country where we can't easily get to him."

Zach clenches his teeth and rubs his temples. He questions the immediate rush to judgment based solely on a single past incident. Boston is invested in catching Salcido and is too smart to leave the country in an FBI vehicle if his goal isn't to be found. It's too sloppy and doesn't fit with his character. Convincing Remsen of that is another thing entirely.

"That makes no sense. Think about it, Matt. He knows we'll track the vehicle. Why would he take it if he was running away?"

"Lack of options?"

"He could rent a car," Emma offers.

"Or steal one," Nadiya adds. "Or even hitchhike like last time."

"Look, I know you guys feel you need to defend him, but the best-case scenario is he left the country without authorization."

"Where is he now?" Zach asks.

"Uh…he's parked outside a residence in Nogales, as far as we can tell."

"Which one?" Emma asks.

"The Lozanos," Zach mutters.

Both women stare at him. It's a kind of clairvoyance they usually only see from their trainee. It also makes sense, and if Zach is correct, it's less likely that Boston is running.

"We're checking…the second-floor apartment is listed under Raul and Rosa Lozano."

"Matt, we need to consider an alternative explanation. He may be going after Salcido."

"By going there?"

"It's a good place to start."

"Then I suggest you find a way to get him back across the border. The cartels have half of the Mexican immigration officers on their payroll. There's no doubt that they know Boston is in Nogales and may go looking for him."

"We'll do what we can. What can Watchtower do?"

"We're going to find someone we trust in the *Policía Federal* to find him and drag him back. Let me know what you come up with."

The call unceremoniously disconnects. Zach stares at the device for a long moment before picking up and checking his favorites.

"Call Boston. He isn't going to answer for me."

Nadiya does as instructed and frowns. "It's off."

"Watchtower can reactivate it," Zach offers.

"Boston will either disable it or place it in his Faraday bag," Nadiya concludes.

Forte frowns. A Faraday cage is built using conductive materials that block external electric fields. In simple terms, it's an electronic isolation chamber that prevents electrical signals or waves from passing through it. Each team member was issued a pouch to place their phone in that serves the same function. There's little doubt that Boston is using his.

Zach is about to dial Dr. Kurota when her name pops up on the caller id, and he connects the call. "Let me guess. Boston isn't in his room."

"How did you know?"

"I'll fill you in when we get there. Meet us in the lobby in fifteen minutes."

Nadiya is already paying the bill when Zach finishes with the doctor and gets up from his chair.

"What are we going to do?" Emma asks.

"Check the hotel and see if he got into the safe."

"Then what?"

"Find Boston before he does something stupid and gets himself killed for real this time."

CHAPTER SEVENTY
"BOSTON" HOLLINGER

LOZANO RESIDENCE
NOGALES, SONORA, MEXICO

I stick out like a sore thumb here. The cargo pants and t-shirt I grabbed at the hotel do nothing to mask a gringo driving a black Chevy Suburban. I'm a magnet for every set of eyes in this small city. If I have the attention of the locals, there's no doubt I've also piqued the interest of the cartels.

I pull off the street behind the target house and climb out of the vehicle. It's still hot under the late afternoon sun, not that I expected anything different. There's no sign of activity in the small apartment. Regardless, I ease up the stairs and check the door. It's locked. I pull out my kit and go to work on picking the lock. It's some of the most useful training I received in Virginia and something I'm surprisingly good at. After about ninety seconds, the tension bar turns the lock, and I enter the house.

The pair of bloodstains on the floor betray what happened here. Nothing seems out of place or missing. This was an execution, not a robbery, in case there was any doubt. I holster my weapon. If Alejandro's thugs were here, I'd be dead by now.

The apartment is made up of mismatched furniture but is well-maintained. The Lozanos didn't have much, but they took pride in what they did have. I'm staring at the photos hung on the wall next to some gaudy metal artwork of the sun when a floorboard creaks behind me. My heart skips a beat.

"Move so much as an inch, gringo, and I'll drop you where you stand," the female voice says in heavily accented English.

"You must be Helio's sister," I say, turning my head into my shoulder and easing my hands up in violation of her only command.

"How do you know that?"

"It's a long story."

"Who do you work for?" she demands.

"The U.S. government."

"Bullshit."

"I would show you my credentials, but I don't want to get shot."

I can see her out of the corner of my eye take a step back and take up a firm shooting stance. She doesn't play around.

"Move slowly."

I do as instructed, turning to face her before pulling out my FBI identification, sans the badge, and holding it up for her to see.

"FBI?"

"In a roundabout sort of way."

"You have a gun?"

I cock my head and crinkle my brow. "Duh."

"Give it to me."

I shake my head, causing her to tighten the grip on her weapon. Afraid she'll pull the trigger before asking me again, I remove my Glock from its holster and hold it by the barrel so as not to appear like I want a Western-style shootout.

"Toss it away."

"That's not gonna happen."

"Then you die."

I sigh and take two steps forward, tossing my weapon on the sofa against the wall. I pivot hard and fast, catching her gun and knocking it from her hands. I'm half-surprised that actually worked. Helio's sister swings wildly and misses as I retreat a few steps. She pulls a knife and charges at me. My training with Nadiya is paying dividends. The move feels like it's in slow-motion, and I instinctively know what to do.

I plant a stop-kick into her chest, arresting her forward momentum. She thrusts the knife at me as I slide to the left to make myself a smaller target. I catch her hand, pulling her forward and then jerking her right arm back across my body. She loses her balance and collapses to the ground, opening up a world of possibilities for me to finish her. I don't.

Instead, I rotate and lock her in an armbar, torquing her shoulder to keep her on her knees. I reach down on the sofa and snatch up the Glock, putting its muzzle to her head. The young woman drops the knife and closes her eyes, resigned to her fate. She isn't groveling, nor does she appear to fear death.

"I told you that it wasn't going to happen."

"Do it."

"Nah. I have zero interest in killing you."

I remove the weapon and release her, walking across the room to retrieve her six-shooter. I half expect her to either bolt from the apartment or rush me, but neither happens. I place both weapons on the small kitchen table and take a seat in the rickety chair.

"Please, join me."

"Who are you?"

"Special Agent Smith."

"Yeah, right."

I smirk. "To be honest, I don't like that alias either. My friends call me Boston. What's your name?"

"Sol," the young woman says.

I let out a laugh and gesture at the artwork on the wall behind her. "Sol and Helio. Your parents must have spent a lot of time in the sun."

"You think you're funny?"

"No, not really."

"What are you doing here? Are you looking for me?"

"Did you kill your parents?"

"No," Sol says, clearly offended.

"Then, no, I'm not looking for you. Are you in the family business?" She looks at me weird, so I try again. "Are you a coyote?"

Sol breaks eye contact, and I close my eyes briefly, not getting much from her. The strongest memory is finding her parents dead on the floor. The rest are all buried underneath that, and I don't have that much time to dig for them.

"I do what I have to for the cartels. That's what survival is. Tell me who murdered my parents because it wasn't one of them."

"Take a seat first," I say, sliding a chair out with my foot. *"Por favor."*

"Why should I?"

"Because it will help you understand that you have enemies, but I'm not one of them."

She looks around, clearly unsure what to do. I sit and watch her patiently. My demeanor may appear calm and collected, but I feel neither. If her sneaking up on me has taught me anything, it's that I still have a lot to learn.

"Where are your friends?

"Last I checked, Phoenix."

"You came here alone?"

"Where I'm going, they can't follow," I confess. "My presence here isn't official business…or strictly legal."

Sol takes my offer of the seat. This is more awkward than most of my first dates. She looks around nervously before settling on my eyes. She leans forward and stares at me, pleading with her own.

"Who killed my parents?"

"The same man who likely killed your brother: Alejandro Salcido." Sol goes pale and closes her eyes as she shakes her head slightly. "I see you know the Magic Man."

"Yeah, I know him," she whispers. "He buys cartel protection. How do you know it was him?"

"That's another long story."

"You have a lot of those, *gringo.*"

"You don't know the half of it," I admit, leaning back. "I'm very sorry about your parents, Sol."

"*Gracias.* They were good people. Very honorable. They never approved of the line of work me and my brother went into. They deserved better children. They deserved to die of old age. If you're looking for Salcido, why are you here?"

"I thought he might have left a guy or two here to wait for you. I need to know where to start looking for him."

"You won't find those answers here."

"Clearly. You don't seem gung-ho about avenging their deaths."

"You don't know jack about Mexico, do you?" Sol asks. I shake my head, not able to argue with that. "Salcido is what we call '*intocable*' – untouchable. He's protected by the cartels *and* the police. You'll never get to him. Even if you do, you'll never get out of Mexico alive."

"It wouldn't be the first time that I died."

"Let me guess, another long story?" Sol asks before following it with a mischievous grin, which I reciprocate.

I like this woman. Besides her beauty, she has intelligence and street smarts that accompany her degree from the school of *hard knocks*. Despite having a tough life, she still manages to maintain affability and a sense of humor.

"The longest of them. Trust me on that. Alejandro Salcido has about a dozen different residences in Mexico. Do you know which one I can find him at?"

Sol laughs. "None of them. He only spends time in a house near the water in San Carlos. It's about four hours south of here."

"I don't remember seeing anything in the records we have on him," I admit.

"You won't. Like I said, Alejandro Salcido is well-protected. That includes his anonymity."

"Okay. Thank you for your help, Sol."

"Not so fast, Boston. I'm going with you. You won't last fifteen minutes in Sonora without me. Argue, and we're going to find out who wins a rematch between us."

Was this woman born in the same batch as Nadiya? It's almost like she's channeling her. The only difference is that I've never beaten Nadiya. It takes only a half-second of thought. I could use someone watching my back, and if Sol is volunteering, who am I to argue?

"Let's go. We'll take my vehicle."

"You mean the big black bullet magnet out front? No, thanks. We'll take my car."

"Yeah, it's far more inconspicuous," I say, staring at her early seventies lime-green Dodge Charger.

"It's faster, uses less gas, and most of all, the cartels will know it's me. And before you ask – no, you're not driving."

She smiles, probably for the first time in days, and I smile along with her. Sol has a certain way about her that reminds me of someone I used to know. That someone was equally irresistible.

CHAPTER SEVENTY-ONE
MAYOR ANGELICA HORTA

CITY HALL OFFICE OF THE MAYOR
PHOENIX, ARIZONA

The press conference to announce and respond to two of Phoenix's finest's deaths was an unmitigated disaster. Those things happen, although not to her. Now she is missing her two trusted aides. Regardless of the setbacks, the wheel keeps turning, leaving Angelica no time to do damage control. Her afternoon schedule was busy, and she welcomed the opportunity to get out of her office and back into the community. She wishes she hadn't.

Angelica stares out the window as they travel west down Washington Street after returning from a restaurant opening. Those events are usually a lot of fun. She gets to try a new restaurant while giving new businesses the visibility that comes with having the mayor show up with the media. Their articles and advertisement are gold, except this time.

The owner of the new Italian eatery probably wishes he hadn't extended an invite. The media came armed with more questions about the fallen officers, misguided assaults on her "war against the police department," and something about illegal campaign contributions, which she still doesn't understand. After running that gantlet, she'll be happy to see this day end.

The car ride back to her office is a welcome respite from reality. She zones out, just watching people walking on the sidewalks. The volume of pedestrians increases as the driver approaches City Hall, and they're all heading in that direction. When they reach the block that the building is located on, she can see why.

A large crowd has traffic blocked. The police escort blares their sirens and flashes their lights, but nobody moves. If anything, more people move into the street.

"What's going on?" the mayor asks her driver.

"I don't know, ma'am."

The driver gets on the radio and starts talking to a dispatcher with the Phoenix police. As mayor, she often travels with a small detail of officers, all of whom she loves and respects. They are consummate professionals, and she trusts them with her life.

"I think it's her!" a man shouts after coming up to the window and peering in. He turns back to a group of people watching him and gestures wildly at her car. "Hey! Right here! It's her."

"What the hell is this?" Horta demands from her driver. He looks as baffled as she is.

A milkshake hits the window, obscuring her view. That doesn't mean she can't see out the back window or the one across from her. A crowd gathers around the car, and Angelica jumps when people start pounding on the vehicle.

"Get us out of here!" she commands, her voice cracking.

The mayor isn't one to get shocked or shaken about anything. She isn't startled easily and rarely feels like she is in danger, even in dark places or while jogging alone. This is different. They're a block from City Hall, and she doesn't think they will make it.

The police start pushing people back, though most don't retreat willingly. The mob is in a rage, and it's focused on her. A path is cleared for the driver to inch forward before finding enough of an opening that he can press harder on the accelerator. It takes a couple of minutes to make the typical thirty-second drive. The vehicle lurches to a stop, and a uniformed officer hurriedly opens the door.

"We need to get you inside, ma'am."

"Why? What is this?" Horta asks, looking around.

A large protest has erupted in the public spaces around the municipal building and courthouse across the street and around City Hall itself. Where they all came from is anybody's guess. None of them were here when she departed for her public events.

"I don't know. We need to get you inside. Now!"

The crowd surges across the street toward them. Another wave flows from the left around the building, screaming obscenities. The police jump in front of the tide of humanity but only serve as breakwaters. There isn't enough manpower here to stop them.

The mayor is being pushed toward City Hall's entrance when she's hit in the head by a hard object. Doubling over, she sees batteries landing on the ground at her feet. The officer and her driver take her arms and hustle her into the building. She looks back from the foyer as officers dressed in riot gear fire tear gas at the crowd. The sight is sickening, but she has to trust that they know what they're doing.

Horta is brought directly to the elevator. Even the lobby of the building isn't safe.

"Are you okay, ma'am?"

"I think so. What is this?"

"It's some sort of anti-government protest," the officer confesses as they ascend to the floor that houses her office.

"How did they get a permit?"

"One wasn't issued. We got wind of it on social media. Nobody expected it to be this large or aggressive."

"Clearly. What are they mad at?"

"Not what, who. They're angry at *you*, Madam Mayor."

CHAPTER SEVENTY-TWO
SSA ZACH FORTE

COPPER STAR HOTEL & SUITES
PHOENIX, ARIZONA

Asami meets the team as they charge into the hotel lobby after parking in the loading zone. They ride the elevator up to Zach's floor in silence and enter the room behind him.

The team watches as the senior agent moves over to the cheap armoire where the safe is held and punches in the code he selected. He opens it and stares inside before sighing and reaching in to retrieve its only content. He turns and holds out his hand, showing the three women the gold FBI badge.

"We're wrong. Boston's running."

"Do you always default to the worst-case scenario?" Nadiya asks. "We've been through this already."

Emma crosses her arms. "You know what your problem is, Zach?"

"I only have one?"

"You never trust Boston."

"Really, Emma? Look around you. We're only here because I trust him."

"No, we're here because you wanted to show Boston that he could use his gift for good," Dr. Kurota chimes in. "To make a difference in this shit world we live in."

"Trust has nothing to do with this. Not anymore," Zach says, holding the badge up.

"It has everything to do with this," Nadiya says.

"Think about it, Zach. If you were going on an unofficial operation in a foreign country, would you bring that? I know I wouldn't."

Zach stares down at the badge in his hand. Emma has a point, but right now, he's not sure of anything. Is this a message, or does Boston want him to think it's one just to prove a point? The latter is something that he's plenty capable of doing.

Nadiya is spot-on – this does have to do with trust, and Zach just demonstrated he has none. His first thoughts about Boston are always the worst ones. But he is quick to change his mind about the man's intentions, even now.

Forte looks at the doctor. "Asami?"

"I don't know. Boston resents his circumstances and values freedom, but I don't know if he's mentally ready to leave unfinished business with Adelmo and the other children. It's a coin flip."

"If Boston wanted to break free of us, he would have done it when we first got here," Emma argues.

"In the dead of night where he could be hours away before anyone noticed. He's left an awful lot of clues for someone who doesn't want to be found," Nadiya adds.

Zach's cell rings with the call he's been expecting. "You're on speaker. What's up, Matt?"

"We have some Mexican Federales scouring Nogales to find Boston. We can't turn his phone on remotely. The Suburban hasn't moved from the last known location, and the analysts believe he's still there. We're tasking a satellite for coverage. Any news on your front?"

Nadiya and Emma shake their heads. Forte can't outright lie to his boss, and there is no way to shade the truth. Matt needs to know what they've learned.

"We found his badge in my safe, and his passport is missing."

"Then that's it. He quit the team and is running."

"That's not the consensus here. We can't get to Alejandro Salcido while he's in Mexico. Any investigation into him would take years and may never uncover enough evidence to bring him to justice."

"What are you saying?"

"I think Boston is going after him."

"That's crazy!" Matt exclaims on the other end of the line with enough volume that everyone recoils from Zach's phone. "It's against the rules."

"Boston knows how many we're willing to break when it serves our purposes. He learned those lessons and is using them himself."

"He's a malfunctioning weapon. That's what he is."

Forte has heard enough. Matt may have the best of intentions, but he's missing the larger point: This is not a Jason Bourne movie. The women are right – they are viewing Boston all wrong.

"He's a human being, Matt, not some rifle you pull out of the gun safe and return when you're done shooting."

"That's not what I meant. It's just that we have invested—"

"You want the investment to pay off. I get it. Why else have we lied to him and kept him locked away in the backwoods of Virginia? Boston needs to be treated like a teammate, not a Watchtower asset only called upon when it's convenient or necessary."

The three women raise their eyebrows and take turns looking at each other. They've never seen this side of Forte before. Neither has he, and it's something Zach has finally realized is a part of the problem. Matt is micromanaging from two thousand miles away. That is going to stop right now.

"You're getting close to insubordination, Zach."

"Then fire me. We are going to start doing this my way, or not at all. Decide."

There's a long pause on the other end of the line. Matt might actually be thinking about it.

"Fine. What do you want?"

"Whatever I ask for, and you'll do it without question. If I want an armored tank division, the first words out of your mouth will be, 'Do you want air support with that?'"

"There are limits to what Watchtower can do," Matt moans.

"Then we're about to test them. I'll be in touch."

Zach ends the call and looks up at the three women.

"That was almost a turn-on," Nadiya says.

"So, what's the plan?" Emma asks impatiently.

"We need to confirm what Boston's intentions are. Then we need a plan to get him the hell out of there, whatever his play is."

"Okay, how will we do that?"

Zach rubs his chin. They could go in covertly, but if Boston is going after Salcido, whatever he does isn't likely to be subtle. That will pose all kinds of problems and may make for an international incident if they don't handle this carefully.

"I don't know, but I have a feeling that helicopters and automatic weapons will be involved."

CHAPTER SEVENTY-THREE

ALEJANDRO SALCIDO

SALCIDO MEXICAN RESIDENCE
SAN CARLOS NUEVO GUAYMAS, SONORA, MEXICO

Alejandro was tired of this call long before his bodyguard materialized in the doorway leading to the veranda to the kitchen. The big man nods, and the trafficker knows it's time to end this conversation. It has gone on for far too long anyway.

"Okay, I've heard enough from you," he shouts into the untraceable prepaid cell phone. "Now it's time for you to listen. I've poured hundreds of thousands of dollars into your campaign, and Lord knows how much into your personal accounts. The details on one police transfer hardly begin to repay that."

"That's not—"

"We have an agreement that I expect you to deliver on," he says, speeding up the delivery before the politician can finish interrupting him. "I don't care what you have to do. The time has come for you to make my investment in you pay off. Until it does, don't contact me again."

Alejandro ends the call and powers down the phone. He signals his bodyguard and sets the phone on a shelf in the corner bar. Jai Snyder is shown onto the veranda.

"*Buenas noches, Señor Salcido.*"

"*Buenas noches.* I apologize for keeping you waiting," he says, moving around the bar to shake the man's hand.

"No apology necessary. I appreciate your taking the time to meet with me. Is everything okay?"

Salcido waves a dismissive hand. "I hate politicians."

"Don't we all? I have to deal with them all the time. Is one causing you a problem?"

"No, it's just some unfinished business in the States. Again, my apologies."

"You have a reputation that precedes you, as a hard worker. I expect nothing less from a man who never takes a vacation, regardless of how this visit to Mexico is being portrayed."

Salcido smirks. "It seems like you're well-informed."

"I wouldn't be good at my job if I weren't. I know why you left Arizona."

"And you think that somehow changes our negotiation?"

"Yes, it does," Jai admits. "Just not in the way that you think."

Alejandro gestures his guest toward the sofa and moves to the bar to pour a couple of tequilas. Jai is an intelligent man and a natural salesman. It's anyone's guess why he chose to work for an NGO instead of embarking on a lucrative career as a stockbroker on Wall Street. Not that Salcido would trust him more if he were one. Maybe less.

"The next question would naturally be what you assume I'm thinking."

"What my thoughts would be if our roles were reversed: that I'm looking to take advantage of your circumstances because you have no better option. It would be an erroneous course of action."

"I agree," Alejandro mutters. "Then how does it change our negotiation? Price?"

Jai shakes his head as the tequilas are poured. "No, my original offer still stands."

"Then I don't understand."

"First things first. I understand that your men inspected my first delivery. What were their impressions?"

"It was a good start," Alejandro begrudgingly admits.

"*Señor Salcido*, we are way beyond games and ruses. If your supply chain is capable of producing a better product, I'm happy to finish my drink and bid you *adios*."

"They were high quality. That was the feedback."

Jai nods. "Value for the price. Wouldn't you agree?"

"Your price is higher than I would have expected."

"That's true, but your operational costs will go down, and so will your risk. The latter is probably more important right now. You will see your bottom line increase while reducing your exposure. It's a win-win."

"And what do *you* get?"

Jai sips his tequila and leans forward. "Access to your distribution network."

Alejandro is a naturally suspicious man. People in this world are inherently selfish and never do things out of kindness. Snyder's deal falls into that category because it's too good. There must be an angle.

"You mentioned that this changes our negotiation. How?"

"Simple. I want to be your sole supplier. You will maintain the stash houses and handle all client transactions north of the border. I will provide you product and handle their transit to you."

Alejandro pouts. There it is. "You realize that I would be placing the health of my entire business in your hands."

Salcido runs his sex-trafficking operation like a business because it is one. They both rely on supply chains, distribution, customer service, accounting, and human resources. Most companies diversify their vendors to avoid a calamity. If Alejandro agrees to this with Jai and dismantles his smuggling operation, rebuilding the network could take a year or more if this relationship goes south.

"I know you look at this as a risk. Allow me to be your exclusive provider for a year. If you like what you see, we can discuss an extension following that. It allows you to cool the FBI investigation while still servicing the needs of your clients. After that year, if you wish to diversify, I won't complain. It will give you time to realize that there's no need."

"Unless you get caught."

"I won't. My organization is above reproach, as is my reputation. Like you, I have built a safety net in Mexico. The government, cartels, and police are all covered."

"Unless you run afoul of the Americans."

"They have no jurisdiction here, and there is no political will to allow the U.S. to solve Mexico's problems when they are inept at solving their own. I'm protected against everyone who matters."

It's a song he has heard sung many times before. You don't live in his world without hearing countless charlatans sing those lyrics, only to discover they're dead or imprisoned a year later. He believes himself to be bulletproof, but only because he's careful. He needs to know whether Jai is as cautious as he is before continuing.

"I agree to your deal in principle."

"Then let's drink on it," Jai says, holding his glass up before both men swallow the liquid.

"The chef is hard at work. Let me pour us some more tequila, and we can talk about all the details before dinner."

CHAPTER SEVENTY-FOUR
"BOSTON" HOLLINGER

APPROACHING THE SAN CARLOS WATERFRONT
SAN CARLOS NUEVO GUAYMAS, SONORA, MEXICO

I stare out the window at the vast emptiness of a dark, barren desert. I can't get over how different this feels. Northern Mexico may not look vastly different than the Southwest United States, but it has a different feel. I've never been much of a traveler, assuming the Caribbean doesn't count. This would be a treat if I thought there was a good chance I would make it out of this country alive.

"You're quiet," Sol says after turning down the radio.

"I was thinking that this must be the loneliest road in the world."

"There isn't much to see between towns and cities on this highway."

I nod in the darkness. "It's peaceful."

"Don't let the stillness of the night fool you. Sonora is the cartels' back yard. There has been a turf battle going on for decades. Even the police have given up."

"It's safer for them to do nothing," I moan.

"And most of them do. None of that explains why you're here...alone."

"All government travel is banned points south of Federal Highway 16 and east of Highway 15. That includes Guaymas."

"And yet you're here. Is that why you left your team in Arizona?"

"It's more complicated than that."

"So you've said. All I know is that you're one crazy *gringo*."

I chuckle and shake my head with amusement. "I have a very motherly doctor who would agree with you."

"I want you to be honest. Why are you doing this?"

Part of me wants to tell her everything, but with only another half hour of driving to reach Guaymas, I don't think I would put a dent in her understanding of everything I have been through or what I can do. I trust her, but I'm not sure it's that much. I choose to keep it narrowed down to motivation.

"Adelmo."

"Adelmo? Is that a person or place?"

"He's a child," I say, adjusting myself in her seat and settling back in. "A few weeks ago, the Phoenix Police conducted a raid on one of Salcido's stash houses. They were trying to take down someone in his network to identify the kingpin, but none of the scumbags there were taken alive. Adelmo was one of a dozen drugged and scared children they found hidden in the cellar. I talked to him at the hospital a few times since."

Sol nods. "You're taking this personally."

"More than you could know," I mumble.

"Is it worth your life, Boston? Because if you storm into Alejandro Salcido's house, that's what it's going to cost you. Are you trying to be a hero?"

It's a legitimate question. It's also deja vu. It's not about being a hero – it's about justice. I did that once before with Gina, and this journey is the result. I'm hoping it works out better this time, but the odds are not in my favor.

"I was a soldier before all this. The best ones don't go into a combat situation with delusions of grandeur. They don't worry or even think about themselves. It's about the men next to them, which is why so many are willing to sacrifice themselves. Nothing in the world is more heroic than that."

"And you're willing to sacrifice yourself?"

"If that's the price to ensure Alejandro Salcido can never do to another child what I've seen him do to kids like Adelmo...yes, I am."

Sol slowly nods in understanding as we enter the small city. It's dimly illuminated, and I can smell the sea from here. She angles the car toward the coastline five minutes later before pulling over along the curb and shifting into park.

"Is this it?" I ask.

"No," she says, pointing out at the view beyond the windshield. "See that house on the corner? That's it."

"Do you know anything about the layout or security?"

"I've never been inside. I just know where it is. What do you need me to do?"

There may be nobody on Earth who wants to see Salcido planted in the ground more than I do – except her. He's responsible for the murder of her parents and likely her brother. This is her fight as much as mine, if not more so. That doesn't mean I want her to charge in there at my side.

"Yeah. Leave this city and don't look back."

"I'm going to help you," Sol insists.

"No, you're not. Head back north and pretend that you never met me."

Sol shakes her head, babbling something in Spanish. "I'm involved. The cartels will know that I helped you. It's the only reason I would come this far south."

"Then leave the cartel and leave Mexico."

"I'm helping. That's the end of it."

The advantage of a long, quiet car ride is that I could finally access some of her memories. Most of them lingered on her parents. One, in particular, was very emotional for her.

"No, you aren't," I say, taking her hand. "When you were a girl, you got in trouble for something. Your father sat you down and told you that, when he was gone, you and your brother would be all that's left to carry on the family traditions. He said that he would live on through you and your brother. Helio is dead. *El sol siempre brillará a través de ti.*"

"The sun will always shine on through you… How could you possibly know that?" Sol asks, astonished.

"It's one of life's mysteries. You will not honor your parents by dying today. You are their legacy. Go live your life the way they intended for you. That's how you avenge their deaths. I will take care of the rest."

Tears roll down her cheeks, just like in the memory of her as a little girl. "Will I ever see you again?"

"Someday."

I offer her a slight smile and leave the vehicle before stopping to give her a little wave. True to her word, she makes a left at the intersection and starts her journey out of the city. A better life is in store for that young woman. I hope she seizes it.

I take a deep breath and exhale. This is a stupid idea. With that thought, I head down the hill toward the house on the water. My stomach churns in my gut with an all-too-familiar feeling.

CHAPTER SEVENTY-FIVE
DETECTIVE BRESHION HURLEY

Breshion leaves the conference room to do some research at his desk computer. He spends too much time at it for his tastes, but the hours he's invested in the conference room have him missing it. No sooner does he log in than his desk phone rings.

"Detective Hurley."

"It's Forte."

"About time you checked in. Where the hell are you guys? We've uncovered some interesting information here. We think that Angelica Horta has been accepting contributions from Salcido through her political action committee."

"That's going to have to wait, Detective. We have a more pressing situation."

"What kind of situation?"

Forte launches into an explanation about how Agent Smith crossed the border and visited Helio Lozano's parents' home. He's sparse on the details. There's no doubt that the senior agent is leaving out chunks of the story. It ends with the shocking conclusion about why he's in Mexico.

"That's the craziest thing I've ever heard. If your man is going there to arrest Salcido, what's the charge?"

"I don't think slapping on handcuffs is what Smith has in mind."

The revelation causes Breshion to sit up straighter. "You can't be serious."

"Unfortunately, I am."

"Where is he now?"

"We don't know. Our colleagues in Washington think that there's a possibility he's traveling south with a woman. Her car was out front of the Lozanos' house, and now it's missing."

"A woman?"

"Helio Lozano's sister. We don't know much about her, but my team in Washington thinks she may run with one of the cartels."

"Given her brother's chosen occupation, there's a high probability of that. Do you think she'd know where Salcido is?"

"Your guess is as good as mine."

The detective leans back in his chair. He's leery of Smith and his motives but admires the guy. He gets things done, even if it's not expressly legal.

"I don't think I need to tell you—"

"You don't. We know the implications and can only guess the consequences. That's for later. Right now, I'm worried about getting Will out of there."

"Agent Forte, Sonora is cartel central. Every one of Salcido's known residences is a stronghold, and you don't even know which one he's at."

"I know the challenges. We have to try."

Breshion understands loyalty. He would be acting the same way if it were one of his detectives in danger.

"Good luck. Understand that the cartels have almost unlimited manpower. They'll know you're coming, ambush you, and the police will stand by and watch. If you cross the border with anything less than an army, you could end up as dead as Smith will."

"Then that's what we'll bring. We'll be in touch."

Breshion hangs up and sees Jamecca staring down at him.

"Good luck with what?"

The detective relays what he learned about Agent Smith's journey south and the FBI's concern about what he's doing. Jamecca doesn't look surprised.

"Where are they going?"

"I don't know. Forte didn't say. Why does it matter?"

"Because I want to help them."

"There's no need. It's an FBI problem, and they can handle it."

Jamecca crosses her arms. "What the hell is wrong with you?"

Breshion looks around the room. There are only a few uniformed officers here, and none of them are paying the duo any attention. That's a good thing. She is acting more like an angry wife than a partner.

"It sounds like you're about to tell me."

"We wouldn't be where we are without Agent Smith and the FBI. We wouldn't be looking at Salcido or contemplating that someone in the city government could be working with him. We owe it—"

"We don't owe them a damn thing. The feds are here to assist us."

"And I want to help them."

"No. I don't want you anywhere near whatever operation they might have planned. I don't want you, me, or this department associated with anything Agent Smith does down there."

"Is that an order?"

Jamecca's tone makes the question more like an accusation. Since the moment they started their relationship, he always feared there would be a day when their personal feelings might interfere with their professionalism. Today might be that day.

"Don't be like that. This has nothing to do with us. Agent Smith's foray into Sonora is extralegal. So is any rescue or extraction mission."

"You don't have any idea what they're doing. It's the federal government. If anyone can secure permission from Mexico, it's them."

"That's right. Them, not us."

"We should know what their plans are. Someone should be acting as a liaison."

"No. I won't agree to this. If you want to take it to Jada, be my guest. She'll tell you the same thing."

"Fine."

Jamecca walks away, heading in the direction of the stairs. For a second, he thinks she might be disobeying an order. She wouldn't be that irrational, or would she?

"Where are you going?"

"Out," she shouts over her shoulder. "It's the one thing I don't need your permission for."

That did get the attention of the other men in the room. Breshion doesn't make a fuss or go after her. He treats it like any two partners having an argument about a case. He can only hope that's all this is.

CHAPTER SEVENTY-SIX

MAYOR ANGELICA HORTA

CITY HALL OFFICE OF THE MAYOR
PHOENIX, ARIZONA

Horta rubs her temples. There are stressful days, and then there are ones like this. Everyone is abandoning her. Friends and allies she has counted on for years have turned on her in the name of political expediency. She is the Hester Prynne of Phoenix, forced to wear the scarlet letter the media has given her.

"Hello, Madam Mayor," Katy says after a gentle rap on the door jamb.

"Hi, Katy. Where's Adrian?"

Her aide looks down at her shoes, rocking back and forth slightly. "He's not coming."

The throbbing intensifies as Angelica leans back and closes her eyes. That's not what she was expecting. Despite the ultimatum, she never once thought Adrian would abandon her. Not now.

"Well, he made his decision. I guess I know where his loyalties lie."

"No, you don't," Katy says in a stern tone.

"Excuse me?"

"Adrian has been nothing but loyal to you."

"He has a funny way of showing it," Angelica snaps.

"And so do you."

"Okay, I guess we need to clear the air between us. What's your problem?"

"*My* problem? Are you listening to yourself? What happened to you, Angelica?"

The mayor feels the surge in her blood pressure. She has never enforced protocol, and her aides typically use her given name outside the office. In here, it's the first time that Katy has ever not called her either "mayor" or "ma'am."

"What do you mean?"

"I went to work for you because you were different. Now you're turning into the same old business-as-usual corrupt politician that you ran against. Why? I want to know."

Angelica rises from her chair and leans over her desk. "First, you went to work for me because nobody else would hire you. Do you want to know why? You're soft, just like the rest of your generation. You won't do what's necessary because you don't know how. You just want to be liked, some teenage girl running for prom queen."

"Wow. I—"

"I'm not done. Second, you aren't the mayor of this city. If you were, you would understand what I'm facing. I would love nothing more than to work with other elected officials to solve problems, but that's not how politics works, even if it's how it should.

Sometimes you have to play hardball, and you need a staff that understands how to do it."

"You've been spending a lot of time talking to Donna, haven't you?"

"That's not what this is about. It's about the media, the protests, and underhanded slimeballs like Andres LaCugna making everything political."

"Where do you think all that criticism is coming from? You're getting bad advice, plain and simple. Donna is the perfect example of everything that's wrong with this country. She's a political hammer, and we're all nails. That's her archaic and jaded view of the world."

"It's an effective one. Had I listened to her earlier, I wouldn't be in this mess. She's teaching me to navigate these waters and how to protect myself."

"From what?"

"That."

The mayor walks over and points to the protest continuing to grow outside the window below. She's under no illusion that this is some spontaneous grassroots assembly of citizens with a legitimate gripe. It's manufactured outrage propagated by her political opponents, and it's working.

"You're wrong. Do you want to know the real reason those people are angry?"

"Sure, please, since you think you have all the answers, enlighten me."

Katy takes a couple of steps closer and meets her gaze across the desk. "They think you're a charlatan who sold them on a woman-of-the-people routine and then got addicted to power the moment you had it."

"Is that what you think is going on here?"

"It's not an original story. I'm sure Donna already told you that."

"I asked you a question. Is that what you think?"

"I think that you're a hypocrite. You've become the thing that you claimed to despise – a slimy politician who puts her own interests in front of the people."

Angelica nods slowly at the slight. She doubts that little naïve Katy will ever see the big picture. The mayor shouldn't have to explain, and taking the time to do so to her foolish media rep would be a waste of breath. Some people just don't get it and never will.

"I'm sorry you feel that way, Katy, because you couldn't be more wrong. But since you do, you're fired. Now get the hell out of my office."

"Gladly."

Katy storms out, slamming the door as she retreats through it. The bang it causes aggravates Angelica's headache more than the brief conversation with her former staffer did. She eases herself back into the chair.

The phone isn't ringing. While her admin sits on the other side of the door, she is about the only person who wants to be anywhere near this office, literally and metaphorically. Angelica is on a remote island surrounded by sharks. This is her fight now, and hers alone.

CHAPTER SEVENTY-SEVEN
"BOSTON" HOLLINGER

SALCIDO MEXICAN RESIDENCE
SAN CARLOS NUEVO GUAYMAS, SONORA, MEXICO

I casually stroll past the front of the house to see if I can notice anything unusual. It's still, just like the rest of this wealthy neighborhood at this late hour. The house isn't large by American standards, nor is it inappropriately ornate. It's a two-story structure that mixes traditional and modern elements, likely with several bedrooms upstairs and the usual common area spaces on the first level.

There is no sign of any guards. That's interesting. I walk down to the intersection and head up the road that opens to four lanes farther east. Lights in the covered veranda attached to the back of the house are on. The raised deck allows for an almost unobstructed view of the marina to my left. It also offers a modicum of privacy for whoever is on it. That makes sense.

I stop to tie my shoe and I hear voices. Sure enough, Salcido is awake, and from the sounds of it, he has company. I cross the street and scope out the closed shops. Content that I have the lay of the land, I circle back and spend another ten minutes watching the front. Not only is the house unguarded, but there's no sign of video surveillance anywhere. That's odd. I expected there to be at least a few cameras watching the approaches and entrances.

Doubt starts to creep into my mind. What if this is the wrong place? What if it's a trap? I have no reason to think that Sol is deceiving me. Salcido killed her entire family, and no allegiance to a cartel would be powerful enough to ignore that fact. Still, going in with guns blazing isn't the most prudent option. I don't want to be wrong and shoot innocent people.

There are no good options for this, so I choose the simplest. I walk directly up to the front door and quietly stand in the covered entrance. There could be hidden cameras or other methods to let the sex trafficker know that an intruder lurks in the shadows. Five minutes later, nothing has happened. Growing bolder, I check the doorknob. It's locked.

I reach into my cargo pocket and pull out a pick set. It takes years of practice to get good at this, or so my instructor warned me. He also said that very few locks are unpickable if you know all the methods to defeat them. That's the key, so to speak: recognizing the type of lock and selecting the proper tools. Fortunately, both the deadbolt and door lock are standard residential-grade hardware. My instructor could probably open this in a matter of seconds. I hope to finish it before sunrise.

I insert a turning tool in the bottom of the keyway and use the medium hook to push the pins up as I slide it deeper into the lock. This was easier in the classroom. After about seven minutes, I manage to slide the bolt back with a satisfying click. If a Hollywood movie is ever made about my life, they will need to speed this scene up. I go to work on the door, and it takes almost as long. With both locks disengaged, I turn the handle and ease the front door open.

The house is dark, outside of a single light in the kitchen and the fully lit veranda. The muffled sounds of a Spanish-language television show echo from a room down the short hallway off the foyer. It could be a study or cigar room of some sort. Someone else is here, after all.

I move into the foyer when I hear the hall door swing open, allowing the television's sound to fill the empty hallway. I sidle up to the foyer wall and cozy up to a bust of someone I wouldn't recognize, even if the space was brightly lit. I ready myself for someone to emerge from the hall. A second goes by…then another. Nothing.

The television drowns out all other noise despite me closing my eyes and listening intently. The volume hasn't changed, so the door is still open. The man is either doing the same thing I am or quietly moving down the hall. Fighting the urge to peek, I patiently wait until I see a massive chest edge out from the hallway. That answers that question.

I form a knife-edge with my hand, making it slightly concave to give it more rigidity. There's only going to be one chance I get at this. I swing my arm out violently and strike the man in the throat. It's like hitting a tree trunk. He lets out a yelp and nothing more. I spin from the wall to face him and drive the heel of my hand into his solar plexus. The move knocks the wind out of him, but he otherwise doesn't move. This man is built like a tractor.

The beast is gasping for air and can't sound the alarm by shouting to his master, so I try to anticipate what he'll do next. It needs to be loud and jarring. I start moving my left hand toward the bust perched on the pedestal. It gives me just enough time to catch his before he can push it over. I grab his wrist and turn his arm before crashing my triceps down on his elbow, snapping his arm in two. The satisfying crack yields another yelp of pain. I did more damage to the man's larynx than I thought.

His left hand reaches behind his back. He's armed, and I'm surprised he didn't have his gun out if he thought there might be trouble. If he gets a shot off, even if it misses, the game is over. His arm thrusts forward, the back of his hand facing up with the gun horizontal.

If he plans on shooting me gangster-style, it's a mistake. I crash my forearm down on his wrist, causing him to drop the weapon. I can see his eyes open wide in surprise. He wildly punches with his left, and I duck. He expects me to counter, but instead, I reach up and lock his throat in a Ranger chokehold. I tighten my grip with the fingers of my right hand to clamp down on the big man's windpipe and carotid arteries while reinforcing it with my left. I keep an eye on his arms to ensure he isn't going for another weapon. So far, he hasn't.

There are a dozen ways to defeat this, so I think about transitioning to a rear choke with more leverage and using my forearm to press against his thick neck. It doesn't look like it'll be necessary. His powerful arms beat on mine, but there isn't much force behind the blows. Thank God. One good shot would release the pressure, and full alertness will be regained within ten seconds. I can attest to that personally, thanks to Nadiya.

I squeeze his throat with all my might. It takes thirty-three pounds of pressure to close off a trachea. With this guy, it may be more. I have no idea how much I'm applying.

The man's legs wobble and then give out, and he slides down the wall. I keep the hold in place. Brain death will occur in four to five minutes. I hold it another minute longer than that, keenly listening for any change to the conversation outside or movement in the kitchen.

The job done, I release the man's throat and secure his weapon. I eject the magazine to ensure it's loaded and do a press check to ensure a round is chambered. It's ready for action, so I creep stealthily around to see if he has any friends who'll miss him. The ground floor is empty.

I could check the upstairs, but the clock is ticking, and it's time to get down to business. I move toward the kitchen, stopping short of the lit area. The two men chat amiably outside, oblivious to the struggle in the foyer. I have the drop on them, provided another bodyguard isn't watching over their meeting.

There is only one thing left to do before interrupting their soirée. I close my eyes and settle my mind, which proves easier than quieting my thumping heart. The show starts immediately, and the memories that flood into my head are horrifying.

CHAPTER SEVENTY-EIGHT
ALEJANDRO SALCIDO

SALCIDO'S MEXICAN ESTATE
SAN CARLOS NUEVO GUAYMAS, SONORA, MEXICO

This has gone far better than Alejandro expected. Jai's terms are acceptable and maybe even generous when considering that the NGO representative knows the bind Alejandro is in. Opportunists would seek to take advantage; valued business partners offer solutions to bad circumstances. He is either the latter or excellent at disguising being the former.

"We should celebrate with another drink," Jai says, clearly enjoying the high-end tequila that Alejandro serves his rare guests at this hideaway.

Alejandro moves to the bar situated in the corner of the airy veranda to find precious little of the flavorful liquid left in the bottle. He holds up the empty vessel.

"I will have my bodyguard fetch us another bottle."

"He can't. He's indisposed."

They both jump at the perfectly enunciated English as a man dressed in cargo pants and a T-shirt walks out onto the veranda from the kitchen, a Glock pointed at Alejandro's chest. Jai jumps up and gawks at the intruder while his host freezes in place, still holding the empty tequila bottle. His thought of using it as a weapon or a distraction to reach his own gun is quickly dismissed.

"Who the hell are you?" Alejandro snaps, the shock wearing off.

"Someone you didn't count on, Magic Man."

Alejandro grins and sets the bottle down slowly. "That likely makes you FBI. You're a long way from home."

"So I've noticed. Sit. Both of you."

Jai looks like he's going to piss himself as he crashes down on the sofa. Alejandro moves slowly and takes his seat on the opposite one, almost looking bored by the exercise. He rests one arm atop the back cushions with his other hand in his lap.

"I would offer you a drink, but we're out, and I doubt you'd accept. Instead, let me congratulate you on finding me. Very few people know about this place."

"Until now," the mysterious man says.

"Yes, that's true. And then you managed to sneak in. It's impressive and likely one of your last acts on this Earth."

Alejandro studies the man. He comes across as sure of himself, almost to the point of arrogance, but there is something off about him – a hidden nervousness buried deep beneath the veneer of confidence.

"For a man with a gun pointed at his chest, you're bristling with confidence."

"This isn't the first time I've had a gun pointed at me," Salcido says. "Each time, it was by men more dangerous than you are."

"Are you sure about that?"

Alejandro smirks. "You are American law enforcement. I pose no threat to you, so you have no reason to shoot me. If you're here to whisk me out of Mexico and arrest me in the United States, I'm afraid you've misinterpreted the situation."

The man cocks his head, offering a grin of his own. "Oh? What makes you think that?"

"I don't care how many people on your team are here. You will never make it out of the city. You likely won't make it out of this house. Speaking of which? Where is your team? They sent you up here to detain me by yourself? Perhaps you are Eliot Ness reincarnated."

"Ness worked for the Bureau of Prohibition in the Treasury Department," the man with the gun deadpans.

"I didn't know that. Then again, I shouldn't be expected to know much about American history."

"Who's your friend, Alejandro?"

"This is Jai Snyder. He's a legend in Mexico and Central America. His organization helps ensure the safety of migrant convoys as they embark on their harrowing trip north. He is…who is a good comparison? The Latin Mother Teresa."

"Look, I don't know why you're here, but I have nothing to do with any of this. I help people," Jai pleads, his voice high as he fights his panic. Clearly, the man doesn't have the stomach for this.

"It's okay, Jai. He's here for me, not you."

The man closes his eyes. Alejandro thinks that he may be concentrating or listening to voices in his earpiece. He thinks about making for his gun stashed on the opposite end table, but he knows he won't make it. The temptation to make a run and tackle him is also dismissed. Alejandro isn't that quick, and his best fighting days are behind him. It could also be a trap, and what this mysterious man wants him to do.

"Are you sleepy, Mr. FBI-man?" Salcido says with a short laugh after the man's eyes open. "Maybe you should have taken a nap before coming here."

"You've been in the sex trade business a long time, Mr. Snyder," the man says. "I would say that you should be ashamed of yourself, but you have no shame. Tell me, do you rape all of the women you kidnap, or just when you feel the urge?"

"I, uh…none of that is true!"

"Yes, it is.

"You're here to expand your empire. You only want to do this for a few more years, so you're looking for a big payday. That's why you're here, right? To strike a deal with the Magic Man. Does he know you plan on betraying him?"

"Turning us against each other won't work, so save your breath," Alejandro interjects. "This is a simple business meeting to see how I can help the less fortunate find a better life in the United States. Nobody is better at that than Jai and his organization."

"Says the man who says I won't get out of this house or city alive."

Salcido laughs and wags a finger at the man. "You're good…very good. Maybe not so sleepy after all. I'll tell you what. I like you, so I'll give you a fighting chance. See, I think you're here alone. Perhaps this is a suicide mission, but it doesn't have to be that way. Leave now, and I'll give you a fifteen-minute head start."

The agent nods like he's contemplating the decision. He checks the entryway to the kitchen. The allure of a hasty escape must be tantalizing. He's a dead man regardless of what he decides to do, not that he knows that. The man's fate was sealed the moment he entered the house. That might have been the case the moment he entered Mexico. Still, Alejandro thinks that a little more encouragement might do the trick.

"Go ahead, Agent Sleepyhead, run. Run fast. The clock's ticking. Is your allegiance to the FBI worth your life? It's your choice."

The man grins instead of beating feet off the veranda. He swings his gun over at Alejandro's guest, who stares at him through wide eyes. Jai opens his mouth to plead a fraction of a second before the weapon burps, and a single, nickel-sized hole appears in his forehead. The entry wound is clean, but the back of Jai's head is now splattered all over Alejandro's veranda.

The trafficker stands, freezing in place only when the weapon is trained on him. The smile disappears from Alejandro's face. A wave of fear and panic grips him as he stares at the armed man in disbelief, realizing just how badly he misread the position he finds himself in.

CHAPTER SEVENTY-NINE
"BOSTON" HOLLINGER

SALCIDO'S MEXICAN ESTATE
SAN CARLOS NUEVO GUAYMAS, SONORA, MEXICO

That was more satisfying than I thought it would be. The idea of this piece of human scum rotting away in prison was my first choice, but I know that'll never happen. This was my equally effective second choice. Jai Snyder will never harm another person.

I turn my attention to Alejandro, who has frozen in place next to the sofa. I almost wish I could take a picture of his face. The trafficker has realized that he's not in the commanding position that he thought he was. I might not make it out of this alive...but he knows that he won't either.

"Your first mistake, *Señor Salcido*, was thinking that I came here to take you in."

"You...you're FBI!"

I cock my head to the side. "Says who?"

"You have no team here...you're a vigilante."

"Something like that. You're right about one thing, Alejandro – nobody can bring you in. You spent years cultivating connections in Arizona. You bought politicians and bribed cops. There's no telling who you have on your payroll. Even with a mountain of evidence, you would face nothing more than a show trial with all the people protecting you and a grateful public singing your praises. That's if you ever see the inside of a courtroom at all."

I am standing behind a woman in front of a group of people. She is talking, but I'm not really listening, and her words drift out of my head. I feel like I'm in my own little world.

Now I'm talking to someone dressed in a suit. He's speaking, but nothing he says is registering.

Another memory starts, and I'm on a cell phone in my office. "It's not enough."

I feel my anger rise. "Thirty-five thousand dollars had better be enough!"

"We have an agreement."

"And I fulfilled my part. Do the same," I say, hanging up.

Another memory comes in, and I'm shaking hands for a group of people with cameras.

The memory snippets are disappointing. I mentioned crooked politicians and cops to trigger them, but only tense or traumatic experiences typically surface. Alejandro paying off elected officials and law enforcement is neither to him. It's nothing more to him than the cost of doing business, just as how nobody remembers going to the supermarket for groceries a month ago. The whole exercise is entirely forgettable.

I expect another "Agent Sleepyhead" quip, but none comes. Salcido knows he's in serious trouble and is either stalling or unwilling to antagonize me any further. He's probably hoping the cartels are on the way. I know how that feels. I was waiting for the cavalry in the moments before Gina shot me a year ago.

"What will it take to make this go away?" Alejandro asks.

I think back to the children in the hospital. What will make their pain and suffering go away? The abuse? The torture? The rapes? The lost innocence? Nothing. They will live the rest of their lives with that burden. Some may get past it. Others it will consume. None of them will be the happy, healthy kids who should be enjoying their childhood.

"What are you going to do, buy me? Get me to drop my guard thinking we have an arrangement that you have no reason to honor once I lower this gun?"

"I always honor my agreements," Salcido says.

"I'll tell you what. I will make an agreement with you. I'm going to show you the same mercy that you showed Helio Lozano."

Alejandro lowers his eyes. He doesn't know how much I've learned about the kid's fate. He might have thought it was a perfect crime, but then again, I'm standing in a house that he was convinced nobody knew about. I don't need to see a memory to know what happened to the coyote, but I close my eyes anyway.

I feel myself smile. It's not a broad smile of joy or happiness. It's more amusement at something the kid in front of me said. Is that Helio? I think it is, but the face is fuzzy.

"I almost forgot. There is one thing you can do for me."

"Anything. What is it?"

My arm moves to my waistband, and I feel the cool steel of the gun resting there. I pull it as I spin. There are other men in the room watching. None of them react to the sudden movement.

I point the weapon at the young man's forehead. It is definitely Helio. His young face matches what I saw in the interrogation room. He has the same surprised look that he once gave me.

"Die," I mutter.

My finger moves to the trigger and pulls it to the rear. The sound is deafening, and now my ears are ringing. I notice the other men covering theirs. They knew this was coming. Helio was never destined to leave this room alive. I lean over and stare down at his body.

The remainder of the memory plays out in my vision once I open my eyes before fading into the pale light of the veranda. Alejandro hasn't said a word, nor did he move a muscle.

"That's what I thought."

"Helio is back in Mexico, alive and well," the trafficker insists.

"Yes, sharing some *enchiladas verdes* with his mother and father, right? No, that's right, you killed them – just like you killed Helio in the storage room of your club."

"You are mistaken! Everything you think you know is wrong."

"Is it? Some things you prefer to handle personally. At least that's what you said to...Javier, is it? You were right about one thing – the FBI never would have looked for Helio in hell."

Alejandro's brown complexion turns white. His first attempts to utter words fail before his next question finally stammers out.

"How could you know that?"

"Do you remember what you told Javier once? It's the problem that you don't anticipate that gets you in the end. I am that problem. As for how I know, well, it's one of life's mysteries."

I can't help but smile. That line is never going to get old. It's also about the only one I can ever use since trying to explain what I can do, even if I were permitted to by my FBI overlords, wouldn't be easy.

"You'll never get away with this. You will be a hunted man for the rest of your days. You can't hide anywhere that my people won't find you. You're a dead man."

I nod slowly. "I have no doubt that you think that's true, Alejandro. There are only two problems...I'm already dead, and you can't find a ghost, much less kill one."

I move closer to him and press the weapon against his temple while my finger moves to the trigger. He doesn't flinch. Instead, he closes his eyes and mutters something in Spanish. I let him finish his sentence before passing down one of my own.

CHAPTER EIGHTY

SSA ZACH FORTE

DAVIS MONTHAN AIR FORCE BASE
TUCSON, ARIZONA

Watchtower has several Defense Department liaisons assigned. Matt once bragged that they had every general serving on the Joint Chiefs of Staff on speed dial. Maybe he wasn't exaggerating after all. The Airmen at Davis Monthan Air Force Base have been more than accommodating to their every need. They've done everything but roll out the red carpet during their arrival.

The team is shown to an empty hangar and is met by several trucks dropping off weapons, body armor, and communications gear. It's a good start, but they'll need more manpower and firepower for this to succeed. Asami won't be any use in a firefight and won't be going. Fortunately, two soldiers walk into the hangar, and Zach knows he's getting his wish. The women stop unpacking Pelican cases full of equipment and stare at the warriors.

"I'm looking for Special Agent Forte."

"You found him."

"I'm Captain Jim Burns, and this is Master Sergeant Yeong Ji. We're from the 10th Special Forces Group."

"You got here fast from Fort Carson."

"My detachment was conducting some training at Fort Huachuca, so we didn't have to travel down here from Colorado."

"How many in your detachment, Captain?" Nadiya asks.

Both Army men eye her, but both are professional enough not to verbalize what is clearly going through their minds. That will enhance their life expectancy.

"I command a twelve-member detachment, ma'am. Master Sergeant Yeong is our team sergeant."

"Do you have your equipment with you?" Forte asks.

"We never leave home without it," the sergeant says.

"You guys must have some serious juice to get us pulled out of training and here on short notice," Burns says. "Can someone tell us what this is all about?"

"We have an FBI agent in Mexico in need of extraction."

The two men look at each other. "Where in Mexico?"

"We don't know."

"That will make things a little difficult, don't you think?" the sergeant asks.

"Our team in Washington is pinpointing his location as we speak," Emma says, beating Forte to the punch.

"Okay, hostiles?" Captain Burns asks.

"Our agent was going after an alleged sex trafficker with deep ties to drug cartels. So, probably a lot of them."

"Let me get this straight. You want us to perform an armed incursion into a friendly neighboring country to extract a lone agent with no confirmed location who's likely being chased by some of the most violent people on Earth?"

"That sums it up, yes."

The captain and sergeant study the faces of the three agents. None of them look like they're kidding or playing some sort of sick joke on his team. Forte can understand why he might think that.

"This is going to be one hell of a briefing to the guys, Ji."

"We've done worse."

"Have we. Look, Special Agent Forte, I normally wouldn't want anything to do with this. But orders are orders, and ours are signed by the Army Chief of Staff himself. So as crazy as it sounds, we'll play along."

"Good to hear."

"Just understand something – I'm not going to put my team in harm's way without more actionable intelligence. Mexico is a big country, and we're not going to be caught flying around it for days without their government's permission."

"Understood. For the record, I'm not asking you to. We will locate our man, and when we do, we'll need your help getting him out of there. If we don't, he's as good as dead."

"Fair enough."

"Where are your men?" Nadiya asks.

"Grabbing chow," the sergeant interjects. "They can gear up and be ready in fifteen minutes after I make the call."

"Then get some chow yourselves. We'll call when we need you. There's no point in your hanging around this hangar waiting on us."

The captain nods and the two men start for the open hangar door.

"Master Sergeant, what weapons systems are you using?" Emma asks.

He stares at her with apprehension. "M4 SOPMOD."

"Block one or two?"

The sergeant glances at Forte, who offers him a smirk. "Weapons instructor."

"Block two. Have you ever fired it?"

"I've fired everything that goes boom. I'm Emma."

"Ji," he says, shaking her hand. "I'm betting you can hit center-mass with all of them. What's your favorite weapon?"

"That's tough. I love handguns because of the challenge, but sniper rifles are so much fun. You can't go wrong with the Barrett M82, but the Finnish SAKO TRG 42 is amazing."

"I've been dying to fire that!" the sergeant exclaims as the two walk off and continue their conversation.

"She might have just made Ji's day," the captain says, watching. "There's nothing he likes more than talking about weapons."

"He's in good company, then. Emma is about as proficient a marksman as they come," Zach explains.

"Level with me, Agent Forte. Who are you guys? No average FBI team could ever get DoD assets, let alone this quickly."

"I'd love to tell you, but…"

"If you say, 'I'd have to kill you,' know that I have a TS/SCI Poly clearance."

Zach smiles. "You aren't read in for this, Captain. Nobody is. Trust me when I say that."

"All right. Secret squirrel shit. Got it."

The military is a community with its own social norms, stigmas, and subcultures. Special operators are no different. Whenever they work with clandestine teams, they evoke a term from World War II: "secret squirrel." Zach heard that the moniker was derived from spies in the European theater who used "squirrel" because Germans couldn't pronounce it. Whatever the origin, it's widely used in today's military, especially among men like this.

Zach's phone rings and he sees that it's from Watchtower. He only hopes they have something.

"Forte."

"Zach, we just located our friend in the lime-green Charger based on some HUMINT and ELINT intelligence."

Zach isn't surprised that they received electronic intelligence on the car's whereabouts. Matt might have gotten a satellite tasked to this or found a way to monitor cameras around Mexico. The human intelligence they collected is another matter entirely. The odds of having a source manage to spot the car anywhere in that country seem remote. That or he wildly underestimates how many sources the U.S. government has cultivated there.

"Please tell me you found it in Tucson."

Matt moans. "I wish I could. Think south of that…much farther south."

"Nogales?"

"Try outside of Guaymas. It's about four and a half hours away on the west coast."

"What the hell is he doing there?" Zach asks, his voice rising.

"Your guess is as good as mine. We're trying to determine if Boston is still with her, and if not, where he is. Get the team prepped. You guys might have a long flight ahead of you."

"Call me when you have an exact location."

Zach hangs up and sighs. It's one thing to cross the border into Mexico. It's another to travel to southern Sonora.

"Washington?"

"Yeah. Get your guys together, Captain. This is going to be much harder than we thought."

"How much harder?"

"We're going to need to find a gas station for our helicopters if we're going to make it there and back."

CHAPTER EIGHTY-ONE

DETECTIVE BRESHION HURLEY

Hurley knows he's on thin ice. It melted when Assistant Chief Fulcher walked into the conference room and realized what her vice team was up to. She practically dragged him by his ear to her office, much like a parent would to a misbehaving toddler. At least it felt that way to the detective.

To make it to her rank and position, any cop has to know which rules can be bent and which ones broken. It's like operating in the Matrix that way. The good ones dance on that line. The disgraced ones cross it and find themselves in the crosshairs of activists, politicians, and media who are determined to take them down. Breshion knows he isn't making that dance any easier for his boss.

After a recap that included his barging into the mayor's office and the disastrous prisoner transport, Jada demands to know why Hurley is investigating her. It would be the vindictive thing to do. All he can do is justify it, which he spends about ten minutes doing with Jamecca and Ritter's help. The assistant chief leans back in her chair when they finish.

"Thank you for this. Will the two of you excuse us, please?"

"Yes, ma'am," the detectives say in unison before leaving and closing the door behind them. Not that the whole office won't know what she says next. The walls aren't that thick.

"Are you trying to get fired? Because you are making it very hard for me not to."

"Do what you need to. We have Salcido. We know that he's working with at least one politician in government, and everything points to the mayor."

Jada was unimpressed while listening to the team walk through the evidence, but she's mulling it over. The case against her is compelling, albeit not close to airtight.

"How sure are you that politicians are getting paid off by Salcido?"

"One hundred percent. The numbers don't lie."

"No, but people do," Jada argues, alluding to the now-likely-deceased Helio Lozano. "And that's part of the problem – it's only the appearance of impropriety. It's not proof. You have none."

"I don't have a smoking gun. I see a pattern of behavior, and we've put dozens of bad guys away by recognizing them. This is no different. The mayor is dirty."

"Okay, I'm almost afraid to ask. What patterns do you think you see?"

"The mayor slashes the budget while she was on the city council. That earns her campaign and political action committee huge cash donations, and she ends up as mayor. Then we take down a stash house, and she slashes vice the next day."

"Along with a half-dozen other departments," Jada argues.

"Window dressing. I think Horta did it to hide her real target: us. Then there's the strange reaction when the FBI arrived. The next day, she announces the Compass Rose Initiative."

"It was drafted by the previous administration," Jada says.

"Yes, and then kicked into overdrive. Adrian Finley admitted that the charter was revised and finished right before the press conference."

"That's meaningless."

"It's convenient timing. Now, with the help of the FBI, we're tracing sizable donations to Horta's political action committee directly from an offshore account that we believe belongs to Salcido. The last deposit was two days ago. Is that meaningless?"

"He donates to a lot of politicians."

"Not in those amounts, and all of those from U.S. accounts that are reported to the IRS. Why not these?"

Jada doesn't have an answer for that one. Like Breshion, and most Americans for that matter, the world of campaign finance is a mystery best left unsolved. Only lawyers and smear merchants in the media spend much time obsessing over the litany of rules the government has laid down for intrepid candidates running for office.

"Okay, let's assume you're right. What do you expect me to do with this?"

"If you don't want us investigating, take it to the brass and open an official one."

"They won't."

"Why not?"

"Politics."

Breshion frowns. If there's an axiom that he believes holds true universally, it's that politics is the number one obstacle to progress. Everything in today's world is about optics. The more visible the target is, the more they are protected to the point that justice can never be served.

In some respects, that makes sense. History is replete with frames and political shenanigans using overhyped claims about behavior or malfeasance that ultimately prove untrue.

Breshion leans forward in his chair. "That's a lousy reason."

"That doesn't make it any less relevant. Detective, you watch the news. Horta's political enemies smell blood in the water and are circling like sharks. We both know that the 'grassroots' protest outside City Hall was anything but. It was organized and supported by people looking to take her down."

"So, what? We let her get away with this, then?"

"I didn't say that," Jada snaps. "You need more evidence. If I take this to the chief, he'll laugh me out of the room."

Breshion throws his head back and drops his arms. He wears emotions on his sleeve, and frustration is one of them. He's in over his head, and he knows it. A little help would be appreciated, either from the now-absent FBI or the suddenly uncooperative leadership in his own police department.

"Keep digging," Jada orders. "Something is brewing over at City Hall. I don't know what it is yet, so keep your investigation under wraps. The last thing we need leaking is that you are looking into the mayor."

"Okay. You need to know that we don't have the resources for this. We wouldn't have made it this far without the FBI, and they aren't here to help."

"You'll think of something."

CHAPTER EIGHTY-TWO

"BOSTON" HOLLINGER

SALCIDO'S MEXICAN ESTATE
SAN CARLOS NUEVO GUAYMAS, SONORA, MEXICO

The sound of my last shot has only now finished bouncing off the houses. The first shot woke up the neighbors, but could easily be dismissed. The second one has caused lights in the adjacent structures to begin to click on. This is Mexico, so while it's not an unfamiliar sound across the bay in Guaymas, it's less common in more affluent San Carlos. I have woken up this small waterfront city, and that's not a good thing.

In the eyes of the law, I'm a murderer. As an FBI agent, I took the law into my own hands and killed two people. It won't matter that I had every reason to kill them or that I knew of their guilt better than everyone except them. I can't prove any of that. As I stand between the bodies of the two dead men, I'm more of an assassin than a law enforcement officer. I nod slowly. I can live with that.

I place the bodyguard's weapon loosely in Salcido's hand. Any diligent forensic investigation would prove in a matter of minutes that Salcido didn't fire it. I'm counting on that not mattering. Even if the Mexican authorities do a forensic investigation, it still provides some reasonable doubt.

I pull my phone out of the Faraday bag and power it on. I fight through all the notifications of missed calls and SMS messages. The team at least has noted my absence and now knows exactly where I am. The GPS signal has already been picked up by Watchtower.

A few pictures of the scene will suffice, so I snap them and power down the device, placing it back into the bag. I move inside the house and find Salcido's office. It's tidy, and who knows if he keeps anything of value here. I snatch a canvas knapsack resting alongside the desk and stuff some papers and a laptop into it, sure to grab the charger and USB cables as well. There's no point in making it obvious that a computer is missing.

With one final look at the office, I turn for the door and freeze. A truck's engine begins to idle as it pulls up outside. A tailgate drops as men bark orders. This can't be good. I move to the window and watch a group of men split up and head around opposite sides of the house. I check my watch. That was fast. Too fast.

With a more urgent purpose, I scurry back to the veranda and the railing beyond my dispatched targets. It's a ten-foot jump down to the ground below and a fifty-fifty chance that I break an ankle on landing. It's better odds than letting these goons find me in the house with a dead human trafficker and a gun in my hand.

I climb over the railing and drop, landing on the uneven ground and rolling to bleed off the energy. I position the backpack on my shoulders and squat low as voices begin to converge on me. I'm going to have to thank Nadiya for teaching me how to fall correctly. Other than a couple of cuts, I'm fine and perfectly mobile. Now the hard part.

This mission didn't have much of a strategy, let alone an exit plan. I didn't think that far ahead. There are only two spare magazines for my Glock, and that isn't going to be enough to get me out of a gunfight with a dozen men should one erupt.

I hear Spanish being shouted in urgent tones above me. The gunmen have found the bodies and will now be searching for the man who left them. I might have a chance if I can cross the two-lane road and fifty yards of open distance between the house and the marina on the waterfront. I could even steal a boat and sail into the bay. That will buy me at least some time.

It's now or never. Voices on the veranda above me urge me to action, and I take off at a dead sprint. A man shouts as I reach the asphalt road between the houses and the waterfront businesses. I'm caught in the open, and bullets begin ripping past me.

The steady staccato of pops precedes the chipped asphalt from bullet strikes tearing at my legs. I duck and zigzag, trying to not give them a clean shot. So far, so good, but as the volume of fire increases, my luck is bound to run out.

I dive onto the concrete sidewalk behind a planter filled with crushed stone and cacti. The landing hurts, but the pain is numbed by the adrenaline coursing through my bloodstream. The walkway is about two feet below the tan concrete barrier of the planter, so I hazard a look over it. Unless they have a sniper in the house, it's unlikely they'll spot me in the darkness.

Men converge from both sides of the house. A vehicle pulls up at the rear of Salcido's residence, and two of its occupants begin to cross the street. With the closed business to my back, I'm pinned down. I have to move.

I take a couple of breaths and pause, unleashing two rounds that strike one of the men crossing the street. The other retreats as about half a dozen men open fire. I slide on my belly, using the concrete wall as cover. When I reach the end, I peer over. They are still fixated on my last location. That gives me a chance.

I push myself to my feet and sprint to the corner of the building. Several bullets whiz past my head once they spot me, and rounds strike the painted stucco façade of the building. The marina is fifty yards away down this asphalt access road. I can make it.

The men are in hot pursuit and no doubt angry. They have the numbers and the firepower advantage. Even if I get two or three more of them, it won't nearly be enough. Escape is the only option.

I have a fighting chance to make it to a boat. The problem is, if I can't start it, there's no way to go. Something tells me that the keys aren't left in these. I have no idea if they even need them — I was in the Army. Without a working boat, that means my options are swimming or death.

There's only one way to find out. I wheel around, turning my back to the water and lining my sights on the shadowy, backlit figures coming down the access road. I fire, retrain, fire, and retrain, just like Emma taught me. Two men fall, but the rest continue to charge.

A foghorn blares off to my right, but I hold my focus. The men coming for me don't. That allows me to drop two more of them before jumping down to the dock. I start to move for the floating dock that leads out into the bay when I hear shouting, gunshots, and screeching tires. Here come their reinforcements.

Headlights grow steadily closer as the vehicle screams down the short access road. I need to take out the driver before it's too late. I line up my sights and move my finger to the trigger. I breathe. Then I stop when I see a bullet hit the car and ricochet off.

"What the hell?" I say to myself.

I have tunnel vision. Situational awareness is everything when you're in danger. That's what Emma preached before every lesson. Despite that constant reinforcement, I've lost mine.

The men are shooting at the car. I don't understand why until the lime-green vehicle spins out and comes to a stop at the end of the access road.

"Boston! Where are you?" a female voice calls out from about ten feet away.

"Right here."

She sticks her head out the window in my direction as bullets start peppering Sol's Charger. The woman is a lot of things, and being cool under pressure is one of them. She isn't even flinching.

"Coming?"

I jump and lift myself over the concrete seawall between the road and dock, and I duck as I hustle around the back of the car. I swing the door open and dive into the passenger side as the thugs increase their volume of fire. Muzzle flashes precede the reports of their guns as bullets start striking the front of the car with a higher frequency.

"I thought I told you to leave."

"Are you really going to scold me for not listening? I'm saving your life."

Sol floors the accelerator. The rear tires spin before finding enough traction to lurch the classic car forward. She hangs a left off the short access road onto the two-lane highway I crossed to reach the marina.

I fire a couple of rounds at the vehicle as we pass it, sending the remaining man who tried crossing the street crashing to the ground. She piles on more speed, and I check behind us for any pursuit. There is none, at least yet. We are far from being out of danger. Sol's miraculous rescue feels more like a delay of the inevitable than a ticket to salvation.

CHAPTER EIGHTY-THREE
MAYOR ANGELICA HORTA

CITY HALL FOYER
PHOENIX, ARIZONA

Angelica wrings her hands to calm her nerves. It isn't working. She has never been in this kind of predicament and wishes she had a staff that she could count on to use as a sounding board. Once upon a time, as in yesterday, Adrian and Katy were those people. Now that times are tougher, she at least knows that she can't rely on them. It's for the best that they aren't here.

The elevator dings, and the doors open to the foyer. It's calm down here, but outside is a different story. Thousands of people are gathered across the street and hundreds more outside the front door. Some are carrying signs. Most are just shouting. Police have managed to contain the protesters, who have grown more peaceful but no less agitated.

The mayor doesn't know what she wants to say, but it has to be something. These people are upset with her because of lies, and they need to listen to reason. Her constituents must understand her position, and a visit with these protesters will allow the media to show her being proactive.

Angelica takes a deep breath and walks toward the door. She is eyed warily by several uniformed PPD officers in the lobby. She expects one of them to stop her until she hears another voice.

"What the hell are you doing?"

"Donna?" Angelica asks after turning toward the reception desk. "How…why are you here?"

"What are you babbling about? I came to see you. You aren't thinking of going out there, are you?"

The mayor stands up a little straighter. "That's exactly what I'm doing. It's leadership."

"It's stupid, and if I have to explain why, so are you. Do you have any idea what will happen if you do?"

"The media will show me trying to talk to them…trying to understand their position and get them to understand mine."

Donna closes her eyes and shakes her head. "You can't talk to the mob. There is no 'Take me to your leader' moment that will make you look principled. You'll get humiliated, and that's the footage people will see in their living rooms."

"I don't think that will happen."

"Then you *are* an idiot. Those people don't want to hear your side or to be reasoned with. They're being told what to believe and are angry about it. Your talking down to them will only feed that anger."

"I won't be talking down to them!" Angelica exclaims, her voice rising.

"That's how they'll perceive it. Look out there. Go ahead and look!" Donna pleads, pointing at the windows and the crowd on the other side of the street behind them. "What do you see?"

"Upset constituents."

"Wrong. First, most of those people probably aren't from Phoenix. They were bused in for the sole purpose of making this 'grassroots' uprising look bigger. Second, they aren't upset with you. They're upset with their own lives. You're just a convenient target to take it out on. That's what modern protests are."

"You've become jaded in your old age," the mayor concludes.

"And with good reason. But, hey, I don't work for you. If you don't believe me, walk out there and see for yourself. Just don't think you can turn to me for damage control after the fact. I can't help people who won't help themselves."

Angelica wasn't sure about this course of action when she embarked on it. Now, a highly respected and influential national political figure is telling her that she's wrong. The mayor respects her opinion and cherishes their friendship, but her credentials and experience don't make her clairvoyant. She could be wrong.

It doesn't matter. The dissent has seized Angelica up with inaction. She has a decision to make and is about to when two men appear at the front door. She recognizes them immediately. The question is, what are they doing here?

"That was ugly," Kevin Demeter says as they are escorted by police through the door.

"Yeah, it was," Andres LaCugna agrees. "At least they aren't mad at *us*. Oh, good, you're here. It saves us an elevator ride. Although an elevator may be the safest place to be with that crowd."

"Councilman Demeter. Councilman LaCugna," Angelica says when the two men reach her. "What brings you to City Hall?"

"Official business."

"We aren't here willingly," Andres grumbles.

"There's some information we need to relay to you."

"What is it?" the mayor asks. Councilman Demeter glances at Donna, and Angelica cuts him off at the pass. "Whatever you have can be said in front of her."

"Sure, if we want it leaked to the press. We all know Ms. DeForest's reputation," Andres says.

"I only leak things that matter from people who matter," Donna counters, causing LaCugna to smirk.

"If you say so."

Kevin hands the mayor an envelope. "The details are in this. We're happy to answer any questions for you should you have any."

"Is that all, gentlemen?" Donna barks, more of an accusation than a question.

"Excuse me?" Andres asks.

"No, I don't think I will. I want you to understand, Andres, so I'll speak slowly. Is...that...all?"

"Does she work for you now?"

"No, which is why I can say whatever the hell I want. If you've done what you came here to do, you should join your friends outside."

Andres recoils a touch before recovering. "My friends?"

"Yeah," Donna says with a smile. "That's what one of the organizers outside called you."

She stops there. The mayor watches as Andres eyes Donna warily and with good cause. She wears a smug look that she could only have learned from politicians and lobbyists in a city like Washington, D.C. It's a game of chicken, and she has no doubt who will win.

"Come on, Kevin. Let's go."

Angelica watches the two men retreat out the door. "How did you know LaCugna arranged this? You talked to an organizer?"

Donna rolls her eyes. "Of course not. I didn't know if he was involved in this at all."

"So, you lied?"

"Welcome to politics," she offers with a shrug. "You just learned something important, though."

"What?"

"He did help organize it. His reaction was all you needed to see. The one thing you learn about politicians in my line of work is to stop listening to what they say and start watching what they do. Open the letter."

Angelica complies and reads the three short paragraphs. "You've got to be kidding me."

"Let me guess – they're dragging you before a special public hearing."

"How did you know?"

Donna gestures to the crowd outside. "It's what I would have done to exploit this situation. Make a bunch of noise that gets covered. That's the 'what.' Then tell the public the 'why' by humiliating you in front of the media, who report it to everyone not paying attention. When's the hearing?"

"Tomorrow."

"Then we don't have much time. That is if you want my help. You need to start acting like a politician if you want to beat this. Or you can go talk to the bloodthirsty crowd gathered outside. It's your choice."

CHAPTER EIGHTY-FOUR
"BOSTON" HOLLINGER

TRAVELING NORTH
SONORA, MEXICO

Sol stomps on the accelerator and screams up Sonora Route 124, away from San Carlos. I check out the back window and don't see any sign of pursuit. There is only one major route out of this town. It's like that in much of Mexico. If they want to find us, it won't be that hard.

"I told you to leave the city," I shout..

Sol grins. "I did. I went across the line and outside the city limits."

"And then what?"

"I came back, *gringo*," she deadpans in a way only a woman can when a man asks a stupid question. I walked into that one. "What happened with Alejandro?"

"I shot him in the head."

"*Bueno.* Good riddance. What was your plan after that? Steal a boat?"

"I thought it was a good idea at the time."

"No, not really. The cartels have enough boats to call it a navy. Assuming you could have even managed to start one."

"Thank you for coming back," I say, settling into my seat.

"Don't thank me yet. We won't be safe until we're out of Mexico, and the hunt has only just begun."

We leave the city via Route 124 and face choosing one of two bad options: Go north where the cartels think we will head or south and farther away from the U.S. border. There's nothing south except certain death, and the border is too far to reach with the manpower the cartels can muster to stop us. There is a consulate in Hermosillo about ninety minutes away. We have a chance of making it there before our pursuers close in.

Sol heads north up Federal Highway 15 as I pull my phone out of the Faraday bag and power it on. I'm about to call Watchtower but decide against it. The journey to Mexico was my choice. I'm not about to endanger my colleagues by asking them to come to my rescue. They don't have the equipment or manpower for that.

"What is that?"

"A phone," I say, using the same tone she answered my question in earlier.

"Haha. I mean the bag you have it in."

"It blocks outside electromagnetic signals from reaching the device."

"So, you can't use it?"

"Exactly. And it ensures that nobody else can turn it on, either."

Sol looks skeptical about that part but keeps her reservations to herself. "Are you going to call someone?"

"No. There's nobody to call."

"You're very strange, Boston. If there is nobody to call, why turn it on? Do you want them to know where to find our bodies?"

"You don't sound optimistic about our chances."

"If you are, then you don't know what we're up against," Sol counters.

She's wrong about that. With the memories I've seen during my time with her, I know what kind of savages she works with. Her toughness and smarts have kept her alive, but she's witnessed these animals commit unspeakable atrocities. They're bloodhounds until they find what they are looking for. And then they're hyenas.

Sol slows the car down and stops in the middle of the road. There is very little traffic in this part of Mexico during the day, and it's utterly desolate at night. None of that explains why she's stopped short at an interchange that reminds me of something I would see in the States.

"Why did you stop?"

"How long have we been driving?"

"I don't know. A little over an hour, I guess. Why?"

"We're turning here. We can't stay on Fifteen."

"Yeah, but the consulate is still twenty minutes that way," I say, pointing out the windshield.

"The cartels will have set up a checkpoint outside the city."

"What makes you think they won't be looking for us on this route?"

"Oh, they will be. We're just making it harder for them."

The decision made, we engage in small talk like we're on a road trip. We laugh, tell stories and try to forget we're fleeing from the most dangerous men on the continent as we turn onto Federal Route 14 and then north on 17 toward Agua Prieta.

After a while, we fall silent as the gravity of our situation sets back in. Sol finally sighs heavily.

"What's wrong?"

"Nothing. I'm just surprised we've lived this long."

"Maybe your route is fooling them."

"Not likely. Only a handful of roads here lead into the U.S. Trust me when I say the cartels know all of them."

"Sol, may I ask you a question? Why did you come back for me?"

She stares out the window for a long moment. "You're an honorable man, Boston. I haven't met many of those in my life."

"Honorable dead man from the sounds of it."

"Probably. At least I will die knowing that I tried to save you."

I shake my head. "That doesn't sound like a fair trade."

"You knew what my father told me when I was a child. You missed one important part: His legacy was one of honor. He would be prouder of me doing this than a lifetime spent doing anything else."

I can't believe this woman works for a cartel. She should be jaded about what life has offered her. Instead, under her beauty lies a heart of gold.

"My turn to ask you a question. How did you know what my father told me? You can't have known that." I continue staring out the window without responding. "Okay, you can't say, for whatever reason. I understand. Just know that we're likely going to die in the next hour or so."

She has a point. Even if we don't, she saved my life. I owe her an explanation.

"I see people's memories."

"What? That's crazy. How?"

"I've had some brain injuries. Somehow, I can just do it. It's a skill I've been honing over the past year."

"Only the past year?"

"Yeah. It's a long story. I promise to tell you if we survive this."

"Deal."

"There is one condition: If I tell you, you can't repeat what you hear to another living soul. There are only a few people who know, and it needs to stay that way."

"Why would you tell me, then?"

"You know a thing or two about honor. Your father raised you well, and you can keep a secret."

"How do you know that?" I stare at her in the dim light the dashboard provides. "You've seen my memories."

I flick my finger in the air, indicating she nailed it. Sol nods, thinking through everything that's happened since we met.

"That's why you killed Salcido. You knew he was guilty."

I perk up when I notice the steep slope rising on either side of us. I gaze out the windshield at the road Sol is chewing up in the car. I then twist to look out the rear window. The last time I had this feeling was in Iraq. It didn't end well.

"What's wrong?"

"There are hills on both sides of us. This is the perfect spot for a—"

Sol slams on the brakes, and the car skids to a stop in the middle of the desolate road. Headlights block the road about eighty yards ahead of us. I turn to see another couple of pairs click on and approach from the rear. There's nothing to do but smell the burnt rubber and wait for them to make their move.

"I don't suppose it would do us any good to get out and make a run for it?" she asks.

I stare at the steep slopes on our sides. We could lose them if it were flat terrain, but it's not. Even if we somehow managed to elude them, we're in the desert without water, not near any towns, and still a two-hour drive to the border. We'd never make it.

"No, it's the end of the line."

"Do you want to surrender?"

"No. Do you?"

She pulls out her six-shooter and checks to ensure it's loaded. "Nope."

"It's been an honor to know you, Sol."

"You too, Boston," she says offering a soft, warm smile before cocking her head. "Can I ask you a question?"

"Sure."

"What is your real name?"

I return the smile. "Eugene."

Flashes erupt from our front and rear, and the car gets peppered with bullets. We climb out of the Charger, taking cover behind the doors. There is no immediate danger from the inaccurate fire at this distance, but that changes when shots rain down from either side of the road. It's a textbook example of a blocked ambush. There is no escape.

We both open fire with a couple of rounds to delay the inevitable. Spending any more ammunition than that is a waste of time. We won't hit anything from here and don't have much to waste.

"Hey, Boston?" Sol shouts from the driver's side door as the return fire punches holes in her car.

"Yeah?" I say, keeping my head down as windows shatter and bullets whip past me.

"For what it's worth, I like 'Boston' better than Eugene."

I grin to myself, knowing she can't see it in the darkness. This woman can keep her cool under even the direst of circumstances. And they don't get more desperate than this.

"So do I," I say with a laugh, likely the last one I'll ever enjoy.

CHAPTER EIGHTY-FIVE
SSA ZACH FORTE

INTERSTATE 17 AMBUSH SITE
NORTH OF SAN RAFAEL DE LA NORIA, SONORA, MEXICO

There are no external lights illuminated or flashing outside the helicopters. The two-ship flight is as visible as a shadow projected against a dark sky. It's a strange experience for Zach and his colleagues. None of them served in the military and they aren't used to flying in a helicopter, let alone one not using its running lights.

Soldiers man Gatling-style miniguns on either door of the bird. Off to the right is the other chopper with Nadiya and Detective Williams flying in a tight formation. The crews are all wearing night vision, bathing their world in a green hue. Unfortunately, there weren't enough to go around. Forte is stuck relying on his own two eyes, neither of which can make out anything on the ground.

He hopes they can get to Boston in time, but it doesn't look good. There's too much territory to cover, even in special operations helicopters flown by the world's best pilots. The drones can help, but they can't eliminate every target, and it only takes one bullet to end their night and Boston's life.

It could already be too late, assuming that a trap isn't being laid for them. Nobody has a clue why Boston drove to this remote part of Mexico, and that's cause for concern. It's something that Matt mentioned both before and after the birds took off. If it is ever discovered, an armed incursion into Mexico will be an international incident and the end of Watchtower.

"Special Agent Forte?" Zach hears over his headset.

"Yeah."

"The drone has located the target vehicle."

"Where?" Zach asks, looking out the door at the ground below as if he can actually see it.

"Ten clicks south…target vehicle is stationary," the pilot announces.

"Stationary?"

"As in not moving," Captain Burns says, turning his head to smirk at Forte.

"I know what it means. Why?"

"Drones have identified at least four hostile vehicles to the north and south."

A flash in the distance interrupts him as he starts to answer. A streak of light tears through the sky toward the ground. The resulting explosion illuminates everything for a mile around it. A second and third streak result in equally impressive fireballs slightly south of the first.

"The drone has engaged several targets."

"Yeah, no kidding," Zach moans.

Forte will never admit it, but Matt did an incredible job marshaling resources. Not only did he get a Special Forces team and two birds from the 160th SOAR, but he also got a pair of MQ-9 Reaper drones from the Air Force. They departed Creech Air Force Base, one covering Federal Highway 15 and the other tracking Boston's cell phone signal. Both are armed with four AGM-114 Hellfire missiles, the standard load with the doubling of that armament now in testing.

The Black Hawk's nose pitches down and adds more speed. A minute later, the drones' handiwork becomes evident. The pilot edges the helicopter over the road, and they pass the first target and what looks like the flaming remains of two vehicles.

Zach can't see anything on the ground other than brief specks of light on the hillsides leading down to the road. The door gunners recognize them as the targets they are, and both miniguns erupt. The hills are showered with tracers as they swivel their guns left and right. Zach peeks out behind him to see the second chopper doing the same.

They pass over the green Charger pinned in the middle of the ambush and then over the second explosion site. The choppers reverse with the grace of a couple of ballroom dancers, and miniguns open up again. This time the helicopter pitches down, causing Forte to grab onto the nylon cargo straps next to him. Captain Burns gives his men in the chopper some hand signals as the pilot flares the helicopter a mere few feet from the ground.

It's a tight spot to land a Black Hawk, but the pilot manages to do it only a few dozen meters from the green car. The SF team fans out on both sides, one stopping to engage a target while the others take up defensive positions.

Zach's heart pounds in his chest as he watches a pair of soldiers bound over to what's left of the green Charger. The windows are all shattered and the vehicle has taken a beating. That's not a good sign. More ominous is that nobody is frantically running toward the Black Hawk. There's no movement at all. They may already be too late.

Bullets ricochet off the Black Hawk's door, causing Zach to fall backward into the crew compartment. The gunner shifts the aim of his six-barrel M134 and fires a long burst onto the hill to his front as the chopper overhead continues to belch lead at anything that moves.

The muzzle flashes from the Gatling gun destroy what remained of his ability to see anything in the inky darkness. Forte regains his footing and looks up. Two figures are being helped over to the chopper by Burns's men. The crew chief shines a light in the pair's faces. The woman looks a little shell-shocked and uncertain. The man looks…impatient. He made it after all.

Forte smirks and nods at the crewman, and Boston helps the gunner usher the beautiful Latina aboard before joining her. Forte glances over at Emma. He can see the look she's wearing even in the dim red light. She already hates his lovely new friend.

The remaining Green Berets collapse back to the chopper and load up. The Black Hawk lifts off and screams north. The soldiers safe their weapons, and Boston is handed a set of headphones that he dons.

"Drone shows more vehicles heading in this direction. We've been instructed to get back across the border ASAP," the pilot says.

"Roger that," Forte responds. "Happy to see me?"

"For once, yes," Boston replies. "I didn't think you'd come for me."

"Honestly, I had to think about it. I'm surprised you're not dead. Now I'm glad that I get the chance to kill you myself. That was stupid."

"If it's stupid, but it works, was it really stupid?"

"Yes. Are you okay?" Forte asks, getting a nod in return.

"I'm tired of getting shot."

Zach inspects his shoulder and sees the gash where the bullet ripped the skin. He was only grazed, so it's nothing more than a flesh wound that will leave a scar. The SF medic pulls a first aid kit out of his pack and removes a field dressing.

"Who's your friend?"

"Helio Lozano's sister, Sol."

"Sol? Are you serious?" Boston nods again. "And Salcido?"

"Roasting in hell where he belongs."

Now it's Forte's turn to shake his head. "There's going to be hell to pay for this when we get back to Washington."

"I'm sure, but we're not going to D.C. yet."

"Why not?"

"Because there are a few more bad guys to take care of first," Boston says as the crew chief finishes applying the bandage.

Forte doesn't know where Boston is going with this, but there's no use in discussing it over an open channel where these soldiers can hear it. That doesn't mean he isn't curious.

"Am I going to like this?"

"No, but Remsen will."

CHAPTER EIGHTY-SIX
"BOSTON" HOLLINGER

DAVIS MONTHAN AIR FORCE BASE
TUCSON, ARIZONA

Emergency rooms have come a long way, even at military hospitals. Private rooms ring the perimeter of a central nurses' station, with wide doors and even wider access for gurneys and the crush of emergency services personnel who come in and out. Despite the better comfort and privacy, I still hate them.

Considering the number of shots fired at me, only one bullet managed to graze my shoulder. The military doctor finished the work the Special Forces medic started, leaving me to be doted on by my female colleagues and mother hen doctor. All three are keen on getting me to talk about everything that happened in Mexico. Fortunately, members of the vice squad stop by to pay a visit.

"Good to see you're doing okay," Detective Hurley says, handing me a coffee before taking a sip of the one he got for himself.

"Yeah, thanks. So far as getting shot is concerned, I'll take it. I'm surprised you came all the way down here."

"And I'm surprised an FBI agent hunted by a cartel in their back yard lived to tell the tale."

"I barely did," I say, nodding at my shoulder.

"I thought I taught you better than that," Emma says.

"Uh, it was an ambush, and there were over twenty of them."

"So?" she asks with a smile.

"Really, Will, what you did south of the border was impressive," Nadiya adds. "Reckless and boneheaded for sure, but impressive."

I catch Hurley stealing a glance at Detective Robinson. Their romance is evident to me, and now I'm beginning to wonder if they are trying to figure out which one of these women I'm sleeping with. Turnabout is fair play, even if they'd be disappointed in the answer.

"Thanks, I think. I wish I could take full credit for it, but I had help."

"The girl?"

"Sol. Without her, I probably wouldn't have made it much past Nogales. She saved my life."

"I heard that you demanded asylum in the U.S. for her."

"It's the least I can do. The question is whether the request will be taken seriously."

"By Matt?" Dr. Kurota asks.

"Or the person I asked to make it," I say as Forte enters the small room.

It was my first request when the helicopter landed at the base. Actually, it was more of a demand. I would not abide the FBI sending Sol back as I fear they would have. After betraying the cartels and helping me escape, she can never go back to Sonora. That means she's stuck in the States, and I want her to have every opportunity to succeed.

Detective Hurley decides to break the tension that is suddenly as thick as a London fog. "What happened in Mexico, Agent Smith?"

Forte nods, and I take a deep breath before explaining how I bumped into Helio's sister at their parents' house. Next comes a synopsis of our trip south and my crashing Alejandro Salcido's meeting with Jai Snyder. There are gaps in the story, the first being why I chose to venture down there in the first place.

"Then what?" Robinson asks.

"I confronted him. He shot at me and hit Jai Snyder in the chest. Then he turned the gun on himself and committed suicide."

Hurley shakes his head, not buying the lie. "Alejandro Salcido was a fixture in this city. The only thing more unbelievable than him running a human trafficking ring is that he committed suicide at his home in Mexico."

"I don't know what to tell you, Detective. That's what happened."

"The laptop you grabbed has been sent to our regional computer forensic laboratory in New Mexico," Forte says. "They should be able to unlock its secrets and provide us enough information to take down the whole network."

Zach's attempt to change the subject is going to fall on deaf ears. The detective continues to stare at me, not at all attentive to the treasure that the computer may hold.

"I'd like to talk to your agent alone, please," Hurley says, turning to Forte.

"I don't think—"

"It's okay, Zach. Give us the room, please."

Zach looks a little sick to his stomach, but he doesn't protest. That surprises me. The request doesn't seem to bother Emma or Nadiya, although Asami looks a little constipated at the thought of leaving.

"All right, Agent Smith," the detective says once they clear the room. "We both know you're lying. I have no power to do anything about it, but I want you to level with me. What really happened to Salcido?"

He stares directly at me with no emotion at all. His question was matter-of-fact, not accusatory.

"I shot him in the head."

The detective's mouth drops. "You're admitting to murder?"

"Call it what you will. Salcido never would've been arrested in Sonora. Even if he'd been stupid enough to come back to the U.S., and he wouldn't have been, there isn't enough evidence to even get a warrant, let alone prosecute him. Not with his connections."

"And Snyder? Did you kill him, too?"

"Jai Snyder was using the convoys his NGO was funding as a supply source for trafficking. He was abducting women and children at rest stops all the way through Mexico. He was trying to expand his enterprise by going into business with Salcido."

"How do you know that?" Hurley asks, amazement seeping into his voice.

"It's one of life's mysteries."

"Seriously, how?"

"I overheard part of the negotiation before I got the jump on them."

I doubt that the detective believes that's the whole story, but it's plausible enough for him to move off the subject.

"Why did you tell me this? I could bring it to federal prosecutors. You could go to prison. Your team might protect you, but what makes you think I will?"

"If our roles were reversed, you would've done the same thing. You know it, and so do I."

The detective doesn't argue. I know his background and why he's so passionate about his job. He believes in the rule of law, but there's a good chance that laws don't apply to Alejandro Salcido. He would have escaped prosecution to continue exploiting people only looking for a better life. The detective might disagree with my methods, but he isn't going to cry about the result.

"So, now what? You go home to Washington?"

I slowly shake my head. "We finish this."

"What do you mean?"

"Salcido had moles everywhere, but I confirmed that he had support high up in city government. Someone with a lot of political clout."

"We've been looking into that. He was on a first-name basis with almost every politician in Arizona, including the governor. He contributed to many of their campaigns."

"But because of the leak, you've already zeroed in on Mayor Horta."

Hurley grins. "Salcido's contributions helped seal her win in the last election. She made cuts to the police department as a councilwoman, including the vice squad. She also shifted personnel around before your team got here. The problem is, everything we've found is circumstantial."

"Then we need to crack open that laptop, and fast."

"Even if we do, that kind of investigation will take months," Hurley argues. "Mayor Horta is already under an enormous amount of political pressure, so the city council may do the job for us. They scheduled a public hearing about Compass Rose for Thursday. It could be enough to launch a recall."

If the entire city government is in a room two days from now, it might provide the opportunity I'm looking for. Of course, I can't tell the detective that. They need hard evidence, and the only way to do that is to see if Watchtower lives up to its reputation.

"We can't have politicians helping traffic human beings. We need to know who was supporting him. I need to get outta this hospital first. Then, let's get our teams together in a room back at vice and get to work."

CHAPTER EIGHTY-SEVEN

SSA ZACH FORTE

The information from Watchtower keeps pouring in. They're sending over gigabytes of information that the RCFL in New Mexico is pulling off the laptop. Watchtower has dedicated every analyst on the payroll to dissect the data and chase down where it leads.

Salcido's network, employees, and buyers are all clearly spelled out. The number of warrants and arrests that will result will lead the national news. His moles and other supporters are more cryptic. Names aren't used, and bribes to them have to be chased down one by one. Every Arizona politician's financial background and private dealings are now under the microscope.

The trafficker knew how to bury money, and no doubt had it transferred around with equal secrecy. Zach is counting on something showing up on the politician's side of the house. Matt either has a federal judge on speed dial to issue the required warrants, or they're taking advantage of their covert status and not bothering. The latter is terrifying. Either way, the teams are hard at work, but the clock is ticking.

The special hearing of the city council on the Compass Rose Initiative is in less than twenty-four hours. Justice may ultimately lie in what Boston sees in that room. What he does comes out of paranormal or fantasy novels, not the real world. Disbelief is the only thing safeguarding the secret. Zach's convinced that Detective Hurley is close to suspending that disbelief.

Forte stands, feeding a need to stretch and loosen his tight joints. He exits the conference room and walks past the desks to the other side of the office to the break room for a cup of coffee. When he sees Boston talking to Emma, he can only think, "Here we go again." There have been too many awkward conversations in this spot already.

"Any luck?" Emma asks.

"No smoking gun yet, if that's what you're asking."

"Did you talk to Matt?" Boston asks. "More importantly, am I getting grounded?"

"No. Remsen is generally pleased with what he read in the report. Expect a conversation about doing the whole Rambo thing in a foreign country, though."

"I thought it was more Jason Bourne," Boston admits.

"Jack Reacher is more fitting," Emma playfully adds.

"Whatever."

"Is that all?"

"No," Zach replies to Boston while eyeing Emma.

"Should I leave?" she asks.

"No, let's do away with the side conversations and secrets. I have no problem with you hearing this. I spoke with Matt about Sol Lozano's asylum request."

"The next words out of your mouth had better be 'We'll fast-track it, and it's all but a done deal.'"

"Yeah, I wish I could say that was the case."

"He said no?" Emma asks, exasperated at the mere thought of the denial.

"Pretty much."

Boston shakes his head. "For more than a year, Remsen has strutted around that training facility claiming that Watchtower isn't like the rest of the bureaucracy – that it's different. It isn't. It's the exact same."

"You're one hundred percent right."

"What?"

"You're right. The people who work at Watchtower have brought the same crap attitude and culture they learned from their agencies there, Matt included."

"So, what are you going to do about it?"

Zach bites his lip. "Nothing. I argued as loudly as I could before Matt made it clear that the decision was made."

Boston frowns. "Nothing ever changes."

"Some things do. You are."

"I'm what?" Boston seethes.

"Going to change his mind. You're going to tell me that if Sol's asylum isn't signed off on in the next twenty-four hours, you're going to tell the world about your gift and how the government has weaponized it against your will."

Zach knows what he just did. It's more than advising Boston on a method to ensure that Sol gets the asylum she so richly deserves. He just handed over the keys to the castle. Boston can use it as leverage to get whatever he wants until Remsen finds a way to neutralize the threat, which he will.

"Are you serious?"

"Despite what you think about me, Boston, I'm on your side. You say that Sol saved your life? That's good enough for me. You could have used Salcido's laptop as leverage, but you didn't. You could have bolted at any point during this operation, but you're still here. You trusted Matt to grant the one small thing you asked for, and he blew you off. So, it's time to bring the queen out and put the king in check."

"Really? A chess analogy?" Emma asks.

"You don't even know how the pieces move, Zach."

"True, but it doesn't make the analogy any less relevant."

"All right," Boston says, nodding. "Make your play. Understand one thing, though: This doesn't square things between us."

Zach hangs his head and stares at his shoes. He has a long road to travel to regain Boston's trust. He knows that, but every journey starts with a single step. Getting him out of Mexico was his first. This is his second.

"I know, but that's a conversation for another time. Let's handle our business here first. We'll deal with the rest later."

Nadiya bursts into the conference room. "Guys, we found something that you need to see."

The group wastes no time. Zach keeps stride with the athletic Nadiya as they reach the conference room to find everyone gathered around one of the laptops.

Hurley looks up, smiling. "Jackpot."

CHAPTER EIGHTY-EIGHT

MAYOR ANGELICA HORTA

CITY COUNCIL CHAMBER
PHOENIX, ARIZONA

The meeting has only been underway for an hour, but it feels like three days to Angelica. She's on an island, alone at the massive oval conference table facing the city council members seated on the raised bench. There are no allies in this fight – only enemies. LaCugna made sure of that, and he's enjoying every moment of this grilling.

"In fact, Compass Rose was not something you were planning until you heard that an FBI team was being sent from Washington, D.C. to help combat the sex trafficking epidemic in the city. Isn't that true?"

The mayor does some soul-searching. She remembers what Donna said about her sucking at politics. Her old, sarcastic friend is right. Angelica does suck at it and decides not to play any with her career on the line.

"Yes, it is."

"From what I understand, that's not what you told Judy Costello. She has explained to this council that you told her the opposite. Is that true?"

"Yes."

There is a grumble in the visitor's gallery behind her. The city council chamber was built to accommodate concentric arched rows for about two hundred onlookers. The seats are vacant during most sessions. There was a line to get into this session, and half of it was turned away. Even the media is here in force. They're grumbling too.

"That's all you have to say?" Kevin Demeter asks.

"There is no defense for my actions. I got caught up in things, and I regret it. Judy Costello is more than just the head of Lantern House. She's someone I consider a friend, and I lied straight to her face. It's not a moment that I'm proud of. All I can do is make amends for the mistake and pledge never to do it again."

"How can we believe you? This is more than just creating an organization to mask your shortcomings as mayor," LaCugna surmises. "You deceived us, the principal members of Compass Rose, both of its co-chairs, and the public. For what? Because you were embarrassed? Or was it because you know your policies led to this in the first place?"

She's a convenient target in this hearing. LaCugna is trying to pin all the ills and mismanagement coming from this council on her. Angelica knows that she shoulders some, but he conveniently forgets that the city council approves the budget. How convenient.

"I think that we would all admit that the budget negotiations in previous years were contentious and difficult choices needed to be made."

"Some were more enthusiastic than others for cuts, if I remember correctly."

"I don't remember your objections, Councilman LaCugna. I do remember you sitting on the sidelines through most of it."

"I was trying to find a solution that worked for everyone."

"Only, that's what leadership is – making choices where there are clear winners and losers. In this case, we asked the public to settle for fewer public services to keep living in Phoenix more affordable. A high tax burden creates a host of economic issues."

"So does cutting the police department to an ineffectual shell of what it should be."

Horta is beginning to lose her patience. LaCugna is trying to get under her skin, and it's working.

"Yes, I'm sure you have heartfelt concern for the victims and have done everything you can to help restore funding since you've been on the council. Right?"

"I resent the implication—"

"Okay, please, let's take the temperature down a little. Mayor Horta, you sat up here with us. You were one of us. There's no doubt that you would be asking these same questions if our roles were reversed. Given your admission to lying about the creation of the Compass Rose Initiative, I don't believe—"

Uniformed officers and men and women in suits barge into the chamber. Most take positions along the sides of the room as Detective Hurley and Assistant Chief Fulcher march into the center. She knows that gait all too well. It's the same one he used when he charged into her office.

"What's the meaning of this?" Kevin Demeter asks from the dais.

"My apologies for the intrusion, Councilman," Fulcher says. "We have important information relevant to your discussion that I think you'll want to hear. If you indulge us, Detective Breshion Hurley from vice will talk you through it."

"Who are these people with you?" another member of the council asks.

"Ma'am, I'm Supervisory Special Agent Zach Forte with the FBI. These are my colleagues."

"The team from Washington," Councilman Demeter concludes.

"Yes, sir."

"This is very unorthodox," Congressman LaCugna adds. "However, in the interests of public transparency, I think we should allow it."

The mayor can only imagine what this could be. The way that LaCugna is acting, it's orchestrated for effect. She is already on the ropes, so maybe he intends this to be the knockout punch. Detective Hurley already hates her, and if they're leveraging the FBI, there is no telling what they could have found while digging for dirt. No politician is as pure as fresh snow.

Angelica watches as the other council members nod. The reporters have perked up, and cameras click as the visitors watching all lean forward in their seats.

"Please proceed, Detective."

"Thank you, Councilman," Hurley says as Jada Fulcher takes a step back. "As you know, we had in our custody a coyote who worked for a major trafficking ring in the area. He escaped during a brazen attack on his transport vehicle, and two officers were killed in the ambush."

"We've all heard about that," Kevin declares.

"What you don't know is that the coyote implicated a member of our community as the ringleader – Alejandro Salcido."

The gasp from the people in the gallery sucks all of the oxygen out of the room. A dull roar of grumbling and side conversations is gaveled down by Councilman Demeter as photographers click away and cameras continue to roll.

"I find that hard to believe," a council member says after order is restored. "It was shocking enough that he was involved in a murder-suicide down in Mexico."

"That isn't the whole story," Special Agent Forte interjects. "Salcido committed suicide at his estate in Mexico when he learned that there was a federal warrant for his arrest on charges of sex trafficking, abduction, murder, and a slew of other charges."

"I...I don't know what to say to that."

"Yes, I know, he was a major contributor to campaigns and charities in the community," Hurley continues. "He was admired, and that was his cover all along. He deceived you and everyone in the City of Phoenix. The details will be submitted via formal reports from the Phoenix Police Department and Federal Bureau of Investigation at a later date."

Angelica looks around the room. There are over a dozen officers and a few FBI agents here. Agent Smith is standing along the wall with his eyes closed, just as he was in her office. She's glad that he's on the job.

"As we speak, members of the Phoenix SWAT and FBI Hostage Rescue Team are taking down his stash houses in various municipalities in Arizona. The information we've obtained will bring the whole ring to justice. There is something else."

Hurley nods at Agent Forte. "It has come to the FBI's attention that Salcido had considerable support for his operation from within the Phoenix government. Somebody in the city's leadership fed him information in turn for financial support. That person is in a position to influence policy and make decisions that would benefit his illegal operations. Isn't that correct, Madam Mayor?"

The bomb has been dropped. It must have been the plan all along. Angelica steels herself for the barrage that's coming. She can already feel every pair of eyes in the room turn in her direction and bore into her soul.

CHAPTER EIGHTY-NINE
DETECTIVE BRESHION HURLEY

CITY COUNCIL CHAMBER
PHOENIX, ARIZONA

Breshion studies Horta as she remains seated at the table. Instead of staring back at him, her eyes dart left and right, searching for the truth. The detective suppresses a grin. The mayor is anxious, and she should be.

The entire chamber silently awaits Horta's response, which is not quickly forthcoming. The silence grows increasingly awkward until Breshion's patience wears out.

"Do you always take this long to answer a question? No wonder it takes government forever to do anything."

"That wasn't a question, Detective," the mayor defiantly argues. "It was a conclusion based on a misreading of whatever evidence you've gathered. If you want a straight answer, then ask a straight question."

"Okay," Breshion says with a smile. "Did you take money from Alejandro Salcido?"

"Yes," Mayor Horta says, eliciting a reaction from those in the room. "He has contributed to my campaign. He contributes...contributed to many of them."

"Were any of these contributions illegal?"

"If you're asking whether I took a bribe, the answer is no."

The detective feels more like a prosecutor than a cop. He stares at her with accusatory eyes.

"Yes, you did," he states before turning to the council. "We have uncovered a series of deposits into your political action committee from offshore accounts. Those funds were then diverted into accounts that we believe you own for personal use. The sums were not insignificant – we're talking about hundreds of thousands of dollars."

The mayor looks puzzled and swallows hard. "I have a personal checking account. I have savings and retirement accounts. That's it."

"That's what you would like us to believe."

"As for contributions to my PAC, I know nothing about that."

"Because you weren't involved," Agent Smith says, leaving his spot against the wall. "You were set up to make everyone in this city believe you were, including us."

Every pair of eyes in the room tracks Agent Smith as he walks over to Hurley. Most of those in attendance are curious, but Agent Forte and the other vice squad members look more annoyed...and confused.

"What are you doing?" the detective asks, keeping his voice low through clenched teeth.

"The mayor isn't behind Salcido," Smith responds in a whisper.

"That's not what the evidence shows. You've seen it yourself. How could you possibly think Horta isn't up to her neck in this?"

"She's being framed. Just let me take it from here. You'll see."

"Agent Smith—"

"You need to trust me, Detective. I promise I won't let you down."

Breshion has every reason to be furious at this surprise change in direction. But he finds himself trusting this agent. There is no way Smith would jeopardize the investigation. There's too much at stake.

"I think you owe us an explanation, Agent Smith," Councilman Demeter says into his microphone.

"Yes, sir, I do. Alejandro Salcido was a master manipulator, but he needed help to stay hidden in the shadows. Mayor Horta was useful with her push to cut services when she was on the city council. That obviously worked out well for him, so he supported her campaign for mayor."

"That's sickening," Demeter muses.

"He supported you as well, councilman. You've done favors for him in the past to clear out tabs at one of his bars. We can discuss that more, or you can let me get to the heart of the matter."

Cameras click, and Jada glances over at Hurley, who offers a slight shrug. He knew nothing about that, but there's truth to the allegation, based on Demeter's reaction. The councilman leans back in his chair, allowing Smith to continue.

"Ultimately," Agent Smith continues, "he wanted somebody he could more easily control in the mayor's office. The reason was the one that got you elected in the first place – you care about the people of this city while everyone around you plays politics. Sometimes, those games force you to make the bad decisions you've admitted to today."

"If it pleases the council, I would like to know if the FBI is investigating or offering an endorsement," Andres LaCugna asks. "Because it sounds like the latter."

"Which is something you would know a little about, Councilman. It's why you sought Salcido's help."

Another gasp erupts from the public. Accusatory eyes that shifted back and forth between the mayor and Kevin Demeter now settle on LaCugna.

"What the hell are you talking about? Everybody knows that Salcido and I hated each other!"

"Publicly, yes. Privately, Salcido was a staunch financial supporter and confidant."

"You had better have proof of that."

"We have your financial records. They were clean, at least the ones we knew about. You did a good job hiding the money, but we know who was doing that for you, too. Salcido used his bars and nightclubs as a cover, just as you used countless investment schemes to hide the money he was paying you."

"That's a lie!"

"Your mistake was contributing hundreds of thousands of that money to your own campaign. That makes it a federal crime."

"You have some nerve!"

"No, Councilman LaCugna, *you* do. You knew about Salcido's illegal activities for years. You don't care about the crimes or the victims of sex trafficking because they didn't affect you. You went after Horta when the Compass Rose Initiative was launched because that affected him. Those were his instructions and what he paid you to do."

"These are all baseless allegations."

"The financial transactions Detective Hurley was talking about were arranged by you and Salcido to frame her for bribery before the next election. You could never have guessed that we would end up with Salcido's records."

LaCugna shakes his head.

"Once you learned that Salcido was dead, you made an agreement with his lieutenant, Javier Barerra. Eager to assume his boss's place atop the pyramid, he agreed to help you become mayor if you would provide the same support to him."

"I don't know any Javier Barerra, and I have never spoken to Alejandro Salcido outside of the odd public event that we happen to both be at. That's all!"

"Never?"

"Never, and there isn't a shred of evidence that could prove otherwise because it's simply untrue."

Smith pulls a phone out of his pocket and hands it to Jada. She glances at him warily as she accepts the device and stares at it in her hand.

"Ma'am, please power that on, scroll to recent calls, and select the third one down."

She complies as Agent Smith turns back to the council. "This phone was provided by Mexican authorities following Salcido's suicide. It's an untraceable burner phone. Most of the numbers that called it are as well."

Smith nods, and Jada presses send. Everyone in the room holds their breath and waits for a ring somewhere in the room. Half the public has their eyes on the mayor. The other half search the room, waiting. Nothing happens, and after fifteen seconds elapse, it's clear nothing will.

"It looks like I'm not your man after all," LaCugna says over the grumbling in the room.

Breshion glances over at the other FBI agents. The two women stand expressionless, but Agent Forte is in physical distress. He didn't know about the phone, meaning the agent has gone renegade. The detective already regrets trusting the man.

Agent Smith pulls out his own phone and makes a call. "Matt, the phone is powered off. Activate it."

After a moment, he nods and ends the call.

"In about ten seconds, please try again, ma'am."

Jada stretches her neck to relieve stress and does as she's asked after the appropriate amount of time. Silence again blankets the room until the piercing sound of a ringtone shatters it. Where it's coming from is unmistakable.

Everyone stares at a nervous Andres LaCugna, who looks like he's about to have a stroke. He reaches into his jacket pocket and retrieves a phone, ending the ringing. He raises his eyes to see everyone staring at him.

Cornered animals are the most dangerous. Every creature, including humans, is wired with a "fight or flight" instinct. When you take away one, all that's left is the other. That's the dilemma facing the councilman right now.

LaCugna pushes himself away from the extended bench on the dais he is seated at and pulls a small revolver from his pocket. That's all that was needed to create panic. The people attending the meeting let out screams as they either dive on the ground or make for the exits.

CHAPTER NINETY
"BOSTON" HOLLINGER

CITY COUNCIL CHAMBER
PHOENIX, ARIZONA

A cacophony of shouted orders from the FBI and PPD drown out what LaCugna is screaming. Through it all, I don't move. Noticing my lack of response, he levels his weapon on me as the panicked yelling dies down.

"That's a little extreme, isn't it, Councilman?"

"Stay back! Don't move!"

"Nah," I say, leaning against the dais. "The moment you point that at someone other than me, it will be the last thing you ever do."

"I don't care!"

"Yes, you do. You don't want to kill anyone, and you don't want to die. That's why you brought that gun here. You don't trust Javier and thought he might want to tie up a loose end. They knew you would be at this meeting, and you wanted to be ready."

LaCugna's mouth hangs open. His eyes dart left and right as the PPD officers creep along the back wall, and the public is evacuated quietly from the seats in the chamber. He takes the weapon and puts it under his chin, obviously feeling like he's running out of options.

"Tell them to stop moving. No closer! I'll do it!"

"Go ahead." The impassive tone causes him to look at me in shock. "You're surprised? You worked with a man who sold other human beings. His men raped and tortured children. He was a despicable human being, and so are you. So, please, go ahead and do the world a favor. Pull the trigger."

"Agent Smith…"

"Shut up, Forte. This is between me and this scumbag. Do it."

LaCugna quivers as tears roll down his cheeks. "Don't make me."

"I'm not making you do anything. It's your choice. This is over for you, either way. Prison and death are your only options. I'm sure the countless victims of the crimes you helped Salcido perpetrate don't care either way. So, if you want to kill yourself, I'm not going to stop you."

I take another step, and his eyes are welded shut as his finger twitches. I move along the bench at the dais. I'm less than five feet from him and choose to keep my arms at my sides. I could try to disarm him from here but don't bother. I would only risk getting him or myself killed, and I've already burned through a couple of my nine lives on this operation. I can sense the outcome of this standoff.

"I don't want to go to prison."

"You should have thought of that earlier. Maybe you figured you were too smart to ever get caught. Or that the price of doing business with Salcido was worth it to become mayor. It's what you always wanted, at least since your father said that you'd never amount to anything."

"My father hated me."

"I know. Your father resented everything about his bright, ambitious, hard-working son. You were everything he wasn't. That's why he beat you."

LaCugna's eyes grow wide. "I never told anyone that."

"No, but you live the results every day. You've spent your life determined to prove him wrong. Salcido offered you an easy way to do that, and you seized it."

"I needed his money to beat that bitch!" he exclaims, pointing at Mayor Horta, who is flanked by two officers with weapons drawn as she refused to be removed from the room.

"That's another tragedy of this, Councilman. You didn't. Your father hated you for all the reasons that would have made you a great public servant without Salcido or his money. You could have run on that alone. You didn't. It was a bad decision."

LaCugna is crying like a baby now. "I didn't want any of this."

"I know."

"I can't live like this."

"I know that, too. But before you pull that trigger, there is something you need to consider: The moment you do, your father wins."

That gets his attention, and I give him a sympathetic look. Part of me wants him to burn in hell for what he's done. The other part understands the journey that brought him to this moment. Children are often products of their parents. His childhood was horrible, not that it excuses what he's done.

"Your father always said that you would amount to nothing, just like him. That you were nothing but a loser, just like him. Now it will come full circle when you end your life...just like him."

The shock on his face tells the story. He removes the gun from his head and stares at it in his hand. I'm not sure he's even aware of his surroundings now. I don't move because I don't need to. PPD officers inching closer throughout our conversation charge from either side of the councilman, disarm him, and drag him to the floor.

In a satisfying twist, LaCugna begins bawling as he's pinned on his stomach and cuffed. He is stood up, and pictures are taken – pictures that I'm sure will be on the front page of every newspaper in Arizona, if not the country. He stares at me through watery, red eyes.

"I've never told another living soul about my father. How did you know?"

I shrug. "It's one of life's mysteries."

As LaCugna is escorted out, the mayor looks on, still processing what happened to her political rival. A smile starts to creep across her face as she stands at the edge of the conference table. Forte gives me a grin as he, Breshion, and Assistant Chief Fulcher join me at her side.

"Madam Mayor, I know this must be a satisfying moment for you, but let me give you a nickel's worth of free political advice: Handle this with kid gloves. I strongly suggest you forgo the victory lap and get back to work. LaCugna may be a scumbag, but he has a compelling backstory that will generate enormous sympathy. You scored a political win, but your hands are far from clean. Don't give me an excuse to find out just how dirty they are."

I walk past Nadiya and Emma, who have holstered their weapons, and they grin at me as I pass. My mentors fall in behind me, giving me a feeling of invincibility in knowing that they have my back. Forte joins us in heading to the Chevy Suburban parked among all the squad cars and their flashing red and blue strobes.

Nothing is said. It doesn't need a recap or further narration or analysis. There will be plenty of time for that later, hopefully after we get on a plane and escape the oppressive heat of the desert Southwest.

CHAPTER NINETY-ONE
MAYOR ANGELICA HORTA

CITY HALL PRESS BRIEFING ROOM
PHOENIX, ARIZONA

Angelica sits at her desk with her head resting in her hands as she reads over her notes. Everything that has happened over the past few days leads to one conclusion: This may be the most crucial press conference she ever holds.

The police and a spokesman from the FBI will walk the media through everything that has happened. It's the political ramifications and the path forward that will be left to her. It's a journey that she's simultaneously both eager to start and loathing to take. With opportunity also comes risk. She knows that now more than ever.

"Ma'am, we're almost ready," Katy says from the threshold to her office.

"Thank you," the mayor says, rising and collecting her notes to stuff into the leather portfolio.

"What are you going to say?"

"The truth."

The mayor moves around her desk and stops alongside her newly reemployed aide. She's thrilled that Katy decided to come back to work for her after a series of sincere apologies and a pledge to never let that happen again. The mayor understands that she is on probation with her media specialist. Trust will have to be re-earned, and that will take time. The mayor is just pleased that Katy is giving her the chance to do just that.

"What about the advice that you said the FBI agent gave you?"

The mayor smiles and makes her way down to the press briefing room. Katy is back, but Adrian is another story. He has soured on politics and is looking to take a position with Lantern House by working on the Compass Rose Initiative. The move makes sense, and Angelica hopes that he gets it. She gave him a glowing recommendation to Judy, her friendship with whom will also undergo a long rebuilding.

Angelica meets up with the chief of police, Jada Fulcher, members of the city council, the FBI, and Judy Costello. After the greetings are finished, they assume their positions on the dais as she moves to the podium. As she expects, the room is packed. This is a massive story in the city, the state, and nationwide.

"Ladies and gentlemen, thank you for joining us today. By now, you have all heard what happened in the city council chamber yesterday. Councilman Andres LaCugna was arrested for providing material support and information to a sex trafficking ring, along with several firearms and public endangerment charges. This is a difficult time for the LaCugna family. I ask you to respect their privacy, especially that of his children, during this troubling time for them.

"Weeks ago, I made it my focus to bring an end to human trafficking in Phoenix. The Compass Rose Initiative was one step in that direction. As I freely admit, my initial motives were not pure. What has happened over the last several days has changed that.

"What we hoped to accomplish by bringing federal, state, and local resources together is being realized. The Phoenix Police Department and Federal Bureau of Investigation broke up a massive trafficking ring in the city. Over three dozen migrants destined for the sex trade were liberated from confinement throughout the Phoenix metro area and Tucson.

"This ring was led by Alejandro Salcido, a prominent businessman and significant contributor to many causes, including Lantern House and political campaigns, mine included. We understand now that he was not doing that out of generosity. It was a means to cover up his despicable illegal activities. We have received reports that Alejandro knew we were closing in on him and has committed suicide in his home in Mexico. The FBI will provide more details on this in a few moments.

"I'm going to hand this briefing off to our police and federal representatives who have joined me up here, but I will take a few questions before I do."

Full-throated questions are shouted from the journalists in front of her. She finally hears out one that she can understand through the noise.

"Are you concerned that other public officials or members of law enforcement could be involved in Salcido's organization?"

"News that sex traffickers were getting support was…well, shocking. Every American hopes that their elected officials and public servants are beyond reproach. This incident has shaken the public's confidence in that. There are always concerns about the extent of those involved with Mr. Salcido, and I'm confident that authorities will continue their investigation until those questions are answered."

"Madam Mayor, rumors are circulating that you targeted LaCugna because he was going to run against you in the next election," Vincent DiPasquale says from the second row. "Is that true?"

After everything, Angelica cannot believe that he is still shilling for a disgraced councilman. He hates her enough to keep trying to find some nefarious agenda behind this. Some people will never change. A partisan reporter is among them.

"Andres LaCugna was presented with evidence of his involvement and responded by pulling a gun in the city council chamber. He threatened the people in that room and himself following his admission of guilt. This was not a witch hunt or political vendetta. It was painful for me to hear that LaCugna was involved. Even though he was a political adversary, and I admittedly didn't like him, he was still an elected official who swore an oath to the people in this city. He violated that oath."

"Will Compass Rose continue?" another reporter asks.

"Absolutely. We have some things to work out, but I hope that, under the guiding hand of Judy Costello, it can go on to do great things for the community. That's if she is willing to remain in charge."

Angelica looks back to see Judy nod at her. It's a good sign that she showed up here. It's a better sign that she seems willing to forgive. It's in her nature. She'll do anything for this city, including putting the past behind her for the greater good. The woman is a saint. Not everyone would have done that.

"In my time as mayor, I have come to realize a universal truth that no politician likes to admit: Not all problems can be solved by the government. It takes all of us to build a thriving community. Judy Costello has been a big part of that. If Compass Rose lives up to its potential, it will be because of her, not me. The best thing I can do is help provide her with the resources that she needs and get the hell out of her way."

"How extensive was Alejandro Salcido's network?" another reporter asks.

"This is a good time to hand this over to the Phoenix Police and the FBI. They are better suited to convey the details. Sir?"

Angelica stands aside as the Phoenix Police chief begins his briefing. Judy glances at the mayor, who is staring at her out of the corner of her eye. They have been longtime friends, and that almost ended. Maybe she is on the path of forgiveness…and redemption. She knows that it will be a long road.

Donna was right – she's a lousy politician. Through all this, Angelica has realized something important: The best leaders usually are. It's why she informed the curmudgeon that she would no longer seek her counsel. It's time to stop playing political games and do what she pledged to for this community. It's the one gift Andres LaCugna has given her, and the mayor doesn't plan on squandering it.

CHAPTER NINETY-TWO
DETECTIVE BRESHION HURLEY

Breshion has never liked his apartment complex. Jamecca doesn't complain about it, even though she should. They're a set of buildings that look like they were removed from Cold War Bratislava, repainted in desert colors, and plopped down around a community pool in Tempe. It's cheap, though, explaining why he can afford it on a cop's salary.

"Did Agent Smith say anything at all to you?" Jamecca asks after Breshion pulls into his assigned parking spot.

"Not a word. That's not what we need to be worried about. It's whether he ratted us out to Jada or anyone else."

Breshion made a deal with Agent Smith and held up his end of the bargain. In his experience, that means nothing to the FBI. There is always a healthy level of animosity and mistrust between local and federal law enforcement. He wouldn't have been surprised if the agent sold him out on the way out of town just because he could.

"Do you think he did?"

"I don't know," Breshion answers honestly.

The pair walk past the pool and up the short flight of stairs to his second-level apartment. Jamecca has every right to be concerned about what Agent Smith will do with the knowledge about their relationship. Their careers are in jeopardy, and the fed holds all the cards. He has no reason to say anything about it. The problem is, he doesn't have any reason to keep his word, either.

Breshion unlocks and opens the door, pausing to drop his keys in a dish perched atop the table in the foyer. They make a loud clanking sound when they hit, and he freezes. Jamecca picks up on it and does the same. He can't put his finger on it, but something is off. It's a feeling that he's learned to trust over his career.

"Someone's been here."

"How do you know?" she asks, confused.

Breshion peers into the living room and spots a bottle of champagne and a dozen roses resting on the coffee table. He pulls his gun, with Jamecca following suit. They creep forward in unison, swinging their weapons smoothly left and right.

"That's a pretty good sign."

"I assume you didn't get those for me," she whispers, spotting the arrangement.

"No."

The pair heads down the hall, with Breshion taking the bedroom and Jamecca the small bath. Both are clear. The apartment is only twelve hundred square feet. There are only so many places an intruder can hide. They check all of them. The apartment is empty.

They holster their weapons and return to the living room. Breshion stares at the bouquet of flowers like it's an alien artifact. Jamecca waits for him to do something before growing increasingly impatient.

"Well? Find out who they're from."

Breshion carefully pulls the card from the plastic holder like it was wired to explosives. He turns it over.

"Special Agent Smith."

"Go on…read it."

"It says, 'Breshion and Jamecca, have the romantic evening you both deserve. No matter what life brings, always find happiness with each other.'"

The detective drops the card on the coffee table and admires the twelve perfect red long-stem roses and bottle of expensive champagne. The man has taste. This isn't something he picked up at some cheap liquor store on the way here.

"How the hell did he sneak that into your apartment? Better yet, how did he know where you live in the first place? You didn't tell him, did you?"

"Are you kidding? He's the last guy I would want to know where I sleep. I have no idea how he could have found out."

"Maybe he asked around the station," Jamecca offers, admiring the beautiful red roses arranged perfectly in the vase.

"Maybe it's just one of life's mysteries."

Jamecca punches the grinning detective in the arm. Her smile fades when she realizes that this could be something other than a nice gesture.

"Is it a taunt?"

"No," Breshion says, allowing himself to smile. "I actually think it's the opposite. It's a promise kept."

Agent Smith may be odd and mysterious, but he's also a man of his word. Breshion's secret relationship with Jamecca is safe, at least from the prying eyes of the FBI. The question is, how long before his own department puts the pieces together?

"Do you like being in vice?"

Jamecca's eyebrows crinkle at the sudden inquiry. "I like being with you."

"You didn't answer my question."

"Yeah, I do."

Breshion collapses on the sofa, and Jamecca joins him, her legs tucked under her. He stares pensively at the roses for what feels like an eternity before she finally shatters the silence.

"What's wrong?"

"Nothing. I'm putting in for reassignment."

"What? Why?"

He takes her hand. "Because I'm tired of us being a secret. I don't want it to be one anymore. We both deserve more than that, and I want to see where this goes. I've fallen in love with you, Jamecca, and since we can't be together *and* work together, I need to move on."

She kisses him softly and strokes his face after their lips part. He knows she can see the pain in his eyes, but also the joy. He never would have contemplated leaving vice before. She's worth it.

"No, I will request the reassignment."

"I can't ask you to do that," Breshion says, shaking his head.

Jamecca smiles. "You didn't, and that's one of the many reasons that I've fallen in love with you. You're passionate about what you do in a way that I never will be. For us to have a shot, it's only right for me to be the one who moves on."

"Then you should understand something about my past...about my parents. Maybe it's time to tell you the story about who they were. There's only one other person on this planet who knows."

"Who?"

He looks at the flowers and the champagne. "Someone capable of keeping secrets. I promise to tell you, but not now. Tonight is about us and our future. Let's put this bottle on ice."

"There's no point," she says, rising from the sofa after he does.

A concerned look seizes control of his face. "Why not?"

"Because the heat we're about to generate is only going to melt it."

She kisses him hard, and they fall back onto the couch. For one night, the demons have gone away. All is right in the world.

CHAPTER NINETY-THREE
"BOSTON" HOLLINGER

WATCHTOWER TRAINING CENTER
SOMEWHERE IN VIRGINIA

It's all starting to come together. Nadiya is still kicking my ass, but at least I'm making her work for it now. This is the longest I've ever managed to remain upright while sparring against her.

We move in a circle. The combative expert tests me with a right that I deflect. I move in to catch her but am too slow, and we begin the dance again. React, don't anticipate, I keep telling myself before catching a glimpse of Forte out of the corner of my eye. It was all the hesitation my tormentor needed.

With lightning speed, she lands a right to my jaw and heel-kicks me hard enough to send me sprawling on the mat. Under normal circumstances, she would be pounding me into oblivion right now. That may be the only thing I have to thank Forte for as I stare at the ceiling.

"Aw, damn it," I moan, clutching my chest. "That hurt."

"Distractions kill, Boston. I would have thought you'd have learned that by now," Nadiya taunts.

"Apparently not."

"Nadiya, can I interrupt for a word with the soon-to-be-deceased?" Zach asks.

"Yeah, sure. It'll give this rookie time to regain his senses and remember things I taught him six months ago."

I roll over, press myself back into the standing position and walk past Zach over to the bench. I squirt water into my mouth and towel off my face, or at least what's left of it.

"I see you can still take a hit."

"Or fifty of them. What do you want, Zach?"

"I heard that you're still talking to the children in Phoenix."

"Yeah, is that a problem?"

He eyes me suspiciously. "I don't know. Is it?"

I scoff and check my jaw as I stretch it out. Nadiya rattled my teeth with that last hit, and I want to ensure I still have all of them.

"I wanted to see how they're doing."

"You could have called Dr. Benito and asked."

"I did. Who the hell do you think was translating? As an FYI, Detective Hurley partnered with Lantern House to reunite Adelmo with his mother. Doctor Benito arranged for me to watch the reunion. Speaking of which, I want language courses added to my curriculum," I demand. "Start with Spanish."

"I'll look into it."

"It wasn't a request."

I'm not in the mood to play whatever stupid game Zach came here for. I haven't asked for much since I've been here, as long as you don't count wanting a little more freedom. I get weapons instruction, physically pounded like a slab of meat, and have had tradecraft jammed into my head for a year now. They can squeeze in a little additional training.

"Anything else?" Zach asks.

"Yeah, an update on Sol's asylum request."

"It will be granted tomorrow."

"Good."

I leveled my threat, and Remsen folded. He may have thought I was bluffing but didn't think that the demand was egregious enough to find out. Good thing. I would have followed through on the threat in a heartbeat.

"You know, Boston, you took to those kids back at the hospital like they were your own. I didn't peg you as a family man."

"That shows just how little you know about me. I never thought of myself as anything other than one until Gina almost killed me. That torpedoed my two-point-five kid white picket fence dreams. You know all about that part, don't you?"

"You got justice for them, Boston," Zach says, not taking the bait in that particular trap. "They have a future now. Let it go."

"I'm glad *you* think so. I don't think a lifetime of therapy will help most of those children have a bright future."

"You don't know that," Zach argues.

"Yeah, I do. Better than anyone. You knew what you were doing when you put me in that room. Don't deny it again. Every time I went back to that hospital, I peered through the eyes of innocents. They were vulnerable children ripe for exploitation by adults who did precisely that. I lived their nightmares and felt their terror. I will never unsee those horrors. If you think you can force me to forget all that, you're sadly mistaken."

"That's the job, Boston."

I shake my head. "Let me hit you in the head a bunch of times until you can do what I do. Then tell me that's the job. Are we done here?"

"Yeah," Zach reluctantly says.

I take the opportunity to get away from this chat as fast as I can. It wasn't speedy enough.

"Boston? There are going to be other missions. This won't be the last time you see something ugly."

"Very true, Zach. Every journey has a beginning and an end. The only question is how far down ours we are."

Forte looks like he's about to hurl. He turns and leaves, allowing me to rejoin Nadiya back on the mat. Instead of immediately starting to rearrange my face, she watches Zach exit the training area.

"That was tense."

"Always," I moan. "Come on, let's get back to training."

"Sure. If you learned anything in Mexico, it's that you need a lot more."

"I got out okay."

"This time."

Nadiya makes a move that I deflect. We go back and forth until she finally gets the upper hand and flips me hard onto my back. She straddles me, pinning my arms down with her legs as her face gets close to mine. This is how she likes to make a point. There are times when getting my ass kicked is almost enjoyable.

"Broadway has less drama than the two of you. For the record, I don't blame you for talking to the children."

"You may be in the minority."

"Nobody here can relate to you. Believe me, if the roles were reversed, they would act the same way. All of them."

"And you?"

She shrugs and moves even closer to me. "The closer I get to you, the more I see things from your perspective."

"Remember that the next time you're using me as a punching bag."

She smiles and helps me up. "Forte looked nauseated when he left. That line you used...you had a dream about him, didn't you? That's why he was freaking out a little."

"No," I say with an irresistible grin. "I was awake and heard Zach say it to the doctor on the airplane ride to Phoenix. He doesn't need to know that, though."

Nadiya grabs my throat without applying pressure this time. "Listen up, Hollinger. If you ever pull a stunt like that on me, the only thing you will be able to eat for months is applesauce. Got it?"

I can't help but smile, even knowing that she is serious. "Yes, ma'am."

CHAPTER NINETY-FOUR
SSA ZACH FORTE

WATCHTOWER TRAINING FACILITY
SOMEWHERE IN VIRGINIA

Zach has a pit in his stomach as he leaves Boston at the gym to get his ass kicked by Nadiya. Under any other circumstances, he would be elated at the unqualified success of their first mission. When he worked in counterintelligence, there was no high like the one he got from a job well-done. This is different.

He joins Dr. Kurota and Matt standing at the observation window and looking down at their golden boy below. Remsen is beaming like a proud father. Nadiya pulls a judo move on Boston and sends him down to the mat with a crack that can be heard up here.

"Ouch."

"I had better get some ice ready. Boston's going to need it," Asami says, excusing herself.

Zach watches as Nadiya presses her chest against his and moves an inch from his face. He isn't fighting. Then again, there isn't a heterosexual man on the planet who would be. Nadiya moves her lips an inch from his and stares into his eyes. He thinks for a second that they might kiss, but they don't.

"I told you he would forget about Tara," Matt says, checking behind him for the doctor. "That woman could get me to forget my own name."

"Not everything is what it seems, Matt."

"Lighten up, Francis," Matt says in his best Drill Sergeant Hulka voice. "Are you still brooding about what happened in Mexico?"

"He could have been killed."

"Yet, he wasn't. He put his training to good use. It was impressive for a new agent to seize the initiative like that. The man has a set of balls on him, that's for sure."

"And Salcido?" Forte asks, not wanting to look at his boss.

"What about him? He was a scumbag that got what was coming. Don't tell me that you care he's dead."

"Matt, we're the FBI. At least, we used to be. This group is not judge, jury, and executioner. Unless our charter changed in the last couple of weeks."

Matt turns to face his subordinate. "What happens in Mexico stays in Mexico."

"Really? That's what you're going to go with? What if he had killed Salcido at one of his bars in Phoenix? Then what?"

"We can play the 'what if' game for hours, Zach. He didn't kill him here. Maybe we dodged a bullet. Maybe Boston is smarter than all of us. Either way, it was a win.

We busted a crooked politician, a trafficking kingpin, took down the entire network, and freed over three dozen immigrants destined for sexual slavery. Enjoy the victory while you can. The next opportunity will be coming in a matter of weeks. Boston is operational, and there are plenty of bad guys to catch."

Matt pats his subordinate on the shoulder and walks off toward the exit and the administrative building beyond it. The agent rubs his chin as he watches Boston put up a halfway decent fight before Nadiya's leg sweep drops him to the ground.

"For a guy responsible for helping bring down one of the largest human trafficking rings in Arizona, you look like you're at a funeral. What's up?"

"For once, Doctor, we're on the same page with Boston. I'm as concerned about him as you are. What did you write in your report?"

"The truth. Boston made significant progress in his remote viewing skills. He employed his training better than most Quantico graduates do. He's more determined than I've ever seen him. His mental focus has increased by orders of magnitude. Getting out of here did wonders for him."

"That's all?"

"Boston is driven but erratic. He's unpredictable and has an animus toward rules and procedures. I also questioned his emotional stability. He saw a lot of horrible things in those memories. Who knows how what he sees in future ones could affect him long-term. Does any of that bother you?"

"What you wrote? No. What it may mean? Yeah, that bothers me a lot."

"What, specifically?"

"Are you psychoanalyzing me, Doc?"

"No," Asami says. "I'm curious."

Zach lets out a heavy sigh. "Boston knows what's coming. Someday, the government will realize that he's as much a threat to them as he is to our enemies."

"We are the government, Zach."

"Only a part of it. If the wrong people find out about what Boston can do, they will seek to exploit him. When they realize that he'll learn their deepest and darkest secrets in the process, what do you think will happen?"

"One challenge at a time, Agent Forte. One challenge at a time."

Asami nods and walks off with the bag of ice, leaving Zach alone at the observation window. Now he knows how a death row inmate must feel on the way to his lethal injection. It's a series of steps to a destination you don't want to arrive at but know is inevitable. The question is, how long will Boston take that walk before doing something to change the outcome?

ACKNOWLEDGMENTS

So, that happened. When I wrote *The Eyes of Others*, it was meant to be a standalone book with a shocking ending. Over the years after its initial release, I realized that I had a problem: There was a lot more of Boston's story to tell.

As a result, it underwent a rewrite. Some of his backstory changed, as did the characters and their roles within the story. The most noticeable addition was a further development of Matt Remsen and a secretive governmental organization codenamed "Watchtower."

Boston is such an interesting character with a unique gift that I thought it deserved further exploration. The door was left cracked open in the first edition of *The Eyes of Others*, so this time I barged through it. Boston is alive and well, although if he keeps pulling stunts like he did in Mexico, I wonder how long he will stay that way. Time will tell.

As always, my heartfelt thanks go first to my readers. I write to entertain and provide a break from reality by introducing you to a different version of it. I have always wanted my novels to at least feel plausible, no matter how unlikely the scenario. *The iCandidate* and *The Eyes of Others* are built on that premise. I can only hope that I pull it off to your satisfaction.

Writing is a labor of love, but it comes at a price. The cost is time spent doing things with those you love. It takes a forgiving and patient soul to marry a writer, and I thank God that my wife has one. Michele, you are my rock and my inspiration. Thank you for all your support during this journey.

To Nancy, Kristina, Ken, Gibson – thank you for all your encouragement as I relentlessly chase this dream. Family is such an important foundation, and I have a great one.

Writing may often be a solo sport, but the art of publishing is definitely not. Thank you to Michael Waitz at Sticks and Stones Editing for helping correct my constant mistakes and inconsistencies. A good editor makes all the difference, and you have helped bring my work to the next level.

Also, another shout out to JD&J for the fantastic cover design. Sometimes I have a picture in my head of what I want, and sometimes I don't. In this case, it was the former and yet you still managed to exceed what I envisioned.

ABOUT THE AUTHOR

Mikael Carlson is the award-winning author of the novel, *The iCandidate* and the Michael Bennit Series of political dramas. He is also the author of *Justifiable Deceit* and the Tierra Campos Saga. The Watchtower Thrillers are his third series currently in publication and *The Eyes of Innocents* is his thirteenth novel.

A retired veteran of the Rhode Island Army National Guard and Unites States Army, he deployed twice in support of military operations during the Global War on Terror. Mikael has served in the field artillery, infantry, and in support of special operations units during his career on active duty at Fort Bragg and in the Army National Guard.

A proud U.S. Army Paratrooper, he conducted over fifty airborne operations following the completion of jump school at Fort Benning in 1998. Since then, he has trained with the militaries of countless foreign nations.

Academically, Mikael has earned a Master of Arts in American History and graduated with a B.S. in International Business from Marist College in 1996.

He was raised in New Milford, Connecticut and currently lives in nearby Danbury.